Praise for
Notting Hell

"A delicious yarn."

—*People*

"A tasty look at the price of excess."

—*Kirkus Reviews*

"*Notting Hell* is one of those books where the saying 'with friends like these, who needs enemies' is definitely true. . . . *Notting Hell* is a witty and sharp novel that makes the Desperate Housewives look like schoolgirls."

—Romance Junkies Blog

"Wickedly funny novel laced with social satire, romantic comedy and clever plot twists. . . . Over meticulously prepared cups of caffè latte, adultery, lust and even love sprout in the most unexpected places."

—*Dallas Morning News*

"Gripping . . . a pacy mix of lifestyle envy, sexual intrigue, and good old-fashioned gossip. A real page turner that will appeal to those far from Notting Hill itself."

—*Easy Living* (UK)

"Acerbic and well observed . . . with her magpie eye for local detail and a couple of good cracking jokes per page, *Notting Hell* is snappy, witty, definitely clever, and hugely readable."

—Nicholas Coleridge, *The Spectator* (UK)

"A tale of the rich behaving badly in one of London's most exclusive enclaves. *Notting Hell* is delicious fun."

—Karen Quinn, author of *The Ivy Chronicles* and
Wife in the Fast Lane

By the Same Author

The Mummy Diaries

The Oxford Myth (*ed.*)

Notting Hell

RACHEL JOHNSON

A TOUCHSTONE BOOK
Published by Simon & Schuster
NEW YORK   LONDON   TORONTO   SYDNEY

To Ivo

ἀνδρῶν ἀνάκτι

TOUCHSTONE
A Division of Simon & Schuster, Inc.
1230 Avenue of the Americas
New York, NY 10020

First Touchstone trade paperback edition April 2008

TOUCHSTONE and colophon are registered
trademarks of Simon & Schuster, Inc.

For information about special discounts for bulk purchases,
please contact Simon & Schuster Special Sales at
1-800-456-6798 or business@simonandschuster.com.

Manufactured in the United States of America

1   3   5   7   9   10   8   6   4   2

The Library of Congress cataloged the hardcover edition as follows
Johnson, Rachel.
Notting hell/Rachel Johnson.—1st Touchstone ed.
p.   cm.
"A Touchstone book."
1. Community gardens—Fiction. 2. Neighborhood—Fiction.
3. Notting Hill (London, England)—Fiction. I. Title.
PR6060.O365N68   2007
823'.92—dc22

ISBN-13: 978-1-4165-3176-0
ISBN-10:   1-4165-3176-9
ISBN-13: 978-1-4165-3207-1 (pbk)
ISBN-10:   1-4165-3207-2 (pbk)

Spring

Clare

I don't know what woke me up—I drank no alcohol last night, I observed the carb curfew, I had only one espresso during the day, plus I did a Pilates class and hours of gardening in the fresh air—but I'm definitely awake now. Wide awake.

Outside, in the garden, a cat is screeching, or a fox. In the far distance, I can hear the rumble of night traffic on the Westway flyover. But it's too early for planes. And it's too soon to get up.

In a minute I'm going to go into the wet room and find one of those French sleeping pills you can buy over the counter, if you're in France. I need to calm down. Two things are twining together in my mind, like mating slugs. First, Gideon's away the first half of next week at the Danish furniture expo, for which he's designed a stool, so basically there's no way I can conceive this month, because he'll be away right in the middle of my fertile period. Second, the lilies. I just forgot them, which is not like me at all.

I'd been shopping with Donna, as she'd persuaded me to invest in a crystal to hang in the hall, to slow down the fast-flowing *chi* she says is surging from our front door and rushing along the stairs and making visitors to our home feel all unsettled and transient. I felt like saying, "Thanks, Donna," but instead I merely pointed out that Gideon wouldn't go for it—I mean, he is, after all, a postminimalist ecotect, which means he is very into rainfall harvesting and wind turbines and recyclable materials, so tinkling water features and repro statues of the squatting Buddha are not really his style at all. But she persuaded me to buy this crystal and hang it high on an invisible nylon thread and promised me the only thing

Gideon would notice would be an increase in wealth and good luck.

"Will it help me conceive?" I'd asked, as I put in my card and pin number to pay for the one she said I needed, which was surprisingly expensive.

"I'm not promising you a Christmas baby, but it will definitely help. So would a brass wind chime in the hallway. Crystals have been a powerful healing tool for thousands of years, Clare. If you follow your own path . . ."

Anyway, we were so busy with the crystal—I managed to talk her out of the Buddha and the brass wind chime—that I forgot to go back to the Moltons and finish up there and put the lilies under cloches or in the greenhouse until I potted them up. So now the toad lilies I bought from Crocus, with their star-shaped pale-blue spotty blooms, might never flower.

To distract myself from thoughts of plants flowering or not flowering and the aching sadness that I, too, might be a flower that never even blushes unseen to waste its sweetness on the desert air, I get up.

I pull up our light-excluding cream blinds—we don't have curtains or carpets or valances, as it's very bad karma to have anything made of any sort of material touching any surface you walk on in outdoor shoes. Then I push open the sash window and lean out.

It's certainly cold, but I don't think it's freezing although the weather girl did say something about a late frost, and I look across the communal garden to the Lonsdale Gardens side of the square. The garden is a classic *hortus inclusus*, but it isn't shaped like a square, it's more rectangular, with two short ends and two long sides that are Lonsdale Gardens and Colville Crescent.

Hardly any lights are on in Lonsdale Gardens, as you would expect, as most of the residents are families with school-age children or bankers or both, and bankers have to get to their desks an hour and a half before their children have to be at school, so this is a place of early birds, not night owls.

The lawned central area of the garden, surrounded by paths, is a dark pool of blackness, but it's easy to discern the outlines of the huge plane and ash trees against the white stucco backs of the houses opposite.

I pull back from the window.

The rear elevation of the Avery house, the last in the terrace, is suddenly bathed in bright white light. Something has triggered the security lights—a fox or a cat, some intruder. I keep staring hard at the house, waiting to see the shadowy shape of a fox padding out into the undergrowth, brush aloft, as if *he* owned the garden, not all of us. But nothing.

Then, just at the moment I would expect the lights to power off again, I see the figure of a woman in white slip down the central path in between the Adirondack chairs and the lead planters, past the old garage covered with dense ivy and creepers, to the gate at the bottom of the Averys' garden. As she pauses to find the latch, she stands bathed in light, and I can make out exactly who it is, in a killer outfit of short white nightie, lush caramel-colored pashmina flung around her shoulders, and green Hunter wellies. Her long brown legs merge into the darkness, and all I can see is the shape of her pintucked nightdress bobbing along the path like a ghost and ducking into her own garden next door.

As the security lights dim, I can come up with only one reason that Virginie Lacoste might be stealing away from the Avery residence at—I glance at my watch—getting on for three in the morning.

A mental image of Bob, in blue shirt and khaki chinos (which is, for some reason, what he is always wearing in my imagination), pops into my mind. Bob is East Coast, rugged, ruddy, Republican, and not, in my book, overendowed with charm.

Virginie is French, blond, *soignée,* and her transition from

Paris to London only serves to exaggerate her extreme Frenchness. It's not just the effortlessly smart way she throws together outfits, or runs her household and business and social life to the click of her fingers, she has this very carnivorous, very amoral, very Gallic thing going on—but still I just don't believe that even Virginie, who seems capable of most things, has the gall (so that's where the word comes from), with all the families of the garden slumbering around, to have Bob Avery under the nose of his sleeping wife and his four children.

Then I have an aha moment—maybe the guilty pair were at it in the garage, not the house. As the Averys never park their Chrysler Voyager in there, maybe Bob uses it to service his mistresses?

Some instinct tells me to note the time and the date. It is 2:44 A.M., 18 March, the day after St. Patrick's Day. For some reason, I think it might be important.

As I lie on my back, in bed, waiting for the pill to take effect, I can't decide whether I'm shocked or not. After all, these gardens, where the rear elevations of the houses enclose a private square, off limits to all but owner-occupiers, are famous for it, as Gideon wistfully tells me. It's so easy to leave a back door invitingly unlocked, and if someone sees you popping into someone's house the back way, your observer won't darkly suspect that you are up to no good with your neighbor's wife—he'll assume you're dropping off that thing you borrowed.

There was one particularly famous time, before all the houses became single occupancy, when the Notting Hill police were trying to catch a serial rapist who'd been preying on young women in basement flats along Elgin Crescent. They put infrared cameras on the roofs for several nights and trained them on the communal garden and waited. Reviewing the footage later, they realized, to their embarrassment, that all they had managed to capture was the lustful crisscrossing of the garden at dead of night by amorous neighbors—among them pillars of the community and prominent financiers. Not surprisingly, the tapes were quietly "lost" before the *Evening Standard* could get hold of them.

But I don't need a camera to prove what I've seen. I'm a direct witness: I know what I've seen. I know what they've been up to, and I wonder if it's any coincidence that today is the day of the Averys' party—a party we've all been looking forward to, not least because tonight we'll find out how Bob and Sally spent six figures on redoing the downstairs kitchen-family room, a room that the previous owners had already redecorated to within an inch of its life, all slate this and Boffi that, only months before the Averys moved in, ripped everything out and started over, which is what happens round here. Houses are redecorated and refurbished on a loop.

And it also means that, later, I'll get to find out how Virginie and Bob act around each other in public, and we're going finally to get a chance to inspect the new billionaire on the block, Si Kasparian, who Mimi is obviously already all excited about even though she hasn't met him yet. I asked her whether she'd Googled him and she denied it, but I don't believe her. Of course she's Googled him. He's a billionaire who's moved on to the garden. She's a journalist with curly chestnut hair, and breasts, and so disgustingly fertile, with her three babies in five years, she could probably self-pollinate if she chose. I know she's determined to get to Si and make him her property before anyone else does.

I get up, close the window, and walk barefoot and naked into the wet room, enjoying the dry warmth of the underfloor heating through the poured concrete floor, the same concrete, in the same soft dove-gray shade, that covers every square foot of floorspace in the house. Gideon goes on and on about concrete, especially when it's made from some waste byproduct like fly ash or slag cement. He says it's a friend to the environment in all stages of its lifespan, making it the ideal material for sustainable construction, but all I care about is how delicious and warm it feels underfoot.

I find a David Mellor tumbler and pour myself some water to counteract the dehydrating effect of the narcotic.

I wake again at 6 A.M. because I hear scrunching underneath the window, and my first thought is relief that I got back to sleep without needing the pill. Then I remember I did take the pill.

My eyes won't open properly so I just lie there for a while. A few minutes later, I hear scrunching again. Someone's running around the garden. I know who it is without bothering to look. Bob Avery. Not only is he American, he has someone to be in shape for and he has something to get in shape for. Virginie, and the garden sports in June.

Most years, we have at least one banker who believes that coming second is for losers presenting himself at the Minor Injuries Unit of St. Charles' Hospital with ankle or groin injuries, and having gravel picked out of his knees.

As the jogging fades away, I clamber out of our huge Savoir bed with its all-white linen and stand in the pounding hot shower with directional body jets for ages. I try to slough off the sleeping pill, and enjoy the feeling of the water drilling into the top of my head and drumming my breasts and stomach before sluicing into the runnels at my feet and draining away into the floor.

I put on some Levi's and some cashmere socks, a gray cashmere sweater over a white agnès b. long-sleeved T-shirt, and pad down to the kitchen. I make a cup of green tea, slip on my fleece-lined lace-up nut-brown Ilse Jacobsen boots, and head out into the communal garden for some fresh air, pausing only to fondle the bud of a mop-headed allium in our garden.

I'll do a circuit, check the frostbitten lilies, the blue toad lily plants *Tricyrtis* 'Blue Wonder,' and make a list as I go. The other day, Ralph Fleming found me on my hands and knees, and he told me I was the spirit of Lonsdale Gardens. I looked up in surprise and saw him smiling down at me, in an awful holey maroon jersey and some baggy cords, a newspaper tucked under his arm, and my heart did a little somersault, and I thought, suddenly, "Lucky Mimi," then the moment passed. I said, "Don't be silly, I'm only potting up blue sage," but it was the nicest thing anyone's said to me for ages.

Mimi

Beep beep beep.

Beep beep. A long male arm lifts out of bed and jabs the clock to silence. The clock is on Ralph's side because Ralph is a morning person and usually springs out of bed like a baby lamb leaping over a ha-ha. But not today, it seems. Whereas I am not a morning person (nor an evening person for that matter, as Ralph points out), so I allow myself to drowse while Ralph fiddles away with the remote control to awaken our new digital television, which carries at least a hundred channels and all the BBC radio ones, too, from standby.

Ralph knows that I can't stand the intrusion of TV in the morning, so what he does is program it to *Today* on Radio Four instead, which he can watch quite happily for hours, despite the unchanging blue screen being completely empty except for the words *Today Programme* and the date, and the exciting news that after the news at 8 A.M. the Education Secretary will be talking about tuition fees. And I know without opening my eyes that, if he's still unusually in bed, his brown eyes are glued to that empty blue screen, he'll be gripping the remote in one hand and what Posy calls his dinkle in the other with the absorption of a toddler sucking his thumb and holding blankie up to his cheek at storytime.

The children, who have all been weaned on PS2 and corrupted by the cathode tube, find it sad that their father actually "watches radio," but I think it's dear. It reminds me of the time we put a long-playing record of *My Fair Lady* on a turntable in a rented cottage in Wales and the children watched it spinning round and round bumpily under the needle for hours as the urbane voice of Rex Harrison poured out silkily from somewhere else. While they're completely blasé about nanotechnology and podcasts, they somehow find proper machinery with real moving parts, like cuckoo clocks or army Land Rovers, rather impressive.

Still, I do think that moving the TV to the bedroom was a mistake.

My former acupuncturist, Donna Linnet, who is *feng shui* guru to the rich and famous of Notting Hill, says that having the telly at the foot of the bed is sapping our *chi*, but that's not the only problem, I fear. Since we got a TV in the bedroom, Ralph watches it, and so do Posy (six), Cas (ten) and Mirabel (eleven), sometimes all at the same time and in our bed, where It is all supposed to happen.

Of course, It happens—it's not total bed death, oh, no, as I explained to Donna (I hope not protesting too much)—but in the very early morning I want to sleep and late at night I also, strangely enough, want to sleep, as lying snug in a toasty bed, doing nothing for nobody, is my favorite thing in the whole world. Not to mention the fact that the loafing presence of three children and also, occasionally, a dog in our bedroom would distract even the most dutiful wife (i.e., not me) from her connubial obligations. . . .

So what usually happens at night is I nod off on my back while Ralph sends himself efficiently to sleep by watching Gavin Esler conduct a long interview with a government actuary about the pensions crisis on *Newsnight*. Then Ralph clicks it off, and we both just about have the energy to murmur, "Good night, darling," and feel a twinge about leaving the thing on standby before slipping into a drooling slumber which is over all too soon (I've always thought it's such a shame that one can't enjoy being asleep more), and in what seems like seconds the alarm clock is beeping again.

Donna says that if we are really determined to put the ka-boom back into bedtime, we should lose the TV and definitely not watch it during our intimate times together. She says that TVs are insistent objects that stare at their owners like dogs wanting to be taken out until they get their owners' attention and emit bad *sha chi*. Then, she says, we should make a statement to affirm what we've done. Donna suggests that Ralph and I should turn to each other after its departure and chant, "Our room is only about passion, rest, and self-nurturing. My partner and I are now able to connect without commercial interruptions."

Whenever Donna talks like this I just nod and say, "I hear what you're saying," and the funny thing is, at the time she's saying it, she sounds as if she's making perfect sense and I want to rush off and do exactly what she tells me. It sounds so obvious and right. But when I tell Ralph later, it comes out all wrong and I sound silly parroting her profound wisdom back at him.

We were up in our bedroom, and Donna was checking which way the bed was facing to see if it was aligned with the natural flow of energy and putting objects such as Ralph's scuffed leather cufflink boxes in pairs as a way of reinforcing close relationships.

I found myself saying, "Donna, angel, my husband's name is pronounced Rafe as in Fiennes, and not as per the roaring sound made by the Metro-Goldwyn-Mayer lion, and only his old schoolfriends call him Ralf, because of his initials, which are R. A. L. F., for Ralph Alec Lorimer Fleming."

Then she shot me a puzzled look. I thought she was going to query Lorimer, which is an unusual name even for someone as highborn as Ralph, but she said, "Mimi, I don't think you and I are on the same page right now. And I'm not sure, to be honest, whether you will ever be in a good place around this issue."

After that, I didn't rebook my weekly appointment. And now my coveted slot's gone to someone whose "needs around wellness" are greater than mine. It's gone to Clare, which is fine by me, what with her unexplained infertility, which, according to Donna, can be helped by *feng shui* and diet as well as all the other obligatory stuff to do with visualization and skeletal realignment, etc.

Anyway, I think it's probably for the best. I'm not sure that *feng shui* isn't mere nineties nonsense for women with too much time and money on their hands, and with our ropey financial situation. . . . And, if I put her plan about getting rid of the new TV and the chanting to Ralph, he might think I'd lost the plot entirely.

Ralph did meet Donna once. I felt that even the lesser task of getting Mohammed to the mountain was quite an achievement. He was very polite, but I could tell he wasn't keen. After she'd gone, trailing clouds of scented oils and leaving empty mugs of herbal tea in her fragrant wake, he slightly let rip and started saying that he didn't see how a grown woman could talk out loud about things like the *li* quadrant of our bagua map without embarrassment. What she was saying did not only make no sense *in English*, it was nonsense *in any language,* and so on.

Ralph likes living with lots of stuff—pictures, furniture, side tables, walnut whatnots, etc.—and he listened icily when Donna delivered herself of her set-piece lecture. "Clutter is anything that gets in the way of the ability to move through the day with grace, serenity, and self-respect," she told Ralph, as she picked up a copy of a long-sold miniature portrait of one of his Fleming ancestors by the school of Hilliard. "Getting rid of clutter makes it easier for you to listen to the quiet voice of intuition, the inner whisper," she murmured, "that guides you toward what you really need to think, to do, to be and to have."

Ralph wasn't, it has to be said, the target audience for this revelation. As she spoke, he gave her his steady look. "What you call clutter are precious things that I love," he said, removing the portrait from her hands before she decluttered it, "not worthless impedimenta to be thrown out on some crazy whim."

So if I mention the ditching-the-TV plan, he'd accuse me of swallowing the whole Notting Hill Mummy thing like one of those little fermented probiotic drinks seething with friendly bacteria, in one gulp.

Still lying here, as the *Today* prog embarks on a heated discussion on the shameful lack of statutory provision of holidays for carers. Hate getting up, and so I'm just thinking about the whole Notting Hill Mummy thing, and how actually outrageous it is that Ralph ever mentions *me* in the *same breath* as NHMs.

A real NHM lives an organic life of holistic therapies and private training sessions in a multimillion-pound house . . . with just a couple of small Filipinas chained up in the basement . . . while looking scrumptious and concerned about the environment at all times. It's all about being beautiful, rich and caring, all at once! About having a Porsche Cayenne . . . as well as a Prius. About having slate solar panels to heat your London home . . . as well as an eight-bedroom spread in Shropshire. It's about having your hair shirt never too far from your Helmut Lang in your walk-in closet.

And I have neither car, am so low-maintenance I never even get my mustache waxed, and the only help I have is Fatty (Fatima is a Portuguese grandmother whom I am ashamed to say I have been known to refer to as "my housekeeper," as if she were color-coding the children's ironed underwear as I speak, who sighingly makes an appearance three times a week).

An NHM is married to a banker, a film director, the owner of a multimedia agency, or the editor of a national newspaper/head of a TV channel. I'm married to a man who does a spot of light consulting and cranks out a few sheets of subscription-only insider info on oil and gas (zzzz—oops. I dropped off for a sec . . .) once a month.

An NHM lives in a house that has all or some of the following: leather floors; rare hardwoods from Japan; a chill-out zone; his and hers bathrooms (his has a plasma screen and connectivity and a glass roof so he can feel like he's taking a shower outdoors while on the phone to New York; hers is a cozy boudoir); climate-controlled shoe closets; filtered central airconditioning; a slate-floored larder; a rubber-floored playroom with a piano and professional recording studio (for the kids' jamming sessions); a wet room; a mudroom; a utility room; and so many acres of stainless steel in the disinfected kitchen you expect a team of morticians in scrubs to pop up any minute and sluice down a corpse or two. And even if an NHM has all of the above and her next-door neighbor puts an ozone pool in the basement, then she suddenly realizes that she "needs" a swimming pool, too, and will literally move heaven and several cubic miles of earth to get one, too.

I live in a faded, shabby but not chic, late Victorian terraced house with none of the above—though it does have glorious views of the communal garden. As I lie here, I look out on golden sunlight on green leaves. Which is, I admit, nice.

An NHM barely works, let alone full time in an office. 1. She's much too busy spending to earn and 2. she's much too tired after a long day ferrying children between activities and attending appointments on only a rocket and shaved Parmesan salad to attend to what our mothers darkly call a husband's "needs," let alone perform gainful employment—she's much too busy being an über-mummy for any of that. Instead, she'll go to yoga or Tui Na to unblock her energy channels, or book an appointment for emergency acupuncture (£100 an hour) after her shattering day.

And a shattering day for an NHM might involve switching to a green energy supplier . . . choosing new wallpaper for the drawing room with her own personal color consultant . . . as well as "coping" with the school run with the assistance of a full-time driver and an omnicompetent, permacheerful, Antipodean nanny.

Here in Notting Hill, you are an NHM if and only if you have met all the following key developmental milestones by the age of forty—but preferably by the age of thirty-five:

1. Have been invited to join a private, celebrity-studded yoga group/book club/Pilates class
2. Have at least one gifted child
3. Have at least one special needs child
4. Weigh less and, even spookier, look younger than your own daughter
5. Employ a family nutritionist, a personal PA, plastic surgeon and a weekend nanny as well as a live-out nanny, a home-work nanny, a housekeeper, and team of alternative therapists
6. Privately tutor your children in the basics, i.e., music, chess, maths, Greek, and Sanskrit
7. Invite your hundred closest friends to a Wigmore Hall–level recital given by your own child, in which he plays a selection of his own compositions
8. Invite a few neighbors round for a kitchen supper which includes at least two internationally renowned foodie friends (locals Sally Clarke, Rowley Leigh, or Alistair Little work well for this stunt)
9. Become new best friends with fab Emma Freud (the Notting Hill Mummy's poster mom) and, whilst we're on that hallowed subject . . .
10. Have a fourth, fifth or even sixth child, as a *famille ultra nombreuse* is the ultimate status symbol for mothers who like to show they've more money and more help to buy them more sleep, the most precious beauty product of all, than everyone else.

And I have achieved none of the above, so I'm not a proper Notting Hill über-mummy, even though I live here. Ralph isn't a Notting Hill über-daddy either, because a blue-chip NHD spends more time on flatbed seats in first class above the Atlantic than he does in bed at home.

Not that we're poor. We're not. We're only "it's a struggle to pay the school fees" poor. We're "we never-go-skiing" poor. We're "we don't have a second home" poor. Which means that by Notting Hill standards, where seven-figure bonuses come as standard and where one of our neighbors recently had several million pounds stolen from his bank account and didn't even notice, we're so impoverished that a certain grim magnificence attaches to our continuing residence in the area.

Our neighbors are a very eclectic, socially mixed bunch: they fall into one of two of a multitude of socioeconomic groups—yes, our neighbors divide into the haves . . . and the have-yachts.

So we live in Notting Hill, and lots of bankers live in Notting Hill, and all bankers are rich. But there's rich and rich, and the bankers round here are extra-super-duper ultra-rich, because they are—as they will happily tell you when you ask them to justify their sick-making salaries and bonuses—the superstars of the financial and corporate and entrepreneurial worlds. If Patrick Molton were a model, rather than a banker, he would be Kate Moss. If Bob Avery were a footballer, he'd be David Beckham. If Jeremy Dodd Noble were a playwright not a ring-tone king (he's very big in Nokia), he'd be Harold Pinter. But we're just normal, and it's hard to do normal in Notting Hill, though I think I make a pretty good fist of it, despite Ralph.

Ralph despises alternative medicine, fashion, expensive restaurants, shiny rich people, swanky houses, and, most of all, he can't see the point of famous people unless they're expert and passionate dry-fly fishermen. Plus, he hates shopping unless it's in two London streets—Jermyn or St. James's, and on his own. So Ralph finds the whole Notting Hill scene, well, a touch brassy and try-hard.

Ralph feels that his family proved itself about a thousand years ago when the first earl toadied up to the reigning monarch of the day, and he regards any sort of showing off or display of excess wealth or social aspiration—all of which are of course endemic to this *pose*code—as vulgar and uncalled for.

As for our neighbors . . .

Trish and Jeremy Dodd Noble. He's a very well-preserved sporty type of fifty-five; she's fifteen years younger. Trish can be tricky and tactless, but I'm fond of her, I really am. They live in a big all-white house on Lonsdale Gardens, two gifted children, no pets. We call Trish "Doors to Manual" for the very good reason that in common with all younger second wives in Poshtershire (i.e., Gloucestershire), where, needless to say, they have a £2 million second home near Little Sodbury, she looks like an air stewardess, in a glossy, blond, Virgin Atlantic sort of way that I only wish I could pull off.

Clare and Gideon Sturgis, who live next door but one. She's my closest chum on the garden, very into her new garden-design consultancy work, very . . . perfectionist (trying not to say anal), i.e., if the children forget to remove their outdoor shoes, her nose twitches, and if you eat a croissant standing up in her kitchen (is there any other way?), she will hand you a side plate. They have no children, but while Clare is deep in bio-panic, Gideon (hairy, dark, and successful eco-architect or ecotect, who cleans up round here) seems to find their continuing inability to breed easier to bear each year, perhaps because he has other consolations, not to mention his fantastically successful practice.

The Forsters. Nice retired diplomatic couple from Notting Hill's more rackety days (i.e., when £30,000 bought you a five-bedroom house rather than a nanny car, sandwiched between us. Two grown-up children, Lucy a teacher and Alexander a rising young star in the Conservatives, a bred-in-the-bone Notting Hill Tory (i.e., eats at Zucca, bicycles, and uses Gideon to refurbish his house).

Bob and Sally Avery. The newish kids on the block, Americans from Boston, bankers, though she's "doing kids right now"; she's a slight blond crop-headed WASP and he's a freckly, rugged Irish type.

The Mathieu Lacostes. Mathieu is a weedy Frog in canary cords and pullovers who rarely appears, and Virginie is a slippery little minx who will no doubt be responsible for triggering early puberty in Cas and all the other boys on the garden in a few years' time.

The Moltons, Marguerite and Patrick. She's rather anxious and translucent but very beautiful, and he's a cheery rugby-fanatic type, very boysy with Max, Charlie, and Sam, who are all down for Eton, of course, and last but not least—Si Kasparian. Though I haven't met him yet. He's this transatlantic, apparently very secretive billionaire (well, he's on the Rich List) whose smoldering photograph (on deck of yacht in open-necked shirt, always the same one) sometimes appears in the business sections. He's just bought 104 Lonsdale Gardens, spent the purchase price again on the refurb, and is about to move in.

I find this exciting. In fact, though I would never admit this to Clare, I've Googled Si a few times, but there's not much out there. Everyone on the garden is playing it cool (it's simply not done to show you're impressed by anyone or anything), but there's no doubt at all that all the women on the garden —me, Clare, Trish, Virginie—are in a covert competition to get to him first and then—if so minded—the winner might graciously let the others in on the act. It's not every day that a brooding billionaire becomes the boy next door . . . so the race is on. This always happens when new blood moves in— when everyone is insanely rich and lacks for nothing, literally the only thing left to acquire is trophy friends who can be counted on to add luster to your many parties.

When I say "everyone" is rich and lacks for nothing, I don't include me. Basically, since we moved here, the neighborhood's taken off into the stratosphere like a Hawker Harrier jump jet, leaving me and Ralph standing alone on the flight deck with our mouths slightly open.

The reality is, Ralph owns this house, and we only live here because his father, Peregrine, bought it for sweetie money in the sixties and passed it on to Ralph (something complicated to do with capital gains and inheritance tax far beyond my comprehension), and it has, apparently, increased in value by around 3,000 percent over twelve years, which I also do not begin to understand.

But now I adore the bloody area, that's the problem.

I'm completely embedded. I love living on the communal garden, it's like a sort of villa holiday with like-minded friends that never ends, only with different rows, not about whose turn it is to do the shopping and cooking and drowning duty at the pool but whose turn it is to organize the renewal of the playbark under the swings or supply the mulled organic wine and hot nibbles on Bonfire Night. Though I should add that Ralph calls Lonsdale Gardens "Flanders" (because every inch of soil is fought over . . . to the *death* . . . and we all take such entrenched positions on life-and-death things like . . . well, where to relocate the compost heap).

And I love working from home and can spend what I regard as a busy and productive morning playing tennis, having coffee with a girlfriend, and then wandering home to squeeze in a spot of work before guzzling my own bodyweight in fried green tomatoes with mozzarella at 202 on Westbourne Grove, which is, unfortunately, one of the most irresistible shopping streets in the whole of London. There was a bad moment the other day when I went out to the market for a cabbage and came back with a furry tweedy piece from Yates Buchanan that cost my whole monthly paycheck and didn't realize I'd forgotten the cabbage till I got home.

This would all be very well if 1. we were rich and 2. I didn't have to work. So I'm a freelance journalist. It sounds quite swish but, in fact, *freelance* is simply the standard euphemism for a person who slobs about the house in pajama bottoms and coffee-stained T-shirt complaining about workload and hustling for freebies—and describing herself, naturally, as a "writer" to attractive men at dinner parties.

After continuing to lie in bed for precisely five more minutes, during which all this thinking somehow contrives to make me nod off again, I go to the bathroom. As a person with latent curls, I have to get in there before Ralph steams the place up with his shower, for important, frizzy-hair-related reasons.

For some reason Calypso's barking in the kitchen. She also barked earlier, at around 6 A.M., because some fitness freak was jogging around the garden, round and round, *scrunch-scrunch-scrunch* on the gravel. The noise annoyingly roused me from the most heavenly dream, all about finding a shop that stocked cashmere sweaters in delicious colors at Primark prices, which I was heaping into a shopping trolley.

Calypso's barking always makes us nervous, even if it's just a few yaps. Luckily, the Forsters are nice doggy people but, on the other side, well, the couple has baby twins and he has to be in the City at 7 A.M., and I know they don't like it. The last thing we want is for the families with babies to restart the Hundred Years War against the families with dogs, because that battle can only end with the doomsday scenario, which is dogs being banned from the communal garden.

And we couldn't live without Calypso. Just thinking of it brings tears to my eyes. She's easily the nicest member of our family, with far the best manners. We'd have to leave this oasis of greenery in the middle of one of the loveliest parts of London. No more watching my neighbors' children grow up alongside my own. No more built-in playmates for those long, boring weekends during term time. No more strolling round the garden at dusk, smelling the honeysuckle and roses, congratulating ourselves on the perfection of our habitat.

Ralph keeps saying we'll have to move soon anyway, because

we're living in an area so beyond our joint pay-grade (true) that we can't afford to shop in it (also, tragically for me, true). But I'm still pretending that we won't, that there will be no exit from the Garden of Eden. Maybe I'm in denial. But, as I say to Ralph, even if I am in denial, it's still a lot better than being in somewhere like . . . Perivale.

"Darling girl, what planet are you on?" he replies, if I ever mention Perivale, with a quivering lower lip.

"There's no way we can afford the *Hanger Lane gyratory*—we're going to have to move to the country and live off the land, like that boy who was at school—you know, Hugh fairly long name."

And then I laugh a brittle laugh, as if he's joking really. "But, Ralph, everywhere is expensive now, country property's *shot up*, and Bridport is fearfully chic now Hugh Fearnley-Whittingstall has started flogging River Cottage nettle soup. It's just that Notting Hill prices are ridiculous—and it's not *our fault* this is where we live," I purr. "It's our *good fortune*, don't you think, darling?"

Whenever I say this, Ralph mutters something about hearing the distant rumble of tumbrils, which, roughly translated, means, I think, that we're living on borrowed time as well as borrowed money.

Clare

I'm sucking in lungfuls of damp morning air. A light mist is lifting off the grass. The sun is flashing off spotless windows. In downstairs kitchens, families are breakfasting with their children. I can see my neighbor Lady Forster in her Formica kitchen, which was no doubt considered daringly avant garde when it was put in but now looks as if it should be in the V&A.

The Forsters are among the very few old-timers around here who've managed to cling on to their houses on communal gardens despite the savage pressure grown children exert on their aging parents to hand down their homes. Apart from them and the Flemings, who are clinging on despite everything, this garden consists of bankers, television executives and leading architects but, mainly, it has to be said, bankers.

Lady F. is listening to the *Today* program, deafeningly loud —I can hear Anne Atkins's smug voice from here—and making a cup of tea in the proper way for Sir John, using a gilded tin tea caddy dating from the Queen's coronation, strainer and milk in a jug. She is wearing her pink candlewick dressing-gown, and the scene is very reassuring in a fifties Britain way. The kitchen has fitted cupboards and tiled worktops in black and white and a lino floor the color of blood-orange juice. Actually, if it was cleaned up a bit, it would be rather now in a retro sort of way.

Lady Forster has a son and a daughter. Son Alexander is a rising Tory MP, rather good-looking, married to Priscilla, who is big in designer leather pet accessories in hot pink and purple colors. Lucy teaches.

I'm fond of Lady F. She's the sort of woman upon whom Empire was built and doesn't complain about anything ever, and calls a spade a spade. Still, Mimi and I often say it's lucky that both she and Sir John are rather deaf.

The Flemings' household is bedlam and, as we don't have any fitted carpets, every footfall on our side echoes like gunshot. So we tend to walk around on the concrete floors in our thick cashmere socks, trying not to slip, especially down the staircases, and try to suggest to visitors that they remove their shoes upon entry, as if we are going to perform a Japanese tea ceremony or something.

As it's 7:55—I know because I can hear "Thought for the Day"—the morning exodus is in full swing. On this garden, lots of the children go to Ponsonby Prep, up at Notting Hill Gate. Even though Ponsonby's only up the road, it's astonishing how many of them are driven the short distance to school, in this day and age.

When I pointed this out to Mimi, she said she was all for walking to school in principle, and mostly did, but the problem was that children did so many extracurricular things these days, demanding close parental involvement, that it was actually quite hard to schlep even a few hundred yards with children and all the stuff they need for school, e.g., a trombone, rugby kit including helmet and mouth guard, three lunch boxes, three satchels, a box of Krispy Kremes for class "snack," plus a handmade model of the solar system that Daddy has spent all half-term making.

I told her I wouldn't know, and she had the grace to blush. I mainly ride a bicycle around and have a Citroën van for the run to Rassells, and disapprove of all this ferrying to and fro—but then, as I said, I don't do the school run. Not yet, anyway.

Wussy's come out. Our cat. He's rubbing against my leg while I sip my green tea a bit more so it doesn't slop over when I do my walk-round (there's the annual general meeting tomorrow night—so always the chance that I'll be nobbled by the neighbors).

Wuss the Puss simply wandered into the house one day and

never left. He had no tag, no chip. After three days, I took him to the vet, the rather smart Mr. Carmichael on Addison Avenue, to have him checked out and neutered. I'll never forget that day. It was the Wrst time I was taking a small creature that was dependent on me to the doctor, and I suddenly knew what it was like to be a mother with a sick child, waiting at the surgery.

Mr. Carmichael called, "Mr. Wussy Sturgis, please," and I realized he meant Wuss. He snapped on some rubber gloves, lifted him onto the white table, and examined him all over. He looked at his teeth, ran his hands down Wussy's legs and did something to his bottom I tried not to notice. Then he cleared his throat and said I needn't bother about neutering because the mite had "very little on that front to write home about." Carmichael then charged me £60 for a couple of jabs, which is pretty standard round here for a couple of minutes' work. At the Food Doctor, my friends are more than happy to pay more simply to be told not to eat "anything white."

I've never told Gideon about Wussy's manhood issues. Men are odd about that sort of thing, especially Gideon, and especially as we're trying to start a family. I've finally given up trying to avoid this unattractive expression, even if it does suggest that the leap from pitiable childless couple to Kennedy-style dynasty is achieved in a twinkling of bedclothes, which is certainly not true in our case.

Giddy dotes on Wuss even more than I do. Part of me had begun to wonder whether us not having children suited Gideon, as he loves having me all to himself and is so busy with his ecotecture practice, and he can be quite moody and critical at times, though I wouldn't go so far as Mimi does. She once described Gideon, to his face, as the only man she'd ever met who "actually seemed to have periods"—a very Mimi remark to which I have never alluded since.

In fact, she talks about Gideon, or "Giddy," a lot. I've even wondered whether she might have a little crush on him. He is, after all, a notably successful architect, still has his own hair, and his work is always appearing in magazines. Not that I'm exactly idle myself, especially now it's spring.

It's that time of year. I'm busier with my one-woman garden-design business than I've ever been. The sun comes out, and some master of the universe looks out of the window for the first time in months and announces, "We must do something about the garden situation," to no one in particular.

When a Notting Hill banker says that, this is what he means. It means he expects his wife to dial in high-end services and get the top person for the job. It certainly doesn't mean that at the weekend they're going to go to B&Q or Homebase and stock up on lawn feed and RoundUp, like normal couples do, because there sure aren't any normal couples around here.

Whenever I see That Film (this is how we refer to *Notting Hill*, the film, just as *Macbeth* is the Scottish play), I find it peculiar that the happy-ever-after shot is of a pregnant Julia Roberts and Hugh Grant lying on a bench in a communal garden in Notting Hill. To me, that scene signified the beginning of narrative tension not the happy ever after.

How they got here doesn't interest me—what I want to know is how they're coping in their new and very alien environment. I can't watch the film without thinking that they or any other celebrity couple wouldn't last five minutes in a communal garden and would soon have to slink off to some nice gated mansion in Hampstead where they don't have to interact with anyone.

When I try to explain this to friends who live in Chelsea or Belgravia or Hampstead, I say it helps to imagine the communal garden not as five bucolic acres of lawned areas and planted beds in bosky Kensington but as a piece of disputed territory like, say, Bosnia. Within the zone, there are any number of warring tribes but, basically, the main factions here boil down to families with young children and no dogs, families with grown children and dogs, couples with dogs and no children, gays, and Americans. The families with small children hate the dog owners. The old people and the gays love the dog owners but hate the families with noisy children and teenagers. The gays love the old people and the dog owners. And everyone secretly hates the Americans, but for all the wrong reasons. So it may be communal but it is, in fact, easily the least kibbutznik five acres of open space anywhere in the civilized world.

Then they get it, especially when I tell them that the man who invented *Big Brother* got the idea when he was living on a Notting Hill communal garden and realized that he couldn't pick his nose in his own drawing room without about a hundred people knowing exactly what he was doing.

Another thing. Most people think of Kensington and Chelsea as a green part of London, but it's not. There's hardly any open space at all. Communal gardens are about as communal as public schools are public. In fact, as Ralph once pointed out when we were lying on the tidy green lawn on rugs, with glasses of chilled white wine and some peppered cashew nuts, one warm summer evening, "The only access most of the council block kids get to grass in this borough is via the dealers at Ladbroke Grove tube." So, if you ever wondered why it is that people are prepared to trample over their own grandmothers in their determination to secure a family house in an ice-cream color, now you know.

And once we're here, you'd think that we'd be much too busy smelling the roses to fret about someone putting a white plastic picnic table outside his back door (only teak or iron garden furniture is allowed), or painting the rear of his house an unacceptable shade of cream (only certain shades of cream will do), but no. Many of us are only truly happy when uncovering lapses of taste and other transgressions in each other and then bringing them up in the garden, or at the committee meetings, in front of everyone else.

Mimi

After turning off the alarm, Ralph sinks back into his pillow. Morning has been broken for at least ten minutes and neither of us has spoken.

I decide to nip into the bathroom to pee before rousing the children. As I'm reaching for the loo paper, "That one, Greg," a man's voice says, from somewhere beneath me. "That big branch, then let's make a start on the willow."

I'd forgotten that tree surgery was happening in Lonsdale Gardens today.

I'd seen the flyer that came through the door from the garden committee about keeping children away from falling branches and stump grinding, which sounded vaguely dental, but I didn't see anything that spelled out that our large splendid ash, its patchy, variegated bark the exact same color and pattern as Mini-Boden camouflage trousers, which has preserved our modesty and screened our bathroom window for many years, was "having work."

I begin to get a funny feeling that someone is watching me.

I'm right. A man in a hard hat and holding a chainsaw is framed in the bathroom window, not two meters from my nose, looking at me. I decide not to grab the towel. After all, I'm in my own bathroom.

Then he raises his chainsaw aloft, as if in greeting.

A tooth-grating whine starts up, and he applies the chainsaw to a large branch, which falls with a sickening, tearing crash to the ground.

I feel a pang. I liked our tree. It looked beautiful and healthy to me. But that means nothing nowadays. I had no idea it was the Keira Knightley of trees, for even radiant damsels who bathe in rain dew with unicorns must "have work" these days.

I flush and leave the bathroom sideways.

"There's a man with a chainsaw sitting in the tree outside the bathroom window, I warn you," I tell Ralph, when I reach the safety of the bedroom. After all, it's not every day this happens. "He just watched me pee."

"And did you enjoy that?" says Ralph, his eyes still drawn to the blank TV screen.

I snort and start going through my underwear drawer, searching for pants, just one pair, that's all I ask. I've long given up on socks and have abandoned thongs for any number of good reasons, but the wholesale disappearance of underwear makes me wonder whether Ralph's loony theory that Fatima is secretly selling all the things we've ever lost on a stall in the Portobello Road to "fund her secret crack habit" is in fact true.

"Why, I ask, are girls so coy about what is after all a natural and necessary function," continues Ralph, swinging his long legs over the bed, wearing only a pair of cornflower-blue pajama bottoms in light cotton, so I can admire his lean torso.

Ralph has very few clothes, but the ones he has are invariably very good. Take the PJs he has on/off today. He may have lost the top somewhere (i.e., Fatima may have sold it on the Portobello Road), but the bottoms are still from Hilditch and Key, and piped in cream silk.

"I've never had the slightest problem even crapping in front of other people," he continues, as Anne Atkins drones on about our shared human response to a Serbian granny who prayed to God and found she was expecting a miracle baby at the age of sixty-seven. "Nor do any other men I know have a problem with it. Christ on a bike! Sixty-seven years old! You've got another three decades of childbearing years to go, what a ghastly thought! In fact, Meems," he says, disappearing into the bathroom, "I'm hearing the Call right now."

"The Call" is short for "the call to stool," an ancient Fleming family saying that I sincerely hope requires no further explanation from me.

After an interval, I hear the flush. Ralph has balls, I have to admit. I can't go *at all* if anyone is within earshot. He teases me about it. I've had three babies but am reluctant to admit that I have a back passage at all, and have to turn the page swiftly when the G2 section of the *Guardian* runs one of its regular first-person accounts of some poor sod's colorectal surgery.

Then I hear the *chugga-wokka-chugga* of our knackered power-shower (installed in the fond hope that we will one day let the house to the mythical people we simply call "Rich Americans" in the summer) start up, and then downpour.

Ralph comes back in dripping, leaving damp footprints on the carpet, and drops the towel to the floor. I give the towel a pointed look, but Ralph ignores it with the ease of long practice. Ralph has always treated any house he lives in as a hotel and has made it clear he is not going to change now, however many times I complain about the troubling and persistent nonappearance of the "towel fairy" and the "shirt fairy" and so on.

He says I should be very grateful I've managed to find anyone to marry me at all, and I don't know how lucky I am to have nabbed Ralph Alec Lorimer Fleming.

Naked, Ralph puts on his watch, which he keeps on his bedside table. It's a very old Patek Philippe. Apparently, this is some kind of heirloom timepiece, according to some American woman he sat next to at dinner, but Ralph just calls it "Grandfather's watch."

"You never really own a Patek Philippe," he says now, as he straps it on his wrist before rubbing his hair dry with another towel and then dropping that to the floor, too, "you merely look after it for the next generation."

He's never said this before. I think he must have been reading my copy of *Vanity Fair* on the loo while doing number two in front of an uninvited audience of tree surgeons, singing, shaving, and managing to drench all three clean towels in the bathroom with water.

Whoever said men are incapable of multitasking has clearly never met Ralph.

When I come down, dressed in an unsightly array of my own and Cas's most forgiving and elasticated garments, Mirabel blurts in a shocked voice, *"Mum!"*

I think she is about to accuse me of stealing Cas's tracksuit bottoms, even though I paid for them and sewed in the nametape, but she says, "What are those marks on your cheek?"

I am so concerned I've broken out that I dash to the mirror in the hall—only to see the faintest impression of pillow pinkly scoring my face. I sigh and rejoin my growing family.

"It's only facial quilting, darling," I say, pouring tea. "You gave me a shock. I thought there was something really wrong."

Mirabel merely raises one eyebrow a minute fraction. This is only one of the ways that she conveys disapproval, but it is one of the most lethal.

It's her age. It was only last year that she spent the entire summer in shorts and bare feet reading the Animal Ark series. One day it was *Ponies in the Paddock*, next day it was *Puppies in the Porch*, and a furry, kitten-soft climax was reached with *Lambs in the Lane*. Now she's a miniskirted neo-nymphet into Green Day concerts ("I must go! It's my destiny, Mum," she wails), black eye makeup and chatrooms, just as Cas will be all wanking and whiffy trainers any day now.

Gloomy thought.

During breakfast, I start telling the children about the man seeing me starkers on the loo, dangling outside the window— "The man, not me, that is," I say—thinking the story might amuse them.

Mirabel carries on crunching her Honey Nut Cheerios and interrupts me, like Jeremy Paxman cutting off a Tory junior minister in mid-flow. "Like, TMI; Mum. Please. You're *old*. You shouldn't be walking around the house naked anyway, at your age. It's just so *mank*."

"I am only thirty-seven," I retort. "And it's my house. I can walk around naked as much as I like."

"Whatev," says my daughter, in a voice intended to convey that her mother isn't even worth the expenditure of a third syllable.

"Your mother's right, of course," says Ralph mildly, sipping his tea, "about the main thing, which is her right to amble about naked. The minor issue of this being *her* house," he sighs, "I am generously letting go." After that, the children stage one of their noisy rows about who finished all the orange juice, during which Ralph sits reading the paper.

Ralph has many unique qualities, and one of them is to continue reading the *Daily Telegraph* while Cas and Mirabel fight over who has the last bowl of Honey Nut Cheerios while I unload and fill the dishwasher at warp speed, trip over the dog bowl, check homework folders, make sure the children have all their kit for sport and music and something mysterious made of balsa wood for IT, and Posy witters on and on in his ear about something to do with the Bayeux Tapestry and Year Two.

He doesn't call it being unhelpful. He calls it Doing. Things. One. At. A. Time. And not losing his head while everyone around is losing theirs, naturally, and blaming it on him, as if he's dug in the trenches at Passchendaele rather than sitting in the kitchen at 67 Colville Crescent at breakfast time.

Clare

At this time of year, March, the grass is a pale newborn green, the color of a Golden Delicious, and is so thick and lush I could almost get my head down and start munching, like a cow. It's sublime out here. The sun's pouring over Lonsdale Gardens, bouncing off freshly painted stucco. The buds are all waiting to unclench like millions upon millions of baby fists, and the blossoms beginning to foam on the cherry and almond trees.

Sniff deeply, and you're not in London at all. It smells so good, with the syrupy scent of viburnum swirling through the crisp early morning air, roughened by exhaust. I could bottle it—this essence of *rus in urbe*.

As I tread over the wet grass in my boots, cup in hand, I note that Stephen has recently hacked up sods of turf in the free-range areas of lawn known as the wildflower meadows and planted yellow primroses at drunken angles.

It's not something I, a plantswoman, would have chosen to do. They're seasonal, but that doesn't mean they're right for here. But Stephen's the gardener. He's the one paid to plant and embellish and maintain the communal garden, not me, thank God. I'm busy enough as it is, as I'm in sole charge of the house and the diary, not to mention present-buying, clothes storage, cashmere care, photo albums, holiday booking, and everything to do with our house and garden, both of which serve as an ongoing showcase for our own style, of course.

Last night. I can't stop thinking about it. Bob. And Virginie. About Virginie. And Bob.

I don't feel as if I've been spying. If you live on the garden, you can't help but see things. We all see straight into each others' back gardens, rear windows—and should live our lives accordingly.

Take Mimi.

I like the fact that Mimi's kitchen is always full of other people's kids eating handfuls of Honey Nut Cheerios out of the packet, but mainly I like it because they're not in *my* kitchen, making crumbs. Gideon would be horrified to come home and find children untidily strewn along the benches and perched on worktops, helping themselves to *his* freshly squeezed mandarin juice from the fridge.

The kids shade in and out of each others' houses like cats. But the adults are more careful to respect boundaries. Having said that, Mimi often rocks up unannounced to my study to use the fax machine, applying her own menial standards of housekeeping and privacy to everyone else, I suppose.

So, unless you move out, you have to rub along. The secret to harmony is to defuse any potential disputes before people start suing each other. Litigation is regarded as an unwholesome American import, sort of like Halloween. We try to avoid it.

Still, I'm not sure Stephen's going to get away with the primroses, though. Someone's bound to bring it up tomorrow night. We're all charming and considerate when we're on our own turf, or in each others' houses, but anything to do with the communal garden manages to bring out the two-year-old in all of us.

I make a note in my pad. Primulas. Underneath that, I write, "Bob and Virginie. Tell Mimi?"

I will decide after I've done a tour of the garden and checked out the scene of the crime.

Most of my clients live on the other side of the garden, on the Lonsdale or so-called right side of the garden, while the Colville side is sometimes described as the "wrong" side.

This used to sound odd to me, before I moved here. When

I chatted to residents, trying to find out who might be selling and which elderly couple might be on their last legs, I used to wonder whether there could really be a wrong side to a communal garden where houses on one side cost two million plus and on the other between three and five million. The answer to that is, as I now know, how could there not be?

There's also a hierarchy of gardens. Our Colville–Lonsdale garden is not nearly as smart as the ones that divide Elgin Crescent and Lansdowne Road, or Ladbroke Square Gardens, or Montpelier Garden. It's more of a family garden; it allows dogs and ball games, and there's a playground at one end. Which doesn't explain why Si Kasparian has just moved here, but he must have his reasons. I write myself another little memo. This one says, "Get on to Si K. asap."

Now I'm out here, looking in on the weed-infested scrubby patch that is the Flemings' back garden. It's funny how I can match people to gardens much more easily than I can to their houses. It's even easier than matching dogs to owners.

The Forsters' garden is scented and contemplative, which is something all retired couples ask for. The hip young couple with baby twins next door to Mimi have turned their garden into an extra room, for barbecues and hanging out in, with cushions and rugs, and a yurt at one end in the summer.

Though some of the private little back gardens here are quite small—we're not talking *parterre* at Versailles, put it that way—size definitely doesn't matter when it comes to the budget. I do lots of gardens in Chiswick, and further north, in W10 and Queens Park, but I've noticed that clients there are quite beady and keep a careful track of what I'm buying, asking whether we really need so many camellias or jasmines, and even cheekily about whether I can pass on my discount. But my Notting Hill clients are different. The more they spend, the happier they are. Also, they never do anything themselves that they can pay someone else to do for them.

I was going to say that families with boys always have

knackered lawns, but the Moltons' little garden here is immaculate, despite the three boys. Well-weeded flower beds. Swept York stone paving. Low box hedging. White plants in chunky terra cotta pots. It's all tidy.

The only mess at all is by the back door, an area littered with Max, Charlie, and Sam's footballs interspersed with pairs of mud-clogged trainers. I can just see the boys running in from the garden into the downstairs kitchen for tea and obediently kicking off their trainers before entering the hygienic home.

It's strange to think that Patrick's chairman of the garden committee. He's got so much on his plate already.

He's a good father, though. When he comes home early from the bank, or the airport, he'll often come straight out in his suit, to find his boys. He'll hang his jacket from a branch, and play keepy-uppy or practice headers with Max and Charlie and the rest, leaping like a salmon and showing his sons and their friends and any mothers who might be watching just what an athletic all-round great guy he is.

He may be chairman but whenever I try to talk to him about plants and his own garden, his eyes very quickly glaze over. So I talk to Marguerite, who is very clear about what she wants. She doesn't want anything rambling and romantic but clean geometric shapes. When Patrick found me clipping the box hedges by their back entrance the other day, he made his usual joke about me trimming my bush. He's made it so often that this time I replied by telling him that he was out of touch and that big bushes were back, I'd read it in *Vogue*, and he roared with laughter.

I'm now peering through foliage toward the back door of *maison* Lacoste, scene of last night's secret tryst.

The Lacoste garden is all-white and, in the summer, highly scented. There's even a statue in the middle, to add a quite redundant touch of grandeur to the setting. At the back of the house, there are shutters drawn across the windows on the lower ground and ground floors. It's a French thing. They are much more private than the Brits, or the Americans, who find the very notion of hedges dividing and separating gardens very quaint. Unless I'd seen her with my own eyes, I'd never imagine Virginie out here in the dark at 3 A.M., fumbling with her back-door key in her bare legs and wellies. And still, part of me can't believe that Bob and Virginie are so in lust with each other that they are willing to dice not just with their marriages but with their standing with the neighbors . . . just for sex.

Of the Lacostes there is no sign. That's normal. Virginie's probably designing Prince of Wales check knickerbockers in her office in South Kensington, and Mathieu doesn't seem to be around that much at all—he's often in Paris doing stuff for L'Oréal.

I stand for a second, looking at the secretively shuttered rear elevation of their elegant, five story mansion with off-street parking and staff accommodation.

Virginie.

She's slender rather than thin and exudes a toned and burnished elegance no Englishwoman can hope to match. Her skin is always slightly bronzed, and her hair is pale gold. It falls to her shoulders like a waterfall and when she turns her head it swishes and falls back exactly into place, like in a shampoo advertisement. Her daytime uniform is a crisp white shirt, the collar and cuffs and shirt-tails of which peek out from underneath a tight merino sweater. Sometimes she pushes her hair off her smooth bronzed forehead with an Alice band, wears Capri trousers and a figure-hugging cashmere cardigan, and looks a bit like the young Brigitte Bardot. She'll come out to retrieve some important trinket the twins have left in the garden or to look for her son, Guy.

When she's in the garden, all the men give her that stare— the one they can't help giving when they see a woman and can't think of anything else but her, and their wives have to nudge them quite hard to stop.

I see Patrick give her this look, especially when she turns around and he can enjoy the sight of her rear end. She's super-slim but has one of those bottoms, like the ones you see gracing the window display of every French pharmacy. Gideon has made a lifetime's study of these ads and can spend happy minutes standing outside a pharmacy studying large semi-pornographic images of tanned female bodies lying naked in the surf advertising products to get rid of cellulite. Even after bearing three children, Virginie has the sort of bottom that doesn't need one single application of Derrière Lifting at all, which must be a sort of miracle from what I hear from all my girlfriends of the lowering effect of childbirth on the rear end. Put it this way. She even looks sensational in *culottes,* or what the magazines call City shorts, with ballet flats, which is possibly the hardest look of all to carry off. When I pointed this out to Gideon, he said that she probably looked even better *sans-culottes* and licked his lips, so I frowned and changed the subject. I wonder if Sally Avery has noticed anything—she's not the type to turn a blind eye, that's for sure.

Mathieu and Virginie have Guy, about nine, shy, with large knees. Then there are the twins, Capucine and Clementine, always dressed identically in palest pink laundered cotton dresses and matching pale pink cashmere, with white socks and pink button shoes from Bonpoint.

Needless to say, the children are bilingual and are all either at, or going to, the Lycée Français, so Virginie is the only West London parent I've met who is not in a permanent state of competitive anxiety about her children's private education. This seems to free her up enormously to do lots of other things, all of which she does well. Not only does she apparently have a new lover. She has three children. A husband. Three residences to maintain, in two countries (there are two houses in France as well as this one). And, most annoyingly of all, she eats.

I once dropped something off at her house. It was lunchtime. I found her sitting on her own in the kitchen eating a very undercooked steak oozing blood, some *dauphinoise* potatoes and green beans, with a pot of chocolate mousse waiting by her plate. She was also well stuck into a large glass of red wine. I found this a cheering sight. I think it was the reverence she accorded her lunch break that impressed me even more than her calorific intake.

Oh, yes, and about five years ago, she launched a mail-order clothes catalogue called BCBG. There is also a baby clothes line, BC Bébé, which she added after the birth of the twins. This is, needless to say, extremely expensive but, according to the founder owner, plugs a yawning gap in the market.

"When I 'ad Guy, I found it impossible to find haut de gamme children's clothes in England in le style anglais," she told me, without irony, *"so I 'ad to make zem myself."*

I haven't looked at the Averys' garden. I know it so well anyway. I'll come back to them later this morning, after I've had my weekly session with Donna, and place some fragrant plants on either side of their Adirondack chairs, in readiness for their party. I might also suggest to Sally that they move Megan's rabbit hutches off the lawn to smarten the place up, even though moving the hutches will leave unsightly sad brown patches . . . and I want to assess Si's garden too—if I'm going to approach him tonight and pitch, I need some ideas.

I've been right round the garden. It took twenty minutes. It's now getting on for 8:30. I'm going to go out to Rassells for some stuff, including more blue sage, for the herb garden by the children's swings, which has somehow become my preserve. On this garden, if you don't have children, it's assumed you'll be thrilled to take responsibility for everything else. Then I am going to Guy Parsons to get my hair done for the Avery party.

After all, Virginie will be there, looking edible in some ultra-feminine cocktail dress—she has wonderful taste in clothes, but if you ask her who she's wearing she just shrugs, as if it's a silly question, that it's not a question of labels, it's a question of quality and fit.

And I don't want Gideon all over her as well as Bob. And as I also want to ambush Si, I want to look my best, and I know how lethal Frenchwomen are (not to mention Mimi, who has been known to launch herself at a key male target like a heat-seeking missile).

But the French—they open their mouths and say something mundane like, "Are not Helena's white roses magnificent?" and otherwise sensible Englishmen lose their grip completely. I sometimes see them staring at Virginie with the same doggy greed you see on the face of a drooling old family Labrador while the Sunday joint's being carved.

If only they knew what I know about her, though. She looks so proper and correct as she goes off to Mass at St. Francis of Assisi every Sunday with the children in their knickerbockers and smocks, but underneath that demure exterior, I know what she is. She has the face of the Virgin Mary but the body of a whore—which is what makes her so irresistible, I suppose.

Mimi

I get back from Hyde Park, where I have suffered the daily indignity of being the only NHM actually walking her own dog (all the others pay walkers and/or personal trainers to achieve exactly the same result), and Patrick Molton's driver is still waiting, which could very well be some sort of local record for how long a driver can double-park with his engine running on company time. The *Daily Express* is folded on the passenger seat. He's got out of the car to have a quick fag.

"Still waiting for his Lordship, are we?" I remark, as I stroll past with Calypso.

The driver rolls his eyes and grinds out his stub on the pavement. "Waiting for his Lordship to arrive back from the airport, so I can then drive him on to work," he answers.

At that moment, a taxi glides up and double-parks outside the Moltons', engine gurgling. Patrick gets out, holding a briefcase and a copy of *The Wall Street Journal*. He gives a hand gesture to his waiting driver and disappears into his house.

The taxi pulls away. The Lexus towncar's engine, an expensive chug, blends in. The air is full of exhaust, noise and expectation. For a second, I think with rueful admiration of Ralph, who uncomplainingly takes the tube to Westminster every day, wearing his shoe leather thin on London's pavements; then I leave the masters of the universe and their drivers and let myself into my own house. I put on the kettle and go straight to the fridge.

I am weak with hunger, even though it's only an hour since a substantial breakfast, during which I polished off Posy's soldiers and also managed to force down two bits of toast all on my own. As I'm cramming slices of M&S Edam reserved for the children's lunch boxes into my mouth, the telephone goes.

It's Clare. I mentally devote the next half hour to her ongoing bio-panic, take the hands-free and start prowling around the kitchen, waiting for the kettle. But Clare doesn't talk about her failure to conceive for the two-hundredth month in a row.

"So, guess who I saw in her nightgown in the communal garden at precisely two forty-four this morning," she begins without preamble. "With the lead piping?"

"Who?" I ask, trying to think who I would least expect to be roaming the communal garden in her scanties in the small hours. "Trish Dodd Noble? Valerie Forster? Colonel Mustard?"

We giggle. However different our lives are, however divergent our incomes, taste in interior décor, standard of tidiness, ability to conceive, etc., I do think we *get* each other.

"Wrong," says Clare.

I think what fun it would be to see her and recover from my walk in her deluxe, child-free house and pad around in her kitchen with its warm concrete floor drinking lattes out of her thick-rimmed white Wedgwood cups and eating home-made hazelnut and chocolate biscotti. Everything about Clare and Clare's life is straight out of the pages of *Elle Décor*. Unfortunately, everything about my life is out of the pages of *Bad Housekeeping*. Clare is a glossy neatfreak. Her oven is a sheeny, smudge-free anthracite £3,000 Smeg range. I am shabby and untidy. My oven is a cream Aga with scratched lids and burnt-on spills inherited from the days when Peregrine and Slinky lived here in the 1970s (i.e., in the years when the All Saints Road was the front line, not somewhere nesting couples went at weekends to buy square bathtubs made of native wind-blown wood and Pilates-wear).

"Don't you want to come over for a quick coffee before I

go to Guy Parsons for my color? I can do coffee because I've just done a Rassells run, and I'm pretty free today apart from my appointment with Donna, getting my hair done and finishing my sketch of the quincunx for Tom Stuart-Smith."

I'm now walking around the kitchen, doing a superficial clear-up and piling dirty cereal bowls in the sink for Fatima to tackle later. As I'm tidying the big pine table I notice that Posy has left her reading folder behind. I also notice that Mirabel has left behind her consent form—running to five pages and including her entire medical history and next of kin—to go on a highly dangerous school trip to the local police station, at least three hundred yards from the school gates. This means I will have to return to Ponsonby in the next hour. I sigh, even though this happens almost every day, sometimes more than once.

Yesterday, I had to go to Ponsonby four times, and I was, on my fourth visit (previous ones had concerned forgotten PE kit, nit-check rota, and a child with a sore throat), congratulated by the school secretary and informed that I was, officially, the record holder for repeat trips made in the course of one school day by one parent. I tried to look suitably proud.

"I'd love to, but I've got to file," I say, in answer to the tempting invite to drop everything and have a cozy coffee morning instead. "As well as go back to school—otherwise Mirabel won't be able to visit Notting Hill police station in Ladbroke Grove for health and safety reasons. How about a quick lunch instead? Two-o-two? Fresh and Wild? Will your appointment be over by then? But don't leave me in suspense. Who was it?"

"Virginie," says Clare.

"Noooo," I breathe. Visions of Virginie in a crotch-skimming babydoll nightie . . . al fresco in the communal garden . . . *sur l'herbe* . . . crowd my mind.

"Yes," says Clare. "And what's more, I can tell you what she was doing in the garden in the early hours, which is even more interesting. She was leaving the Averys' garden and coming back into hers."

We agree to meet at Fresh and Wild at 1 P.M.. sharp to discuss these important and exciting developments.

This gives me three hours to research and write my piece, and to go to school with missing and forgotten items, which is oodles of time to compose my "It's Your Funeral" weekly column for the *Daily Telegraph* Saturday mag.

What I normally do is approach the usual suspects—actors, politicians, artists, writers, self-publicizing crashers—and invite them to customize their own funeral: choose the location, cremation or burial, music, hymns, readings. It's the old list format, but I love doing it and people *loooove* to be asked to do it. As in all the best columns, the secret is to flatter the subjects to produce almost all the material themselves. All I really do is a bit of selecting and subbing. And, as I point out to my detractors, who say it's morbid, bad karma, gloomy, etc., the £300 I get a pop definitely puts the fun into funeral for me.

Last week, for example, I had a marvelous time with a major-general. The old boy spoke in masculine, clipped tones, had seen live action in Northern Ireland (Bloody Sunday) Kosovo, Iraq—the works. To my surprise, he was absolutely thrilled to bits to be asked, or so he said. "Plan my own funeral service?" he said. "What did you say your name was again? From the *Telegraph*? Aren't you some relation of that rugger chap on the television? I think that's a very jolly idea," etc., etc. I modestly agreed I was Con's older sister, and soon our conversation was burning as merrily as dry kindling.

Then the maj.-gen. went on, "Come to think of it, if I get the entire kit and caboodle shipshape and Bristol fashion now, it'll save Marjorie and the children no end of trouble when I do finally decide to *porp orf.*"

As I dial the number of Dame Janet Hubbard, the master of an Oxbridge college, who I am interviewing for "It's Your Funeral," I find myself distracted by the vision Clare has revealed of the previous night.

I should be thinking about Dame Janet's seminal work on the

Ancient Greeks' influence on the sexuality of the Victorians but, instead, all I can think of is Virginie's moonlit flit from her lover back to base, witnessed only by Clare and a few rabid foxes. In order to rank the newsworthiness of the event in my own mind, I have to give it a tabloid headline. The best I can come up with is: "NIGHT-MERE"—that's in big black shrieking letters—and underneath: "French Mum's Affair with U.S. Bank Boss."

I admit it's not great, but it does tell me that Virginie and Bob may be big news on our garden, but Clare's massive local scoop is unlikely to have the *Washington Post* or *The Wall Street Journal* looking to its laurels.

As I sigh and replace the receiver, I realize I am feeling slightly . . . envious. Frankly, whenever I hear about another mother slotting adultery into the school run, my main feeling is one of admiration. I mean, with her three children, cooking, BCBG—her thriving mail-order clothes business—her houses, where on earth does Virginie find the time and energy? I sit and stare into space for a while. Then I put Si Kasparian's name into www.factiva.com and search U.K. nationals to see if he's moved on to the garden yet. Nothing I read gives me this vital information, as the last twenty-six or so stories in the thread clearly concern some development in London Docklands to do with the 2012 Olympics, and I don't even bother to open them.

So, it's a gossipy lunch with Clare at Fresh & Wild, the Westbourne Grove mecca for organic fundamentalists, where even the drugs they do in the loos are certified additive-free, and a party tonight . . . where I might be introduced to Si Kasparian—that is, if he's moved in yet. Not that I'm interested, I tell myself.

Still, things are definitely looking up.

The phone rings again, just as I have given up trying to get through to Dame Janet and am busily checking my e-mails and checking out the Chloë skirts on net-a-porter.com.

Aagh! The morning is ticking away, and I have achieved nothing.

"Yes!" I bark, as if frantically busy. If you work from home, it's very important to convey to those who take the tube to toil in offices and only have twenty days' holiday a year that your day is much more busy and important than theirs. Otherwise, everyone treats you as an unpaid, full-time concierge service.

"It's Jane Fraser," says a cut-glass voice.

Jane Fraser is my other main source of freelance income. I immediately soften my tone. She is in fact Lady Jane Fraser but never uses her title. The youngest daughter of an earl with an ethereal beauty that belies her temperament, Jane is tougher than a sack of nails. She is one of those very upper-class girls who spurns her blue-blooded background and spends her entire adult life parading a succession of unsuitable bad boys, married men, or black lovers to underline this point. She is defiantly single and, though she works for the *Mail*, she reads the *Guardian*.

"Jane!" I cry, in tones that suggest that now she's rung, my cup of happiness doth truly runneth over.

"Busy moment? Okay moment? How are you? Ralph?" Jane asks, rhetorically. I know she doesn't really want to know about my dull middle-class life in a poncy white neighborhood because that sort of thing bores her senseless. If I answered, she would only start stifling yawns down the receiver.

"Quite busy," I reply. "Nice to hear from you. How are you? How's morale?"

Jane ignores my pleasantries, just as I have ignored hers.

The first few features I did for her, she was noncommittal. I tried harder and harder each time and sent needy little e-mails after I'd filed, assuring her I was standing by for changes and rewrites. But she didn't seem interested in offering any after-care to her writers at all.

I had a breakthrough moment with Lady Jane about a year ago—or so I thought. I did a big piece about Johnnie Boden, who runs the mail-order empire, terribly nice, and why we middle-class mummies were all obsessed with his catalogue and clothes and Norfolk beach shoots, complete with Agas and ponies and chintz and mummies wrinkling their noses to the camera in their raspberry funnel-necked lamby tops.

I did my homework, went to Johnnie's Chiswick house, had tea off willow-pattern china with the mini-Bodens, my name for his three scrumptious daughters, and everything. I did the interview with Johnnie, during which he spoke exclusively to me about Eton, his Oxford years, his teenage spots and red hair. I chummed up with his sizzling wife, Sophie.

The piece ran over four pages. Postlayout and prepublication, Jane called me. "Mimi," she said.

"Yes, Jane?" I said, expectant. I knew the piece was good. It explained the secret of Boden's success, which is that he conveys to mummies the importance of not only looking nice but being nice, and that being cheerful isn't a privilege that comes with middle-class comfort, it's a *duty,* and so on, and I came up with a killer headline, which was "Johnnie Boden Weather," accompanied by a pic of a teenage Johnnie, complete with spots, in a boater on Eton's Fourth of June. It was the highwater mark of my journalistic career, I felt. But the question was— did it hit the spot for Jane?

"I think that's the best piece," she said, as I murmured bashfully into the receiver, "I've ever read . . ." she continued, promisingly, "in the *Daily Mail . . .*" she trickled on, as my tail lowered a little bit, "on Johnnie Boden," she finished.

"That's incredibly kind of you," I said, my tail now tucked firmly between my legs. "It reminds me of the huge compliment that Lucy paid Mr. Tumnus the faun when he confessed to kidnapping her and told him he wasn't bad at all, he was the nicest faun she'd ever met."

"How amusing," said Jane.

When I told Ralph, he roared with laughter, and said he

was gladder than ever he wasn't a reptile, which is upper-class for journalist.

"So, Mimi," says Jane, in businesslike tones now. "I don't know how much you have on your plate, but the editor thinks you'd be perfect for a longer feature for us, give you a chance to stretch yourself a little. And I do think you'll have fun with this," she says, not even Faint Praiser sounding entirely convinced.

When Jane refers to the editor, I know what it means. It means she is obeying orders.

When she says "perfect for me," it means that three others have turned the offer down flat and she will not take no for an answer. And when she says something will be a chance to "stretch myself" a little, she means she thinks a three-thousand word Mimi Malone spectacular is long overdue.

"Um. What is it?" I ask.

"Adultery," says Jane. "What are the rules of adultery? Are they different for men and women? Talk to your rich friends. They're all at it. Talk to serial adulterers. Comb the cuts, so we can have a sidebar with the rules according to men and rules according to women, and run a rogue's gallery of notorious adulterers."

I try not to groan out loud. "Such as?" I inquire.

"Well, there are hundreds, aren't there? You know, like" (long pause as Jane tries to think of serial adulterers) "um, that Kimberly woman."

"Off the record, presumably?" I confirm. I don't want the piece thrown back just because I've made up people's names/concealed their identities in order to protect their children from being teased in the playground.

"Only if you have to," Jane concedes, making this (apart from the fat fee) my typical nightmare commission. I'm asked to investigate the exact subject that no one in his right mind will ever talk about. I have to spin it out over a few thousand words and invade as many people's privacy in the process as I can. And get photos.

If I didn't have to pay three sets of school fees every three months, I would tell Jane where to stuff the editor's idea.

But I can't. If I say no, she may never ring me again with one of those cushy commissions—"My Perfect Weekend," say, or "When I Am Forty"—which I can knock off in an hour without stirring from the kitchen table or even lifting the telephone to make one call. The sort of pieces that aren't solid enough even to be called fluff—they're so insubstantial, they're *lint*.

"That sounds great," I hear myself saying in a bright voice. I am already thinking about gathering material, maybe at the Averys' tonight, picking up some nonattributable background quotes while I poke around the Virginie/Bob storyline, which sounds promising.

Still, as I accept, I tell myself this is the last time I agree to write a trashy, vulgar, low-down piece just because we're living beyond our means in a rich man's neighborhood. Dame Janet's line is ringing.

"Hello?" barks a deep voice.

"Oh, Dame Janet, hello there, it's Mimi Malone from the *Telegraph*," I say, in my oiliest tones. "I do hope you received my letter, and that you've had time to think about your own" (I usually emit a light laugh at this point, as punctuation) "funeral arrangements."

"Yes," answers Dame Janet. If I didn't know this was Dame Janet, the world's living expert on intercrural frottage in Periclean Athens—let no one accuse me of not doing my background research—I'd have sworn I was talking to a man.

"I don't think I'm going to be much use to you, to be frank," she growls. "I'd always planned a rather unusual send-off."

"Ooh," I say, encouragingly. Sometimes these are the best ones.

"I want to be cremated, but I have decided against any sort of service or memorial," she says, donnishly. "Instead, I have already set a sum of money aside for my closest friends to have a private audience with my favorite paintings in the front rooms of the Royal Academy. I've made a list of the paintings, and it's up to my executors, including the Oxford Chair in Fine Art, to make sure they are all brought together for the occasion."

Then Dame Janet rattles off a list of paintings: Terbrugghen's *St. Sebastian Tended by Irene,* self-portraits by Samuel Butler and Filippino Lippi, the Bellini triptych in the Frari church in Venice, and their exact locations in the Uffizi, the Ashmolean, etc.

"Goodness," I ooze. "How very original, Dame Janet."

I ring the *Telegraph* and break the news that Dame Janet's a nonstarter. They keep me on hold for ages, and when the magazine editor comes back on the line she says, "Don't worry, Mimi, we've got plenty of your Funerals in hand—why don't you crack on and do Iain Duncan Smith? And while you're at it, why don't you churn out a little featurette for *Weekend* about people who have already built their own mausoleums—or should that be mausolea?"

"I'd love to," I say, through gritted teeth, and pick up the telephone to ring Robin Lane Fox in his rooms at New College, Oxford, and he tells me all about his final resting place in Lefkadia, Macedonia, where a vaulted tomb, already frescoed with images of the great man's three favorite hunters, sixty-petaled roses and Bactrian dancing girls, is waiting to receive him.

Clare

If you go to Westbourne Grove midmorning on the day of a big local do like the Averys' party, it's a bit like drowning. You see the panorama of your current life pass before your eyes, on their way to 202 or Tom's or to Question Air for some Seven jeans or a key piece from the latest Vivienne Westwood collection. You begin to wonder if anyone has jobs at all, before realizing, of course, that for many women, and most women around here, shopping *is* their job.

I'm in Ottolenghi on Ledbury Road, having had a very interesting hour with Donna, who I have to say gives awfully good value for her £100 an hour. She made some really revolutionary suggestions that she thinks could unblock me and Gideon, all of which I am pondering while picking up some things for tonight's late supper. Ticky Bains is here, spending £17.50 on some roasted butternut squash with chili and some fine green beans dressed with garlic and sesame. We say hi.

I leave Ottolenghi and pick up a latte from Tom's to take into the hairdresser so I have something to sip while I think about what Donna has said, and the Lockharts are in there, prominently breakfasting with Emily Mortimer, the actress, on pancakes and eggs and muesli with Greek yogurt, porridge with blueberry compote, honey and banana, the works.

Both the Lockharts and Emmy have brought their toddlers along as accessories and are sitting at the round table in the middle of the upstairs café eating this big fat brunch, surrounded by people working on their laptops. It's a charming scene—but somehow this rich combination of creativity and fecundity on a weekday morning means that when I get to Guy Parsons for my roots I'm in a scratchy mood.

It wasn't Ticky, it was Gigi Lockhart.

Ticky's lovely. I'm devoted to her. She and Ed (a barrister who has cleverly attracted the epithet of Best Brain on the Bench) throw a party every Christmas. Early in the day, she supervises as all the furniture is carried out of the house, swaddled in gray blankets and placed in a pantechnicon that waits down the road. They have to suspend two residents' parking bays in Lansdowne Road just for the party—it must be an organizational nightmare—and even Ticky, who has an MBA and used to run a division of DHL before children, admits the logistics are quite a challenge.

Then, several hundred of us crowd into the big house, with its pillars out front, and feast on *zakouski*. There'll be hot savory mouthfuls on white china spoons and waiters circulating with trays of canapés: tranches of pinkish foie gras on baby buckwheat blinis, slivers of beef with fresh white horseradish or baked cherry tomatoes stuffed with risotto.

As the witching hour approaches, waitresses start pirouetting with platters of tiny baby puddings, like chocolate mousses on a crunchy praline base and mini ices in waffle cones, for us to pop in our mouths. At 10:30 P.M. exactly, the host starts flicking the lights on and off, to signal time.

It's definitely one of the very best parties of the year, partly because, it has to be said, when it comes to the following year, Ed and Ticky sit down with the guest list. Armed with a Berol italic marker, they work through the pages and strike thick black lines through 10 percent of the list to make sure the party mix stays fresh, which is so important.

No, it's Gigi, not Ticky who makes me want to hurl myself under the wheels of the number 23 bus. She brings out something in me that I thought I'd left behind when I resigned from my position as *House and Garden*'s editor-at-large to concentrate full time on garden design and our new house and on following my dream: bringing up our baby on a Notting Hill communal garden.

You never know where you are with Gigi. She's heavenly on her own. But anything to do with parties, she's a monster. For her, entertaining is not a way of seeing lots of old friends at once. It's a lethal weapon. She ignores you unless you're talking to someone interesting, in which case she'll rush up and say hello. It's always the same with her—old friends must die so that newer, shinier ones can live.

That's the way things work around here. I can guarantee that if Gigi introduced Hugh Grant to her worst enemy, her worst enemy would go around saying what an angel Gigi is and how nice the Lockharts are and what terrific parties they give.

When I get back from lunch with Mimi at Fresh & Wild—she asked me in a nonchalant way, playing with her quinoa salad, whether Si Kasparian was in residence yet in 104 Lonsdale Gardens, I couldn't enlighten her—I feel sleepy. It was my broken night.

I have a long nap, till 3:30 P.M., then I make some tea, do my e-mails, place my orders, then pull on my Ilse Jacobsen boots, head out to the garden, and march across the grass to the Averys' and the Kasparian residence. I've decided to give the Averys' "yard" a once-over as a lovely surprise for poor Sally, our hostess tonight, and I also want to make damn sure that when Si hires someone to do his window boxes, it's me he hires and not one of the other Chelsea Golds touting for business in this area—it's not a money thing, of course, it's a pride thing.

As I'm picking stones out of heavy clay soil by hand and chucking them into my barrow, out comes Megan with some raw cabbage leaves. She joins me. Megan's the baby—it goes Kurt, Margaret, Kevin, Megan. I think she only does school in the morning. She's all dressed up, and I rest on my spade to watch her feed her rabbits.

Scrimshaw, the golden Labrador, is pawing at the back door, and when Megan's carefully replaced the doors of the cages, she lets him out, and he hurtles through the air and explodes into the communal garden and runs round in circles, round and round, working off energy. I watch him and decide that even if we don't have a baby I'd still never get a dog. In fact, I am so far from being a dog person, now we have Wussy, that I would even go so far as to say I am a cat person.

"What are your rabbits called, Megan?" I ask.

"My rabbits are called Graydon and Toby," she says in a tiny American voice.

"Those are nice names," I say, which is the cue for Megan to tell me a long story about how Graydon always bites Toby and they had to buy a separate hutch for him.

As she says this, I look at Toby and notice that he is sitting in the far back corner of his cage, twitching, while Graydon is glaring at him and pressed to the front wire mesh of his cage, and it strikes me that even the pets on the communal garden fight each other. I lay aside this negative thought, just as Donna has taught me, by saying, "Delete, delete, delete," under my breath, as if I am getting rid of unwanted spam.

Megan takes advantage of the pause to dart into the garden, making me feel that she was waiting for me to finish so she could escape.

On the lawn, in a patch of sunshine (the tree cover makes spring and summer lovely and shaded), Mimi's chatting to Trish Dodd Noble. Mimi's holding a tennis racket in her hand and Calypso is waiting impatiently, drooling, for her to strike a tennis ball so she can fetch it.

I watch Scrimshaw dig a hole in the lawn and follow that up by leaving a packet in a border underneath a *Convolvulus cneorum*. I make a mental note to bring up the perennial problem of poop tomorrow at the AGM.

Megan bounds across the grass: in her white tulle dress with a creamy collar and puff sleeves, her white ringlets bouncing, she makes a glorious contrast against the liquid green of the spring grass. She is clearly wearing her party dress for tonight, and leaps to the eye with the same luminous impact of the Angel Gabriel in a quattrocento painting of the Annunciation. She is indeed a picture of innocence.

When I think of what I saw last night, I can't help thinking of those poor children being wheeled out as props for tonight's entertainment as if Mom Sally and Pop Bob and their four blond children are the very model of a wholesome American family, whereas I know, and now Mimi knows, and therefore soon everyone on the garden and beyond will know—not for nothing is my friend called "Radio Mimi"—that they're not.

And that could be interesting.

Mimi

Bugger. Shit.

In the garden just now, I asked Trish, i.e., Doors to Manual whether Anjelika (the au pair) or Tracy (the nanny), might possibly be free to babysit for a couple of hours. I almost begged. I'd spotted Megan in her party dress and it reminded me that 1. the Avery party is tonight and 2. I don't yet have cover.

Last time Tracy babysat, I'd suggested to the strapping Kiwi that she might, er, possibly, perhaps get on with some ironing while we were out? I'd waved toward the washing basket, containing a tangled pile of Ralph's double-cuff shirts, as if this was a perfectly normal request. I was suddenly feeling rather resistant to paying her top whack of £8 an hour to watch DVDs and drink Diet Coke and call New Zealand on my home phone while my three children, whom I had tucked in myself, slept on.

Trish said she'd ask, but I have to assume the worst. So I have three choices:

1. Go on my own and leave Ralph in charge, i.e., come back to find children still up, hurling hot chocolate around a hurricane-struck kitchen
2. Call Fatima and see if I can persuade her to come back for an hour, which means a grumpy put-upon Fatty tomorrow
3. Sneak out with R.A.L.F. and leave the children in front of a DVD

Option three could be a no-no. For a start, Ralph disapproves. He always had nannies as a child, who only took, out of choice, one half day off a fortnight, so he can't begin to understand the endlessly dreary *Mein Kampf* every modern mother has with childcare. But more to the point, if something went wrong and the house caught fire while I was out partying at the Averys' £4 million house, I just know what the headline would be.

Malone is my maiden name, which I have kept for work and dinner parties with attractive men, and for when I am receiving money I have earned from the sweat of my own brow. Everywhere else, e.g., at the doctor's surgery, at school, at the butcher's, I am Mrs. Fleming. My system seems to work very well, especially for me—when the money's incoming, I am Mimi Malone, and when it's outgoing, I'm Mrs Fleming. Anyway, I can just see some sub chortling as he arranges the words "The Homalones of Notting Hill" over a picture of my children huddled in blankets outside the smoldering ruins of my "£1.5 million family home" and a vinegary news story detailing how we nipped across the garden to hose ourselves down with free champagne while the children's home blazed.

So I have no babysitter, and we're in the kitchen. Well, we're always in the kitchen. It's on the lower ground floor, so I had it painted throughout in New White by Farrow and Ball—it sounds very dull but is actually lovely and creamy, which makes the cream Aga look like the color of bad English teeth, which is the only color for Agas, I think. It has a wooden planked floor, and the antique Welsh dresser on the side wall is hung very artistically (I think) with my Cornishware. Most of it isn't Cornishware at all but is blue and white china, assorted, but I call it Cornishware, because that sounds more artistic.

We all sit at a round scrubbed pine table at the garden end of the room, to feel the benefit of our leafy location, so there's quite a lot of rushing from the kitchen end and back and tripping over dog bowls and dropping things.

The kitchen needs what estate agents call "freshening" or

"updating," but we can't be bothered with that. It's reasonably clean and cozy, especially with the Aga on. A house without an Aga is like a woman without a womb, I once said to Clare. Ralph mildly remarked that this wasn't perhaps the best observation for a woman of Irish peasant extraction who dropped her babies into the potato fields, etc., to make to a close friend of forty grappling with years of unexplained infertility. To which I replied that one can't always tiptoe around everybody's neuroses all the time; otherwise we would all go mad.

One whole kitchen wall is covered with a selection of the children's pictures. I am a demanding curator. If a drawing or painting is not worth keeping, I say I'll put it away in "my very special secret place," as I gaze in wonder at some hideous daub in maroon and brown and stuck with macaroni.

"Yes, of course I can see that the big crumple of tin foil," I cry, "is the ship and the little crumple is the mermaid, darling!" Then, of course, I sneak it among the papers in the recycling bin when they've gone to bed.

The few pictures that survive this cull are stuck up with Blu-tak, alongside team photos of Cas in the Under-12s. I also like to keep a collage wall of all the photos we get sent at Christmas of families skiing/in the Caribbean/on safari/standing outside their new country houses.

I love keeping those cards as a memo to self that even if our ship did come in, I will never mail photographic proof of our good fortune to our four hundred closest friends.

That said, the truth is that Ralph and I much prefer to receive one of these pictorial boast-cards than twenty boring ones showing a snow-clad Palace of Westminster. I mean, when it comes to Christmas cards, there's no such thing as too vulgar—and I would only hesitate before sending one out myself because sadly we have nothing to boast about.

Anyway, tonight, we are having a perfectly balanced supper of fish fingers (essential fatty fish oils), baked beans (lovely roughage) and oven chips (bursting with potato goodness). A supper of fish fingers is, let's face it, a lot quicker than making fish pie from scratch—and has the added bonus that the children will actually eat it, or almost all of it.

"Will it taste of burnt?" asks Mirabel, as I open the oven door and fan away some acrid smoke.

"Um . . . not too burnt," I reply in a bright voice.

I have a reputation for burning everything I cook, especially baked goods. Once I made a batch of scones in Slinky's Aga, which I wasn't used to. When Cas bit into it, he lost a tooth. Ralph loves domestic goddess moments like that. I told Cas that the Scots might have the Stone of Scone, but Cas had "the scone of stone." My brilliant pun was only slightly ruined by Ralph pointing out that "scone" in this instance was in fact pronounced to rhyme with "spoon." After the scone incident, which came hard on the heels of the awful time the children unanimously voted a moist sponge Sweet Treasures cake filled with buttercream and raspberry jam, covered with pink icing and decorated with sweets made by Lord Sainsbury, as more toothsome than the blackened discs made by their own mother, I have also stopped making birthday cakes.

After the fish and chips, I am planning to treat them with choccy puds while I break the news about the party tonight, in the hope that Posy develops a positive Pavlovian response to my leaving the house. I remove the puds from the fridge in readiness and glance at Posy's picture of me with a huge head and massive stomach and stick legs that I have stuck on to it to inhibit me from spooning Ben and Jerry's Phish Food from the tub into my open mouth.

Underneath the picture Posy has written:

MY MUM
my mum has brown hair my mum has small eyes my mum has
a big nose I love my mum

"Darlings," I say in a cheerful voice, squeezing ketchup for them, even Cas, out of long habit, as they point to the right place on the plate. "Daddy and I are just popping out to Megan's mummy's house, you know, Scrimshaw's house, for a drink, and then we'll be back." (There's no point in saying the Averys' house, as the children only identify other grown-ups by knowing which children or pets own them.)

"Eeuw!" says Mirabel, as I souse her plate with that watery ketchup juice that always dribbles out of the squeezy bottle before the sauce arrives (Ralph calls it "the pre-ketchup," which is disgusting).

Posy wails, "Not again!" her cornflower-blue eyes welling viscously, like a Cries Real Tears Barbie, and bites a rosebud lip. The tears tremble on the brim of her lower lid, in a meniscus of emotion.

Posy hates it when we go out.

"Just chill, will you, Posy," says Cas, placing oven chips into his mouth four at a time, keeping his eyes on the few remaining in the baking dish, even though they're burnt. He's been playing rugby.

"But, darling," I point out, "I haven't been out all week. Apart from your instrumental concert! And that doesn't count, it was a school thing. And it went on for ages. You mustn't be sad. I'll be back in an hour."

"Yeah, we'll be fine, Mum," says Cas. "Mirabel will go into her chatroom to talk to her minger dynasty mates, and I'll spend the evening looking at porn on the net."

"My friends are not called the minger dynasty, Cas," replies Mirabel, in a shocked voice.

"Yes, Casimir, don't be rude about your sister's friends," I say. "And you are not to go online, any of you. I've got parental controls, you know. I can track your footprints, so you'd better not try anything. Anyway, I'll be back before you know it, Fatima's coming over shortly. If I find you on the computer, there'll be . . ." I pause, conveying a fatal lack of authority, "hell to pay."

None of the children react at all to my threat, because they know that what I've just said is a lie.

It's what I always say. They know and I know that after three glasses of champagne, I will be faint with hunger and tottering down the road to one of the Italian *osterias* on Kensington Park Road (we call it the "Hi" street because you always have to say "hi" about fifty times as you amble down it, latte in hand). They know that the chances of my heading straight home after a party to read three bedtime stories, each one tailored to the individual child, as prescribed by the parenting Nazis, are vanishingly small.

I clear the plates and present the little glass ramekins of chocolate soufflés prepared by Lord Sainsbury. As they dig in their teaspoons, I admit that actually I'll probably miss bedtime and issue complex instructions about music practice, homework, reading in bed, tooth-brushing, hairbrushing, and lights out before I tackle the next obstacle to a night out, which is Ralph.

I make my way upstairs to Ralph's brown-paneled study on the ground floor. When Peregrine lived here, it used to be his study, and Ralph's bedroom was called the Nursery (pronounced, for some reason, "nurshry.") Life was so much more civilized then, as Ralph never fails to point out.

"Bad news," I say. "We're supposed to be going out tonight." As I expect, Ralph groans, as if in pain. "It's only to the Averys'," I say. "On the garden."

"Remind me who they are again," says Ralph, even though the invitation has been sitting in his study for a month, though it has, admittedly, slipped behind the card from the Ladbroke Association inviting us to go on a guided tour of the communal gardens . . . and another exciting invitation to participate in a charity quiz (£30 a head) to benefit the "impoverished gentlefolk of Kensington." I find these words have an improbable, oxymoronic quality—the same as the shop called Inspirational Basketware outside Taunton or a recipe inviting me to make "hassle-free gnocchi" from scratch in the *Guardian* food section.

I'm prevaricating because, the truth is, I *had* forgotten to mention the Avery invite.

And if I want him to accompany me to things, which I do, very much, I have to virtually ask him in writing and submit the request the previous year.

I quickly give Ralph the run down, in an encouraging voice, as if I am persuading a tearful toddler that playgroup will be really fun! and Teddy and Arthur will be there!

"Bob's that tall Boston Irish chap, early forties, Shearson Lehman, brown hair, blue eyes, freckles. I've pointed him out to you, coaching softball in Hyde Park on Sunday. Jogs," I say, as Ralph continues watching the screen.

He has a letter in his hand. I refrain from saying that Bob is knobbing Virginie Lacoste, according to Clare, because Ralph makes a point of rising loftily above unsubstantiated gossip.

"Sally's his wife, Boston Brahmin, with family compound in Nantucket. Used to be a management consultant but now *doing kids*." I say "doing kids" in a very poor imitation of Sally's Boston accent. "Slim, blond, boyish, you know, she's the one that walks Scrimshaw, that sweet golden Labrador puppy"— Ralph looks up in mild interest as he is very fond of dogs—"wearing those funny pasty-shaped snowboots from L.L. Bean. Kickboxes."

Ralph raises his eyebrows.

I don't bother to say that Sally'n'Bob met at Harvard Business School, dated for two years, moved to New York, married, had four children (Sally barely looks old enough to be married, let alone to have produced four blond children) and are now big players in the Notting Hill American community.

"Will there be fayre?" he demands to know.

"Oh, Lord, yes," I reassure him, breezily, as if reassuring the toddler that there will be biscuits and Ribena. "Of course there'll be food. Mountains of it. Oodles of it. Wall-to-wall canapés."

"And I suppose these people, the Laverys, are deeply impli-cated in the Amschluss?" he queries next.

"The Amschluss" is Ralph's technical term for Manhattan's ongoing annexation of Notting Hill. In general, he is not in favor, even though the influx is one of the key reasons why our house, bought for sixpence ha'penny by Peregrine in the sixties, is now worth a silly amount of money. Holland Park and Notting Hill are afloat on a sea of dollars. Ralph is unimpressed by this, and is also unimpressed by the fact that many of the new Notting Hill couples he meets manage to combine pointless good looks (her) with meaningless amounts of money (him).

So I lie and tell Ralph that I don't think the Averys are as yet big in the Amschluss. I want Ralph to like them, you see, and people like Ralph, who've been around the neighborhood for decades and remember Notting Hill in the days of race riots and Rachman and beatniks and Anita Pallenberg, don't appreci-ate the positive impact on the service economy of Americans as much as desperate housewives and domestic divas do.

Secretly, we find the upscaling of the raffish neighborhood very convenient. Places stay open longer, and restaurants deliver, and sluggish shopkeepers come face to face with the impatient demands of New Yorkers asking for things to happen "like, yesterday," and that sort of thing. I mean, Felicitous, where I pick up a daily coffee, is open from school-run time till something like eleven at night so busy bankers can pick up some sake-marinated salmon with griddled asparagus on their way home. Which is nice, you must admit.

On the other hand, it can get too much. On 4 July, the Stars and Stripes hang out of the sash windows of early Victorian houses, and barbecues and Budweiser parties occur in the back gardens or "yards," as the American bankers in their aprons pointedly call them, as they toss hot dogs on outdoor grills.

Which is all fine and dandy, apart from the late-night firework displays around 4 July. These, in our view, are unnecessary, loud, and tend to rev up anti-U.S. sentiment in Notting Hill even faster than an unprovoked air attack on an innocent Sudanese aspirin factory.

It's getting on for 6:30 P.M.

We are almost at the local news segment of the Six. And not even Ralph can pretend to be interested in the annoyingly titled segment called "the news from where YOU are." But he watches it anyway, of course. Even though he's asked about fayre, I still don't have a result. He conveys the distinct impression that he would prefer to stay at home reading a book, or indeed rereading the Farlows catalogue, instead of talking to a whole lot of women about their children's schools.

"Oh, God," he groans. "Mimi. Why are you doing this to me? Why?"

"Ralph," I say sharply. "Please. You really should make more of an effort. They're *neighbors*. We've got to go. It's what living on the communal garden is *all about*. You'll have a lovely time when you get there," I continue, more soothingly. "We won't stay long. I'll call Fatty and see if she can come back for an hour or so." I don't tell Ralph my top-secret plan to totter over to the little Italian restaurant we call Listeria and scare up a table for two if no one scoops us up for supper.

"By the way," I say, changing the subject before he protests further, "what's in that letter?"

"Just another letter from an estate agent, asking if we would ever consider selling," he replies, his eyes on Fiona Bruce's creamy décolletage as she recaps the headlines.

"Oh," I say. Then I race up the stairs two at a time to get ready before Ralph changes his mind about going out, or raises the subject of flogging Colville Crescent yet again, or displays any more of his . . . *Eton disorders*.

After prolonged exposure to Crusty and Tim, Fucker, Hooray, and John, not to mention R.A.L.F., I would say I am possibly the country's top consultant when it comes to such disorders; if pressed for a definition, this expert would say that Eton disorders encompass a wide spectrum or family of syndromes, but into this wide spectrum fall a deep reluctance to leave one's own house, a similar reluctance to make new friends (all Ralph's closest friends were at school with him and bonded over sixth-form wanking competitions), deep suspicion of anything smart or fashionable or expensive, a horror of appearing in newspapers, a disinclination to buy anything but green and tweedy clothes with special little flaps to do with game and cartridges . . . I could go on.

And as soon as Fatty arrives, I'm out of the door like a speeding bullet. Ralph exits more reluctantly. In a couple of minutes, less, we're at the Averys', and I fling our coats at a maid and immediately plunge downstairs, avoiding the straggle of waifs and strays in the drawing room.

Several neighbors surround Ralph and pat him on the back, drawing him into the gathering. This always happens. With Ralph, everyone knows that it's touch or go whether he'll come, because he's either away or sitting at home contentedly in front of one of his Understanding Trout series of fly-fishing DVDs. So when he makes a rare appearance, the host and hostess are, inevitably, terribly pleased. On occasion, people even clap when he turns up, but I get the feeling they applaud in the same way that economy-class passengers on a flight from Kathmandu on Afghan Airlines might clap when the pilot plops them down in Baghdad in one piece (i.e., more out of gratitude than joy).

Clare

Gideon and I would never cross the garden to go to some social function, even though we can lock our garden gate and kitchen door and set the alarm just as easily from the back of the house.

No. The form is this. If you are invited to something on the garden, you change and go through the front door, to signal the demarcation between chance meetings in the communal garden and planned occasions that go in the diary.

As we walk up, my kitten heels clacking, we can tell immediately there's a big turnout for the Averys. There are cars waiting, double-parked, with drivers puffing on cigarettes up and down the street, their smoke mingling with the clotting scent of cherry blossom. Gideon sneezes twice as we stand on the threshold. Hay fever.

Patrick Molton is standing on the doorstep. He is doing that vigorous waggling thing men do with their forefinger in his other ear. I'm about to say something about the AGM tomorrow night and the announcement, when I notice he's talking into a mobile, so I shut my mouth. When he sees us, he turns his back. This is unlike Patrick, who is usually very hail-fellow-well-met and always clapping Gideon on the back in a matey way and asking me about the patter of tiny feet.

The funny thing is, I don't mind all that from Patrick, because he is essentially kind, although it is odd to think that everyone on the garden's monitoring my ovulation schedule almost as carefully as I am.

As we wait for the door to be answered, I wonder who the Averys will have doing the food and my stomach makes an unladylike noise. "Darling!" Gideon murmurs.

I'm a little surprised by the number of drivers in the street. After all, the Averys have only been here nine months, but they've clearly already arrived. If they'd moved from Manhattan to Wales, let's say, it would have taken them years before the neighbors spoke to them in the village shop. Here, the reverse applies. Now, this part of London is totally beyond the means of all but the richest of the rich. So the newer you are to the neighborhood, the higher up the money tree you are. The only people who are moving into the neighborhood are multimillionaires many times over, like the Averys, and the only people who are moving out are the *nouveaux pauvres*, like the—I almost said, like the Flemings, but of course they haven't moved. Not yet anyway, though Ralph does seem to suggest that it's only a matter of time.

As we pass Patrick to enter, I can hear him talking softly into his mobile. He thinks we can't hear, but he's not to know I have pin-sharp hearing.

"Look, gorgeous," he is saying, in caressing tones, "don't worry about the money, babe. You understand? I told you in New York, didn't I? I don't care if it's three hundred a week or three thou a week, I want us to have it. We've got to be more careful, babe, I'm not sure you weren't spotted in the lounge. So just do as I say, woman. That's an order." As he's talking, he's running his fingers through his thick brown hair and looking rather boyish and excited. I wonder whether they are investing in a flat or renting somewhere. It must be for Maria, their housekeeper—but on second thoughts, it can't be. Not even Patrick, who is flirty and touchy feely with all females under fifty, calls one of the staff—and a rather dignified mature woman at that—"babe."

My suspicions are heightened further upon entrance.

The first person I see inside the drawing room (first impression—white walls, spot painting by Damien Hirst, Allegra Hicks rugs, large sculpture of dog fashioned of twisted coat hangers) is Marguerite. Which rules her out conclusively as Patrick's interlocutor.

I don't dwell on this, because Patrick calls everyone sexy and gorgeous, and he could quite easily have been talking to his stockbroker, for all I know. But I register it—Mimi will be riveted, especially as she's got to write some huge article for the *Daily Mail* on exactly this subject.

A roar rises from the basement kitchen, where clearly all the action is. In the large drawing room, there are ten souls trying not to look lost and forlorn. When Gideon and I come in, ten pairs of eyes snap to us.

I wave at Marguerite. She is talking to a work colleague of Patrick's at the bank, so I decide not to break in. I know that we've got to descend immediately, otherwise we'll be stuck up here in no-man's land.

I'm anxious to find Mimi and Virginie. I want to observe her body language close up. Obviously, if Virginie ignores Bob, the host, all evening, then she is, definitely, seeing him on the side. That's such a giveaway. But I find myself dawdling over the photo gallery that lines the stairs. I do find family photographs irresistible. Here, three generations of Avery white teeth, bare feet, brown arms, and happy grins are showcased in matching pale-wood frames hung at eye level.

I know that the Avery family has a compound somewhere, in Nantucket. But I didn't know that the family en masse looks so like an advert for estate planning in the pages of *The New Yorker* as styled by Calvin Klein.

I pass Ralph coming up the stairs with his jacket in his hands. So that means Mimi is down there, and it's hot. "Don't you think they all look like some advertisement for pile cream?" he remarks, as he comes up and finds me poring over the gallery. "Or incontinence pads. Live life to the max—with new super-absorbent incontinence pads from Snug Night."

We linger together over the highly posed tableaux of Sally's tanned and vibrant mother and distinguished-looking father surrounded by their grandchildren by the ocean, in crisp white cotton shirts and chinos.

Then he moves to pass me. There's not much room. I flatten myself against the wall, but he, gentleman that he is, insists that he wait as I continue on.

As I pass, I hold up my hand to thank him. He takes it lightly, raises it, looks me straight in the eyes, inclines his head so his fringe flops over his eyes, and then lets my hand go.

In that second, I feel my chest seize up and my hand tingle as if I have been struck by lightning. I feel hot. It is all I can do to place one foot in front of the other and descend the staircase.

My head is buzzing. All I can think is—Ralph! Come back!

But, instead, I carry on down, churning inside, to the big, airy double aspect basement with a highish ceiling (they *must* have dug down—everyone who underpins does) which easily accommodates the crowd. I catch my breath and, on the last step, I pause to inspect.

I like the way the sheeny high-tech kitchen contrasts with the nubbly texture of the stone flooring. I also like the unsentimental emphasis on functionality in what is the hub and heart of the family house. At one point, before they did the work (the rule round here is to spend the purchase price again on remodeling the house), the Averys consulted Gideon on what they called an informal basis, which meant they wanted free advice, of course, on the pretext of saving the planet. Gideon nudged them in the direction of a retail architect. Gideon's not free to air, even to neighbors.

But the interior couture of the kitchen is hard to take in now because in the center of the room, there's a striking new addition to the domestic furniture: a whirring, circling steel carousel complete with five tiny Japanese men in white bonnets, two of whom are chopping and slicing and arranging plates of sushi and then loading them on to the moving belt. For a while I watch one slicing blue-purplish tuna and milky-white sea bream, then popping the sliced fish on top of the rice, shaped like baby white mice. Then he adds little cylinders of grated daikon, and radishes carved in the shape of roses.

A third chef is lifting and shaking tempura from a deep-fat fryer, while a fourth prepares more aubergines, carrots, asparagus, and courgette flowers and dips them in batter. And the fifth is whisking dirty plates from the diners feeding around the carousel and tossing them into a deep stainless-steel sink, where the mixer tap by Philippe Starck is pouring a continuous silver stream of water.

All this is a nice touch. The Averys invited us to their "block party" for locals, but having Itsu in to cater makes it's a bit more than that—it's making a statement.

I look away from the sushi to the garden end and note there's another Damien Hirst on the far wall and two blond suede squishy sofas facing each other against each wall. Above the fireplace, a vast plasma screen, showing sports.

All around, there are low-lying storage cupboards at skirting height and shallow benches of reinforced concrete, so Sally can quickly hide away all the sort of clutter that litters every surface of Mimi's kitchen. I also think she's smart to run low seating against the walls. It frees up masses of space in the center of the room, and means the space isn't too busy with chairs.

My eye can't help going back and back to the sushi carousel that's trundling plates round and round. It's rather hypnotic to watch, this steady trundle of plates, so orderly, and so Japanese and ceremonious amid the discourteous throng of a London party.

It all reminds me of something; I can't think what it is. I half close my eyes, as Gideon leaves my side and heads toward Bob and the guys watching the Super Bowl tape, swiping a beer as he goes. These men in dark suits and white shirts, the hubbub, the competitive feeding frenzy, and the cackle of gossip.

"You know what this reminds me of?" I say, as Mimi approaches. "Penguin feeding time, London Zoo."

Then I spot Ralph, now trailing in her wake. My stomach clenches.

I repeat my observation for his benefit, gesturing to the men in their black and white plumage hurling gobbets of raw fish down their gullets.

"Yes," he drawls. "You're right, as usual. Its pure Lubetkin, isn't it? You're so clever, Clare."

I love the fact that Ralph is visually observant and notices things. We discuss the use of concrete in architecture and its renaissance as a hard-wearing environmentally friendly alternative to stone.

Mimi looks puzzled, but Ralph merely crinkles his greeny-yellow eyes at me and changes the subject. Neither of us bothers to explain to Mimi that Berthold Lubetkin constructed the modernist concrete penguin pool in the thirties, or that concrete is a beautiful material, because Mimi would find that sort of conversation at a drinks party terribly nerdy.

Mimi

Ralph and Clare start rabbiting on about some geeky architect—Clare's never been one to wear her Cambridge learning
lightly—so I melt away to score some sushi and find useful
people to talk to who might give me new columns and other
work.

All my best gigs come this way.

"Don't forget to choke down some fayre," I remind Ralph,
as it would suit me fine not to have to rustle up something
eggy on a plate later, if we're not going to eat at Listeria,
that is.

I scan the crowd and identify my next target—the editor of
a Sunday newspaper. I treat parties like military campaigns.
But the editor is chatting up Cookie, a supermodel turned
actress turned knitwear designer and, as I drift off, undecided
whether to make it a threesome or not, Clare reaches out and
taps me on the shoulder.

"Oh, yes—are you two going on to something after this,"
she looks at us both, "or are you free for supper?"

I look at Ralph inquiringly, and say, "Well . . . I was about
to tuck into the sushi but I'll try to hold back if you're offering
to feed us later." Obviously, I am gagging to go, as I will drive
any distance, climb any mountain, for a hot meal I haven't
had to cook, shop for, and wash up after myself, but I don't
want Clare to see that.

"Fine with me," Ralph obliges, which surprises me. He isn't
usually so pliant when it comes to accepting impromptu
invites.

Clare gives Ralph a grateful look, and makes her way over
to Marguerite Molton, who has finally escaped a colleague of

Patrick's and is talking to Sally Avery about the benefits of clever milk fortified with omega oils.

As I usually see Sally, Clare, and Marguerite in their day clothes in the garden or in the street, I note how good-looking all three are, in very different ways, when they scrub up. Sally, mine American hostess, is wearing low-cut black tailored trousers that show off her narrow form, ballet flats and a wrap top in a dusky pink and black paisley print. Clare is looking expensive and pared down in a Prada shirt-dress tied at the hip and obviously very pricey heels that look as if they are woven out of raffia, and her bare legs gleam. Marguerite is wearing a tailored shirt with exaggerated cuffs and a frilly bit at the front, and a pencil skirt with a complicated pleat at the back and some detailing at the waistband that announces to sharp-eyed female observers that it is probably very expensive (i.e., is much more likely to be Balenciaga than Boden).

Ralph heads over and kisses all three women warmly, tells Marguerite, who is looking tired, that she is looking beautiful in that shirt and that he "loves a bit of ruff," and then he introduces himself to Sally, very correctly, and then takes his leave of all three with a little bow and plunges into the scrum around the carousel with the resolute air of a man who has been forced to play British Bulldog as a six-year-old new boy at prep school, and for whom nothing thereafter can hold any terrors again—not even talking to three women at length about their children's gluten and lactose intolerances.

Ralph and I take the opposite approach to parties. He thinks they're an unnecessary waste of time and energy. He says that once you're married, there is no purpose to talking to members of the opposite sex and drinking to excess. He also claims that cocktail parties make him anxious because he can never think of clever ways of ending the conversation; whereas I am always trying to think of clever ways to end conversations, because what makes me anxious is not how to escape from a long chat with someone, it's how to release them from the obligation of talking to *me*.

My preferred method is to pinch the bottom of a passing male. I find it gets attention much faster than hovering on the outskirts of a group waiting to be included into some conversation about someone's recent acquisition of a third home in an undiscovered part of Puglia.

I decide, after a brief hesitation—my fingers hovering over grey-flanneled buttocks—not to pinch the bottom of the editor, because he's in the middle of a pitch. He's trying to hire Cookie!

"I loved that thing you did for Susie Forbes at *Easy Living* on the rise of, um, pediatric asthma and links to diet," the editor of *The Sunday Times* is saying to Cookie, as I mentally congratulate him for doing his homework. "And it made me think: you'd be brilliant at writing a parenting column about children's food. You've got kids, you know all about hiding vegetables so kids don't know they're eating them, and fish oils and stuff, and it would be a great synergy with your fashion career. Think about it."

He swigs on his beer, while Cookie picks up a wasabi-coated peanut, contemplates it, and then puts it into her mouth. She looks intent and pensive. In my experience of very thin and beautiful women, when they look this intelligent it invariably means they are thinking about their calorie intake.

I watch in interest. I've just had a wasabi-coated nut, and it was like mainlining horseradish into my eyeballs. Frankly, it was so bad that it almost made me think that cocktail parties should become nut-free zones, too, like all planes and schools and canteens, but I decided this was a depressing thought and cast it aside.

A second later, she spits it out again, into a demure fist, and wipes tears from her eyes. I wonder why the editor's so keen on her—after all, I think to myself crossly, she's got no track record as a *writer* at all—and then remember that there was a mouthwatering picture of Cookie on the cover of last week's *Sunday Times* Style section. She was wearing nothing but a pink cashmere fur-lined stole and some matching pink cashmere socks and mittens from her new adult collection, and spooning Ben and Jerry's into her mouth, legs crossed over what Posy calls "her private."

I abandon Cookie and co. and head to the carousel for Japanese food. As I wait for a plate of hot prawn tempura to sidle within reach—something in me balks at masticating a mouthful of wet fish while talking to one of the *Guardian* Media Top 100—and then lift it off the conveyor belt, I hear someone cry, "Mimi! Over here."

On the other side of the room, Gideon Sturgis is talking to someone, and while Gideon's speaking, that someone's eyes are resting on me. Not on the supermodel. Not on the editor of the *Sunday Times*. Not even on any of the crowned heads of Notting Hill, i.e., Richard and Emma . . . (Curtis/Freud), Matthew and Elisabeth (Freud/Murdoch). Not the Sebastian Faulks, not the Edward Faulks, the Steyns, the Griggs, or the Camerons, who are graciously also attending this engagement. He's looking at *me*. I know. I checked on either side of me.

I look back at him.

I don't know what it is. There's something about him that gets me. His stillness. His concentrated sense of purpose. Like José Mourinho sullenly contemplating a poor Chelsea performance during a patchy away game, he is intent, focused, and somehow . . . all-powerful.

I do not change my expression much, merely aiming for a sultry return of gaze, which is quite difficult, as I have taken a large bite of prawn tempura and am sure that an oily smear has glossed my chin and that I am bound to have a crumb of batter somewhere on my cheek.

The man is familiar from somewhere. Short, dark, cropped hair, graying as it curls over the ears. Hooded eyes. Dark eyebrows like slashes across his brow. A Mediterranean complexion, and the shadow of stubble. But then . . . everyone round here is familiar from somewhere.

I'm not going to make the elementary mistake of assuming I know him. Last time I did that at a Notting Hill party given by Paul and Marigold (Johnson), the hatchet-jawed man I thought I was enthralling on the key subject of the praline granola from Clarke's (no apologies—it's so good, I could go on for hours) turned out to be Tom Stoppard. We gaze at each other, shamelessly. Gideon keeps waving at me.

"We could call it 'Scrummy Mummy'!" I hear the editor of *The Sunday Times* persist hopefully. "You wouldn't have to write it yourself, you know," he adds, suddenly reaching out and tapping me on the shoulder to indicate that it's my turn now. "We have people to do that, Cookie."

Then, in a flash, I know who it is. It's Si Kasparian. I mean, I've Googled him often enough, haven't I? It's just he's so much better looking than in those online photos . . . which don't do justice to that thick curling hair . . . the swarthy complexion . . . and those dramatic eyebrows.

My new neighbor. The philanthropist, yachtsman and art collector, married to . . . flower name—not Veronica, not Hyacinth, certainly not Nigella . . . got it.

Primrose.

My God, I think. He's gorgeous. He's a billionaire. And he's my next-door neighbor, practically, and on the right side of the garden, too.

And now, using my social search engine, I bring up an interesting fact. Si is divorced.

Which means that he is, officially, Out There.

Even if I'm, officially, not.

Something goes liquid in my stomach, and it's not the prawn tempura, because Gideon and Si are now jostling toward me, while the editor of *The Sunday Times* is beaming down and asking me how my column is going, which I always think is code for "I don't read/much care for your column, by the way."

"Mimi, have you met our distinguished new neighbor? Si, this is Mimi, Mimi, Si. You've got to watch what you say in front of Mimi, ha ha, she's a journalist," Gideon babbles.

"Ha ha," I tinkle.

It is an iron rule that only those who are most unlikely to say or do anything remotely noteworthy or vaguely interesting ever make this remark. But as Gideon has introduced me to the most alpha male in the room, I am prepared to overlook this. The best thing that one friend can do for another, socially, is to introduce her to someone interesting she hasn't already met about a million times, an almost impossible feat, unless you are Gigi Lockhart, who picks up celebrities faster than my children pick up bugs in their hair.

"Mimi Malone," comes a dark brown voice that causes the hair on the nape of my neck to lift slightly from the skin.

"You're not nearly as pretty in the flesh as you are in your byline picture," it rumbles. He has a deep voice. A very deep voice, which sort of rattles as it emerges, as if it has to exit through the bars of a cave. I shiver, as if in shock. I am almost hypersensitive aurally. I can't bear the noise of anyone eating, or snoring. In fact, I have been known to move cinema seats away from popcorn-bag rustlers and to wake a gently slumbering Ralph up to tell him he's "breathing too loudly."

"Ha ha," says the editor, and backs away from our group to nobble Peter Bazalgette, the media mogul.

I give Si my cool stare (as sometimes practiced in the mirror before parties) so he can examine me and retract this remark, although I know I am to take it as meaning the opposite.

I am, in fact (and I do know how vain this sounds), slightly prettier than my byline picture, especially when I am responding to male attention by blooming like a cabbage rose in a cottage garden. Also, I am beyond thrilled that he knows who

I am—what a wonderful opportunity to pretend that I haven't a clue who *he* is. It really gives me the heads-up.

As we study each other, something happens.

When he looks at me, it's as if he *sees* me. As if he *knows*.

The room seems to go silent, and I hear a noise in my head. And I recognize it, even though I have never heard it before.

It is the marriage-wrecking-ball crash of lust colliding with something in my head. With greed. With desire. With need. With naughtiness. With whatever, or whatev, as Mirabel would say.

I have lived happily with my husband for twelve years. We have three lovely children together (well, lovely to us, anyway). We have a dear, tatty old house in a smoking-hot location. And yet. And yet.

When I look into the eyes of this man standing at Gideon's side, who is staring at me as if he'd like to pop me in his mouth, whole, like an edamame bean, I feel my moral compass spinning out of control.

I have the same response I get when I leaf through the endless catalogues that come with the weekend newspapers. Lakeland Plastics. Something of Stow. White Company. Picketts, etc.

Before I glimpse the catalogue, I never knew that a double-egg poacher or a pink leather passport cover or a goose-down mattress topper even existed.

Now I know I can't live without one.

A voice comes into my head. For some reason, it is Michael Parkinson's.

"So, Mimi, when did you first feel attraction for" (pause for knowing laughter from audience) "the billionaire businessman Si Kasparian?"

Attraction doesn't quite cover it, actually. As his eyes bore into mine and a smile tugs the corners of his mouth, I think I may be ovulating on the spot.

"Well, I'm sorry to be such a disappointment," I reply. He

takes out a packet of American Spirit from the back pocket of his Levi's, and a Dunhill lighter.

"So why Notting Hill?" I ask archly. I mean, everyone knows that it's a place where rich people play happy families, not a hunting ground for lonesome playboys. "Don't tell me you moved here because what you really, really want is to provide a terrible distraction to all of us mummies?" I nibble, provocatively, I hope, on some chicken teriyaki that a cute gap-year waiter boy with a Marlborough mop of shaggy dark hair is bringing round.

"Well," Si says in his slow, mid-Atlantic growl, looking at me sternly, "that would be nice. If I only I could get any of you, what are you called?—*yummy mummies*—to notice me."

I like the fact that Si italicizes the dread expression "yummy mummies," but I suspect him of fishing.

"I'm having point of entry problems into the neighborhood. Who's my in around here? Who do I need to know? Is it you?" He sparks up his cigarette and takes that delicious first suck at it. A few American guests look over in horror, and start fanning the air ostentatiously, which he ignores.

I am finding this terribly exciting.

Nothing quite so exciting has happened to me since someone stopped me in the street and asked me whether I was Mimi Malone and I said, yes, blushingly, and the woman said, with satisfaction, that she thought so and wasn't that funny because I looked very like that Con Malone off the telly, only *older,* of course. Ooh and *he's goooorgeous,* she added, accusingly, as if she could not forgive me for not being him.

But right now I'm thinking my time has come. Every dog has his day, and I manage to drag my eyes away from his for a second to give a rapid sweep of the room to assess the competition, which is, as I suspected, hotting up.

At least four predatory females are waiting to swoop on Si as soon as I'm done with him. Clare has got her beady eye on us. Trish Dodd Noble is grinning in our direction. And among them is Virginie, looking more delectable than ever in some indefinably chic tailored skirt and blouse.

She is keeping an eye on me as she chats away to Trish Dodd Noble, who I bet is droning on about Francis and Melissa, the painfully gifted Dodd Noble offspring—I think one or both won music scholarships to Westminster and St. Paul's Girls School.

"I'm not nearly important enough," I say. "In fact, I would say that knowing me is a positive bar to social acceptability. If I were you, I'd go off and find some very respectable charity-fundraising matron to chat up, immediately."

But he doesn't leave. But, luckily, Gideon does. So we are in a *tête à tête* that I am determined to prolong as long as I can. At one point, I even do that awful thing, the thing I loathe above all else, when Trish tries to break in—I hold up the palm of my hand, as if I'm stopping traffic, to keep her at bay. And she darts me a look, but I can't say I care.

The reason I do this is because Si is in the middle of telling me, in a serious voice, one that makes me want to wrap my arms around him, about his divorce ("Nothing can prepare you for the pain of accepting that something's over and moving on") and about how Primrose wanted to stay on in Eaton Square ("It's her home, after all, and it was the least I could do").

In answer to my query about Notting Hill, he speaks about how he had a flat here in his twenties and how he had wanted to be on a communal garden ever since ("and I've got various investments here"). He makes little of the fact that he's richer than everyone in the room put together. And he makes much of the fact that he has no children . . . the killer combo.

I tell him that I am half-Irish on my father's side and admit to Gideon's charge of being a journalist. I don't, for some reason, mention the fact that I'm married with three children, no money, and a mongrel.

As Si talks, his eyes flit between my eyes and lips, and I notice he occasionally looks down to my best feature, which

I have boosted with a cleavage-enchancing bra from Agent Provocateur on Westbourne Grove, which opened in the neighborhood with a poster campaign bidding "Knickers to Notting Hill." With another man, I might find this sleazy. With him, I don't. I've never felt this urge to remain in a man's presence before. It's as if some pheromonic force field I've never fully felt is yanking me toward him.

"So what does Si stand for?"

"Selim Imran," he answers. "I grew up in the States. Everyone has a nickname there. Mine was Si."

I can't help asking where he was educated, explaining it's an English obsession, and he says, "Andover then Yale then Harvard," which I presume means the Business School, and then I ask him how old he is. "About forty-eight," he says, blowing out smoke as he says it. This makes me feel very young and generally frisky, as I am only about thirty-seven and a half. I ask him whether his house is finished.

Si replies that it's almost ready, he has a great team, but he is looking for someone to do his window boxes . . . I say, what, you mean someone who can *feng shui* the window boxes, saying "fung schwee" in an ironic voice, and he says, "Whatever." I'm sure he didn't mean *feng shui* his window boxes, but the fact is, Donna does *feng shui* gardens, too—when it comes to your alternative-therapy needs, she is a one-stop-shop. But what I'm thinking is that Si is confecting a reason to contact me again, and I am goosebumping. All over.

During all this, my husband, who has nobly accompanied me to this gathering, is in the room. So are my friends, and neighbors. I have everything a woman could want—house, health, husband, hair, husband with hair . . . I have children, work, friends, family, an Aga kitchen and richer friends with large country houses with even bigger Aga kitchens to stay in.

And yet, when I come to look back on this moment, and write my blinking piece for Lady Jane, which turns out to have been commissioned in the nick of time, I know what I'm going to put in.

It's not necessarily planned.

It happens.

And I'll write that it happens even when you have everything you want, and yet, you still want more, just as it's possible to find a tiny crack inside after a huge, stomach-distending Christmas dinner and manage to squeeze in some plum pudding after all. I'll write that it's perfectly possible to cast aside twelve years of constancy in the blink of an eye. It's not a moment of madness, when you put at risk everything you hold most precious. Because it isn't.

It is an "I man, you woman" moment. A "me Tarzan, you Jane" moment that tells two people exactly how much they need to know about each other if they're going to take something to the next level.

Which is not a lot, to be honest.

Clare

Gideon opens a bottle of Lynch-Bages and wields the corkscrew like a scalpel. A Notting Hill party is like a sudden death. It demands an immediate postmortem. "So what did we all think of the party?" he asks unnecessarily, pouring wine, while I slice the fillet, *tiède* and oozing bloody juices, lay the meat in parallel slices on the warmed plates and then spoon on garlicky *dauphinoise* potatoes made with double cream and Gruyère. I wipe any splodges from the edge of each large plate with an unbleached linen cloth.

A dish of steamed green beans sits on the table, along with a cold pale rectangle of unsalted Normandy butter and a whole squat loaf of *pain Poilâne* the size of a cartwheel. You can buy it in halves, but that looks less splendid and sustainingly feast-like than a whole loaf.

"Very interesting," I say. "I thought the sushi was an inventive touch, and it also meant that people didn't all leave at nine. If I'd known, I wouldn't have made dinner."

They all reassure me that they'd much, much prefer to be here in Colville Crescent than standing up eating raw fish, and I feel happy. It's lovely to be home after the party.

At Mimi's insistence, I tell those who don't already know about my vision of the previous night. It receives an attentive audience. "Mm," says Ralph. "Virginie at large in a skimpy nightie in the small hours. That's my kind of nocturnal emission, I must say."

"Are you sure it was the Averys' house?" says Gideon, almost sulkily. I am being nice to him, as he flew in overnight from the West Coast, and that always takes it out of him, even though he had a flatbed seat.

"I can't think what she'd see in him," he whines. "If I'd known the bar was set so low I might have had a go myself."

"Gideon, of course I'm sure. The Averys live almost opposite us. She came out right by the old garage at the end of their garden."

"Mm. Well, there's no doubt she's easy on the eye," muses Ralph. "Was she at the party?"

Virginie's always exerted a grip on the male imagination, and the knowledge that she is flitting from house to house wearing very few clothes has merely served to tighten it. "I didn't see her."

"She sure was," I answer. "But she was deliberately avoiding Bob. I noticed. She talked to Sally and Marguerite and the Dodd Nobles and everyone, but she very noticeably didn't even say hello or good-bye to Bob, which is conclusive, really."

"I *saw* her but didn't *talk* to her," says Mimi, looking dreamy. "Wasn't she looking stunning? She does sexy secretary better than anyone I know. I wish I could wear a tailored shirt under a tight jersey like that and not look like a lumpy bumpy schoolgirl. Plus, I thought she was slightly thinner than usual, that's a giveaway. Women who are having affairs always stop eating—apparently," she adds, slightly hurriedly, addressing herself to her plate.

"Yes, she was looking pretty," I say, handing Ralph his plate, which I have heaped extra high. Mimi has many fine qualities, but gourmet home cooking isn't one of them, and I do love putting a plate of really good food in front of a man. "When I saw her, I asked her about last night." All eyes are on me now. "Yes, I asked her what she was doing running around the garden at two in the morning in her underclothes."

Even though the beef is cooling fast on their plates, everyone suddenly grabs their glasses and takes a slug, still looking at me.

"Well, she merely laughed." I give an impression of Virginie's dirty giggle in a French accent. "She just laughed and she said, '*Oh, you saw me, did you, ow funnay, I deed worn-der if anyone would see me.*'"

"And?" asks Gideon.

"And then she said that she had heard the sound of a sprinkler going in the Averys' garden, and she thought she would be *une bonne voisine* and go down and close it off. And we sort of left it at that, because then Sally Avery came over and they kissed and Virginie gushed about what a *tellement amusante* party it was, and obviously I wasn't going to have this conversation anywhere in the vicinity of Sally, was I?"

"I still don't get it," says Gideon. "I thought the Americans and the French were at each other's throats over the war. Bob's a prowar Republican capitalist fascist pig. He probably owns a gun. A home arsenal of guns. Pump-action shotguns for pig shooting. Like the French, I opposed the war. I'm a Labour-voting pacifist architect with a social conscience. I went on the antiwar march." He looks around and shakes his head. "So why doesn't she want to screw me?"

"Perhaps it's a case of *de gustibus nil disputandum,* dear boy," murmurs Ralph.

"Perhaps it's a case of take a ticket and wait your turn," says Mimi.

Gideon looks hopeful at the prospect, like a child at the rustle of a sweet wrapper, and then everyone starts eating again.

"I have to say, I take my hat off to Virginie, though," I continue, when it's time for the next course, picking up the same thread as I lay an oozing slab of Gorgonzola on the table together with some crumbly pure-butter oatcakes, also from Clarke's, and another bottle of Pauillac, for our next course. I then mix in a garlicky dressing over chicory and toasted walnuts, having decided at the last minute to hold the Roquefort, as we were having cheese.

"She was terribly chummy with Sally for a woman who's

having an illicit affair not just with Sally's husband but with her next-door neighbor to boot. Talk about fouling the nest."

"But hold on, Clare," says Ralph, cutting a large slice of Gorgonzola. "Before you start accusing Virginie of shitting on her own doorstep, hold your pretty horses. Virginie's a little minx, I quite agree—and if only she'd been tripping out of my garden instead of Bob's, but never mind, ours not to reason why. She said she was turning off the sprinkler. I don't see how you quite convert that statement into a conviction that she and Bob are mating right under wife Sally's freckled little East Coast nose."

"Because, Ralph," I say, quite firmly. "Because you forget that I know all the gardens inside out. I am the gardener, well, Stephen is, but I do lots of the little gardens. And," I continue with emphasis, "the Averys don't have any sprinklers. I was in there today, doing some weeding, and I happened to notice. And even if they did have sprinklers, it's been raining so much that there would be no reason whatsoever to have them on at this time of year anyway."

Ralph and Gideon look slightly disgruntled at this, while Mimi has her very concentrated look, the look that tells me that she is absorbing information very hard so she can reproduce it later, usually as copy.

"I can't believe it," she says. "You wait for ages, and three adulterous liaisons come up at once."

I laugh, and Mimi and I exchange a look. At the Averys', I passed on my intelligence about Patrick Molton and said that I was pretty sure he was talking to his mistress on his mobile. She'd said, "To one of his mistresses, more like." And I'd already told her about Virginie. That makes only two. Mimi is always prone to exaggeration, but still, I make a mental note to ask who the third pair of local adulterers is.

"Amazing to see Si turning up like that," says Gideon, changing the subject. "Very surprising. When I did his house in La Garde-Freinet, in my early minimal period, ha ha, he'd give these parties for the Rothschilds and the Guinnesses and all the smart set, only he, Si, the host, wouldn't show up, so Primrose would have to do it all on her own. Which she was very good at, but I couldn't help feeling it was a little selfish of him and sorry for her. She's rather nice, actually," Gideon says.

"I sometimes think I'd be much nicer than I am if I didn't have to worry about money," says Mimi. "Anyway, Gideon," she continues, slightly flushed now, "I should point out that, historically, women have been known to suffer worse fates than having to host elegant Provençal soirées for the local *gratin* single-handed. I don't imagine that Primrose was doing the *pissaladière* herself, somehow, do you?"

"I think he's rather attractive," I butt in, to change the subject. The last thing we want is for Ralph and Mimi to have one of their arguments about money. "Don't you, Mimi?"

Mimi is drinking her red wine rather fast and looking rather flushed.

"Who?" Mimi asks.

"Si Kasparian."

"Si?" Mimi looks down at her plate.

"Mm. Suppose I do . . ." She breaks the biscuit on her plate into fragments, before looking up and very directly at Gideon.

"How do you know him, Gideon?" she asks suddenly.

There is a pin-drop moment of silence while I file away the scene in my mental album of Good Times.

Me and Giddy—me, slim and straight with brown hair, Gideon rough-hewn, with his yellowish Levantine complexion, stubble and black curls—in Prada and Paul Smith; Mimi with her chestnut mop and pink cheeks and her bosom, wearing a flouncy skirt and a vest top and cardigan; Ralph, with his aquiline profile, like a Roman emperor, his long limbs in rumpled cords and his floppy brown hair that's always a shade too long and curls over his collar.

I click the shutter—snap—to capture my friends in our state-of-the-art designer kitchen, enjoying first-rate food and wine that I have sourced from the neighborhood's unparalleled range of Italian delis and vintners. Sometimes I recognize that seeing everything as a potential photo shoot for *House and Garden* is a possible affliction but, according to Gideon, you can take the girl out of Vogue House but you can't take Vogue House out of the girl.

"Well, I worked for him in the mid-1990s sometime, on the house in France," says Gideon. "So it was a business relationship. He's not a friend of mine, if you see what I mean. Couldn't have impressed him much. He got John to do the cottage in the Berkshires. And the apartment in New York, I think."

"That's John Pawson," I say, in case Mimi and Ralph aren't in the loop when it comes to celebrated architects and their client lists.

"Or, on the other hand, he may have got Pawson because he never paid me the final third of my fee," says Gideon, smiling wolfishly.

"Are you serious?" says Mimi, looking shocked, fork laden with chicory en route to mouth.

"Don't worry, angel, I never thought he would," Gideon said, swigging from one of our crystal wineglasses. "I always frontload my fee on the basis that you never get the last installment anyway. It's how the rich stay rich, poppet. We know each other's dirty tricks."

"What's the house in the Berkshires like then?" asks Mimi, casually.

"Usual thing," says Gideon. "Six bedrooms, seven bathrooms, ten thousand square feet, cathedral-height ceilings, fieldstone fireplace, lake-style heated pool and waterfall, Adirondack-style pool and guest cottage."

"Sounds ghastly," says Ralph.

"Sounds great," says Mimi, at the same time.

"Actually, I remember now," continues Gideon, "John didn't

do the cottage. He made his excuses, something about log cabins not being his thing, and just did the Park Avenue apartment for Si, which is supposed to be wonderful. You know. Majestic. Monastic. The stuff of *Architectural Digest* wet dreams."

While we're finishing the cheese, Gideon makes a suggestion.

"Shall we have an intercourse cigarette upstairs?" he asks, pulling out his softpack of American Spirit cigarettes and looking around the gathering.

"Who's ready for an early exclusive preview of the new Gideon Sturgis panoramic roof terrace and solar-paneled roof before pudding? Before the rest of the world gets to see it in *World of Interiors* May issue?"

"Oooh—I'd love to," Mimi says, her pink cheeks getting even pinker.

Mimi stands up but Ralph stays put. Perfect. Gideon can show off to Mimi and I get Ralph on my own.

"Clare, I don't know how you do it," says Ralph, with a sigh, as they disappear upstairs, cutting himself another oozing slice of cheese, which he has to scrape off on the side of his plate. He takes a handful of oatcakes, and reaches for the butter. "You cook like an angel, you're even prettier now than you were when you were at Cambridge. Apart from the fact that you have a completely ridiculous house and a husband of such epic ludicrosity that he should appear in the *Guinness Book of World Records,* I'd marry you."

"But Ralph—you never knew me at Cambridge," I point out, accurately. "You were at Edinburgh." I'm such a poor flirt. "Anyway, we like the house. And Gideon's not altogether ludicrous, you know. Ecotecture is the only way forward. And he's very good at it. He really believes in what he does." Now I'm sounding earnest.

"I'm only teasing," says Ralph, though he isn't. "You know we love coming here. But I don't think I could stay here for even a night. It's too grand for us. I mean, where's all your furniture? Where on earth do you put all your stuff?"

I smile at Ralph, and he smiles back at me, and there's a moment's silence during which something kindles between us. I remember the crackling touch of his hand, dry and warm, on mine, and my breathless descent to the Avery party thereafter. "Gideon gives me everything I want," I say to Ralph, my heart thudding.

And then, while the others are on the roof, I for some reason tell him about the one thing that Gideon can't give me. I tell about our problems in that area in a woman-to-man way as if Mimi hasn't already, endlessly. I tell him from the heart, and when I've finished, both our eyes are brimming. We have definitely connected in some way tonight.

After that, we talk about something else completely—he asks me all about my qualifications from the Chelsea Physick Garden, and then he tells me about his work, which he dismisses as "dull beyond your wildest dreams" but sounds absolutely fascinating. I mean, I know a little bit, the high oil price, reserves and so on, and the problems with getting gas from Russia out to Western Europe through pipelines, but Ralph's geopolitical knowledge of the industry is clearly second to none.

He nonchalantly tells me he's been hired as a consultant by a big oil company to liaise between all the government departments and BP and this other company over the impact of excavating an oil field off the coast of the Isle of Wight, on top of his Russian consulting work.

I tell him it sounds as if he's doing fantastically well, and he shrugs and says that thing that always alarms me, that it's only a matter of time before he has to put the house on the market, and that Mimi simply can't accept that they are living way beyond their means, that she won't hear of moving and changes the subject every time he brings it up.

But then I hear the others clattering down the concrete

stairs, and Mimi and Gideon come back, both saying how cold it was on the roof.

Mimi and Gideon are fairly quiet after that—her lips have gone blue—so we all eat our raspberries from Michanicou, the most expensive grocer in the Western World, with some golden Jersey double cream from the Grocer on Elgin, and I put the kettle on for herbal tea.

We have finished three bottles of the Pauillac and, even so, Gideon is all for opening some port, even though I give him discouraging looks. There is something glittery and hungry about him tonight, even though he made the sweetest little speech about me when I was dishing out the raspberries. Then Ralph comes to my rescue.

"I think I'll stick at the *post mortem*, not the *most portem*," he says and everyone groans. Ralph is famous for his terrible puns. "Gay tea for me."

I can't help clearing up as soon as there are dirty plates on the table, and Ralph is so polite, he takes it as a hint to leave rather than a sign of my compulsive tidiness. We all four go to the front steps.

"Safe journey," cries Gideon. When people on the garden entertain each other, we always say this at the end of the evening, just as we say, "Have you come far?" at the beginning.

"Yes, drive safely!" I add, as the Flemings walk, waving, the few steps from our house to their house.

"Well done, darling, that was lovely," says Gideon, when we're lying in bed, with the blinds down, me in my new Bonsoir pajamas. "You are such a wonderful hostess. What a good dinner."

He snuggles up, naked and hot and hairy, and I can feel immediately that he is erect, and I know why. It was that minx Virginie. As I reach down and take him in a firm grasp, he starts nuzzling my throat, at the bare skin, and tries to lever himself on top of me.

I scoot down the bed and manipulate his limbs so that I am

lying between the V of his open legs and his erection is slapping impressively against his belly. But he pulls me up again. He doesn't want that. So I wriggle quickly out of my crisp PJs, fold them along their crease lines, and lay them on the floor beside the bed, and hold out my arms to him. At the key moment—which comes rather fast for Gideon, who is usually very generous—he collapses on my chest, smelling smokily of cigarettes and blue cheese, which isn't as horrid as it sounds.

I lie on the damp patch, which is, as usual, on my side, imagine changing the bed linen first thing in the morning, and work out that I'm not due to ovulate until lunchtime, 28 March, which is in ten and a half days' time, and try not to mind about either.

Mimi

Fatima looks rather boot-faced when we stagger in, slightly the worse for wear after, in my case, two bottles of Kirin beer and the thick end of a bottle of red wine.

"I go quickle, quickle," she says, tapping her watch.

"But it's only eleven thirty, Fatty," I say, stifling a hiccup. "Don't you want Ralph to run you home?" I continue, hoping she says no.

Fatima lives at the far north end of the Portobello Road, in the Latin or Arab quarter of North Kensington. On a good day, she brings the children custard tarts and sweet coconut cakes from Lisboa, which I usually snaffle before teatime. I do think it's very important for women of my age not to get too thin—it makes us look so stringy and anxious.

"How were the children? Did Posy settle all right?" I ask, throwing down keys and clutch on the ledge by the front door.

"Childrers she fine, my pretty darling," says Fatima, her face softening. "Bye bye." She lets herself out, and Ralph double-locks behind her.

I won't allow myself to review the evening until I'm in bed. Of course, I am longing to share all my gossip with Ralph—but I can't.

First, that thing with Si Kasparian at the sushi party. I'm not saying that our conversation was very scintillating, but that wasn't the point. The point was that we were introduced, and then we were superglued together for the rest of the evening. The charge was flowing like nobody's business.

When I tore myself away to go and have a late supper with

Clare and Gideon, I felt as if I'd left a piece of me behind—especially after that leave-taking . . .

What with going to the Sturgises for supper, I haven't yet had time to relive the moment at the party when I finally said good-bye to Si and, instead of kissing my cheek, or my hand, or not kissing me at all, he leant toward me and very lightly kissed my neck—and my knees buckled.

And then! Gideon Sturgis! Solar-paneled roof, forsooth!

If you're taking dinner off a famous architect and he suddenly turns to you and suggests you might want to see some clever thing he's just designed, it's only polite to go along.

So, we're together on the top landing. Above our heads is a glass roof. It's not a very clear night, but through the glass I can see the night sky, the clouds a dull orangey color.

"Open sesame," says Gideon, and pushes a small silver button flush with the white surface of the wall.

Then the retractable roof retracts. It's completely silent. And I have to admit, very impressive, and even quite sexy in a James Bond kind of way. It almost makes me see the point of Gideon, if he could build something as clever as that, but not quite.

"Wow," I say. Then Gideon pops open a hidden cupboard by pushing on a hidden spring-loaded panel, like Caernarvon discovering Tutankhamen's tomb. His hand looks very black and hairy against the spotless white paint, and I begin to get that iffy feeling, and my mother's warning voice pops into my head, saying, "Do be *careful*, darling—are you quite, quite sure this isn't a *goat alert*?"

Gideon withdraws a lightweight stepladder from the concealed cupboard.

"After you," he says, opening it with a flourish, like a waiter flapping a napkin.

So I'm in my gypsy skirt from Whistles and a very smart £6 Ladybird vest of Mirabel's from Woolies' on the Portobello

Road. I leave my beaded flip-flops from the Cross summer sale on the ground and I step on to the ladder barefoot.

Gideon holds it.

"After you," he says.

I start climbing. It's all going to be fine. I am going to go out on the roof, say how wonderful and clever Gideon is, and then come back down.

But when I'm midway, i.e. my top half is poking out on to the Sturgises' roof and my legs are still within, there is a sudden billow of wind. I clutch at the parapet and feel, to my dismay, cool air fanning my legs, then, even worse, hot, panting breath. When I look down, I can't see Gideon at all. His head is completely concealed in my skirt.

"Gosh, I'm terribly sorry, Gideon," I say, relieved that Clare is not here to witness her husband's nose buried in my gusset.

"Don't apologize," Gideon says huskily, his voice muffled. "Don't mention it. I may just stay down here, if that's all right. I've definitely got The View."

Then I step rather ungracefully off the ladder and out on to the roof and hug my chest, as it's quite breezy and chilly up here on the roof in the dark. Gideon slithers up the ladder a few seconds later.

I try to say something intelligent about the design of the slidy roof and the importance of renewable energy in order to pretend to us both that the skirt incident never happened but end up chattering something about how I've never seen the crescent from this angle before. I also make a throwaway remark about chimney pots. And the number of satellite dishes. All of which is a little silly, I know, because I have, strangely enough, never been up here on the Sturgises' roof before, so how could I ever have seen my own house from this particular eyrie, but something about Gideon is making me nervous.

"Sorry, are you cold, Mimi?" he says, after going on a bit

about the hydraulic mechanics of the device, and how strong the glass is, and the ethics of light pollution, as I try not to let my teeth clack together.

Then he tosses his cigarette stub over the parapet into Colville Crescent below.

"Maybe I shouldn't have brought you up here." There is a funny note to his voice.

"I am, a bit," I answer, thinking that he will call it a day and we can go down for pudding.

Instead, Gideon comes and stands directly in front of me, very much in my space.

I am too surprised to speak. I wonder if he is going to tell me something I don't want to hear. That Clare has cancer, or they're moving to New York, or something equally discombobulating and thought-provoking.

But he doesn't speak. He puts his arms round me and sort of nuzzles me in a bear-hug, and rubs his hands vigorously up and down my back. "Better?" he asks.

I can't think what to say. I am rigid with cold, and now shock.

But he doesn't wait for an answer.

He comes in even closer, and then, he comes in very close and sort of sniffs my whole face, like a truffle hound seeking out some buried nugget in the mulch of the Piedmont, so close I can feel his stubble grazing my face, reminding me of the dogs I see every morning in Hyde Park, joyously circling each other nose to tail. And then—schlurp!

His lips fasten lampreylike onto mine, and his tongue is rasping against my teeth, prizing me open and thoroughly exploring the inside of my mouth. And, in the meantime, his arms have an independent agenda of their own.

I would be fibbing if I said that this was all *entirely* unpleasant. For one thing, it was a whole lot less cold. And like any self-respecting woman fast approaching forty, I have no strenuous objections to men—men, women, children, dogs, you name it—finding me irresistibly attractive.

So I went along with fiddling on the roof for a few seconds, but mainly because I couldn't think what else to do, how to extricate myself without seeming frigidly prissy. I wasn't Frenching the hell out of him, put it that way. And also because that thing with Si had got me going, rather.

I think, on the whole, that going along with it even for a few seconds was a mistake, because soon I feel something hard and big and proud pressing into me. At this point, I knew I had to do something.

"Sorry," I said, breaking away for air. "I feel giddy."

"Oh, darling," murmured Gideon, steering me further from the edge but not letting go.

"Oh, baby, do you get vertigo?"

"No, I feel you," I said. "I feel Giddy." Then I laughed. "Ha ha . . . is there a special hidden button I should push to make it retract back again?"

What was I thinking of?

Gideon took my hand and put it on his crotch. I could feel his heat and his throbbing bulge through the thin linen of gray Paul Smith trousers. He left my hand there and then snaked his up under my skirt, and he did something . . . quite technically advanced . . . down there.

Now, this was going too far. A snog is one thing, but I didn't want Gideon Sturgis thinking I'm going any further.

I absolutely am not. If I'm going to leap into bed with anyone who isn't my husband, it's not going to be Gideon Sturgis, especially as it is now crystal clear that he is a confirmed goat. Not to mention the fact that Clare is my garden best friend.

My mother, Mary, has a theory about this, which I think she has even written up in her *Saga* column. She says that when a man finds a woman attractive, other men know, without knowing they know, and are also drawn to her. She has a special name for this beautiful thing. She calls it "flies on carrion," and the implication is, I'm afraid, that Gideon is aroused not so much by me but by the pheromones released by my own attraction to Si.

"Stop, Gideon," I ordered, reflecting how strange it was that when Si kissed my neck, I shivered with pleasure, but when Gideon sucked my tongue and gave me a thorough digital examination, front and back, I felt nothing more than a mere animal arousal. I straightened my knickers, which had wound their way around my right buttock. "Please. You must stop."

We went downstairs, and neither Clare nor Ralph noticed anything, and Gideon got even more jacked up on vintage Pauillac. Then we mashed lovely thick cream into fresh raspberries from Michanicou, sipped peppermint tea made with real leaves, and sloped off back home to Fatty (i.e., quite an evening).

After Fatty goes I climb the stairs. I plant a kiss on each sleeping child's damp face and turn off their tape machines and straighten their duvets, and check that each has a pile of school uniform to pull on in the morning. Ralph takes Calypso out to powder her nose, and checks the back door in a man-of-the-house way.

When we flop into bed, Ralph starts talking again about perhaps taking out a small mortgage to tide us over so I clamber on top of him. I haven't finished with this evening yet. I feel life is rich again with possibility, and I want to share my bounty.

"Oh, darling," he says. "I'm too tired."

"What were you and Clare talking about?" I ask, as I kiss his smooth forehead and ears and stroke his hair away from his eyes.

"You," he says. He always says that.

"No you weren't," I say. "Go on, tell me."

"She was talking about Gideon and how he seems to have lost all interest in sex since she started calling him on his mobile and making him leave the office and race home to have sex when her temperature went up. Woman stuff," Ralph replies. "You know. About eggs, and stuff."

"And what else?" I ask, kissing the smooth place on his forehead, above his eyebrows, that smells more purely of him than anywhere else. When I sniff him there, I get a homesick feeling that tells me I've missed him, without realizing.

"But I rather suspect the reason they haven't had babies yet is fairly simple, and it's not because Gideon isn't a perfectly good sperm butler," he continues in a muffled voice, as I am dandling my *embonpoint* by now over his mouth.

"Is that all?" I ask. It's always hard to get anything out of Ralph.

Ralph doesn't answer this.

"Anyway, what did you think about that little speech he made about Clare over pudding, which was a carbon copy of the one he made at her birthday last year," I suddenly remember, "about Clare's life being 'both her lasting achievement and her work in progress,' which is basically saying, isn't Clare clever to have hitched her wagon to fabulous me. It made me feel so sorry for her. So why do you think they haven't managed to have babies yet?" I ask.

"Well . . . That gray cashmere sweater with no shirt underneath, and those black suede loafers worn without socks, not to mention his entire house—"

"Oh, come on, their house is gorgeous," I protest.

"If you ask me, Gideon's so far into the closet he's practically in . . . Narnia."

"Shut up," I order. "Don't make me laugh now. And you're wrong about Gideon being a poofter."

Not only is Gideon a full-blooded heterosexual, he would

shag a wall if it was wearing blue mascara. But I don't tell Ralph why I'm so sure.

"I think it's much more fashionable to be a closet hetero and have a secret straight life, not a sad secret gay one, and Gideon would never dream of doing anything untrendy," is what I say instead of telling Ralph.

Then I buck and rear over him, feeling athletic, and Ralph, despite an initial show of reluctance, gives every sign of enjoying the proud sight of his naked wife rampant.

We go on in this vein for a while, and things are coming up roses for us both, only I've forgotten that Calypso is lying like a faithful hound at the foot of a carved medieval effigy by our creaking bed, so when it comes to the crisis point where we're both shouting, "Now now now," and "Yes yes yes," to each other in tortured yelps, she jumps up on to the bed with a volley of barks, convinced that one of us is killing the other one and not sure which one of us to maul to death and which one to rescue.

"Quiet, Calypso," roars Ralph. "Aaaargggh."

"Aaarrgh," I return.

"How was that for you?" I ask, smugly, as he flumps back on the pillow, panting. "Vesuvian," he says, stroking my tummy with his long, elegant fingers. "You know, I sometimes think any chap who manages to ride a filly over the finishing line deserves a place in the Winner's Enclosure. I often think there's been some mistake and wonder why I'm not doing a lap of honor round the bedroom, to the roar of the crowd."

"I know, you men do awfully well," I say. "I don't know how you do it. What I don't get is how, after all that effort, I have only burned up 150 calories. It just seems such a tiny amount, given how exhausting it is."

It's true. My satisfaction that my husband and I have just performed coitus is slightly offset by my mental calculation that I have burned off exactly the number of calories contained in one Clarke's oatcake with butter, and I must have eaten at least seven.

"I can see why going to the gym has replaced sex in most people's lives. It's so much more efficient than having sex," I observe, in a drowsy voice.

"And so much more fun, too," says Ralph, turning away from me, grabbing a pillow, and going instantly to sleep.

Clare

19 March. Annual general meeting of Lonsdale Gardens. A hundred people perched on chairs clutching three-page agendas. The three Molton boys scudding about in their matching stripy blue-and-white pajamas, holding bowls of blue tortilla chips. I love these unchanging annual events, these punctuation marks in the garden year.

"Thank you, Charlie," I say, taking one from a proffered bowl. The Molton house is, like most around here, a nut- and gluten- and dairy-free zone. Marguerite, for whom diet is religion, stands in the kitchen opening bottles of organic white Burgundy that John Armit delivered that morning and which have been chilling nicely in her Sub-Zero drinks fridge with humidor attachment.

Patrick usually allows us all to chatter for ten minutes or so before he opens proceedings. I am buttering up Lady Forster because I haven't told her yet about our plans to embed tiny uplighters in our front garden, which I am in the middle of redoing this year to resemble an old vegetable garden with big horizontal bands of box hedging, herbs, poppy "Patty's Plum," phaeum geraniums, wild strawberries, sweet garlic, and so on. Stripes make a small garden feel wider.

"Thank you for coming, all," says Patrick in a raised voice.

This is the cue for us to take our seats on folding chairs that are kept in the shed and only brought out for occasions like this.

Mathieu and Virginie come and sit fairly near the front, Mathieu looking formal despite, or should that be because of, his ensemble of tweed jacket, ironed jeans and canary yellow lambswool pullover slung over his shoulders. Virginie is working the *matelot* look today, in a Breton striped T-shirt in navy and white over a pair of white sailor trousers by Chloë with gilt buttons over her hipbones and some flat navy pumps. She is all tiny ankles and wrists.

The Averys come to sit next to them in the row.

Virginie doesn't look at Bob (she doesn't realize what a giveaway this is) but beams at Sally and pats the free chair next to her. Sally sits down. Virginie leans across and whispers in Sally's ear. Sally blushes. Then, after a pause, she whispers something back in Virginie's gold-locked ear. Virginie throws her head back. Bob and Mathieu, meanwhile, are studying their agendas calmly like good boys throughout this girlish scene.

Trish Dodd Noble then goes to take a seat next to Patrick at the rostrum, as is her right. She is treasurer and Patrick is chairman, but the way she goes about it, you'd think she was running a FTSE 100 company single-handed—which, now I come to think of it, she did. It's just that like many women around here, she has simply transferred her organizational skills to the domestic sphere, with resounding success.

"I have apologies from three committee members who can't be here," says Patrick, in his "I am the bull, you are the herd" voice, as Trish riffles through some paperwork with a professional eye and taps a Mont Blanc pen on the tabletop. "Jonathon is on book tour in the States, Sir Marcus is at Highgrove," Patrick looks around to check that we are all suitably impressed by the grandeur of the extracurricular activities of the garden committee, "and Sue's mother's ill so Sue is sadly unable to be here. Anyway, moving on to new members, now, before we get stuck into the main business."

I feel myself go a little pink.

"Clare Sturgis is kindly stepping into Lady Forster's shoes and taking over as secretary." He looks at me, and claps his hands together softly. "Clare, welcome to the committee.

We're all delighted and honored to have such a towering figure in the world of horticulture taking on more of a role on the garden."

There is a round of polite applause.

"I would like to start things off by warning you that I intend to follow my tried-and-trusted method of dealing with any garden problems that may arise by simply responding with the same two words to anything you might say to me," Patrick pauses for laughter before adding, "Yes, dear."

The laughter rumbles on, with the self-satisfied timbre emitted by an exclusive group of people who have managed to acquire desirable properties and an agreeably high-end set of neighbors at the same time. Sometimes the AGM can feel not like a bunch of neighbors talking about pea shingle and bedding plants but the meeting of a bloodstock syndicate that wins the Grand National not once but every year.

Ralph pats my thigh. "So, Clare, how did That Prick persuade you to take that poisoned chalice?" he whispers in my ear.

"I'm a pushover," I whisper back. "One packet of poppyseeds and I'm anybody's."

Ralph chuckles and Patrick glares at him.

Then Patrick gallops through his chairman's report. He summarizes the tree surgery and there is input from the members about whether to replace the felled trees and, if so, with what. This sparks furious debate from the members about the relative merits of saplings and more mature trees, which leads one resident, one who I'm definitely going to have to watch like a hawk, contradicting Stephen the gardener sharply and telling us all that she, unlike all of us, knew what she was talking about because she was a member of the International Society of Dendrology.

Stephen then gives his annual gardener's report and tells us all about reseeding and topsoil and the belated sprouting of a smyrnium, during which I hear Ralph emit a tiny snore.

Then Patrick thanks Stephen and we all clap, and then

Patrick rattles through the accounts for last year (the insurance seems to double every five minutes), the budget for next year (the garden levy is going up again, not that anyone here will notice).

"Dates for your diaries now," Patrick continues, waving to son Max to refill his glass.

Max arrives with the dish of hummus and rice cakes instead. Patrick looks aghast, so son Charlie comes up with a bottle.

"That's better," says Patrick. "Thank goodness at least one member of my family knows what I like." I look at Marguerite, who has had all the Moltons on a strict diet since I can remember. She's looking pinched; her cheekbones jutting, she laughs along with everyone else at the sight of a small boy in flannel pajamas carrying a magnum of Burgundy.

Marguerite is extremely beautiful with glossy dark hair, intense blue eyes, and papery white skin but is not, according to Gideon, sexy. "She's too thin, she's got no tits and her hipbones jut out," he says. "It would be like screwing a garden rake."

"Garden Sports and Summer Party is twenty-five June," Patrick is saying now, briskly. "As I repeat every year, this event can't happen without many willing volunteers. Obviously, the marquee will go up on Saturday morning, but I need strong chaps out on the lawn to mark out the pitch and hammer in stakes. I know that some of you garden ladies are organizing the cricket tea, sorry, you know what I mean, the usual refreshments, prizes and so on, already—thank you for that, ladies, in advance, it is much appreciated by all, particularly the ice-cream stall." Patrick beams at us all again, cozily.

"When will he just shut up?" Ralph mutters.

"Lastly, it's never too early to remind you that we also need helpers for Bonfire Night, that means you, too, Ralph, and help with the construction of our bonfire. I don't need to tell you how important it is that our Bonfire Night display is better in every way than the one in Montpelier Garden, and I think I'm right in saying that the per household contribution this year has been set at seventy-five pounds."

Patrick moves swiftly on. "Don't everyone feel you have to rush off, there's some naughty hummus to finish up, ha ha, can't think why, not to mention some very fattening celery sticks."

There is a generalized stirring, but as half the meeting rises to its feet, Patrick waves his agenda and calls the meeting back to order.

"Oh, yes, sorry, can you all take your seats—I've forgotten Any Other Business," he calls out. "I don't know whether any of you have heard, but Woody Allen, the director, approached the Dodd Nobles, as he wanted to set a scene for his new London film with that blond pouter, you know, errr, argh, whose name escapes me" (several residents call out "Scarlett Johansson") "on the garden."

He turns to Trish, who is trying and failing not to look too excited. In Notting Hill, it is social death to appear the slightest bit celebrity-struck.

She picks up the thread. "Yes, um, Patrick's right, *Woody* came to tea a couple of weeks ago," she says, with transparent exultation. "He was very nice, and I took him through our garden into the communal garden." She pauses, so we can all visualize her *tête-à-tête* with the legendary director and revise our opinions of her upward. "He seemed very keen. So then, of course, I rang Patrick, just to check whether Woody could shoot the scene on the garden," she continues. "I wasn't sure what it says in the bylaws."

"I don't care what it says in the bylaws," interrupts Patrick with a smirk, "I think we're all agreed that we can't have film people taking over and making life intolerable for the residents. We can't go about tripping over catering trucks and cables and starlets. We said no to Richard Curtis when he asked if he could shoot That Film, so we say no to Woody Allen."

"I suppose so," says Trish, in a flat voice, clearly disappointed.

"So that's all right then," says Patrick, opening his folder. "Issue closed." There is some whispering as the old guard, such as the Forsters, are informed who Woody Allen is, and some murmuring about how Patrick is absolutely right to keep cameras and Hollywood riffraff out of our own magical glade.

"Moving on! Last bit of other business now—we've had some plans copied over to us," Patrick says briskly, pretending to consult his notes, "from the Averys."

Everybody at the meeting listens. I feel the Averys just in front of me, and the Lacostes suddenly go very still, as everyone looks toward them and looks away again.

Patrick explains that the Averys are planning to rebuild their garage, which is a low-lying building that nestles, if you think of the garden as a rectangle, just below the top right-hand corner and sits on the slip road called Lonsdale Rise that connects the long sides of Colville Crescent and Lonsdale Gardens.

He says the detailed plans are available for public inspection at the Town Hall, but that if any member of the committee wants to see them, he, as chairman of the garden committee, has some photocopies—somewhere. He thinks. He adds that he thinks planning permission may have already been granted but the Averys, as a courtesy, are mentioning it now, even though it's all been conducted through proper channels and so forth.

At this, I feel the hairs rise on the back of my neck. Before I can stop myself, I stick my hand up. "Patrick, if you don't mind, can you explain why a matter of such importance to the whole garden hasn't come up before, particularly if, as you say, it's too late to object now?" I ask. "I mean, the Averys' garage is right on the communal garden."

Patrick shrugs. "I can only presume that the relevant parties were contacted independently, and there weren't the requisite number of objections," he says.

Bob Avery rises to his feet. "That's about the size of it, Chairman," he says, in his deep Bostonian drawl. "Letters went out to the neighbors on either side and to those opposite with a direct outlook on to our property, but my wife Sally and I were very fortunate to secure planning consent and are going to start the works this summer, while almost all of us are away and won't be disturbed by the noise."

"That's a heroic assumption," Ralph says out loud. He and Mimi are among the very few residents on the garden without a second home in the depths of the English countryside and a third home abroad.

And that's it. Patrick doesn't say any more, we stand around for a little bit and then leave.

As I walk back home with Ralph and Mimi, I let off steam.

"I can't believe no one else smells a rat, and we only find out about this after planning permission's been given," I fume. "I know how these things work. It means we haven't got a hope of stopping it. How do we know the Averys aren't planning some huge pile on the communal garden, where Bob can service Virginie in peace? I know what Americans are like. They say they've got a cottage on the Cape and what that means is an eight-bedroom beach house with pier and ocean frontage. At least now we all know what that sushi party was about," I continue, as we round the corner from Lonsdale Gardens to Colville Crescent.

"How could we all be so stupid? The Averys cleverly bought us all off right before Patrick announced the existence of the plans at the AGM."

"Calm down, Clare," says Mimi, taking my arm. "Don't think the worst of them. They just want everyone to love them and to be included, like all Americans. They're no different from anyone else. They tried for planning permission—and they got it. You get so worked up about anything to do with the garden, my love. I'm not sure you taking on this additional burden of being secretary's such a good idea. You mustn't feel that everything that goes on in the garden is your responsibility. It'll drive you completely bonkers and block your *jing luo*. You'll need daily sessions with Donna if you go on like this, not weekly ones. It's really not good for you."

I know what Mimi means—she is implying that my infertility is a *stress-related condition* rather than a proper illness, and therefore all my fault, and this makes me even crosser.

"What the fuck are *jing luo*?" demands Ralph. "And who's Donna?"

"They're the invisible pathways of *qi*," Mimi answers him. "And Donna's *feng shui* guru to the whole of Notting Hill, you've met her at least twice." She says *feng shui* in the pretentious way, "fung schwee," just to annoy him.

And Mimi and I chorus, "Do keep up, Ralph," and disappear into our respective addresses.

Mimi

By the time we get back from the AGM, it's past 8 P.M. and Fatima clucks as she leaves. She doesn't like working late two nights on the trot, and I will have to make it up to her at the end of the week.

All is quiet.

Cas is playing FIFA 2006 on the PS2 down in the playroom, in flagrant contravention of a house rule. He's lying on his back on the beanbag, holding the controls, with Calypso lying devotedly alongside.

I start asking him something about his trombone practice and whether he's done all his homework (it was making a desert island complete with contour lines and dormant volcano), having seen no firm evidence of said project in the kitchen, but he just says, "Shush, Mum, I'm playing a game." I stand for a moment admiring his curly chestnut mop and dark lashes and skin like a dusky apricot, then pick up his school shoes and throw them in a basket by the back door.

Cas doesn't think it matters that he never does any homework because he knows that when he grows up he will be a striker for Chelsea, drive a Maserati, and live in a mock-Tudor gated manor outside Chobham with a footballer's wife.

Sometimes, I find myself in agreement with Prince Charles about the inflated expectations of the younger generation, but I love Cas too much to tell him how tiring and frightening being grown-up really is, in much the same way that our mothers neglect to tell us how painful childbirth is. There's no point. We discover it anyway as we go along.

I climb three flights of stairs to the top landing, tottering slightly and breathing heavily. After three glasses of white wine, the contrast between my surroundings and Marguerite Molton's house (our house has carpet dating back to 1961 and smudgemarks all over the walls; hers is a pristine box) are not so glaring.

I push open the girls' door, pausing only to re-affix the P that has dropped off the words POSY'S ROOM, words which are stuck on the door in these sweet painted letters from Cheeky Monkeys that I put in Posy's stocking last Christmas.

Underneath this charming sign, Mirabel has stuck a poster saying PARENTAL ADVISORY—WARNING—DO NOT ENTER. On top of that, she has Sellotaped a new announcement, which says, COME TO THE DARK SIDE—WE HAVE COOKIES. Another sticker says, SAVE THE EARTH. IT'S THE ONLY PLANET WITH CHOCOLATE. Mirabel is on the computer. So no surprise there.

As soon as she gets home, she changes out of her school uniform and into her other uniform of ra-ra skirt and a crop top, even though she is only eleven and the only people who will see her thus clad are her own relations. Sometimes I show her pictures of fetching Mormon girls in Utah wearing ankle-length skirts and pigtails and say, "Now, that's what I call appropriate dress for an eleven-year-old," as she puts a finger down her throat.

"Mirabel?" I say, leaning against the door.

Mirabel keeps tapping at the keyboard. Doesn't look round.

"Mirabel?" I repeat.

"What."

"Are you talking to the pederasts?" I ask.

"Yes," she answers, in her "like, duh" voice, which means I have yet again asked a silly question.

"Have you done your homework?"

"No," she answers, in the same tone.

"Okay, good girl," I say.

Posy is sitting on the floor in their bedroom sorting out her collections, still wearing her gingham smock from school, and my heart is warmed by this rare sight of an actual child absorbed in childish things.

While Mirabel chats to her child molesters and exchanges filth with her schoolfriends, Posy can spend hours quite happily playing with her collection of dinner napkins and moist cleansing wipes. She color-codes the napkins and sorts out the towelettes by country of origin, and then puts them neatly back into two Start-Rite pale-blue shoeboxes.

If you ask her, she will explain that they are called "moist towelettes" in America, *"fazzoletti"* in Italy, and so on, which is quite fascinating, if you like that sort of thing, for about two seconds. At the last count, she had 153 different towelettes, or should I say *"Erfrischungstüchen,"* from twenty-three different countries. As I tell her godparents and grandparents, if you want to make Posy happy, you don't need to buy her a video iPod or take her to *Mary Poppins,* "Just send her a little sachet containing a lemon-scented handwipe from an obscure airline in the post," I say. One day, Ralph predicts, she's going to meet a man who has the largest collection of paper airsick bags in private hands—and Posy's prince will have come.

So all is quiet on the western front, and I tell the girls I'm going to have a bath. Need time to think.

I have been unable to think straight all day. After all, I gave Si my mobile number and I saw him input it into his Black-Berry under the name Mimi, and I felt sure he'd call me today, even if it was only to solicit a number. I was relying on him to . . . strike while the iron was hot.

As I was dragged bodily from the Avery party, I turned back for a second and went up to him. I gave him my smoldering look and said, "Anyway, new neighbor, I'm leaving you now. I haven't enjoyed meeting you At All. But if you do need someone to *feng shui* your window boxes, call me." Although as I do, as it happens, know someone (i.e., Donna) who *feng shuis* window boxes, this was clearly a shameless come-on.

A shameless come-on that I must accept was heard by about a hundred people at the sushi party.

Including my own husband.

And then—shiver shiver—he'd kissed me on the neck, and that was my cattle-prod moment.

But so far, no call. My mobile has barely rung all day, apart from Doors to Manual checking that we're still on for dinner tomorrow, an endurance test I have yet to break to Ralph.

As I got through the day, the AGM, etc. (where Si didn't bother to show), I tried telling myself that property billionaires have other people to take care of everything. Window boxes are unlikely to be high priority. But still, all day, I've been secretly hoping that Si was going to call and ask for the number for the window box guy, just to *make contact*. Only he hasn't.

Ralph is in his study (he's off to Kyrgyzstan—something boring to do with a gas pipeline). And I'm now in the bath, adjusting the taps with my toes and trying not to get my hair too wet at the back while reading a damp copy of *Private Eye*.

I've brought my mobile into the bathroom with me. In fact, I've been taking it into the loo with me, just in case I'm right in my hunch, which is that the one piece of the jigsaw missing in Si's life, despite his yacht *Salome*, a new five-bedroom house in Lonsdale Gardens, Park Avenue apartment, country estates in both the Berkshires and Hampshire, and limitless resources, and despite the fact that he hasn't called is . . . me.

I lie in the bath and feel calmer. I give myself a reality check. I tell myself that I've had my frisson with Si and my grapple with Giddy and, now, the fun's over. Time to return to normal life, with all its quotidian frustrations and little joys . . .

At which moment, my mobile rings. As it rings, it vibrates and starts skittering toward the edge of the bath, so I grab it before it falls in, and before I have time to compose myself and answer in the sensuous, languid, come-hither way I have been rehearsing mentally all day—the sort of voice, in fact, that suggests I have never bought a packet of nine economy loo rolls and hung it on my shopping trolley even once in my life.

"Darling," says a voice that is definitely not Si's, because Si's is deep and dark and crunchy, like chocolate fridge cake.

"Who is this?" I say sharply. I am a married woman, after all. I cannot submit without some protest to some man, not even Si, calling me darling on my mobile while I am lying naked in the bath (Okay, well, whoever this is doesn't know that).

"Forgotten me already?" the man says, and I realize with a prickle of dismay who it is.

It is Gideon.

"I've been thinking about you all day," he says. "Can't get you out of my mind. Last night. On the roof . . ." There is a heavy panting sound.

I sit up, so that the water sloshes off my body and makes a slopping noise.

"Are you in the bath, baby?" Gideon asks.

"Yes," I say, thinking it's a mistake to admit this, at it will convey the reality that I am naked. And wet. And hot.

"Sounds good . . . might come over and join you."

"No, you won't," I hiss, looking toward the door and praying that no family member is within earshot. "You can't. I've locked the front door."

Of course, this is a lie, because Gideon could quite easily enter our house from the back. People are always coming in and out of each others' houses at this time of the evening—to borrow a cup of pine nuts or Italian ooo flour, return glasses left out in the communal garden, or simply to catch up on the gossip over some chilled Pouilly Fumé.

"But I can still get in," Gideon says, sounding creepily determined. "I've got your keys in my hand, if I'm right, having identified the Fleming family keys to number 67 Colville Crescent as the ones with a Marge Simpson enamel key ring on them. We're key holders, remember."

"Ha ha," I gurgle. "I'm touched, Gideon. And I'm sure the children will be thrilled to see you."

"Aren't they in bed yet?" Gideon asks, sounding less enthusiastic. Childless couples have no idea that when you have children, they don't just disappear at inconvenient moments like bedtime, or weekends.

"No, and nor is Ralph," I go on.

"Oh," says Gideon. "I thought Ralph was in Batustan or somewhere."

"Kyrgyzstan," I say, wearily. Why is everyone so completely clueless about Ralph's work? I wonder whether I should find it insulting—to *me*.

"His plane was delayed. . . . Look, Gideon," I say, praying no one's outside the door listening. "It's very sweet of you to be so keen, and all that, but this is a Really Bad Idea. You must see. Clare is my Best Friend. You live on the Same Garden as me. It's Got To Stop."

To my slight surprise, Gideon laughs, and hangs up.

I hate to admit it—but I feel slightly disappointed that he has given up so soon. As I wash with the children's SpongeBob Squarepants sponge, which has somehow found its way into the "master" bathroom, I console myself with the thought that it's all for the best, definitely.

I pad downstairs to get supper together and trip over the hands free telephone one of the children (i.e. Mirabel) has left lying on the stairs. I key in 1571, to see if there are any messages. There's one.

It's from Jane Fraser. I brace myself. It probably means she wants the adultery piece, with photos and quotes, ready soon. She asks me to call her.

I call her mobile, as not even Faint Praiser would be in the office at 9 P.M.

"Oh, Mimi, oh yes, yes, hi," Jane says, clearly having forgotten why she'd rung me. "Look, I know that you're doing adultery for us, but we want you to do an interview too, if you're not too busy," says Jane. "You are, for all your faults, one of my most reliable freelancers. Now—d'you know who I mean by Si Kasparian? You should do. According to 'Londoner's Diary,' he's just spent five million pounds on a house right near you. He doesn't give interviews, but he's your neighbor . . . Do you think you could swing it? Do the usual thing, you know, pretend you want to do a piece about his charitable foundation, called the Primrose Path or something, and then write only about him and his murky business dealings and deeply perverted private life and children's suicides, right? We'll pay you top dollar."

"But Jane, wait a minute," I say, opening a bag of rocket that says "Please wash before use" and emptying it into the salad bowl, "he doesn't have children."

"Whatever, but he's just bought a house on *your* communal garden, am I not right? The one you invited me to last summer, for that ghastly evening thing, where all these jumped-up City people were wandering around congratulating each other on living on the garden and smelling the honeysuckle? God, that horrendous disco in the marquee . . . all those Goldman Sachs partners swigging from champagne bottles and grooving on down to 'Le Freak' by Chic . . ." She trails off, and I can almost hear her shuddering.

"I'm glad you enjoyed it so much," I say, opening the fridge and peering in to see what I could give Ralph for supper. "Remind me to ask you again this year."

Jane laughs her cool, highly bred laugh.

"And Si is my neighbor, yes," I go on, with modest pride. Having smart neighbors is one of the very few things I can boast about, after all. But I don't add anything. I am thinking too fast.

I'm trying to work out what to do, while also trying to work out what to make for supper—could it be pesto . . . again? If I added some toasted pine nuts and crunchy lardons, why not?

Ralph's wonderfully easy to please. He's so grateful to be

fed every night, just as he's genuinely grateful that all my bits are roughly where they should be. I couldn't ask for more, really, but, right now, Ralph's niceness and decency are merely an obstacle in my path. If only he were a monster who beat me and abused the children—then it would all be *sooo* easy. . . .

"Then that's great," enthuses Jane, as if it's all agreed. "We're thinking of calling it 'The Napoleon of Notting Hill.' Two thousand words sound about right?"

"No no no, Jane, hang on a minute," I interject. I need time to think. I stab a packet of lardons with a carving knife and empty them into a frying pan with a slug of oil, open the Aga lid, slam the pan down on the hotplate.

I can't do an interview with Si. It's too obvious, too *forward*. Female interviewers have been coming on to their subjects like there's no tomorrow since the chief exec of General Electric left his wife for a younger model from a business paper.

No, I definitely don't want to do the interview (plus, all the people I've ever interviewed wind up hating me), but I do want the excuse that being *asked* to do the interview has handed me on a plate.

So I tell Jane I'll give it a try, but not to expect much. Also, I remind her that I know nothing about big business or big businessmen, and she could always suggest the Si interview as a City profile. I mention a couple of other freelancers. "I'd have rung them first if I was commissioning the profile," I say, in pious tones, as if I always have the interests of other journalists close to my heart.

"Thanks for that, Mimi. Let me know how you get on, anyway," says Jane, and rings off. She knows she hasn't closed the deal.

The fizzing in my stomach that started when I met Si is now so loud it's almost audible, as if I've swallowed a whole tube of the children's effervescent Redoxon tablets. I go to my desk in the sitting room, take a cream card and a white envelope, and hunt in vain for a fountain pen.

Then I put a lead on Calypso, shout to Ralph that I'm taking the dog round the block, and walk round to Lonsdale Gardens, where I drop a note through Si's letterbox. The billionaire is in residence. All the lights are blazing. This is what my note says, in full. Of course, the card's one with all my vital statistics on it, from London address to mobile number to blood group.

19 March
  Dear Si [I eventually scrawl in green felt tip—only working pen I can find] *The* Daily Mail *has commissioned me to interview you for a big piece, but I have declined. I have told the* Daily Mail *that you're not nearly interesting enough. If you want to persuade me otherwise, you have my number.*
  Yours,
  Mimi Malone.
  PS I hated it when you kissed my neck. Please never do that again.

As I walk home, sniffing the delicious, suggestive scents from all the blossom-laden trees, I am seized with regret. I hear my mother's wise voice enter my head. "Men only respond to one thing, darling," she always says. "Scarcity."

I think she means that men like to be hunters, or something like that, and they want the womenfolk to sit hunched in the cave, skinning the sabre-toothed tigers around the fire, pretending they don't care that the cavemen are *just not that into them.*

Even so, what I've done isn't so bold. For a start, it's Work-Related, and second, I think even Mother would agree that the Rules can be suspended when an attractive single billionaire is clearly panting after one like a hound.

Clare

When the lift doors open, a large sign directs me again into a cool, open-plan office. There are notices and plans pinned up everywhere, a seating area, a computer, a photocopier. I briefly try to imagine what it must be like working here all day, every day, and then a rather attractive man in cords walks in, with long blondish hair. The young woman who has been working at a screen looks up.

"So what did you get up to last night," she asks, "after?"

"Builders' Arms," the man replies. "Big mistake." He rolls his eyes.

"Tell me all about it later," she says, raising her eyebrows at him and turning to me.

I notice that she is sitting underneath a photograph of herself, which tells me that she and two young men with sideburns are the Local Planning Services Team. So the blond in cords is probably an architect. That explains why she's flirting with him.

I resist calling her by her name, even though I now know it from the poster above her head (Caroline Pery) and ask whether I can see the file relating to 100 Lonsdale Gardens, the Avery residence.

"Is it a closed application?" asks Caroline Pery. "Because, if it is, you might have to wait until it's got from the basement, that's where closed files are."

"I think it's closed—well, they've had planning permission," I say, my heart sinking. "How long would I have to wait?"

"About five minutes, maybe," she answers, and I smile.

I thought she was going to say five hours, which would mean missing my Pilates class (my back's gone again after intercourse with Gideon—though it could be all the repotting I've been doing of the spring bedding plants). And lunch with Marguerite.

"Do you have a reference number?" she asks.

I say no and she searches for it by address.

"Ooh, lots of planning applications on this house," she says. "Roof conservatory . . . basement extension . . . OSP . . . mansard . . . all refused so far, till this one, by the looks of things. Shows that persistence pays off."

"But they've only been in there for nine months," I say. "And the house is huge anyway—one of the largest in the street."

"That makes no difference in my experience," Caroline answers. "However big the house is to start with is immaterial. People get greedy for more space."

"Well, in this case, the space is supposed to be for a car not for the family, but I'll believe that when I see it," I say, smiling back, as the computer searches for the file. I think she's marvellous now she has demonstrated her efficiency.

She tells me I'm in luck, the file hasn't gone to the basement yet.

I sit and contemplate an aerial photograph of Peter Jones until Caroline returns with a yellow folder marked "100 Lonsdale Gardens." I sit with it at a desk, feeling businesslike.

Stapled to the inside front cover, there's a list of all the houses most directly affected by the rebuilding of the garage. These are the ones that the authorities are obliged to contact. Obviously, the houses on either side, i.e., numbers 96 to 104, which include the Lacostes and Si Kasparian, and the ones beyond that are listed, and then I realize, with a slight shock, that our house is also listed, as we directly overlook the Averys' rear elevation.

Before I go on to read the whole file, I summon Caroline and point out that, according to this, we were sent a letter, but if we were, I never received it. She comes over and then she silently leafs through the folder and shows me, on file, a copy of the letter we were sent, and says that a yellow notice was pinned on the lamppost outside our house.

"You were contacted and given a chance to object," she remarks. "You had two months." Then she shows me a red dot on a map of the garden square, to show the location of my house and the location of the lamppost and the location of the garage.

"That's odd," I say. "I don't remember either receiving the letter or seeing the yellow notice—and I am usually a noticing sort of person." I wonder if Gideon received the letter, but as the post usually comes midmorning, when he's at work in Soho, I don't see how that would have happened.

I work through the file, but there's not much to see. A letter from the executive director of the planning and conservation committee to the chief administrative officer, which deems the proposal to knock down and rebuild the garage neither "major, controversial, nor sensitive." A letter from English Heritage, saying that they have no objections. In fact, the only objection during the two-month consultation period seems to come in a letter from the chairman of the Ladbroke Association.

I take the letter out of the folder. It doesn't look very professional on a small sheet of Basildon Bond. The type wavers up and down the line.

"Are we sure this new so-called garage will not be used as an extension of the residential accommodation in 100 Lonsdale Gardens and therefore affect the amenity of adjacent properties?" queries the Hon. chairman of the association, whose signature I cannot read. "And will it be the same height and over same footprint to match the existing structure?"

I try to check this last point—a good one—but the architects have declined to fill in the blank space where the planners have requested that they enter the square footage of the new building. I point this out to Caroline, who tells me that I can work out elevation and square footage from the architect's drawing.

"I know I can, but I find it odd that they've left that blank," I say.

I then say to Caroline that it's pretty odd to use an expensive firm of architects to rebuild a garage. I mean, why bother? It confirms all my suspicions, which are shared by the Ladbroke Association, as does a brief glimpse of the plans. The old garage was one story, with a flat roof and no windows and a garage sliding-up-and-over door. The new one is two-story structure with a peaked glass roof, eight French windows, little balconies.

I stab my finger at the plans and march over to Caroline Pery.

"Look," I say. "Why would a Chrysler Voyager need eight French windows and a glass roof? To see out?"

Caroline shrugs. "That's their business," she says. "If they don't use the garage as a garage, that's one thing, but they can make it as fancy a garage as they like."

So the only letter of objection to this monstrous carbuncle, this new domestic residence which is set to dominate Lonsdale Gardens for years to come, was from the NIMBIES on the Ladbroke Association—who object to everything, on principle.

Only one letter of objection to the erection of a brand-new two-story house with a glass roof on a Notting Hill communal garden in a Conservation Area. And as I know only too well, the planning authorities don't stir at all until they have received at least three. I heave a sigh, my heart a stone in my chest.

On the next page is a copy of a letter to the Averys' architects. It is signed by the executive director of planning and cosigned by the head of development control and the area planning officer. The letter states that, as there was only one objection, the proposed rebuild of the Averys' garage had been granted under delegated approval. In other words, the planning committee never even checked over the plans.

I close the file and hand it back to Caroline Pery.

This morning's work has proved one thing beyond any doubt. We couldn't have made it easier for the Averys if we'd handed them their garage (two-story house worth up to a million) on a silver salver.

Mimi

"Mum, I hope you haven't forgotted again," says Posy, as we walk to school, the shops way.

There is a light breeze blowing. The trees are shimmying all the way down Elgin Crescent, shaking their booty of blossom on to the pavements. Calypso is nosing ahead of us, checking out all the driveways that have ever given sanctuary to pussy cats. Calypso is terrified of cats, but she has to pretend to us for obvious reasons that she is intent on chasing them. It's what dogs do. She's even frightened of squirrels. And bunny rabbits.

I am dressed with more care than usual, just in case . . . you know.

Skirt from Whistles, same as last night, the one I am almost beginning to call my Results Skirt. Little pink cashmere cardie from the charity shop on Westbourne Grove (one of the most welcome fashion trends of recent times is the way that grungy old clothes from Oxfam are acceptable all over again—as "vintage.") And finally, to round off this carefully thought out ensemble, off-white Converse sneakers, no socks. There's no point in wearing fuck-me shoes if you're walking children to school—though lots of more high maintenance mothers do.

We cross Ladbroke Grove. Since they installed a traffic light with a green man and a red man, this can take up to five minutes, so I have plenty of time to look around. "You never answer when we ask you things anymore, Mummy," complains Posy.

"Green man," I cry, to my children's embarrassment, and we march over.

"Do you have to shout that every time we cross the road?" asks Mirabel. "Like, TE."

"Um, forgotted what, darling?"

"That you're coming to Circle Time, and that it's my Special Assembly," says Posy importantly, so I can hear the capitals in her voice.

"Of course I haven't!" I cry. Posy knows I'm lying, and this makes her sad, because lies make baby Jesus cry. "How lovely," I say, when what I'm thinking is, of course, "Oh, shit."

This means I won't get back home till 11 A.M. and, more to the point, I'll have to switch my phone off in case it rings in the middle of a six-year-old's revelation that she has some new ballet shoes. Yes, circle time is when adorable small children (mainly belonging to famous people) announce their "news." This can take up to an hour, if you add in the special songs that we all have to sing while perched on tiny chairs and the sessions of show and tell and the time the teacher spends pleading with the one child moping in the Home Corner (which should, frankly, be renamed the Second or even Third Home Corner) to join in, poppet.

Oh, yes, I remember as if it were yesterday the day Emma Freud's shining-eyed, scrumptious daughter announced that her mummy had another baby in her tummy. Like most other mothers there, I shriveled inside—only the very rich and very rested, with round-the-clock help and bottomless energy and funds, can even contemplate the marriage-wrecker otherwise known as Number Four.

I also remember the day Salman Rushdie's son solemnly announced that he was going to miss the class trip to Kew because of his daddy's "next wedding" in New York. His melting dark eyes were black-lashed saucers.

"I'm a page," he said, as we all nodded, our eyes welling at the little boy's mention of such a sophisticated celebration. It certainly had all the ingredients: models, bestsellers, ex-wives, and full magazine coverage not merely of the triumph of hope over experience but the even more remarkable victory of wife number four's breasts over gravity.

Today, we all sit uncomfortably on little chairs, our thighs touching. Anoushka, Posy's teacher, is also perched on a doll's chair in a demure pencil skirt that has ridden up to show a stretch of honed withers, and opens the session.

"So who's got news today?" she asks, in her husky voice, leaning forward so that we can just see the shadow of cleavage. There is no getting away from it. Anoushka Brooks is hot totty. Smokin' hot totty.

She has silky thick black hair that slightly clings to her neck so she spends a lot of time twining it around her long fingers while she talks. She has rather high, jutting breasts, a perfectly flat stomach and perennial legs, but she doesn't ever make the mistake of showing off these attractions—she only allows occasional, accidental glimpses.

She never, ever wears clothes that show her midsection or any part of her stomach, let alone the area from navel to pubis. She has completely grasped, in fact, that when it comes to the sexual allure of dressing, more is more.

So, today, she is wearing a tailored, slightly stretchy white shirt that cleverly reveals the contours of her sensational torso, with elbow-length sleeves, the skirt, has bare glossy legs and a pair of kitten-heeled flip-flops.

A forest of pudgy little arms goes up, and all the shiny morning faces clamor, "Me!" "Me!" "Me!"

I look around Posy's cozy, colorful classroom. Huge rectangular sheets of colored paper have been pinned all around the four walls of the room. On this frieze, a childish collage of the Bayeux tapestry, including the pictorial highlights of the comet, Edward and Harold at Westminster, Harold's landing at Ponthieu, Harold's arrow in the eye, etc., marches around the four sides of the light first-floor room in surprising detail. I suspect the hand of Doc H. as well as Miss Brooks in the narrative, but it's still impressive even so, if only for the effort put into the display.

A couple of men put their hands up, too (when Anoushka's

taking the class, it's amazing how many masters of the universe decide to put their children first for once and arrive late at their merchant banks).

Anoushka pouts at the chaps—one is an internationally bestselling author; the other runs an advertising agency in Soho—and shakes her head. "Luca!" she says, pointing an elegant wrist adorned with a Tiffany watch. "Luca Sebastian! What's your news, darling?"

Luca, who has been sitting on the carpet along with Posy and the rest of the class of around twenty little moppets, hops to his feet. All the other Lucas in the class sit down again.

Luca S. is the only child of an actress who graces the covers of magazines aimed at women in their thirties who are doing it all. On the covers, Luca's mother looks replete, nourished, at ease in her glowing skin. At the school gates, she looks famished, tired, unairbrushed, and just as anxious as all the rest of us.

"We did go to a big houth but then I did go to the little houth," Luca announces in a proud lisp.

Everyone smiles at the charming vision of Luca in his sailor suit. Then, some of the fathers glance surreptitiously at their watches. Luca's news is clearly going to take a while.

"That's very interesting, Luca," approves Anoushka. "Where was the big house you went to? Was it your country house?"

"No it wathn't but Mummy goes there with Ed for thpecial weekends," says Luca, "And I go to the little houth. That's where I go while Mummy and Ed have a little thleep in their thwuite."

Everyone falls about, rocking on the little chairs. This is unexpectedly informative.

Jake McGuire, who has been sitting beside me, eyeballing Anoushka, whispers in my ear. In my current state of high alert, I find the hairs on the back of my neck rising instantly.

"Want me to translate?" he whispers. "Luca has been to Babington House in Somerset, right? That's the big house. But Luca has obviously been dumped in the crèche all weekend by his mother's new boyfriend. That's the little house."

Luca's own mummy isn't around to hear her private life being revealed to half of W11, but that doesn't matter. It is the way of these things that some other mother or nanny will give her a full report later. There's nothing people enjoy more than passing on the news that one's child has won a prize or given an embarrassing little thpeech in the sad absence of his parents.

"It was such a shame you missed it," they say, looking pleased and patting your arm as your face falls. "He was soooo sweet. You'll just have to make sure you come next time, won't you! It was in the school calendar, you know! We all had a letter about it the week before!" etc., etc.

After Anoushka has squeezed the last drop of information from Luca (she has perfected the art of extracting world-class gossip from the children of celebrities), it is time for Golden Pears.

Luca sits down. He has performed to all of our satisfaction, especially as the whole parent body knows that Luca's father isn't called Ed. So far as we know, Luca's father is a film producer called Jim.

I feel myself warming toward Luca's mummy. It's always nice to discover that other parents are perfectly capable of getting up to all sorts of energetic and probably illegal high-jinks at Babington House, making full use of the Playroom and the Poolroom (both little-people-free zones), while Luca is left to play with Stickle Bricks in some outhouse for hours with only a Ukrainian nanny for company.

I'm all in favor of those who continue the rock-and-roll lifestyle even after they are fully occupied with the hallowed duties of Motherhood. They provide such a refreshing corrective to all those actresses who give birth and call press conferences to announce that fame and fortune no longer matter to them even the tiniest bit. The actress (fill in name of Oscar-nominated hottie) is, like, so grounded in reality now, she tells *Hello!*—and all she cares about is (fill in blank of new baby daughter with silly fruit name).

I like Golden Pears, particularly as Posy is always winning them. Posy is such an obliging and diligent little girl, and Anoushka seems genuinely so fond of her.

Jake McGuire's son Noah gets a Golden Pear for "holding his pencil correctly during writing practice," and we all clap. Parents are conditioned only positively to reinforce everything any child says or does, as if the sky will fall in otherwise. I suppose it all starts with toilet training. After all, if one congratulates a child for performing a bowel movement, then we are teaching children to believe that minor or indeed involuntary achievements are, in fact, acts of distinction, and one is then forced to keep this up from the first triumphant time on the potty for at least twenty years until they leave home.

Saffron, Posy's best friend, gets a Golden Pear for "her wonderfully imaginative costume for World Book Day." My heart sinks a little. Saffron came as an Oompa Loompa, you see, in a clever little grass skirt and full body makeup done by a professional.

It's not my fault that Posy came in her school uniform. How is one expected to remember things like World Book Day, when children are supposed to come into school dressed as their favorite character from "literature," on top of everything else?

But then it gets worse. Much worse.

"Not only did Saffron wear the most original costume, but she also sang a special little song, didn't you, Saffron?" Anoushka purrs. "And would you like to share that special little song now with everybody, Saffron?"

Saffron rises to her feet and takes the stage with all the

confident puff of Cecilia Bartoli dazzling the audience at Covent Garden with her coloratura.

"Oompa Loompa doompadee doo," Saffron tweets.

Saffron's mummy's eyes are bright with tears of pride. Annoyingly, I feel tears prickle behind my lids, too, but I've noticed that pregnancy permanently alters the tear ducts and the vocal cords, making one liable to cry and shout, noisily, and at the slightest provocation.

"I've got a perfect puzzle for you."

The adults in the audience start nodding their heads and tapping their feet, to show what slaves to the rhythm they are underneath their conventional exteriors.

"Oompa Loompa doompadah dee,
If you are wise you'll listen to me."

"Fantastic, Saffron! Shall we give her a clap?"

We all clap. Saffron takes the curtain call, looks slightly disappointed that she hasn't been invited to perform an encore, then subsides.

Then Charlie, Marguerite's middle son, gets a Golden Pear for "trying hard with his spellings," and Marguerite gives a thin smile. The Moltons are terribly ambitious for their sons, as Patrick wants them all to go to Eton, but all of them seem to have learning difficulties of one sort or another, requiring daily after-school sessions with expensive private tutors.

And then, at last, Posy's name is called. We are all feeling rather hot and impatient by now, but it would be very bad form to leave before the end.

"Posy Fleming," coos Anoushka. Posy scrambles to her feet and stands by Anoushka, who has been standing while doling out the little Golden Pear badges, allowing us all to admire her cleavage again as she pins each pear carefully on to each child's sailor top.

Posy looks pink with excitement, and I admit I'm breathing a little faster, too. I hold my breath as Anoushka reads from her sheet.

"For being so helpful and emptying the Year One wastepaper baskets," she says. "Well done, Posy."

There is a brief stunned pause, during which no one looks at me. We all clap. I go up and kiss Posy. "Well done, my darling," I say. She nods bravely.

As we're filing out, Marguerite is hovering to speak to Anoushka, as are several of the groovy daddies. Anoushka is so adorable that not only do all the mothers queue up devotedly at parents' evening to talk about their six-year-old's fine motor skills, but all the fathers do, too.

After assembly, all the other mothers head off to Pilates or to yoga with their Ayog mats, or to their personal trainers, or to the hairdresser, but I have to walk Calypso, who has been sitting very patiently with the school secretary, and then I have to go home and work, on my own, which I will be doing for the next couple of days, as Ralph's in Kyrgyzstan. I find it easier just to say that Ralph's "in the Stans," when people ask, as if there is an equivalent of "the Hamptons" somewhere coastal in the former Soviet Republic. That usually does the trick.

Creatives have the attention span of a border terrier puppy and are bad at hiding their panic that if they actually ask either me or Ralph about his work in oil and gas, we might actually tell them.

As I trudge back, I find myself singing the song of the Oompa Loompas and not feeling as sorry for myself as I might.

I walk down the Portobello Road. By now, the morning is in full swing. Traders are shouting. Their huge voices carry from one end of the road to the other.

"Punnet of blueberries! Two fruh pahnd! Lovely blueberries! Two pahnd! Loverly peaches four fruh pahnd! Two mangos a pahnd, two mangos fruh pahnd!"

They stand around nursing Styrofoam cups of tea in fingerless gloves. Soon the council will be selling the mews houses where they keep the produce and barrows to property developers, and there won't be a fruit and veg market on the Portobello Road ever again.

I walk down this bustling street, waving and smiling to the traders, who get up at 3 A.M. to sell potatoes and onions to locals, people like me, who actually find it a bit easier to order it all online from Ocado. I buy some blueberries from Herbert. I say, "Wotcher," to Ed at the flower stall. I buy some rocket from Cheryl, who is the third generation of her family to run a stall here and worries she is the last.

The one-armed man is playing the accordion, jerking from side to side. The Rasta with very unnatty, gray dreads is playing his steel drums at the junction of Talbot Road and the Portobello, and the two chirpy women who run another flower stall are jiggling away to the bouncy strains of "Rat in the Kitchen." The smell of fried onions and bratwurst and wieners sizzles from the German sausage stand.

A queue of homeless tramps is forming outside the peaked redbrick Victorian façade of the Salvation Army HQ, waiting for their daily bread and soup. Layabout writers in chinos are sipping Fair Trade espresso at the Tea and Coffee Plant and reading the *Guardian,* lighting up American Spirit cigarettes and inspecting the Brazilian girls en route to work in Ay, Mañana, or any other of the dozen or so coffeeshops within a five-hundred meter radius of the Electric Cinema. In the Electric Brasserie, film producers are meeting with agents, and yummy mummies are meeting with yummy mummies.

I cut down Westbourne Park Road and pass builders going to NuLine wearing cut-off denim shorts, woolly socks and workboots, street traders, mums with buggies on their way to Tesco, shop girls at the discount shoe boutiques and Woolies.

Now is the time for the normal working denizens of W11, but not for very much longer. By lunchtime, the beautiful people will reclaim the streets and meet for a fusion lunch at E&O, for wilted spinach and tenderized steak at Mediterraneo.

It is, as I predicted, 11 A.M. There are high white clouds in the blue sky, a stiff breeze and the promise of rain later. I switch on my mobile, and it beeps. Twice. *Beep beep.* Then *beep beep.* The sweet soundtrack of my life.

I have missed two calls.

Yippee!

Clare

"Let's sit in the corner," says Marguerite, placing her bag on the table nearest the mirrored end wall of the Grocer on Elgin and sitting down on one of the molded plastic Charles Eames chairs. It is nice and quiet in here today, and has the reverential hush of a place entirely dedicated to the sale and consumption of the finest ingredients.

I pounce on the bag.

It is a beautiful thing—a bucket shape in duck-egg palest blue with a birdcage embroidered on the front, and three birds, two yellow and one mint-green. It is most definitely a beautiful thing, but it is not Marguerite's usual understated style. This is—obviously—a Lulu Guinness piece.

"Oh, that," she says. "Patrick gave it to me. I almost gave it to Maria" (Maria is the Moltons' housekeeper) "but I thought it was a useful size." As she speaks, she brings out a ring-bound notebook from within its girly cavity, as if to prove her point.

At the mention of Maria's name, I have a sudden vision of her at work. A rather proud woman of a certain age, her half-moon glasses hanging on a cord round her neck, she is rendering smooth and creaseless a piled tangle of Patrick's shirts, her soft sighs in syncopation with the exasperated puffs of the steam iron as she thinks of her four children back in the Philippines. Before she even gets to the ironing, I know that Maria will have removed every smudgy fingerprint from every stainless-steel surface of the kitchen and deep-cleaned four bathrooms.

I wonder whether, when and if I ever have children, my social conscience about hiring Third World mothers away from their babies to look after my own children and abandon theirs will desert me. Then I delete the thought.

"I think we should order," I say, waving to the Parisian waiter, Emanuel. I love the Grocer, even though I was also very fond of the snug independent bookshop, Elgin Books, it replaced. The owners have made a wonderfully airy and restful place to escape from the crush of tourists traipsing up and down the Portobello, with an atrium ceiling, white walls, huge bunches of lilies, and dark hardwood floors.

"I'm starving," I say, because I am.

Since I came back from the Town Hall, I have bicycled to BeautCamp Pilates, bicycled back, showered, and now I'm looking forward to lunch.

I like the fact that when you order, they make up your dish from scratch, fresh. They have excellent suppliers. But I can see it's not an ideal bill of fare for Marguerite. Everything seems to have wheat or dairy in it, to both of which she professes to be intolerant. Put it this way, there's no full-fat spread in the Molton household. They use omega butter made from "essential seeds" instead.

I twist gingerly so I can see the blackboard. My back hurts. Marguerite also ponders the menu, her mouth slightly turned down at the corners. She is wearing a dark brown narrow shirt dress from Prada, with breathing holes punched under the arms for ventilation, and a pair of Prada trainers. She is so thin that even her knees are pointy, and her hands look red and very slightly raw.

"Have the minestrone," I suggest.

"No," says Marguerite, her eyes on the blackboard. "I'm going to have the prawn and soba noodle salad with mushrooms, chili and soy."

She has the same frowning expression of concentration I see on the faces of women at the chill cabinet in Fresh & Wild as they wrestle with today's big issue, the one that takes up a lot more head-space in these women's minds than global warming,

Third World debt, or child soldiers—is it going to be a Totally Cheesy sandwich of grated carrot cheddar or a tofu and seaweed wrap?

"Ooh, Marguerite," I say. "Noodles."

If Marguerite's eating carbs, things must be really bad. Marguerite once explained to me that her aim was to have the family eating raw whole foods, organic, of course, and that she hated the idea of "meat decaying in the boys' colons." She went on to explain that, ideally, food should be eaten when it's alive, at the peak of its energy and life force, and that the moment you pick, chop, let alone cook a vegetable, its enzymes and nutrients start to deplete. I love Marguerite, but all this doesn't make her the easiest of lunch dates.

"Noodles, I really need noodles," she says, sighing. "Comfort food."

Emanuel, the snake-hipped waiter with heavy black stubble, takes our order, then replaces his pencil behind his ear.

"Okay," she says briskly, her blue eyes blazing. "The other night. Week before last. The power cut, remember?"

I nod. Of course I remember. I'd gone into the communal garden to see whether the whole neighborhood had been cut off, or just us, and Bob was out there lighting flares and wearing a pair of seersucker shorts, moccasins and a navy sweater, and we talked about the "outage."

"Anyway, for some reason, the power cut disabled the telephone system in Lonsdale Gardens. I called the electricity company on my mobile, to ask how long it was going to be. It was about ten thirty, I suppose, when I finally got through," continues Marguerite. "They said a couple of hours. But, then, as I was getting ready for bed, I suddenly remembered all the prepared meals in the freezer and worried that they would spoil. What if the power didn't come back on? Or if it did, at five A.M., after they'd begun to defrost, and then started to refreeze? I just didn't want the boys to risk eating them if they'd defrosted beyond a certain point—it's not really safe—and I needed to know."

I nod as if this is the sort of thing that I find myself worrying about, too, in the long watches of the night.

"So I decided to call the electricity board. Patrick was in bed. *He's* certainly not losing sleep over hundreds of pounds of meals hand-prepared by the boys' nutritionist, as you can imagine. But, by this point, my mobile battery was low, really low, and I worried that by the time they answered, my mobile would be dead. And I couldn't charge it up, of course, because of the power cut." She pauses.

At this juncture, Emanuel brings us our lunches—mine is vivid and bold like a Fauvist painting, with its slash of golden char-grilled chicken, the dark green rocket, and the brilliant red of the peppers and tomato. Marguerite's wet noodles and prawns are in a white china bowl, a gray concoction lightened only by the green sprinkling of chopped fresh coriander.

"So, I thought, I know, I'll use *Patrick's* mobile."

I sort of know what is coming now, but I quickly eat some char-grilled chicken on flatbread with my cherry tomato and rocket salad on the side, and drink some fizzy water.

"And there it was. This text message. Up on the screen." Marguerite has been holding it together quite well until this point, but her voice cracks a little now. I reach out and stroke her arm. But she moves it away, in order to open the notebook by her bowl. "Hope you are asleep, angel boy, I miss you, kiss kiss kiss," she reads out, an angry red flush standing out on her high white cheekbones. She looks up at me, and her eyes are very blue.

"Can I see?" I ask, and reach over the small table for the notebook, narrowly avoiding drenching the evidence for the prosecution with my £2 glass of Welsh spring water. I give a quick look round the Grocer, but all is as it should be.

All the food packs are arranged in a pleasingly symmetrical way in open chilled cabinets of stainless steel. The floor is expensively planked hardwood from sustainable forests. A huge display of lilies spreads its scent over platters of cloudy meringues studded with violent bloody blotches of baked raspberries. We are alone in the café section round the corner, apart from two young women with buggies trying to have a conversation over slabs of tortilla. We are out of earshot of shoppers contemplating the beef stew and lamb shanks (which look like plasma products at a blood bank in their shrink-wrapped sachets) and buying little servings of tabbouleh and falafel.

"Sure," she says, handing over the notebook. "I just thought I'd make a fair copy of the contents of his mobile phone's inbox. There weren't any voice mails—I've noticed he deletes them as soon as he's heard them."

For a second, I wonder whether Marguerite's secretarial approach to what is, in fact, a messy domestic drama isn't a little odd. But she is terribly organized about everything else —so there's no reason to suppose she won't be methodical about her husband's betrayal. She's even copied out the date and time that each message is sent—presumably to cross-reference against the family diary.

> hope u r fast asleep, angel boy, night, I miss u xxx (received 14–03 at 0014)

> walking to wk, thinking of u, missing u, will txt l8r xx (received 15–03 at 0730)

> angel hope u r ok, @ flat tonite, let me know if u can get away l8r for bite or 2mrw am! (received 16–03 at 1400)

> baby yes going to pub w wk mates shd be @flat by 730 will get food cu cant wait xxx (received 16–03 at 1804)

There are more, but I've seen enough. I hand the book back. The language of text messaging is so ugly—those awful formulations like "l8r" and "pashun8"—I can hardly bear to look at it. Marguerite flips to the next page in the notebook, where she has made notes to herself.

"Oh, God, Marguerite," I say. "Poor, poor you. So what do you think he's up to? Who is she? Do you think we know her? I rather doubt it. From the texts she sounds about twenty—all this stuff about going to the pub after work."

Marguerite is deep into her notebook. I realize what I've pointed out. If Patrick is sleeping with a woman of twenty, his mistress is twenty years younger than his wife. Marguerite, luckily, does not seem to notice the generation gap—it's almost as if she is resigned to this cliché.

Although, I have to admit, there is an almost enjoyable twist to this.

Patrick is always patting our bottoms and saying things like, "Gosh, Clare, I had no idea you had such a sexy figure." He said that to me once when I was wearing a pair of tight jeans from Seven and some pink Hunter wellies for breast cancer and was wheeling some bags of fertilizer from the garden gate. "I always like a pair of peachcutters on a girl."

So it turns out that Patrick's all-too-obvious lechery is, after all, a brilliant double bluff.

The awful thing is, I can't quite concentrate on the predictable news of Patrick's adultery. After all, I heard him cooing into the mobile to some mistress or other about some flat already, so Marguerite hasn't told me anything I don't already know . . . at one level, anyway.

It's on the tip of my tongue to talk to Marguerite about the Avery garage, about which I feel quite as betrayed as she does about her husband's adultery. But I don't. This is perhaps not the moment, I see, to complain about new build within the curtilage of a semidetached house on a communal garden.

"If Patrick has been seeing this or any other whore behind my back, I'm going to kick him out," she says in a cold voice, looking me in the eyes. "I'll take him to the cleaners. I gave up my job at Morgan Stanley to be his wife and mother to his three sons. To have his shoes polished by a valet every week. To have a three-course dinner on the table every night. Dinner with candles. Napkins. Fresh fucking *ficelle* every day from Maison Blanc, even though I've explained to him about the effects of gluten on the mucosal lining of the small intestine a million times."

I nod, as if I am fully aware of the adverse effects, too, and I'm with her on this.

"I can't forgive this, Clare. I gave up my job at Morgan Stanley because he said men whose wives worked never made partner and those who had a full backup team of support staff at home always did." Marguerite isn't crying. She's too angry. I think it's the first time I've ever heard her swear.

"Well, now I'm going to work. I am going to work at getting my revenge, and I think he'll find that I'm very good at what I do. After I've finished with him, he'll wish he'd employed me," she spits, "instead of marrying me."

"Marguerite, love," I say. "I do think you need a tad more proof before you go thermonuclear with him. Text messages are notoriously easy to misinterpret, aren't they? I think you should go over this with Mimi. Aren't we all having supper at the Dodd Nobles' tonight?" I want to convey that I think it's a mistake to approach Patrick's obvious infidelity with such terrible zeal, because who knew where that journey would take them.

"I can't exactly raise it at the Dodd Nobles'," says Marguerite. "But I might tell Mimi. I'm not going to confront Patrick, yet. I'm going to stalk him instead."

I look toward the door to see why I've just felt a cold draft, but it's closed.

"How about one of those meringues with raspberries to split with our coffee?" I ask.

"No, thanks," says Marguerite. "You have one. I can't do sugar or caffeine, even in a crisis."

Mimi

Mitchell, the maître d' at E&O, can obviously smell the pheromones or hear the dog whistle or whatever it is that males can detect on their bitches, because he's put me and Si in a booth against the back wall, in the sort of snug in the bottom left-hand corner of the large sleek restaurant, with its slatted dark-wood wall, pendulous white lights, and black smoochy banquettes.

Si is sitting with his back to the plate-glass window on the "Hi" Street so he can't see the parade of locals sauntering past en route to lunch dates with their agents and film directors.

On my mobile, his message had been simple and direct. "Si Kasparian," he had rasped. "Got your note, Mimi. I suggest we discuss over lunch. If you can't meet me at E&O at one today, leave a message with my secretary, Diane, on 7727 1130." He rattled off the number so fast I had to listen to the message three times before I caught it.

E&O was a smart choice for us for many reasons. 1. the food is scrummy, 2. it's very public, and 3. it's very near. If he'd suggested anywhere out of W11, the implication would be that we didn't want to be seen, and why would we not want to be seen? We haven't done anything wrong. We have nothing to hide!

I have decided not to dress up but dress down for my meeting with Si. Of course, the official agenda is the interview. But the real agenda is something else entirely which I'm not admitting even to myself.

I slightly regret my decision to dress down when I spot that Kate Moss is directly across from us with her daughter in the midst of a mother-and-baby group. For some reason, supermodel mummies like to meet up not in the comfort and privacy of their own homes but in very public places like the Electric Brasserie or E&O and anywhere else photographers from *Heat* might be lurking. And when it comes to dressing down, Kate is the undisputed Queen of Grunge.

Lila keeps running up and down between the tables. Because she's Kate Moss's daughter, everyone is more indulgent than usual and beams down with unfeigned rapture at the tousled scrap, even though she keeps grabbing the paper tablecloths and almost upending several hundred pounds' worth of fusion Asian Rim cuisine onto the polished wood floor.

Occasionally, Kate scoops up the child and pops her back on the bench next to another mother and child, who are both dressed from top to toe in pretty patterned frocks from Dosa.

Kate's brown legs are bare, and she is wearing thong sandals and has tied a silk scarf around her hips. Lila is dressed in a Fair Isle sweater over a lawn smock and is wearing the must-have mini Mukluks that I have seen in Yates Buchanan for £150. A tweed princess coat with a velvet collar from Young England keeps falling off the banquette onto the floor. The waiters keep reverentially picking it up.

Kate is looking so scrawny in the flesh that I long to run over and tell her to tuck into some Thai beef and noodles, but of course I don't.

I am tempted to make my usual crashingly obvious observation about movie stars and models, that they are invariably tiny with huge heads and eyes like headlamps, but I don't want to draw Si's attention to Kate Moss for the good reason that Kate is not only staggeringly pretty but also weighs about as much as her own daughter.

One of the things I love about E&O, as well as the famous chili salt squid, is the way that the owners have run long rectangular mirrors along the walls at chest height, tilted into the room, so, in order to check out the celebrities on other tables, it is not necessary to pretend one is not looking at them at all.

If I want to stare unnoticed at Jeremy Paxman or Henry Porter or Ivo Dawnay tucking into a plate of deep-fried oysters (which of course I do), all I have to do is give a glassy look into the mirror as if I am concentrating very hard on the representation of the Sunni minority in the new Iraqi parliament, and no one will ever know that I'm actually goggling at an attractive male.

We're sitting opposite each other. Between us sit walnut-wood open-topped jars containing chopsticks, paper napkins, and knives and forks, which at least gives me something to play with during the rather stilted lulls in the conversation during which we dart each other sidelong glances and then look away.

My skirt is sliding up and down the black leather banquette when I move. I have slipped off my LK Bennett wedges, also from last year, because they have given me a small blister on my little toe.

Si is wearing a suit with a very blue open-necked shirt which has mother-of-pearl buttons and oversized collar and double cuffs. It is a bit flash and loud for lunchtime but, then, so is E&O. The blue tone of the shirt makes his skin look darker than I remember. I am noticing, too, the pepper and salt in the locks curling above his ears and at his temples, and that his skin is a completely different texture from Ralph's.

Ralph was a blond child and his skin is dry and smooth and a nice dun color that blends with his brown hair, whereas Si is piratically swarthy, with an open-pored complexion and the perfect quantity of chest hair (i.e., not a burst-mattress-on-skip sort of amount but just enough black tendrils to suggest surging virility).

I'm breaking the chopstick pairs apart and playing with the salt cellar, dribbling it out in a white stream onto the paper tablecloth while giving Si my Lady-Di-watching-open-heart-surgery look from beneath my lashes, until I realize how suggestive this is, and stop. On the table in front of us is a bowl of bright green edamame drizzled with sesame oil, and we are drinking beer.

We are talking—God knows why—about the changing face of Notting Hill and I am saying how ghastly it is that all the useful shops have closed and reopened as boutiques and coffee bars selling plastic sandwiches and smoothies.

"I mean, in the old days, this street alone had a toy shop, a laundrette, an electrician's, and a florist, off the top of my head," I say, as I suck a bean out of a pod. "And now look at it—there are at least four Italian restaurants, two coffee shops, six girly overpriced boutiques selling clothes to stylists and nowhere to take a broken toaster or buy a birthday present for a six-year-old boy."

I want Si to think that I am very grounded and not at all the shallow sort of person who browses in shops selling kaftans embroidered with Swarovski crystals or £200 jeans with artfully frayed hems and holes in the crotch—though of course I would be like a shot if I had the money.

"The sad truth," I continue, knowingly, "is that Notting Hill no longer exists for the people who live here. Notting Hill is only for tourists. So, therefore, Notting Hill is over. Ooh! Yum." Two bowls of chili salt squid, to which I have long been addicted, have arrived.

"So why are you still here?" Si asks, giving me what I now know is his crinkly, amused look, as I dip a ring of squid into the viscous red sauce.

"Because," I answer, munching, "I love it here. I've lived here most of my adult life. The children have grown up on the garden," I look Si mistily in the eyes, "and it's their world. The other point is, if we sold up in Notting Hill, we wouldn't get so much more for our money. I know our house is worth masses, my husband's had it valued, but you can't buy a maisonette in Shepherd's Bush for less than a million nowadays, so what would we gain by moving? I'll tell you. The only thing we would gain is that people would stop saying to us, 'You could always sell your house and move to Shepherd's Bush, you know,' as if that's the answer to all our problems, and we're only staying here out of some sort of misguided, snobbish obstinacy. But I don't want to move to Shepherd's Bush," I continue, now working my way through Si's portion, without embarrassment. "Although, it's true, most of our great friends have moved to the Bush, we have loads of friends here, even if they are way out of our league in terms of income."

As I speak, I make a note to stop talking about us as if we are terribly poor. And make a note to stop talking so much, period.

The one thing I have learnt about living among the super-rich is that they are acutely aware of the outstretched palm. The rich naturally want to feel that they are loved for themselves, not for their ability to pay, so I resolve to correct the unfortunate impression that I might have already given that I am On The Take.

In fact, we Flemings *are* relatively rich compared to the national average income, it's just that the combined revenue of our communal garden square, in one quarter alone, probably exceeds the gross domestic product of Denmark.

"But the truth is, we're not ever going to move," I say. "Well, I'm not. Over my dead body."

"And how does your husband feel about Notting Hill?" asks Si. So far, we have been careful not to mention him by his name.

"To be honest, not as strongly as I do, even though he's been here longer," I reply. "I'm so embedded here. The children's school, the garden, the neighbors, the shops. His main objection is that Notting Hill is a good ninety minutes away from a decent chalk stream. When his family first moved here, it was all poofters in antique shops and boardinghouses. . . . No, what bothers him is the fact that it's too far from the

Test. He increasingly doesn't see the point of people and increasingly does sees the point of standing thigh-high in a river, surrounded by ducks."

I then bang on a bit more about the fact that it's all coffee shops and boutiques, and the only people who can afford the houses are American bankers. "It's been a case of bankers goes the neighborhood," I say, and Si roars gratifyingly with laughter, as if I'm easily the most amusing person he's ever met. Then I explain that developers are block-buying the Portobello Road and driving out all the little Pakistani men selling pens and ribbons and Afghan slippers that smell of sick.

I hope I'm not talking too much, and not mentioning Ralph too much, or being too critical of developers, but Si really does look interested, so then I rattle on about Ralph's work in the field of oil and gas and his love of country pursuits, deliberately making him sound like a cross between John Paul Getty, Paul Gallico, and Armand Hammer.

I am picking at my black cod with miso, but I'm no longer hungry. Si is eating now—marinated beef with ceps and some sticky rice. He is picking up the mushrooms with his chopsticks and leaving them on the side.

"You're as fussy as my daughter," I say, watching him. I notice that whenever I talk about my children, he doesn't really pick up the ball and run with it. This makes me think that he doesn't think of me as a mummy at all . . . or even as a journalist . . . but as a *woman* . . . which I can't help but find intoxicating.

The mood has thickened between us. We are two beers down and at that difficult stage where mutual attraction is making polite conversation seem pointless.

I give up on my cod and look over at Si's plate.

"Good?" I enquire.

"Want to try?" he says, pushing it over.

"A tiny bit," I allow. I pluck a mushroom with my fingers and pop it into my mouth and swallow it. It is cold and slimy but otherwise featureless (i.e. it tastes like most mushrooms). "I always tell the children that they can't tell me they don't like something until they've tried it at least once, but I don't think that applies to mushrooms. I do think they're a bit young for oral ceps."

Si laughs again. We are getting on famously. I allow myself a little gurgle at my own joke, too, to keep him company.

"Well, your kids may be a little young, I agree, but oral ceps can be a lot of fungi," he says, looking at me.

I feel myself going red and hot and uncomfortable. Suddenly, it's as if all we both want to do is rip each other's clothes off with our teeth and make animal growling noises. I start to say, "Is it just me—" when he interrupts.

"So, Mimi Malone," he says, staring. "Let's get down to business." I go even pinker, and some words struggle in my throat. For a wild second, the mad idea that he is going to offer to . . . *buy me* enters my head.

But then he continues, "Your card. The interview. What do you have in mind?"

I feel too hot in my cardigan. I hold a glass of iced fizzy water against my pink cheek. Then I put it down. Then I start taking off my cardigan.

Si doesn't hide the fact that his dark eyes are on the jouncing of my breasts as I wriggle out of the sleeves, and I also cannot fail to note his thick black eyelashes.

"My game plan is to avoid if possible this commission I've had from the *Mail*, which is to do an interview with you," I answer. "They want to call you the new Napoleon of Notting Hill. Please say no. Let's just not, okay?"

I sip my beer and look at him. My heart has started hammering, and I'm remembering what it was like when he kissed my neck.

"Well, I never usually do interviews, but I might be prepared to make an exception in your case. Would you give me copy approval?"

"I never usually give copy approval, but I might be prepared to make an exception in your case," I say, lowering my eyelashes. "Would you like photo approval too?"

"Very much," he says. "When do you want to start?"

As we've been talking, both of us have been leaning into the table between us. I lean back and, with my right foot, I point my toes and insert my foot inside his trouser leg and very gently stroke the inside of his calf.

It is very bad of me and very wrong of me and very silly of me, but I just can't help it.

Si doesn't react at all but reaches into an inside pocket and takes out a bill-fold with a silver clip. I make a show of rootling in my bag, but he restrains me, which is just as well, as I have only found two shockingly soiled nit combs and no wallet.

There must be ten red fifties in his heavy clip. Without asking for the bill, he places two fifty-pound notes on the table and weights the notes carefully with the salt cellar. I feel like saying that we've only had two starters and four beers and two main courses and that probably only comes to eighty quid, but I stop myself. This isn't the moment to reveal my thrifty streak.

"We're out of here," he says.

When we leave E&O and exit on to the "Hi" Street, it seems very bright. A man in a peaked cap opens the door of a Bentley, which is waiting on the double-yellow line. "Lucky you didn't get a ticket," I say, giggling.

"I would have done if I hadn't taken the precaution of paying the parking warden not to patrol this corner earlier, miss," the chauffeur replies, doffing his cap.

I like the fact that Si's chauffeur calls me miss and pray it's a reflection of my peachy bloom and not the average age of Si's female rides.

"How very sensible of you," I say. "But it's okay. I only live round the corner. I don't need a lift."

"Get in, Mimi," says Si. "Don't make me walk you home,

for God's sake—I never walk anywhere around here because you have to stop and talk to people every five paces, and I can't face it."

I climb in. The chauffeur goes round the other side and opens the door for Si.

I could get used to this.

"Thank you, Hunter. You know, round here, I have to keep crossing the street to avoid women asking me to dinner," Si continues. "Like your friend Trish Dodd Noble. She asked me at the party where I met you to come to some dinner tonight. I said I was terribly sorry, I couldn't come, but she called me the next day and said she loved spur-of-the-moment entertaining, she was very spontaneous herself, and said I was very welcome to change my mind. She said tonight was going to be very casual. Kitchen supper."

"Well, I'm going to be there," I say, sinking into the cream leather seats. "And I should warn you, Trish Dodd Noble's idea of casual is about as casual as a . . ." I try to find a comparison that will mean something to Si, "presidential inauguration. Anyway, I'm not choosy. I'll go anywhere for a hot meal."

"In that case, how incredible, I may just be free after all," Si says, and half-turns toward me.

My heart starts to beat and I realize that I have left my Brora cashmere cardigan, my main Christmas present from Ralph last year, on the leatherette bench and, in any other situation, I would be running back to retrieve it, knocking over small children and little old ladies in my panic, but not now. Now I don't care a fig.

Between us, the air is clotted and heavy, as if a thunderstorm is about to break.

I look out of the window, mainly to try to ascertain whether anyone on the "Hi" Street can see us, and feel detached from the restaurants and kaftan shops and the girlie boutiques selling scented candles and baubles, as if I'm sitting in the first-class cabin of an airplane.

"Don't worry, no one can see you. No one can shoot you either. We're bulletproof," Si says, closing the glass divider between us two and the back of Hunter's neck. Hunter's head doesn't even twitch but, for a second, my eyes lock with his in the rearview mirror, and we both look away quickly.

"That's a relief. Um . . . how do you know where I live?" I ask, stroking the cream interior leather trim of the armor-plated Bentley as we glide along.

I am not looking at Si, I fear I will lose all self-control so, instead, I continue stroking the armrest of my seat and try to look as bridal as possible.

"Because you told me," Si points out. "On that card you sent me." Si is reminding me—slightly ungentlemanly of him—that I made the first move.

"Is that where we're going?"

"Not immediately," says Si, and reaches out a dry, warm hand toward mine. At his touch, I melt into his arms without being aware of moving a muscle and feel his mouth on mine.

When Gideon kissed me, and even when he . . . digitally remastered me down there, it was like a medical procedure. When Si kisses me, I feel electricity setting off little charges from head to toe, and I never want to stop. Si is a very good kisser. He doesn't do energetic tongue-sucking, and he has no interest in hard lip-biting, which can also be somewhat challenging. Instead, he kisses my nose and the corners of my mouth and plants little kisses on my neck. His breath smells of cucumbers. And he nibbles at my lips, and fingertips.

Hunter pulls up discreetly a little way from my front door, and I sink back. I am hornier than a rhino's face and, from the look of things, so is Si. Even the back of Hunter's neck has gone a little pink, as if he'd spent the day at Lords watching a one-day cricket match and forgotten his sunhat.

I realize that Si is the first man who is not my husband I

have kissed like that since I got married, and I have not kissed Ralph like that for ages. I also acknowledge to myself that what I have done is very bad and very wrong—well, of course it is, that's why it felt so good—and that things must end there.

A kiss is not just a kiss.

If I take this further I know I am stepping on to the road to couples counseling . . . divorce . . . sobbing children . . . the shattering of my reputation as a solid burgher of Notting Hill . . . the division of assets . . . the sale of Colville Cres. . . .

All this to be rapidly followed by me driving from my sad little flat to Ralph's set in Albany, which he shares with a lovely young girl from Sotheby's fine art department, on Christmas Day, with all the presents and the stuffed stockings in the back of the car, and then heading back to Perivale, on my own, a divorcee, weeping hot tears of regret and recrimination as I ponder all I have lost.

So we are not going to go there. I am going to dig deep, hold it together, and keep this thing very, very real. Which means opening the door handle, stepping outside on to the pavement, and not looking back as I let myself into my own front door.

Which is what I am going to do. Very soon. Now, in fact.

Si and I look at each other for a long second or two, and he says, "Well?"

"Thank you very much for a lovely lunch," I say, using my best manners. But I still don't get out. I feel as if some centrifugal force is pinning me to the soft pigskin seat. A voice inside my head tells me to get out before I get carried away, not to risk all that is fine and true and decent in my life for a snog in a Bentley with a billionaire I don't know.

"So. Mimi . . ." His voice is very low, very slow. "Would you like to come back to Lonsdale Gardens and . . . do that . . . Napoleon interview with me now?" he asks. "I hope you've got your tape recorder, because I'm very fussy about quotes."

"No," I say.

I don't say, "I can't," or "Not now." I don't need to explain why. But I still don't get out of the car. I check the rear view mirror to see if Hunter is watching, and this time it is me who turns to Si.

"Not tonight, Josephine," he says, but he takes me in his arms.

Clare

Ralph and Mimi have finally made it, looking, if possible, even more rumpled and disheveled than usual.

We're all drinking champagne on the balcony, because Si Kasparian and Gideon want to smoke and Trish won't allow anyone to smoke in the house, not even her trophy guest, who is, unquestionably, Si.

To have persuaded Si to come to a "cozy kitchen supper," which is Notting Hill for "catered £200 a head dinner" must count as one of Trish's finest hours. At least I can nail the garden business with him now—if only I could get a word in. The proximity of an ex-client and billionaire who appears regularly on the business pages is also intoxicating Gideon, who is now trying to impress Si by talking about the country house he is designing for the Saatchis.

"It's a tough brief," he is saying. "He can't ever be more than forty-five minutes from Selfridges. So I told him we should be thinking Bucks or maybe the Chilterns—that's an easy commute—and then he says he needs to be at least ten minutes by car from the nearest other house, in other words he wants *über* remote, not forty-five minutes from the Ivy remote! I told him, I said, 'Charles, trust me, what everyone wants now, is a piece of wilderness.' I said, 'Charles, all this can only work if we build in the West Highlands and you 'copter into Central London whenever you want to eat or shop,' ha ha."

Si draws on his cigarette, and I can tell he's only half-listening to Gideon.

Mimi and Ralph are in the drawing room with Trish and Jeremy, being given champagne and healthful little nibbles. Si is definitely distracted, but then so would I be if I was having to listen politely to the greatest hits of Gideon's career, much as I love him.

So it's me and Gideon, Trish and Jeremy, Marguerite and Patrick, Si Kasparian, Mimi and Ralph and, any second now, I know that a very well-groomed nervous young woman will arrive trying not to look too conspicuously single. That will be Si's date for the evening.

I mean, poor her. Think of coming to a dinner party knowing that it's all married couples, like animals marching into the Ark two by two . . . oops. I just spilled some champagne down my gray silk Armani blouse. I lost concentration, for a second.

The most exquisite girl is now greeting the Dodd Nobles and the Flemings in the drawing room, and both Gideon and Si's tongues have hit the floor. Not surprisingly. Si's date is a complete show-stopper. She's top-to-toe in Top Shop, but she can carry it off brilliantly with that hair, and those legs.

"Sorry to drag you outside because of my filthy habit," growls Si, throwing the stub into a lush camellia, which needs cutting back. His eyes are on the girl. So are Patrick's. And Gideon's. And Mimi's. "But I think we can all go in now."

We troop into the drawing room, and Trish introduces the beautiful girl to me and Si and Gideon as Anoushka Brooks, who is helping Melissa with her maths, a form teacher at Ponsonby Prep. It quickly transpires that she's Posy's form teacher and Charlie Molton's, too, so of course Ralph and Mimi and Marguerite and Patrick are delirious with joy at her appearance—the hold these private schools have over parents never ceases to amaze me.

"Well, I can see why all the fathers make such an effort to do the school run now," sniggers Gideon. "Are you known as Looks Brooks by any chance? Or Miss Nookie, even? I find I miss nookie all the time—" he roars with laughter—"don't you, Ralph?"

"Shut up, Gideon," I say. "Please don't be so silly. I do apologize, Anoushka."

I wander round the ground floor of the Dodd Noble house while Gideon drools over Anoushka.

The Dodd Nobles spent some time in Scandinavia in the 1990s, while Jeremy was heading up Nokia's corporate responsibility division. Trish has clearly fallen for the restful plainness of the Gustavian style. All the walls are white, and the furniture is white, and even chandeliers and the frames around the mirrors and paintings are white, and there is an all-white kitchen, too, with a white-painted wood floor. Their interior decorator has certainly stuck to her brief.

There's a marginally warmer feel in the drawing room, because it's not painted bright white but a soft gray. Whereas the rest of the house has these wide, white-painted, oak-planked floors throughout, in here the floor is laid with very soft antelope-hide in an ash-blond color, hand-stitched with fine leather thread. On the antelope-hide floor-covering, there are a pair of oversize fuchsia velvet sofas, scattered with huge velvet cushions in clashing plum and scarlet shades and dotted with mirrored sequins. It's as if the Dodd Nobles are saying, we like the purity of the Scandinavian style, but don't be taken in. Underneath, we're hot-blooded Latins.

Trish is following me with a platter of bruschetta as I nose around.

"I love this paint," I say to Trish, gesturing toward the pigeon-gray drawing-room walls.

"What is it?"

Then Trish tells me it's Slipper Satin from Farrow and Ball, as recommended by her color therapist. She says the old cornice took three months to reveal, and was then painted six times in distemper made of egg-white and sealed with herbal resin. Most of the party has drifted over by now so we all gaze up at the cornice admiringly.

"Hope you like it," says Jeremy. "I told Trish she had an

unlimited budget. And she still exceeded it." We all laugh.

Instead of sitting down and talking to Trish, I start examining the photographs arranged in rows on top of the ebony Steinway grand. There's a black and white shot of a shirtless Jeremy on a yacht, Trish in a bikini on a yacht, one of Francis sailing, Melissa skiing, Jeremy windsurfing, Jeremy snowboarding, and a family group photograph that I dimly remember last seeing on a card last Christmas. In this shot, they are standing in front of their latest acquisition, an eight-bedroom house in Shropshire, which they bought just as everyone was recovering from the blow of their purchase of the rectory in Little Sodbury. All these photographs are mounted in identical silver frames.

I'd love to see their new country house and, no doubt, I will soon, in *House and Garden*. Their spreads in London and Gloucestershire have already been, appropriately, spread over several pages in British *Vogue*, an article which Ralph and Mimi flicked through in my kitchen when it came out. I remember Ralph saying that, "with the honorable exception of the Sturgises, it's not Dodd Noble at all to have your house in a magazine, but Dead Common."

"I think we're almost ready for the light entertainment program," announces Trish, giving us all a bright smile and handing round canapés.

I draw Mimi aside.

I whisper that Francis and Melissa are clearly going to treat us to some little concert, for, as we all know, both the children of the house are music scholars, and that she and Ralph have got to behave.

Mimi looks appalled. "I'll never get Ralph to go out ever again if this goes on for too long," she whispers, glugging her champagne and scooping chili and garlic seeds from the Food Doctor into her mouth from a little bowl, leaving a spoor of seeds on the ashy pale-hide carpet. "I had to move heaven and earth just to get him here in the first place, you've no idea, *and* promise I'd go to the Scottish Gamekeepers Annual Dinner in return. We've barely recovered from Posy's concert at Ponsonby! I'm sure I told you—the first ten or so children all played "Michael Row" and "Ode to Joy," but it went on and on, you know, there were forty pieces to get through. Some wise parents stood by the door and managed to sneak out after they'd heard their own child, but Ralph and I made the mistake of sitting in the front row, so there was absolutely no escape," she goes on audibly. "And, by the end, these child prodigies, Posy's age of course, were playing entire concertos by Rachmaninoff and Schoenberg, which we had to sit through till the bitter end. I can't tell you how grim it was."

I inwardly marvel that only Mimi could start and finish a long anecdote that manages to insult both the hosts of a soirée and at least one of their guests, Posy's teacher, Anoushka, at the same time. Outwardly, I gaze at her in horror.

She looks puzzled and then realizes her goof. "Not that I'm not looking forward to the recital very much, Trish!" she ends gaily, and we all shriek with relieved laughter that it wasn't worse than it was.

Soon after, Francis and Melissa enter the drawing room. We all race to find comfortable seats on the sofas. Francis sits at the piano and Melissa disappears again and returns with a cello. Francis is a rather good-looking boy, with a shaggy quiff that he has greased to stand in a cockatoo crest. On the back of his T-shirt, it says, YO, and on the front it says BITCH, and he is wearing a pair of jeans so baggy and low-slung that they would puzzle Sir Isaac Newton—nothing is keeping them up and yet they somehow stay up.

Above his D&G jeans—the words DOLCE AND GABBANA span his waistband—several inches of Calvin Klein boxers are clearly visible.

Melissa is wearing a purple suede miniskirt, boots, and a denim jacket. She is not beautiful but has the coltish advantage of youth, even over Anoushka, who is in her twenties.

"Ur, hi, guys," says Francis. "We're going to, like, play some Beethoven and stuff."

Ralph leans over. "Francis's trousers appear to have reached a new low," he whispers to me.

"Shh," I say.

"Now, come on, Frankie," trills Trish. She is gripping her glass of elderflower spritzer so tightly that her knuckles are whitening. "Introduce your piece properly!"

Frank looks stormy.

"Okay, then, I will! Francis and Melissa are going to play Beethoven's Sonata in F opus 55 no. 1, one movement, the *adagio sostenuto,* followed by two of the twelve variations on 'See the Conquering Hero Comes' from *Judas Maccabaeus,* by Handel of course."

"Whatever," says Francis, opening the dense score on the music stand of the grand piano. Melissa opens her score. Then she flicks her hair. Then she picks up her bow and places the cello between her open legs, which is an undeniably sexy action, and looks over to her brother. Then she flicks her hair over to the other side.

"Wow," says Si, in a deep, warm, sincere voice. "I'm sure looking forward to this. I'm so glad I came after all, Trish. You were right to twist my arm."

Mimi giggles out loud but pretends to be choking on a canapé instead and fools no one. Trish gives her a sharp look, and I think that Mimi better watch her back.

Luckily, Trish is so caught up in the thrill of the moment, her own children being such a credit to her, she doesn't pay that much attention to Mimi's latest insult.

After that, I decide not to look at either Ralph or Mimi at all during the first five minutes of the recital, which are taken up with tuning, in case I lose it, too. It is only when the teenagers' exquisite playing fills the large room with celestial sound that I feel I can afford to relax and look around the gathering.

Si is staring at Mimi. When she notices him staring, he half-closes one eye at her. She raises an eyebrow and looks away toward Melissa, whose hair is shielding her face in a honey-colored curtain.

Marguerite is smiling fixedly and obviously trying not to look at Francis's bottom, of which even more is now visible as he shifts about on the piano stool.

Ralph is looking around the room, no doubt assessing the furniture and paintings and wondering how little of it is inherited.

Mimi looks rather on edge and is sitting up very straight on one of the fuschia sofas, next to Patrick Molton. I notice that Patrick's leg is touching Mimi's. On the other side of Patrick, Trish is sitting, looking proud and happy, and not moving at all.

Jeremy is standing up behind the sofa, knocking back champagne and staring at his daughter with a sort of naked expression of devotion.

Anoushka is watching the two teenagers perform with an expression of professional interest on her face that reminds everyone she's a teacher, her knees turned in a ladylike way to one side. We all clap hard at the end.

During dinner, everyone swaps garden gossip, and Mimi and I exchange a look. I wonder whether she's going to bring up the headline story, which is Virginie Lacoste and Bob Avery. She does.

"Do tell everyone what you saw in the garden the night before the Averys' party," Mimi says, her eyes gleaming.

Suddenly, I feel shy. I feel I've told this anecdote too many times before. So I merely say that at three in the morning, I woke up worrying about some lilies and looked out of the window to check for frost, and saw this ghostly vision of Virginie in a nightie, trailing out of the Averys' house, and how she'd pretended to be turning off a sprinkler.

"Yeah, right. She wasn't turning one off, she was turning one on, the little strumpet," says Gideon. "Bob Avery's sprinkler."

For some reason, he absolutely gets off on this Virginie story.

"Anyway, that's not what we should all be worrying about," I conclude in a headmistressy voice. "Frankly, I don't care what Virginie and Bob are up to, but what I do care about is the Averys' wretched plan to rebuild their garage on the communal garden."

Then I brief the company briskly on what I discovered at the planning office. That I've studied the plans and scoped out the new build, that there's an architect involved, that it's a two-story edifice with a glass roof and, to all intents and purposes, is a separate house. Not a garage.

"Jeepers," says Si, whistling. "How did old Bob Avery get that one past the planners?" Then he tells the assembled company that he wanted to change the sash windows on the back elevation of his house but wasn't allowed to. And then Jeremy says that when they painted the back of his house duck-egg blue, he received forty-six letters of complaint from people around the garden. And he had to change it back to magnolia.

"Quite right," says Mimi in a teasing way.

I bring the conversation back to the garage. This is such a good opportunity, with Patrick here. I feel that we could, collectively, make some headway.

"Come on, Patrick," I say. "You're chairman. We can't just let them get away with it. We've all got to band together and—"

"Sorry to interrupt, Clare, but I just want to announce that Francis has very kindly offered to play for us again," interrupts Trish.

Ralph and Mimi look up from their raspberry *crème brûlées* with almond *tuiles* in dismay. I have to say, they always do full justice to all hospitality that blows their way.

"But I don't need to break up the party!" Trish goes on. "Frank's electric keyboard's in the chill-out zone next door, so none of us have to move. Melissa's gone out," she adds, as if we were all concerned as to her daughter's whereabouts, even though, the truth is, Melissa could have been visiting a crack den for all I cared.

Murmurs of "How lovely," and "Gosh, what talent" emanate from the group as we fortify ourselves with more wine.

"Will someone please explain to an old man what a chill-out zone is?" asks Ralph plaintively, an explanation which Jeremy Dodd Noble, who paid for its installation, is only too happy to supply.

"So what's Francis going to play now?" Mimi asks.

"Actually—it's one of his own compositions," Trish replies, gaily. "He's been composing since before he could walk."

And so, for the rest of the evening, we listen as Francis's atonal composition, which he has multitracked with layers of instrumentation, organs, drums, sax, and a strange screeching noise on a computer, echoes around the basement. We sit through it nobly, as Trish is monitoring our enthralled response to every note closely. When it's finally over, we're so relieved that we give him a huge hand and shower him with compliments.

Frank glowers modestly and scratches his quiff and tells us it is a genre called "like, post-trip-hop-rap-garage with scratching." We all nod as if we know exactly what he's talking about and feel very old. Then, he says, hand tugging at his quiff, he's like, er, also in a band at school, which is more sort of, um, house than, like, garage.

"Oh, that's fantastic," says Mimi.

"Francis, does your band by any chance do patio, too?" says Ralph, snorting. And then we all roar with laughter. And we look around at each other laughing and think what a lovely evening it's been.

Then we reluctantly get to our feet, so that none of us are left behind to have a nightcap *à quatre* with the Dodd Nobles.

I walk home with Gideon.

Mimi walks home with Ralph.

Si drives Anoushka to her flat in Lancaster Road in a large midnight-blue Bentley Arnage. He wouldn't hear of her taking a minicab up Ladbroke Grove at this hour.

Marguerite walks home with Patrick, who immediately gets out his mobile and starts texting.

Trish and Jeremy stand picturesquely in the doorway of their home, as featured in *Vogue,* waving and shouting and laughing, "Safe journey."

And I feel, deep in my heart, that even though the Averys may be hell-bent on ruining ours, there is nowhere, absolutely nowhere, quite so worth living as in a Notting Hill communal garden.

Summer

Mimi

Here we all are again, same place, same time, every year.

The May Fair, where we all are, is held, as always, up at the church at the smart end of Ladbroke Grove. It's where we had Mirabel and Casimir christened, but not Posy, because we had a slight falling-out with the vicar after the service for Cas.

As I remember—God, it seems so long ago—two of Casimir Alec Malone Fleming's godparents, two godparents we had handpicked for being solvent and responsible, peeled off to Maison Blanc for croissants and café crèmes during the sermon. The vicar took a very dim view but not dim enough to stop him from coming to the after-party at Colville Cres. later. Even after three flutes of champagne, he was still going on about how Alan and Natalia's dereliction during the service boded ill for their contribution to our only son's "Christian upbringing under the kindly but watchful eye of the Lord."

Ralph is at home claiming he has to work on a special report he's been asked to do on the effect of the oil-price rise toward a hundred dollars a barrel on the fiscal outlook.

"Have fun," I said, as we left him snoozing quietly on the sofa, the Business section of *The Sunday Times* in his nerveless hand.

The sun is shining, the sky is blue, white clouds scud. The grass is green, the trees are wearing their summer leaves, there are crowds of people at the church. I should be feeling that God's in his heaven and all's right in W11, but I'm not. I feel as if I'm wearing a happy mask, even though *le tout* Notting Hill is up here.

I shepherd my flock past the barbecue that's filling the air with smoke from burnt Lidgates sausages and Lidgates burgers (both from an organic farm in Essex, carved from cows and pigs all of whom David Lidgate presumably knows by name), and past a lady doing a brisk trade in onion bhajis, and pretend not to see a huddle of celebrity yummy mummies breast-feeding on the grass.

I am amused to see that standing sentinel above the lactating starlets are Mrs. Richard Curtis, a mother of four, and CNN's Christiane Amanpour.

I pretend not to ogle the A-listers as we press past them into the dark but bustling interior of one of the few places of noncelebrity worship in the parish, where I tie Calypso to a brass hook on a heavy oak door.

Inside, my eyes take some time to adjust to the gloaming.

The pews are pushed back to clear space. The entire nave is occupied by tables laden with doilies and old china and manned by little old ladies; a candyfloss stall, tombola, raffle. There is also the usual assortment of upper-middle-class women selling printed silk scarves/cushion covers/painted wooden frames/beaded kaftans and other overpriced artisanal, gifty things of limited utility and zero appeal.

I long ago decided that this sort of itinerant activity involving trestle tables, inventories, cash-taking, and stock proves irresistible to the sort of woman who has children and when the children grow up decides she wants to "play shops" all over again. Only this can explain the popularity of pashmina and jewelry sales held in private houses before Christmas. I've also spotted that a few of Ralph's friends with stately homes are taking this to a new level—the really smart women with titles and country estates are all playing "farm shops" now.

The children wander round disconsolately. After a bit, I take them downstairs. In the crypt, there's a crowd three deep storming a tea table covered with plates of baked goods, and two ladies sloshing peat-colored steaming tea over pale green cups and saucers from a couple of steaming urns.

I rather like the fact that Notting Hill residents, for one

afternoon a year, forget all about perfecting their interiors and children and instead go around pretending they are living in a Devonshire village circa 1947, greeting the vicar, rootling through the white-elephant stall, buying plants and falling on the tea table as if they haven't seen an iced bun or flapjack containing white sugar, white flour and real butter all year, which they probably haven't. It makes us feel part of a normal community, admittedly in much the same way that the Queen connects with her subjects by doing the washing-up in her Marigolds once a year after a shooting lunch at Balmoral.

And alongside the tea tables, yes, here is lentil central, the Fair Trade stall. As usual, it is manned by Lucy Forster. She's only twenty-eight, but the hot look she is clearly striving for is . . . spinster of this parish. She wears sensible shoes and Alice bands as if her life depended on it.

When she was in her early teens she apparently went through such a passionate pony phase, Lady Forster told me, that her future was a choice between "horses and horses." Lucy is terribly nice, except she always says everything three times, so that should be terribly terribly terribly nice. And nice though she is, prolonged exposure to Lucy, whose all-time heroine is Princess Anne, makes one contemplate setting fire to one's hair and then putting it out with a hammer, just for the sheer hell of it.

Now Lucy hails me as I'm coming through the Sunday School entrance as if she's just spotted the fox leaving his earth and needs to alert the whipper-in.

"Mirabel, Cazzers, Posypie," she yodels, above the chatter of women in artfully casual floral tea-dresses from Marni and Chloë talking about what private schools their children were all going to in September, "Here, here, over he-re."

I push my flock in Lucy's direction, wondering how I am going to escape making a purchase of Fair Trade coffee from a female-only Nicaraguan collective. "Hallo there, Mrs. Fleming, I mean, Mimi," she says, fixing me with a delighted eye, as we swarm up, "Isn't this the nicest, nicest, *nicest* fête? Don't you think?"

"No, I don't think," mutters Cas, at my elbow. "The bric-à-brac," his voice drops to a whisper, "is a bit shit."

"So, you three—have you had tea yet?" asks Lucy, in the children's general direction.

"We're just about to," I say, even though we've only just had lunch. But on a Sunday, what else is there to do but move swiftly on to tea?

"Before you tuck in, please have a quick dekko at my stall," sings Lucy. "All in a good cause."

"Ooh, yes, how lovely," I say, my hand hovering over a two-pound bag of brown rice, even though the children will touch neither brown rice nor wholewheat pasta as they say it tastes "hairy."

"Is this the only size you've got?"

"'Fraid so," says Lucy, handing it to me. "How decent of you, Mrs. Fleming. Rilly. That will be five pounds."

"Five?" I squeak. I find this is always happening. At Lidgates, I ordered a leg of lamb, and they trimmed it and bagged it and handed a ticket to the cashier, and when I got my checkbook out they said, "seventy-five pounds fifty" and I screeched, despite the long, well-dressed queue behind me, "for a leg of lamb?"

And the cashier looked down her nose at me and said, "Yes, mod'm."

So I paid. Basically, in order to get a sense of Notting Hill prices, think how much what you have just bought *should* cost, double it and then add £8.50.

"I know," sympathizes Lucy. "But five pounds probably feeds the"—she grabs a bag and reads the side—"Federation of Small Farmers of Khaddar's wives and kiddies for a week. But don't worry, Mrs. Fleming. If you find you haven't scrummed it all down by September, you can always pop over and give it to Mummy. She'll be happy to have it for the Harvest Festival display at the old folks' drop-in center."

After that, I rather lose the will to live, fall on the tea table, and eat a piece of coffee and walnut cake, a brownie, a cucumber sandwich, and drink three cups of tea. Then I feel better, but only briefly. Posy unties Calypso from a peg in the vestry, gives her an egg sandwich, and we potter home.

I check my e-mail for the seventeenth time that day and ring my mobile from the landline to check it's working but am not comforted.

Then I go upstairs to recover from having eaten two large meals within the space of an hour and a half and find that, instead of writing his report on the impact of high energy prices on the oil-importing sector, Ralph is now lying asleep on our bed with his shoes on, *The Sunday Times* Business section covering his snoring head.

I feel I am going mad, and it's all my fault.

Clare

We're supposed to rotate, among the four of us—Trish, Mimi, Marguerite, and me—but Mimi's house is frankly not big enough and very untidy, and we all tacitly agreed never to go there as, if we do, we get dog hair all over our designer yogawear.

I like Marguerite's house for yoga. It's nice and empty, and seriously clean. It's even better than my house, because Gideon tends to time his home visits just as we are all lubricating our joints with a series of asanas, and he can't help making lewd observations. Anyway, Marguerite likes it that we all go to her.

I think now she's finally kicked out Patrick, she needs our validation and continuing support, which is very understandable. So we've been gathering the past few weeks at Marguerite's, and even Trish, who is very competitive without realizing (she has just sent us all engraved invitations to some further recital Melissa and Frank are giving for charity), is going along with it.

Each of us has brought our own little rolled-up mat and laid it out in the upstairs drawing room of the Molton house. It has a polished wood floor, grand piano, Rug Company rugs (moved for the yoga class), and some ancestral family portraits of Patrick's glowering down at us from the walls. The French windows on to a small balcony are open, and Marguerite, who is always cold—my theory is it's because she never eats protein—goes to shut them.

Mimi is lying down quietly on her back. She seems tired. A bit low. Trish, who is a very bendy sort of person, is doing some stretches in a pair of black Asquith leggings and a crop top.

Lauren, the instructor, charges in, and the room fills with her positive energy. She's already held three classes this morning but she's inexhaustible. Her life's mission is to bring yoga into our already overcrowded lives, and I don't think she realizes there's only so much health and beauty maintenance one can fit in a day, and most of us have weekly if not daily sessions with Donna as well as beauty treatments and therapy to factor in, too.

Lauren goes over to give Marguerite a big, consoling hug, I seize the moment to bring up the subject of the garage. I know yoga class is supposed to be "Me" time and a moment for us all to focus on our bodies and our breath, but I can't help it. It's just been occupying so much head space. And the Averys are really making tracks now. The basic structure is up and they're putting in services.

I can't help wondering what did happen to that letter we were sent by the council, and whether Gideon had got to it first. I asked him a couple of times and he got irritated, saying that, as an architect, he would have taken careful note of anything like that and not thrown it away.

But something's not right. I know the council sent us a letter, to our correct home address, because I saw the date-stamped hard copy of it *on file*. And I also know that as an architect himself, Gideon is pro-build. He likes big shiny new erections in the middle of quiet green spaces.

"What I fail to understand is why the Averys are intending to ruin the quiet, contemplative nature of the square with a building that so aggressively encroaches into the garden," I say, as I join in Trish's stretches. I wipe my hands in case they are sweaty and push against a white wall, first one leg and then the other.

Marguerite and Lauren are still locked in a mutually supportive embrace, with closed eyes, in the middle of the room.

"Then there's the fact that all these new floor-to-ceiling windows being built will look straight onto the garden from the so-called garage, which sets a dreadful precedent. Think of the light pollution they'll shed," I continue, into the wall.

"The thing that surprises me," says Mimi, lying supine and staring at the ceiling, which is absolutely bare, as there are no overhead lights of any sort in the drawing room, "is that the Averys are relative newcomers and, in theory, should be trying to ingratiate themselves with us all for years and years before trying anything remotely funky."

"I agree," says Trish, unrolling her mat by the window and lying on her side, so we can admire her chiseled stomach as she does her inner-thigh crunches.

"When I think of the hell we went through with our underpinning, which we waited to do until we'd lived on the garden at least five years, out of respect for everyone else. Do you remember, after we'd underpinned, that awful business, when the Woolwich tried to sue the garden committee for failing to pollard the willow?"

"How can we forget?" says Mimi, her eyes shut. "And I also haven't forgotten that Virginie rang you up and said that if your insurers sued the garden committee, you would be in such bad odor that you would *"'ave to move."*

"And we'd been here even longer than them!" shrieked Trish. "We bought the house just before Francis was born. It's not as if we asked the Woolwich to sue the garden committee! We *begged* them not to."

Trish has become flushed with the memory of that difficult time.

"Well, they didn't, thank God, but I agree it must have been a nightmare," I say.

"It's funny how we all seem to take it in turns to be persona non grata on the garden," says Mimi. "The Dodd Nobles have had their turn over the underpinning, then the Lacostes for putting in their fountain, then the Grays had to get cover for their water feature, and now it's the Averys. And don't forget that when I was pregnant with Posy, Virginie rang *me* up on some pretext and also told me we would *"'ave to move,"* too, and I asked why, and she said because the Colville Cres. houses are so small, and I said we'd fit in somehow and Virginie declared, *"But you will be all squashed togezair—you will be like council 'ouse tenants."*

We all laugh at Virginie's brazen rudeness. The Flemings may well be the poorest family on the garden, but none of us would dream of rubbing their noses in it like that.

"Well, I think the Averys are laboring under some crazy delusion that this is somehow a free country and they can do what they like on their own property," I continue. I have thought about this hard.

"They are failing completely to absorb the reality of communal garden living, and that is that it is the observation of the unwritten rules and unspoken protocol that gives the place its real value. To erect an intrusive building just because you've got planning permission for it, in the teeth of neighborly opposition, is missing the point entirely."

There are murmurs of agreement, and then Lauren claps her hands and we all shut up.

As we do some deep breathing with our tummies, I lie there thinking about impotence.

Not that Gideon has any problems at all in that department. The reverse.

It's me. I just feel so impotent.

There's nothing I can do to stop the monstrous carbuncle. I've been round the houses with the planning department. If the Averys don't put their car in it, then we can do something. But we have to wait until the horrible eyesore is finished before we can prove that it's for the four kids and the nanny, not the gold Chrysler Voyager. I've sent several letters to Caroline Pery suggesting it is rather unusual, even in this postcode, to have a garage with central heating and plumbing and broadband, but she's written back pointing out that the Averys can put in gold taps and a fitted pigskin floor from Bill Amberg if they like, so long as they put their car in it.

Well, we shall see about that.

As for the other thing . . . it's just not happening. As I breathe deeply, it occurs to me that every other woman present has a child. Trish has Francis and Melissa, Mimi has Mirabel, Casimir, and Posy, and Marguerite has her three boys—even Lauren, a single mum, has her whey-faced daughter, Fennel.

In the spring, I'd told myself that if I wasn't pregnant by the summer, I'd think radically about the options.

Lauren tells us to kneel on all fours, and as I'm holding my tummy tightly tightly into my spine, I have my fantasy. The one I've started to have since I saw Virginie creeping out of Bob's yard but which features me and Ralph instead, and better underwear.

At the conclusion of this fantasy, I suddenly think of something he said over dinner in March, probably as a joke, but it makes two things *clunk-click* into place.

Mimi

"So, tell me Mimi, what is going on weeth Patreeek et Marguerite? Why is 'e leeving in a flat in Ladbroke Grove? Eez too terribul."

Among Virginie's many appealing characteristics is her voice—broken English in a French accent.

Ralph says that she should be continuously miked up to a phone sex line and she'd never need to sell babygros with piecrust collars again. I pointed out she doesn't *need* to sell them anyway, she just enjoys playing shops. Virginie, like almost every woman I know except me, doesn't *need* to work—she only does it *pour s'amuser*.

Virginie and I are standing glumly on Lonsdale Gardens at the site of the eyesore, which is what residents have taken to calling the Avery garage under Clare's encouragement.

I have done yoga class and am now en route with Calypso to the dry cleaner to pick up Ralph's suit for his meeting at the DTI tomorrow. I have taken the long way round, so I can perambulate slowly past Si's house in Lonsdale Gardens. Which is very sad of me. Then, I don't have much on this week till Friday, when we're supposed to be heading down to stay with younger brother, Con, and his saintly blond Austrian wife Gretchen in Petts Bottom, Kent.

It's funny. In the old days (i.e., less than three months ago), I'd be looking forward to a family weekend out of London and taking the children to collect the eggs at the farm and going on a walk after a heavy lunch of *Tafelspitz* and *Erdapfelsalat*.

Now the whole prospect fills me with dread. I'd much prefer to stay in London, making little trips past Si's house to see which lights are on and eagerly carrying out little favors for Ralph.

But it's really amazing how fast the garage has gone up since the AGM, at which time it was only a twinkle in Bob Avery's eye.

It took a couple of weeks to excavate the site, during which time caterpillar tractors trundled in and out of the main garden gates and we all had our bikes nicked. The old garage was knocked down and bundled in bits into skips, which meant suspended bays and parking tickets.

The noise was deafening, and Ralph took to coming home every day from Westminster or the Isle of Wight and cheerfully asking, "So, Meems, did the earth move again for you today? Are your nice new friends the Averys still digging for Britain?" etc.

I told him how intolerable the noise was and it was all right for him because he worked in an office.

And then they started plowing deep into London clay. Down, down, down. Then the foundations went in.

Ralph refused to get worked up about it, even when I told him Clare had counted eighteen power points and cable outlets in the "so-called garage" and what looked suspiciously like wall sockets for a cable for TV and broadband. Clare is monitoring every development like a hawk.

"Well, a Chrysler people-mover has to be comfortable," he said, as I reported on the latest technological mod-con to be installed in what we were all told was a two-car garage. "Clean, dry and with access to pay-per-view porn is the least any car in this part of London is entitled to expect."

Now, Virginie and I stand together, shoulder to shoulder, mesmerized by the continuous noise and activity on the site. Men with mud-smeared torsos are cutting stone slabs, using power drills. Jackhammering the old York stone around the garage and hurling fragments onto a pile. Smoothing render onto interior walls. From the street, we can look straight into the empty shell of the new build.

Virginie was parking outside 100 Lonsdale, the Avery house,

as I was ambling past, so I halted to watch her long brown legs emerge from her new top-of-the-line Volvo XC 90, then a clutch of tennis rackets, and then her neat self, all clad in pink and white.

"Been playing tennis at the club?" I ask her.

"Yes, I 'ad a lesson with Christian," she answers. *"Ee wanted to work on my . . . net-play."*

Virginie and I both play at the Holland Park Lawn Tennis Club, though I'm an off-peak member, as it's cheaper. Every time I go, young and musclebound South African coaches seem to be vying to improve Virginie's ground strokes, a mission which requires them to stand behind Virginie with their pelvises pressing into her pert buttocks, gripping her slender brown forearm with their slightly sweating brown hands.

Virginie, as you might expect, has a very decent line in tennis kit, all embroidered with the Lacoste croc, lest we forget what her own brand is.

Today, she is wearing a tennis dress trimmed with baby-girl pale pink and matching toweling socks. Say what you like about her being a scheming minx stealing another woman's husband, she's always a pleasure to watch, and she looks so relaxed that I find myself rather envious of the way that Virginie is fitting adultery into her routine as easily as a tennis lesson at the club. I think it's a French thing. I found it—I'm using past tense because it seems to be over—terribly strain-making.

"Let's see . . . it was after the AGM and the Averys' party it all sort of exploded," I say, in answer to her question about the marital status of the Moltons. "Marguerite suspected something was up and Patrick was seeing someone else because she'd found these incriminating texts on his mobile."

Virginie sniffs with disgust.

"The silly woman," she remarks. *"I would nevair do that. Eez asking for trobble."*

"I rather agree, but still," I continue, as we watch an

electrician refer to an architect's drawing in his hand and with a pencil mark out yet more power points in the lower ground floor of the eyesore.

"So she decided to stalk him."

Virginie tuts and shakes her head as if she simply cannot believe the childishness of it.

I then rattle through the rest of what I know, because I'm faint with hunger and want to get home to see if I've got an e-mail from Si, who is in the States, and has been on and off for a month, refurbishing his yacht *Salome* in Rockport harbor and spending a lot of time in New York, and generally making me feel very not needed on voyage.

"When she started reading his mobile phone inbox every night, she knew beyond a doubt that he was seeing at least one woman," I explain. "There were also steamy messages from a couple of others, so Marguerite had to confront the fact that Patrick was not only being unfaithful to her now but had been so serially in the past."

Virginie stares impassively into the foundations, so I get on.

"Then Patrick, for some reason, took to deleting the texts as soon as he'd read them and deleting voice messages, too. Marguerite had already got Clare to ring the number of the main mistress, as it were, and when Clare called she said it was either a teacher or a mother at the school gates, because there was all this playground-type noise in the background making it difficult to hear. Anyway, then Marguerite rather cleverly had an idea, which was to hack into his Hoare's bank account online."

"*Un instant,*" commands Virginie. "*So the mistress is another muzzer or a teacher or even a nannay, okay, but why would Marguerite be interested in 'acking into ze bank account of zees putain girlfriend?*"

Three men stripped to the waist have come to sit on the ground-floor level of the garage, reading the *Sun* over their tea break and wrapping their jaws around huge Subway sand-wiches from the Portobello Road, and eyeing Virginie. In her shortie tennis dress, Virginie emits a gentle glow of sheer provocation.

"No, not the *putain* girlfriend's, not whore, Hoare," I say, trying to make sense. "Patrick's account at Hoare's Bank, spelled H-O-A-R-E," I explain. "It's a sort of gentleman's bank where you have to be about fifty thousand pounds in credit on your current account otherwise they don't want your business."

Virginie purses her lips in approval of such an exclusive high-end operation. She believes in quality above all else. If she calls an item *"haut de gamme,"* that is praise indeed.

"Because she suspected he was paying her rent," I say. "It was terribly easy, because if you want to read his statements online you have to input name, password, and either a memo-rable place, name, or date. So Marguerite tried the name of Patrick's nanny when he was a little boy when he lived in Hampshire, the name of the Hampshire village on the Test he grew up in, and his birthday, and she was straight in."

"Mais what about ze password?" asks Virginie.

"That was easy, too," I say. "Patrick always uses the same password for all his online and e-mail accounts because other-wise you never keep track, so she knew it already. Even I know it."

"And what eez eet, in case I ever need to 'ack into eez accounts?" asks Virginie, pouting slightly at the news that I know some-thing she doesn't.

"Well, it's crumpet, of course," I say. Virginie looks a bit blank again, but this time I don't bother to explain.

"So she hacked in and immediately saw that Patrick was renting a flat somewhere up Ladbroke Grove because twelve hundred pounds was leaving his account on the fourteenth of every month and going to an account held at Barclays, Ladbroke Grove, for Chesterton's Estate Agents, Lancaster

Road, W11. Then she confronted him. At first he denied every-thing and went shouty crackers. Then Marguerite waved his own set of keys to the fuck flat in front of Patrick's nose."

I then told Virginie that Patrick didn't come out with his hands up at all. Instead of admitting it sorrowfully, he'd banged on about the lack of spice in married sex life . . . the need to reconnect with his younger self . . . problems at work . . . Marguerite's preoccupation with the children's diet and sched-ule, and so on—i.e., all the same excuses that married men have used since the dawn of time and will continue to use till the crack of doom.

"So she kicked him out then and there," I conclude.

Virginie gasps, as if I've just told her that the top-five restau-rants in the whole world are not French but British.

One of the builders nudges another and calls over to us. "Anyone for tennis, heh heh?," and they all nudge each other again and wink at us.

"Patrick tried to tell her it was all over with the girl in the flat, but Marguerite was so angry that she said she didn't care if it was over or not, that wasn't the point. She'd got the whole thing planned out. She'd packed an overnight bag for him. She'd got a male friend to come over and drive him away. She'd spoken to a lawyer who told her that she'd be in a much stronger position vis à vis the settlement and custody of the children if she was in possession of the family home and Patrick was pernocating elsewhere." I say this last bit in a lawyerly voice.

"Poor Patreek," Virginie sighs, drawing out his name again, like a caress. *"He works like a pied-noir at ze bank, fourteen hours a day, to provide ees wife and keeds wiz everay leedle thing, and ee make one leedle meestake, and ee loses eet all. Pouf!"*

She manages to make an expressive gesture with her hands even though she is holding three brand-new Donnay tennis rackets in their cases.

Virginie then pronounces on Marguerite's failings in that

department with all the authority of a staunch Catholic who has broken her own marriage vows.

"*She is making a beeg meestake, Mimi . . . she 'as er cheeldren, er 'ouse, beaucoup d'argent, what more does she want from eem? Tous les hommes . . . le cinq à sept . . .*" She continues in this vein for some time. "*Un mariage blanc . . . les besoins . . .*"

As I ceded any occupation of the high ground the moment I met Si Kasparian, gave him my mobile number, and then sent him a card the next day two and a half months ago, I find myself nodding agreement with Virginie.

As she rattles off her disdain of Marguerite's lack of sophistication, she looks at me with what I can only describe as complicity and finishes with the set phrase that all *citoyens* of the francophone world use to foreclose further debate.

"*C'est normale, non?*"

She gives me one of her narrow looks, like a cat contemplating whose lap to sit on next. I wonder if she knows. And, if so, how she knows.

And then I wonder if she knows that all I can think about is *him* and *that*, and all I care about is *him* and *that*, and whether she can see it in my face just as I can see it in hers. There is something behind her eyes as she regards me, making me terribly aware of my skanky morning attire compared to her immaculate getup, as if she is searching out the same look in mine.

But then I remind myself that in almost any situation, the other person isn't thinking about you, she's thinking about herself and, on that basis, it is extremely unlikely that Virginie has given my affairs of the heart a moment's thought.

"So what's your take on all this then?" I say, waving my arm at the Avery garage.

Virginie shrugs. Her shoulders and eyebrows move upward. We move off together, me with Calypso to pick up Ralph's suit at the dry cleaners and head home, and Virginie to shower and reappear in some natty tailoring, cashmere sweater slung around her neck.

"They 'ave planning permission—thair is nothing we can do," she says. *"Let eet go."*

"Well, I'll try," I say. "Anyway, I've got to go home and work, get Ralph's suit, and clean behind the fridge."

Virginie looks at me with what I take to be admiration.

"Really, Mimi, you are incredeeble," she breathes. *"I don't know 'ow you do eet. But oh yes—you and Ralph only 'ave one house, don't you, of course you 'ave more time than ze rest of us for ozzer sings."*

Having planted her dart, she waves and walks quickly toward her front door in her short tennis skirt, and we all watch her, half-hoping that she might scratch her bottom and make all our days.

I always thought that a man with a wife and a mistress had it all, but a woman with a husband and a lover was merely overextended but, as ever, Virginie is proving us all wrong.

I get home and realize that I'm not bothered by Virginie's *banderilla,* her insinuation that my life must be a picnic because I'm not saddled with two or even three second period homes in glorious locations. I wish, in fact, that I could take her breezy attitude to life and to love.

The truth is, I don't really care about the new garage and wish that Clare, who is clearly having some sort of nervous breakdown, would stop banging on about it whenever I see her. Nor do I care much about my work at the moment, and think that asking people to plan their own funerals is daft and—as for writing silly features, like that terribly ill-advised adultery piece, I will never do it again.

I'm not interested, though I try to pretend I am, in Ralph's new project, even if it does concern deposits in the Middle Jurassic Great Oolite Foundation of the Weald and Wessex basin of southern England, which is apparently even more thrilling than his work with former Soviet satellite states.

Plus, all the things in my life that I used to draw pleasure and satisfaction from—my work, my family, my marriage, my friends—now irritate me to snapping point.

It's cricket this term, and Cas keeps launching a tennis ball against the kitchen wall, looking godlike in his whites. It bounces on the floor, then the wall, then if Cas fails to catch it, Calypso skitters after it with her nails scratching the wooden floor, barking. "Stop throwing the ball around the house," I snap.

"I'm not throwing the ball, Mum, I'm practicing my googly to leg stump," Cas informs me, as if that's all right then.

That's irritating.

Posy follows me around and stands behind my shoulder while I'm working (i.e., checking my e-mails for nonexistent messages from Si and looking at the Toast catalogue online) and keeps telling me things that happened in school and fills whatever room I'm in with her innocent tweeting chatter.

That's irritating.

Mirabel comes home from school and goes straight upstairs without looking at or talking to me and changes into a horrid selection of clothes to go online in the grooming suite, where she remains until suppertime.

That's irritating.

Ralph is suddenly being very solicitous and asking me if I'm all right because I'm not my "usual, sunny self," and suggesting that we go off, just the two of us, to Bologna or Bordeaux for the weekend, somewhere we can just lie in bed and only rouse ourselves for "long, Lucullan feasts," whatever they are.

That's touching. It's also irritating.

But what is truly dementing, of course, and what makes me want to weep hot tears of self-pity, is the fact that I have handed myself on a platter to a man, a man who grazed contentedly for a little while and then has apparently decided to go out to the Ivy . . . without me.

And in doing so, I have broken the First Law of Adultery (all the more shaming because I wrote it myself in the

Femail section, and then enumerated a further nine), which is, of course, Only Sleep with Someone with as Much to Lose as You.

Why didn't I think of this a little more when I let slip to Si that I'd been asked to review a country house hotel off the M1 for the family-travel section of the *Telegraph*?

It was the week after our lunch at E&O.

In theory, I was to take the children. We would occupy one of the "family suites" in the wing near the crèche, pool, and spa. We would eat dinner in the wood-burning-pizza restaurant with its organic range of children's meals. The children would go into one room, and Ralph and I in the other. They'd been longing for it for weeks. Ralph, though, was only coming because I'd begged him to.

"But we have a perfectly good house at home," he'd protested when I read to them all from the brochure about the super-king-size bed with organic mattress, ozone pool, spa, bike trails, four different restaurants, and plasma screens in the bedrooms. "We have a perfectly good bed of our own."

Needless to say, the children were counting the days, especially Mirabel, who has an unattractively developed taste for luxury in someone so young.

But then I pulled the plug.

I told the *Telegraph* that the children were all busy with improving activities, as if my weekends were a ceaseless whirl of taking my children to tennis, ballet, and music lessons, not to mention chess club and philosophy group.

"It's just the nightmare weekend for us to go *en famille*," I lied. "Cas has got nets at Lords. Mirabel is auditioning at the Guildhall. Plus Posy has been invited to join her friend Natassa at Saturday-morning Greek school."

"Goodness, Mimi," Celia, travel editor, had remarked, suitably impressed. "I never had you down as one those pushy supermummies we read about."

I did not correct her impression but allowed a pious pause before saying, "So what I propose is I go on my own and allow Ralph to take charge of the weekend and prove what a superdaddy he is. I was thinking that it might make a good little sidebar, in fact—Mum goes off to pamper herself for once at spa leaving dud Dad to hold the fort. What do you think?"

"Like it, like it," said Celia. "Do you think you could persuade Ralph to write it?"

"No," I said truthfully.

Then I'd told Ralph and the children that the PR company had balked at paying for us all and had limited the invitation to me. I'd moaned and groaned and said the last thing I wanted to do was go on my own to some naff version of Babington House near the M1, and how I would have a miserable weekend missing them. As I heaped lies upon lies, I almost convinced myself. The children were outraged, of course, but quickly mollified when Ralph, who was thrilled at being let off the hook, told them he'd take them to Pizza Express and they could get a DVD out.

It's amazing how easy it is to buy off one's own children, when one has to.

It's amazing how easy it is to lie to those one loves most, when one wants to.

And then I'd taken Si. Well, he'd met me there. He took his own room of course. We'd agreed to that. It was a bit tricky checking in, because I had arrived by taxi and I wanted to go up to my room straightaway and steel myself mentally for the momentous next step.

But there was a PR girl ready to meet me in the lobby. She told me that there were refreshments in the room for the kids and could I have tea on the loggia with the hotel manager after I'd unpacked, and I looked at her in puzzlement—then it dawned on me that she thought that the family were all still coming. I'd lied to Ralph and to Celia, the travel editor, and to the children and to myself, but I had forgotten to lie to the hotel. Not that it mattered.

I threw her off, pleading an urgent e-mail, as if we busy journalists were always on the phone to the news desk with breaking stories (i.e., complete fiction), and went up to the room, which was sumptuous, with suede throws and pouffes and a vast bed and a six-foot plasma screen, all as promised. I don't know how my legs carried me up to my suite where I knew I would break my marriage vows, but somehow, they did.

The management had thoughtfully provided a kiddie DVD selection, fruit, and tall tumblers of room-temperature milk that they had covered with cling-film, and platters of chocolate-chip cookies. I tipped the milk down the sink and checked out the bathroom: warm, well-appointed, spotless, and, if anything, even more luxurious than the bedroom.

I nibbled a cookie and opened up my laptop on the desk, which was adorned by a large suede blotter containing writing paper and envelopes. My laptop still had one program running. I had a quick look before closing it down and saw that it was the plan for Iain Duncan Smith's funeral, with my brief comments in brackets as I was taking down his ideas.

I clicked out of it, in a hurry now, because I realized that it was almost four and Si would be checking in any moment— and what I should have been doing for the last few minutes was buffing up my own running order and not wasting time on Iain Duncan Smith's.

Just as I was shutting myself into the bathroom, there was a knock on the door.

"Two minutes," I shrieked, carrying my voice past the bathroom, through the suite and out, I hoped, into the corridor beyond to the PR girl intent on taking me on a protracted tour of the hotel.

I tore off my dress and pants and then, after a moment's hesitation, put a bath hat on to protect my hair. To be honest, if you live as I do in considerably more fear of frizzy hair than of being dragged into a side alley and violated horribly, you have no choice.

I hopped into the bath, which was located as is now customary in the middle of the huge warm stone floor, and rinsed the taxi and the M1 off myself while standing up with the needle-sharp handheld shower.

This took about a minute.

Then I put on a fluffy robe and ran out to open the door, drying my feet as I went on the soft cream wool rug edged in suede.

When I opened the door, the hotel PR girl was nowhere to be seen. And Si was standing outside, in the corridor. He just stood there, and looked at me.

He was wearing perfectly weathered jeans, an old leather belt and a navy fisherman's sweater over a white shirt. His hair looked shorter than I remembered, and I wondered whether he had cut it. He looked browner, too, and I wondered whether he'd been on *Salome* in the interminable week that had passed since I'd last seen him.

He looked at me, and laughter was crinkling the corners of his dark eyes, and I noticed again that his eyelashes were short, but thick and curly.

He reached over to me and plucked off my shower cap, his mouth twisting downward as he tried not to smile.

It was when he didn't mention how silly I looked that I knew it was going to be all right. That he was going to be kind to me.

"I can take real good care of you, you know," he said, as we fell into bed, and tenderly made me think that, whatever happened, it would be wonderful, and that if I didn't spend the rest of my life drifting on a cloud of bliss, there would have been some terrible mistake.

Three thoughts occur during all this, which I mentally file under Life's Great Mysteries to be looked at later.

1. Why is it that I am too tired to have sex once a week with Ralph but energetic enough to have sex seven times in less than thirty-six hours with Si, with coital interruptions only for three-course meals and long baths in a petal-strewn tub or for padding around the suite in huge fluffy robes eating chocolate truffles?

2. Why do I not feel more guilty about this but instead have to repress the urge to boast to strangers in the street about the fact that I am for the first time in ten years having red-hot monkey sex with a billionaire who looks a tiny bit like José Mourinho, if you look at him with your eyes half-shut?

And 3. I thought that if Virginie could do it and incorporate it into her school run, then so could I. Forgetting that she is a stone-cold French superfox and I am an English wife and mother, which is, I now realize, a not insignificant difference.

I thought I could do it once, and then return to my nice, clever, handsome husband and darling children renewed and refreshed and somehow luminous, as if I'd spent the weekend at Bliss Spa instead of shagging for Britain at The Grove, "London's Country House," Hertfordshire.

When I came home, I was so thrilled to see them all at first, I almost cried. I fell on Ralph, who said, "Steady on, old girl, you've only been gone one night," and patted me, I had a prolonged group hug with all three children and, when that was over, I gave Calypso a cuddle, and she was so pleased to see me she peed on the hall carpet.

And then, about half an hour later, I thought I would die if I didn't see Si again, and when Ralph started talking about what we were going to do in the summer, as we made the children's supper in the kitchen, raising the ghastly prospect of long weeks out of London with no trysts with Si, I found myself cold with panic.

I started saying things like, "Maybe you should head up to Scotland with the children and I can join you after I've cleared the decks here," and "Perhaps we should think about spending the summer in London for once," while Ralph looked at me with a strange expression.

I hate being in London over the summer. I'm usually out of there like a bat out of hell, and we do a week in the Borders, subsisting on Slinky's kitchen garden and Perry's cellar, followed by a week in Kent with Gretchen and Con, for heavy but plentiful Austrian fayre, including a boiled sausage dish that made Posy sick and Ralph nickname Gretchen "Retchen," a nickname that has unfortunately stuck, and then we have a fortnight on Studland Bay in Dorset, near Mum and Dad. So we usually spend at least a month somewhere else, altogether, as a family.

But if Si's going to be in London, the awful, shaming truth is that's where I want to be, too—even if he's not here.

Clare

CS Action List 17/06

1. Write Planning Dept again re floor covering in garage query underfloor heating and Perspex roof—for car???
2. Rassells for groundcover & gap fillers cosmos & tobacco plants & Phostrogen & Rapid Green & chicken wire
3. Cut down old flowerheads in Lacoste gdn plus drop note to Si re overdue chq for his spring plants
4. *Papaver rhoeas* seeds for borders & love-in-the mist
5. Treat bald patches of lawn in Avery garden where Scrimshaw's dug holes esp and reseed and protect with chicken wire
6. Puddle-in remaining perennials in containers by Stephen's shed
7. Order new bunting and check old stakes for garden party
8. Dong Quai and false unicorn root
9. Ralph

I am pondering this list in the kitchen over a large cup of green tea and the *Guardian* and wondering whether to cut myself a sliver of the lemon polenta cake sitting under cling-film in the fridge left over from our dinner party last night. Cake's always denser and somehow more flavorful the day after you make it, and yoga always makes me hungry, especially when we chatter a lot, too. Which reminds me: I must tact-fully mention to Mimi that she does talk rather a lot during the class, disrupting the energy flows and harmony, and Lauren doesn't like to mention it herself. Lauren's so nice.

The kitchen is spotless, I can smell the lilies in the middle of our oak table, and the Miele is humming soothingly. In a minute I will hear a popping noise that means the tablet release window has sprung, and I will get a little shock, even though I've been waiting for it. Stephen is mowing the grass outside. I can hear him, and smell it, but I can't see him.

I suggested that it could be left a week, as it's been so dry recently. Stephen agreed with me that the grass hadn't seen much growth and then went ahead and mowed anyway, which annoyed me slightly. As Donna says, I must learn to tune out the things I have no control over and worry only about the things that I can do something about—only then will my energy channels start to unblock properly.

I planned to spend this morning putting some summer sparkle into everyone's gardens and pepping up the tired grass and a million other things, but I have only one item from my list on my mind.

I know he said it as a joke, but I can't help wondering what his reaction would be if I put my extraordinary, breathtaking proposal to him seriously. He's got such good manners that even if he appeared to be charmed or even amused, I'd never know if he was appalled, underneath. His good breeding swings into action.

Right. I'm going to stop thinking about that for a second— it's too distracting in every way—and do a quick check on the garage, as when I was in Lonsdale Gardens yesterday, there was a large van, and a couple of men were wheelbarrowing in load after load.

"What is it?" I asked. I felt entitled, as they were leaving the garden gate open as they went to and fro, which is against the rules. Security on the garden is a huge concern, as so many of us leave our back doors unlocked for hours during the day. If the garden gate's open, burglars can simply walk into our houses and help themselves.

"Tumbled Marble Opus Romano," one read out, after

checking on his manifest. "Shedloads of it, too. Masses of it. What are they building here—Brighton Pavilion?"

"No, it's actually a garage," I replied. "What color's the marble?" I am thinking about all the oil and petrol leaks, and marks from rubber tires, of course. "Gray?"

"No, this lot's white," he replied, and tore off a corner of the plastic wrapping to show me.

At which point, I honestly felt like marching up to their garden gate, bursting into their kitchen, finding Sally and taking her by the scruff of the neck. I mean, does she really think that she can get away with putting WHITE CARRERA MARBLE in a GARAGE? It's like advertising the fact that they've won planning permission for a garage to house their car but are clearly building a (rather grand) house.

Needless to say, I fired off a letter to the planners about it, also mentioning the power points and broadband and cable and air-conditioning and all the other creature comforts and modern services that their car appears to need.

But now I'm standing by the garage, and nothing seems to be happening. The work seems to have stopped anyway. The loads of white carrera marble are sitting there, under tarpaulins. There are no white vans hogging all the pay and display bays; the site is deserted.

Squirrels are jumping from the pollarded plane tree, and I suddenly realize how noisy the works have been, every weekday since March.

Now the workers have downed tools, I can hear the traffic on the Westway again and the noise of the buses rumbling down Holland Park Avenue and Ladbroke Grove, and take a deep lungful of sweet garden air.

I'm just digging out my mobile to call Marguerite to see what on earth's up, when Virginie appears, in tennis whites.

In fact, she appears coming down the front steps of the Averys, as if she owns the place. She sees me standing gawping at the garage, and she flashes a white-toothed smile at me and tosses her head.

"*Oh, hi there, Clare,*" she calls out to me. "*Don't you know?*" For a wild second I think she's telling me she's moved in with Bob, that's it's all over with Mathieu, that I am the last to know. But she's gesturing to the garage.

"Well, anyone can see that work's stopped—but why?" I know it can't be my letter. I only sent it yesterday.

"*Treesh went to the Town 'All, she saw ze plans, she meazhured, and she discovair zat ze roof on ze garage was too eye. Ze Averys 'ave to stop work until an eenspection, and probablay, wheel have to lower ze roof by two inches. Quelle galère! Also, she 'as to redesign ze glass roof. Poor Sallay.*"

I mentally take my hat off to Trish Dodd Noble. The Averys didn't know what they were dealing with.

Until Trish came on to the committee, we coexisted happily with a score of "outside keyholders" on streets like Clarendon Road who had keys for historic reasons lost in the mists of time. Meanwhile, every house on the garden is entitled to one, numbered, key. But Trish is exterminating outside keyholders one by one, with Dalek-like efficiency. Now, if you want a key to the garden, you can buy a twenty-five-year lease on one through Savills, for a mere £25,000.

I replace my mobile in my bag and mutter something about the work stopping for a while probably being on the whole a good thing.

Virginie gazes at the garage, but without the mandatory expression of distaste that we have all taken to adopting as we pass by.

"*Eeet looks a lot better now, doesn't eet?*" she asks. "*Such things always cause contrariété, c'est normale, but I think we will all get used to it and, bof! We move on. Hein?*"

In this spirit, I don't express the glee I feel that at last someone—clever Trish—has managed to throw a spanner into the works, but I stand there marveling at the sheer size of the construction the Averys have pulled off. It is, quite simply, huge. And about as congruous with the usual stucco and greenery as—well, the I. M. Pei pyramid at the Louvre does spring to mind.

Not that Virginie seems to notice. I've noticed that the French really only care about something if it directly affects them. They go on about *fraternité* but have no feeling for other people at all.

"Well, we might get used to it, I suppose," I hear myself saying.

Virginie shrugs, shoulders her tennis rackets, and pops into her front door.

Mimi

What a miserable week.

I've barely slept. Been playing a lot of Nick Drake, enough to make the chirpiest person suicidal, let alone someone who has apparently been ditched by the man for whom she has Risked All.

Si's in the States, and Ralph has gone back to Kyrgyzstan, for what, the fourth time this year? For a man who wanted to devote the first half of his life to women and the second to fishing, he spends a lot of time on . . . neither.

Faint Praiser hasn't called since I failed to write the Si Kasparian "profile" (i.e., hatchet job). She's also been a bit off since I discovered that one of the old dogs I interviewed for the piece, Taki, who kindly supplied me with his Top Ten rules of adultery, was one of the loves of her life, and she didn't take kindly to his Rule Seven, which was: "Marry a beautiful woman, preferably upper class and sure of herself, and then cuckold her with lesser beings, uglier and coarser women."

As Lady Jane is both very highborn and very pretty herself, and not remotely coarse, she naturally took umbrage, and she also took issue with Taki's Rule Four, which is "Never raise your voice and never show anger." Jane called me and said, "Thanks for the piece, Mimi. Might I point out though that rules four and seven certainly never applied when he was cheating on his wife with *me* for four and a half years."

I'm also getting signals from the *Telegraph* that "It's Your Funeral" might be reaching the end of its natural life, as is the way with newspaper columns, so I'm in a panic about money.

On the family front, things are coming apart at the seams.

I occasionally get a text (but only from Ralph in Kyrgyzstan.)

I also occasionally get a text (but only from Mirabel from the grooming suite upstairs).

And my perfect angel has suddenly become so teenagery that she will communicate only by text, which annoys me but Cas even more, but only because I'm still refusing to buy him a mobile, too. Cas is cricket-obsessed and is begging me to let him do nets at Lords at the start of the summer holiday, which I am resisting, for no particular reason—just a profound sense of gloom.

But do I get so much as a text or e-mail or missed call from Si?

And, tonight, we are driving down to glum-wellied Petts Bottom in the drizzle for a weekend that was put in the diary about eight months ago by Gretchen and which I can't wriggle out of now.

Ralph—I hope—will fly into Gatwick and join us by teatime on Saturday but, the chances are, I won't see him till Sunday night.

This is the only weekend we can go, as Con has now taken a flat somewhere in exciting Stratford near the Olympic Village and is going to be working most weekends between now and 2012, as he is deeply entangled in the London Games, a state of affairs that Gretchen, who my parents regard as a living saint, has accepted with her usual Job-like forbearance.

On the girlfriend front, Clare is going around, most unusually, like the cat who got the cream, and is occasionally permitting us (i.e., me, Marguerite, and Trish during yoga) to stray on to topics other than the garage, which is all up, apart from the roof. This makes me wonder whether she's finally got a bun in the oven or, as she rather gratingly calls it, an "autumn crocus."

Marguerite is still refusing to let Patrick come home, even on garden business, and let slip the other day that she quite likes the fact that Patrick is living in his "fuck flat" (she's become rather frighteningly potty-mouthed since the split) because the house is so much tidier without him.

I've called Clare a few times, and once or twice she's called back, but I still don't get the feeling that she is falling over herself to spend QT with me.

I can't remember the last time she made me a double latte with Suchard sprinkles on her gorgeous curvy green Gaggia, or asked us to supper. In the spring, we seemed to be dining *chez* Sturgis every other week.

Si left without giving me any new numbers to call him on, and he hasn't called me. So much, frankly, for me being the only tree in the forest. So much for me making him feel like a moose in the mating season.

In the end, I cracked. I simply couldn't play it cool. I e-mailed him and asked him whether taking long trips to the States to refurbish *Salome*, his yacht, wasn't simply an elaborate way of dumping me, as a farmer drowns an unwanted kitten.

I kind of lost the plot and begged him to come clean as to whether he thought we were On or Off, as we've seen each other precisely three times since the shagathon at the Grove and had sex precisely twice.

He sent one back, a couple of days later.

Mimi . . . I've been tied up 24/7 on the yacht and a business deal . . . in fact I was thinking that you might have moved on. I've told you not to take my absence or delayed replies as omissions. I'm just not very good at communicating like this. Back in June. Can't wait to . . . see you.
Si.
PS And in case you were wondering, my e-mails are only accessible by me, the CIA, the Justice Department and the IRS. So—fairly secure, in other words.

Of course, I pinged a storm-tossed e-mail back, but another silence has fallen. Which I find totally shattering. I know that Si has my mobile and my e-mail address and can contact me on his tri-band Ericsson at any time. I think I may have even hinted in the e-mail that Ralph was in Kyrgyzstan on very important global business, and so I was footloose and unescorted.

But he hasn't.

I can only conclude that the worst has happened. We had our *Brief Encounter,* and he's worried the next movie to come to a theatre near him is *Fatal Attraction.*

As I wrote in the *Daily Mail,* under my own byline no less, "Sex for men is an end in itself but, for many women, it is the rosy-fingered dawning of a Relationship."

No wonder I'm feeling such a chump. I haven't been reading enough self-help books. I haven't even been reading my own articles carefully enough.

But it's my fault. He's not married. I am. I'm the one to break my First Law, not him. What's more, on the second occasion we did it, I broke my Second, which is "Never Do It at Home."

I don't know why I wanted him to. It was a mistake. Colville Cres., ancestral London seat of the Flemings since 1962, didn't seem to work its antique, shabby charms on him as I thought it would.

As soon as It was over, he had a quick cup of coffee and shot out of the door, with his postcoital American Spirit still smoking in his well-manicured hand. I think he was, to be honest, a little taken aback by the living conditions, even though I had tidied like a maniac for at least half an hour before our "lunch" date.

All of which makes me think I've broken the Third Law, too, which, according to my own article, is "Adultery is Like All Good Business—A Question of Saying Yes or No at the Right Time."

If I ever have to write an adultery piece again, which I won't, I know what to amend that to. "Adultery Is Like Crack Cocaine. If Someone Offers You Some, Just Say No."

Anyway, after the slightly sticky moment in Colville Cres., he suggested I "drop by" the following week to his sumptuous bachelor pad on Lonsdale Gardens but, on that occasion, I got the funny feeling that he wasn't comfortable with me being there, either. I wanted to have a good poke around his hinterland, check out his bookshelves (long on books about leadership by Rudolph Giuliani, mainly), open his bathroom cabinet and look for condoms, and so on, but something held me back. He seemed edgy when I was there. So I left.

And since then . . . and apart from that one e-mail, nothing.

Zip, zilch, gutterball.

A big fat zero.

And now I've got to dash to Fresh & Wild to meet poor Marguerite for lunch. She says she's got some interesting gossip for me, so I must peel off my tracksuit bottoms and put on something more Westbourne Grovey, i.e., something feminine yet edgy that will not make me feel too middle-aged and frowsy when I inevitably bump into Stella McCartney buying vegan baby food at the chill cabinet.

I decide on Converse sneakers, no socks, skinny Superfine white jeans that aren't so skinny on me and a Gharani Strok top that floats serenely over my lumps and bumps, and hope that if I do see Stella, she will see that I am channeling Liz Hurley. I've often noticed that any shop that purveys peace and gastroenteric well-being at premium prices has many more bad-tempered customers in it than a famously harmonious shop like, say, Ikea.

The staff, a wholemealier-than-thou bunch handpicked for their inability to speak English, work slower and slower the more people they have to serve. Somehow the combination of the slowness of service, the purity of the produce, and the beautiful people treating their bodies as temples is less calming than you would imagine. Fresh & Wild is not merely a whole-food supermarket, butchery, fishmonger, and café. It's a war zone.

Last month, a woman exited the store after a light, gluten-free lunch and found a traffic warden in the process of writing her a ticket and affixing it to the windscreen of her Mercedes jeep. She picked up a brick off a skip and hit him over the head with it, knocking him out. She ripped off the ticket, laid it on his prone body, then she hopped into her car, reversed into the car behind, and drove off at speed, almost killing Ruby Wax on the pedestrian crossing. Presumably, the woman felt that braining a hard-working Ghanaian immigrant after spending his entire annual salary on a morning's groceries was a very appropriate climax to her ethical retail experience.

I enter into the fruit and vegetable produce side of the store, which wafts conceit in the same way that supermarkets pipe the smell of fresh-baked bread at their customers. Every so often hidden jets spritz the fruit with mineral water with a sound like a Russian babushka sighing—*paah!*—over the loss of her family dacha in the steppes.

Today, there are so many young women with off-road, all-terrain 4×4 buggies on the stairs gazing intently at tomatoes on the vine that I have to thread my way past them to reach the cafeteria-juice-bar-baked-goods section. En route, past the kelp, I stop to have a quick look at the customer notice board. Someone has pinned up a note complaining that the store still doesn't have the special olive oil from the Kazakhstani collective she asked for *at least* a month ago—even though she left the telephone number and e-mail of the one stockist with the resident homeopathist.

While I'm sitting at a high table trying to decide whether to have a juice or a smoothie, a catfight breaks out behind me. It is between two women who were both reaching at the same time to grab the last packet of Sproutpeople pea shoots at the chill cabinet.

"I'm sorry, but I had it first," one snaps.

"No, you didn't, you only grabbed it because you saw *me* reaching for it," the other screeches back.

A shop assistant summons the assistance of not one but two security guards but, by the time they arrive, the two women have established they both took Lolly Stirk's Pregnancy For Yoga classes together as *primigravidae* and are already exchanging hugs and birth stories.

Which only reminds me—as if I need any reminding, that is—that just as all Notting Hill children are either special needs or gifted, no Notting Hill mummy can ever admit to having had a normal, painful seven-hour labor. Parturition is either over in five seconds thanks to whale music and breathing, or is, of course, a life-threatening blue-light-flashing thirty-six-hour hospital drama ending in emergency C-section, performed, of course, by London's top ob-gyn consultant.

After they're both done with birthing, they move on to the perennially fascinating subject of what they put in their children's mouths.

I hear one say to the other that she's so into this place because they have all the best stuff, and when something sprouts, "It's, like, at the peak of its life force and energy." I make a mental note that people talk about whole food these days in just the same reverential and boring way they used to talk about Ecstasy in the 1980s.

I cannot bear this for much longer (the converted do so love to preach to each other), so I go up to wait in line to order a root juice of beetroot, apple, ginger, and carrot. I see Marguerite arrive, looking almost translucent in her whiteness. She is wearing tailored city shorts, heels, a wonderful, puffy and delicate Victorian blouse, and a Belstaff biker jacket and, I have to say, she totally rocks, despite her pallor.

She usually looks very grown-up in Prada and Lanvin and so on and, seeing her today, I suddenly wonder whether this all might be the making of Marguerite.

She spots me at the counter and I point to our table, so she sits down and glances at a leaflet trumpeting the credentials of all Fresh & Wild's marvelous, caring, communitarian organic suppliers.

After my mandatory twenty-minute wait, I carry my tiny carton of juice (ounce for fluid ounce, more expensive than Cristal) back to our table and kiss Marguerite's cool white cheek.

"Shall we just get the food ordeal out of the way and then concentrate?" I suggest. I know this can take some time. Marguerite doesn't do tea, coffee, alcohol, dairy, red meat, wheat, or toxins. No one can understand how she and Patrick, a burger-chomping, red-blooded male, ever got it together.

We go up to the food counter.

"How about some sesame and ginger tofu teriyaki?" I say, as we study the smorgasbord of dishes, "with a spelt wrap? That must be fine, surely?"

Marguerite finally asks for two rolls of pink sushi made with avocado, cucumber and beetroot "pâté" rolled up in sheets of nori, and another small portion of courgette "pasta" with cashew mint cream, reminding me that she always serves her boys "spaghetti" sauce atop a depressing tangle of no-carb cabbage rather than spaghetti.

We wait what seems like an age to pay while the staff chat among themselves and ignore us, so I combine our trays and Marguerite waits at the juice bar for her smoothie. Then I finally go back to our table, me with my little bottle of Fiji water. While waiting, I read the label.

"One of the purest waters in the world issuing from a virgin ecosystem of aquifers deep beneath the volcanic highlands and pristine tropical forests of Viti Levu," it says.

Sometimes I think that if Fresh & Wild sold little bottles of fresh Swiss mountain air, we'd buy that, too.

Marguerite is carrying a sludgy green liquid in a plastic lidded cup with a sacramental air. "What is it, seaweed?" I ask. "Something that looks that disgusting has got to be good for you."

"It's a smoothie made of almond milk, dates, figs and algae

gathered from a lake in Oregon," Marguerite replies, taking a small sip. "I know you all laugh at me. But you should try it. It's utterly delicious."

"I'm sure it is. So?" I ask, forking in salmon. "What news?"

"Well," begins Marguerite. "Do you remember the Averys' party?"

My heart does a backflip.

"Yes," I say encouragingly. Just remembering my first encounter with Si, I can recall the snap of attraction, the crackle of electricity, the pop of possibility. It's almost making me lose my appetite.

"And do you remember that Clare said that she'd seen Virginie in the garden?"

"Of course," I repeat, wondering where this is going. "She went on about it for months."

"Well," says Marguerite again. "Just before that, Patrick was away. On a business trip, I thought. But when I was going through Patrick's diary and credit card statements again, to try to work out how much our joint outgoings are and so on for the financial settlement, and also to see how much of our money he's frittered on this girl, who he claims he's not seeing anymore, by the way . . . anyway, I discovered something interesting."

"Oh, yes?" I say, noncommittally, deciding it's better at this juncture not to mention that the reason that Marguerite lives so high on the hog is because Patrick works a fifteen-hour day on a hamster wheel in the City, every day, and it's *his* money he's spending.

"Yes. I discovered that he withdrew four hundred dollars in cash from a Chase Manhattan ATM on Fifth Avenue on Tuesday the fifteenth of March, from his personal, not the household account, at two P.M. Funny that, as he told me he'd been in Bahrain." She spears a sliver of courgette "pasta" on her fork.

"So I confronted him a couple of days ago, and he admitted

that instead of going to Bahrain, he'd been in New York." She picks up her knife and cuts a small slice of "pâté."

"Go on," I say.

"He said that he wanted to be completely open with me, that he wouldn't hide anything again and knew the error of his ways, and I could ask him anything—but I was too dignified to interrogate him. I don't see the point. I still don't know who it is, and I don't want to, now. He's assured me it's over. And then he told me that on the red-eye flight back to Heathrow on the Thursday, he was in Business with Bob Avery. He said that the bird, in his words, flew carriage. As if that made everything okay."

"Oh," I say, feeling slightly let down. Two men on a plane. Where's the story?

"Don't you see what this means?" Marguerite says, and a pink flush mantles her cheeks and throat. "What it means, Mimi, is that Virginie couldn't have been screwing Bob the night before the party. Virginie couldn't have been with *Bob* in the Avery house when she was wandering around—he was on the red-eye with Patrick."

"Oh, I see," I say slowly, as the penny has taken its time to descend. "I do see." Of course. Clare was lit up with the scandal the morning of the Avery party, and I think I even had lunch with her that day and we both agreed that Bob was a goat and that Virginie was a very naughty minx.

I am silent for a moment.

"So have you told Clare the shock news that Virginie isn't having an adulterous affair with her close neighbor Bob Avery in plain sight of the whole garden and illicitly being unfaithful to Mathieu, her husband?"

"I thought you could," Marguerite says. "I can't face it. I can't say I care a lot, to be honest. I'm dealing with too many issues around my own marriage."

We've finished eating. "So who *was* she with in the Avery house?" I muse.

"I don't know and I don't care," says Marguerite. "My guess is that she was telling the truth. She heard the sprinkler, and she went to turn it off. Though knowing what I know about what everyone on the garden gets up to, I'm not surprised no one believed her."

I am working up the energy to go up to the counter, queue, order a latte, and wait.

"Oh, when I looked at his diary online, by the way, I realized why he'd been in New York then, not Bahrain. I forgot to say."

"Why?"

"Because it was St. Patrick's Day. He was in New York. Patrick in New York on St. Patrick's Day. With a young mistress. How could anyone, least of all Patrick, resist that?"

When I get home there's an e-mail from Si. It says he'll be back "toward the end of the month," and he hopes I haven't been pussyfooting around the neighborhood with any of the tomcats, which is a slightly mixed metaphor but nonetheless cheering, especially as he signs his e-mail, "Moose."

I then spend the rest of the afternoon packing for Petts Bottom so we can beat the Friday traffic out of London. On days when I have lunch, my working day starts at 10 A.M. and stops at 1 P.M., as I can never get anything done after lunch if I have to be at school at 3 P.M.

It all proves the point that I frequently make to Ralph, which is that ladies who lunch are much, much too busy to work. I know I am.

Clare

It's the day of the long-awaited Garden Sports and Summer Party.

I'm up early, because Patrick and I are rendezvous-ing at nine sharp by the shed, along with Trish and Alexander Forster, the Tory MP son of the Forsters, Lucy's older brother, who always comes to the summer Garden Sports with his young family.

The marquee is being erected at the west end of the garden. It's the same every year—a large white tent with one side open to the elements.

Inside, over the grass, the marquee people lay a green tarpaulin floor, one section in the middle a square of lino tiles, for the dancing.

It's a humid, sticky sort of June day, heavy with the promise of heat, and the grass in the communal garden has that withered, browning look to it even though we're not even in July yet. It must be global warming. Stephen's stopped mowing, a fact he confirmed to me when I found him planting out the summer bedding earlier in the week, and we had a chat about the polar ice cap melt rate.

As I walk along the path, I see that several families have left out paddling pools from yesterday evening, and huge water pistols like Uzis and cricket bats and tennis balls litter the grass. As I pass, I pick up detritus and align it for collection on the benches along my route, sighing softly as I bend over.

"Well done, old girl," says Patrick. "Well turned up," when I reach the team at the shed.

I do not like being hailed as "old girl," because it is uncomfortably close to the truth, but today I find I don't care. I love

Sports Day. With the races, the homemade lemonade, the dripping ice-cream cones, the little prizes and rosettes, it brings us all together, and we try to forget any ongoing disputes, for the sake of the children.

Patrick's in his weekend mufti of khaki camouflage shorts, a pair of old gym shoes and a gray T-shirt.

Alexander Forster, the thirty-eight-year-old shadow secretary of state for Northern Ireland, is in his off-duty uniform of moleskin trousers, a Tattersall check shirt, loafers, and witty bright pink socks, to show he's not remotely dull.

He is accompanied by Lettice, in Liberty lawn and shined-up Bonpoint shoes the color of conkers, and Cosmo in a tiny Tattersall shirt identical to his father's, which I think comes from Virginie's catalogue. I have to hand it to her. She's unbeatable when it comes to purveying *le style anglais* to the English upper classes. Cosmo's outfit is completed by corduroy knickerbockers, the same Bonpoint button shoes. Their Jack Russell terrier, Humphrey, is getting under our feet.

The Forsters live in Westminster, in a tall thin house with a patio garden, and thus spend their downtime—when not in Alexander's Essex constituency—in our garden.

"Let's get on with it, shall we?" says Alexander. "I've got to do Andrew Marr tomorrow and I know sweet FA about decommissioning." As he speaks, something starts ringing in his pocket and he takes out a BlackBerry, jabs at it as if he's not quite sure of what he's doing and puts it back, frowning. "Someone asking whether you're going to stand as Leader, Alexander? Isn't it time the Tories had a new leader?" says Patrick, unlocking the shed. "You haven't had a new one for at least, what, eight months."

Patrick is a Tory, of course, but that doesn't mean he treats his fellow Tories with any more respect than he treats anyone else. He's nicer to me, and I'm Labour, than he is to his own race.

"Bloody Sundays," replies Alexander. "Papers, I mean."

We take out the stakes from the shed, and I am lightly tasked with untangling the bunting. Patrick and Alexander mark out the running pitch and string colored fairy lights among the smaller trees, which will look magically festive in the dark greenery later and imprint the bright blobs of yellow, red, green on the children's imaginations.

"Humphrey! Humphrey! Come here!" bellows Alexander suddenly. He had just popped back into the shed, and the dog has wandered off somewhere.

"Humphth's in the danthing tent," lisps Lettice, who calls herself Lettith.

"Well, can you go and find him, Tithy?" instructs Alexander. "He hasn't produced his packet today, so better keep an eye on him."

"Oh, yes, hurry up, poppet," echoes Patrick. "We don't want any *merde* on the dance floor, do we?" He starts singing. "It's *merde* on the dance floor . . . or you'd better not kill the groove, ha ha."

I laugh, but not too hard, to show that I am tough on dog mess but not on the causes of dog mess. When we first arrived, the main battles were between the owners of babies and the even more ferociously protective owners of dogs and, as I had neither, I've learnt how to walk the line between both camps. We watch Lettice/Lettith/Tithy totter unsteadily under canvas.

"So, Clare, how's the nipper situation these days, if you don't mind me asking?" continues Patrick.

I've noticed that while English husbands invariably use the word *situation* whenever they are seeking a service update on any aspect of life they regard as the preserve and responsibility of the wife, American men use the word *status*.

Marguerite is always dealing with the tutoring situation, the homework situation, the Eton situation; Mimi's always dealing more prosaically with the mice situation, the MOT situation and the dry-rot situation. Whereas Bob's always saying things like, "What's the status on the Christmas Caribbean vacation this year?" And I am asked about the "nipper situation" as if it's nothing to do with Gideon at all, which is exactly how Gideon sees it, at any rate.

Patrick looks at me and pushes the hair off his damp forehead. It's hot and sticky, and there's that expectant atmosphere of the day, and children are already rushing around in excitement, firing off supersoakers, squealing, and racing each other in heats on the racetrack, impatient for the festivities to start.

I notice the difference in Patrick. I wonder whether his bonhomie is something to do with the prospect of having a day with his children on his home turf, whether Marguerite has relented, or whether he's simply having the time of his life in his bachelor flat with his mistress. I report briskly that there's little to report on the fertility front. No puff of white smoke yet.

"Well, I think you do bloody well, old girl," he replies. "I mean, presumably you bought the house because you thought you'd be hearing the patter of tiny feet, so I think you do bloody well," he repeats with fervor, "and, *personally*, I'm delighted that you're on the garden committee."

Patrick is looking at me with earnest brown eyes, the way Calypso looks at Ralph, and I realize he is not a boisterous playboy at all but a man who has been playing second fiddle to Marguerite's nutritionist, her therapist, her interior decorator, her yoga instructor, and of course her children, for far too long.

I decide not to ruin the moment by bringing up the business with the garage yet again, and hand him one end of a line of red, white, and blue bunting left over from the Golden Jubilee in 2002 and rather tired, to say the least. "That's very sweet of you," I say, looking round for Alexander. However, instead of marking out the track with stakes, he has sloped off, so there are no stakes yet to tie the bunting to.

Patrick hands his end back and I gather the bunting in my arms.

"Listen," I say, an idea forming. "I'll go to Bob Avery and drag him out to help bang in the stakes on either side of the racetrack. It's a two-man job. The others should be out here, anyway, pitching in. There's no reason why you should be getting everything ready all on your own. There's no reason why Bob shouldn't be made to help. Then I'll do the bunting."

"No, don't worry," he says, automatically. "If I can't manage on my own, I'll go and find that slacker Ralph Fleming."

When he mentions Ralph's name, I trip over the bunting. Patrick holds out a gentlemanly hand and I pick myself up.

"Well, I'll go to Bob's first, and if I don't get any joy, I'll fetch Ralph," I say, brightly. "He only just came back from Kyrgyzstan last night, so first I'll see if Bob can help with the banging-in and then I'll go to Ralph," I repeat firmly.

I wait for Patrick to make a crack about Bob and banging, but he doesn't, and I realize that he wouldn't—pot and kettle.

I leave the bunting on the grass outside the Averys' house and walk into their garden, taking my time to dawdle past the garage. It is still minus a roof. The first thing I notice is there's a spanking new gas-fired barbecue the size of a Smart car on the York stone paving outside the kitchen.

There is no sign of Sally, nor indeed of the children. I presume she has dropped them off at the Saturday-morning rock-climbing session at the Westway, or something equally strenuous, while she has her kickboxing class.

Bob is in the kitchen with a Starbucks coffee in a tall silver thermos mug in his paw, reading *The Wall Street Journal*. I hover politely at the gleaming glass doors, waiting for him to wave me in. I hate to be outside someone's house looking in and then have them think I've been spying. I realize I haven't been inside the Averys' since the sushi party, back in March, back when it all started with Patrick and his mistress, and with Bob and Virginie.

Today, there are children's school bags, reading books, invitations, and homework folders strewn on the long narrow table down the middle of the room, and the clever bench seating I admired back then has attracted a coating of mobile telephones, Mini iPods in sugar-almond colors, swim-goggles, scrunchies, and baseball mitts.

"Hey, Clare," says Bob, sliding open the huge glass doors that separate his kitchen from his garden. "What can I do for you?"

That's the thing about Americans. They remember your name, but they don't do small talk. If Gideon has a business lunch, he says that English people only ever get down to business over coffee. With Americans, he says, "Business is over by the entrée."

"I like your new barbecue," I say. This is a lie. What I really think is, why on earth does Sally pay me to design the garden if they're going to ruin the whole effect by plonking a huge stainless-steel grilling machine in the middle of it?

Bob grins and strides over to it. "Oh, yeah," he says, stroking the stainless-steel lid. "Lazy-Man Country Club series. Three big ones not including tax and shipping."

That's another thing about Americans. They are so unembarrassed about talking about money.

"Where are Graydon and Toby?" I continue. Not having children of my own, I find it strangely easy to remember not merely the names of other people's children but even the names of their pets. I did tell Sally to try to keep the hutches off the lawn in the spring, but they don't seem to be in the kitchen or outside.

"Long story," laughs Bob. "Graydon finally achieved his lifetime ambition, which was to aggress Toby to death, so after Toby went to the great warren in the sky, we gave Graydon to the housekeeper's daughter and we got a couple of hamsters instead. Chip and Pin. Then they died. So now we got a couple new ones. Nip and Tuck."

"Oh, right," I say. There is a silence, during which I have to explain why I'm there.

"Bob," I begin. This is going to be difficult. I have abandoned plans to try to get Bob out there and helping, even though I had a great segue into it when he mentioned his barbecue was a Lazy-Man.

"I'm aware that I haven't properly spoken to you since the AGM, when Patrick told everyone about your plans to erect the new building."

"Uh huh," says Bob, sipping his coffee. His eyes are on me and very steady. As I look at him, I realize he must be about five years younger than me.

"Well, I can see there's no going back now, the garage is pretty much up, but I just hope you realize the strength of opposition to it throughout the garden. I just feel I should let you know that at the committee meeting, there was an almost unanimous feeling that you and Sally have taken us all for something of a ride. You told Patrick you were building a garage. You told the authorities you were building a garage. But it's a house, and with all those windows and the glass roof, it's going to be an eyesore that will ruin the peace and darkness of the garden not just for us but for generations to come."

I pause for breath. I have one shot at what I want to say next, and if it misses the target, I am going to press the nuclear button. I have, after all, been waiting with my finger poised since March.

"I can't persuade you to knock it down, I know that. But I do think that you will go a long way to soothing ruffled feathers—and you must take it from me, there are a lot of ruffled feathers—if you do something about the roof. I beg you. On behalf of the garden committee." I don't have authority to speak on behalf of the garden committee, as I'm not in fact the chairman, but I reckon that Bob's too new around here to know that.

"Don't put on a glass roof."

Bob has been staring at me flintily during the course of my appeal. He hears me out. Then he exhales and places his silver Starbucks mug on the lid of the Lazy-Man and squints over toward the garage, which is so white and so big that it's too dazzling to look at in full daylight.

"Clare, I know you want a fight, but I'm afraid there's nothing left to fight about. The garage has been granted planning permission. You all had the chance to look at the plans. You all had the chance to object. I know that you personally were sent a letter. And I even sent the plans to Patrick, so that folks who couldn't be bothered to schlep to the Town Hall could see his set. What more could I do?"

I hear the sound of children. I know I don't have much time. I certainly don't have time or, suddenly, the energy to explain what people are upset about. If he can't now see the fact that we all mind that the rustic integrity of the garden, intact since 1850, has been irrevocably breached by the quite unnecessary erection of a white shining monument to the Avery family's insensitivity, he never will.

"I take your point, Bob, but I don't think that sending the plans to Patrick was the fastest way of publishing them, as he never told anyone he had them. Whatever. But what I will say, Bob, is that people know more about you than you think."

My voice sounds funny to me, but I plow on. "And if you don't play by the rules, you will find that things can turn very nasty on a communal garden. You haven't been here that long, you know. You don't know how things work. People know things you may want to keep secret. Feuds start. And they don't end." This is dreadful. I sound like something out of a daytime soap.

I walk swiftly to the end of the garden to his gate and gather up the bunting in my arms. It smells of shed. Bob stays where he is. As if he's protecting the Lazy-Man.

I can now see the shapes of Megan and Kevin and Margaret and Kurt bouncing around the kitchen like popcorn popping in a microwave bag.

"I just think you'd better spit it out, whatever it is you're saying," he calls over to me, as the commotion from his house rolls toward us, a tsunami of children and voices. I walk back a little way toward him.

"You know what I'm saying, Bob."

"Actually, I don't, Clare," he says, quietly.

"I'm saying that unless you do something about the roof, I'm going to tell your wife about you and Virginie." I cannot believe that I have just threatened a neighbor with exposure in this way.

Bob looks at me in bafflement, and then his face clears and his eyes sparkle.

"Oh, Clare," he roars, smiting the top of the Lazy-Man with a beefy hand, causing his mug to skitter across the polished steel surface. "The foxy Frenchy? The camp cutie? Oh, bless you. Bless you. You have *totally* made my day."

"Well, I'm glad, in that case," I say, feeling stupid. What on earth does he mean?

He follows me. "And Clare—"

"Yes?"

"Let me offer some neighborly advice, honey. Instead of worrying about how I'm betraying *my* wife, I think you need to go talk to *your* husband."

"*Gideon?*"

"You said it," says Bob, taking a slug of coffee. "Or you could wait here and we could talk to him together. We have a meeting scheduled for 10 A.M., right here."

"What about, may I ask?"

"You mean you don't know?" demands Bob, looking surprised. Then his face clears. "You don't know, do you? Oh, boy." He takes a checked Ralph Lauren handkerchief out of his shorts pocket and polishes the lid of the Lazy-Man.

Then he squints across at the garage again, and it all clicks. He's hired Gideon to do the roof. This must mean that they've abandoned the peaked glass thing and they're putting on one of Gideon's signature retractable roofs. My first thought is, thank goodness they've seen the light; a retractable roof is a much less light-polluting option. My second thought is not a thought. It is a feeling. It makes me realize that I am right to have done what I have, because if Gideon has done this, I am right to make my own future and follow my own path, just as Donna has ordered.

"Oh," I say. "Oh. Well, I'd better go home and start doing the lemonade." I make to leave.

"Oh, Clare," he calls after me, summoning me back. "What you said about the importance of not starting fights with the neighbors, or whatever?" I stand still. "You think I'm going to make nice, don't you? Well, we did. We gave a party, and I didn't notice anyone not coming. Now the in-your-face rich Americans want to change something on the precious communal garden and, suddenly, you don't like us anymore. We're *vulgar*. We don't understand how things are *done*. Well, sorry about that. We got planning permission. We've spent a quarter of a million pounds, all in. So it's just tough shit. You lose. We win. You're only Bush League, Mrs. Sturgis, and I suggest you stay out of the way of big hitters. So stop with the whining, will ya?"

I head back across the browning grass, breathing heavily, my forehead beaded with sweat.

First, I am going to go home and take half a homeopathic tranquillizer and prepare myself to confront Gideon about his betrayal when he gets back. (He said he had a meeting in NW10 and would be back after lunch. Which I now know means a site meeting, or what he calls a "shite meeting," with Bob and Sally across the garden, and lunch with someone else, God knows who.)

I'm going to get him to admit that he hid the letter about the garage and went behind my back. That he lied to me. And took down the yellow notice outside our house.

But before any of that takes place, I have some very important business to transact—with Ralph.

I hurry into the kitchen, remove my shoes, and run lightly upstairs to the wet room. When I see our marital bed, with its smooth, white, pure surface and perfectly plumped white pillows, for some reason I avert my eyes.

Mimi

"No, Mirabel, you are not, for the last and final time, going to wear my thong," I hiss, pushing knickers and tights and bras down into my overflowing top drawer blossoming with lingerie and shoving it closed.

Mirabel not only regards *mia casa* as *sua casa*, she regards all my clothing, jewelry, shoes, and even underwear as hers, too.

"But Mu-um," says Mirabel. She has even gone so far as to put it on underneath her ra-ra skirt and crop top, and is standing in front of the full-length mirror looking at her rear end cloven by the thin black band of cotton. I am beside myself. I can barely deal with my own sexuality let alone the burgeoning evidence of my daughter's.

"Do you really want everyone to see your bottom during the races this afternoon?" I snap, noting how peachy and perky her behind is compared to mine, which has a hangdog look, so hangdog that the very few times I was naked in front of Si, I made sure I walked out of the bedroom backward, like a subject taking leave of his monarch. Posy is lying on the floor on her back, watching Mirabel with admiration.

"Mum," she asks suddenly. "Will Mirabel go to an *organic* university?"

I cannot do Posy's enchanting question justice right now. "Hold on, Posy," I reply, "Probably she will, by then, but I'm just sorting something out with Mirabel."

"If you don't want me to wear thongs, then why do you have them in your drawer?" continues Mirabel remorselessly.

"One, it is none of your business what I have in my drawers and two, my underwear is *my* underwear, and three, thongs are unhygienic." I do not elaborate. With her low tolerance for things mank and gross, I do not think Mirabel will appreciate being told that a thong is basically an uncomfortable way of wicking germs from the back to the front bottom.

"Whatev," says Mirabel, except she doesn't, she holds up her two thumbs together and points her index fingers in the shape of a W.

"So take them off and put on some of the ones I bought you in M&S," I order, standing in bra and pants in front of my wardrobe. I am trying to decide what to wear for the garden sports. This is a very important decision. On the surface, my attire has to convey the droopy femininity of an Edwardian tea dress. Underneath, its pantherine swiftness has to assist me to a historic victory in the women's (aged sixteen to thirty-nine) race.

So my bra is a sports bra and my pants are white stretchy cotton.

I am looking at my body with interest. Since the thing (I'm not sure how to designate it, to be honest—doesn't seem to merit the word *affair*) with Si, I've lost weight. I can't deny this is a bonus, even if it is sadly the only one. I may be wretched, guilty, and heartbroken, etc., but I'm also under nine stone for the first time in ten years.

I decide on a navy gingham cotton skirt cut on the bias from the Marilyn Moore shop in Elgin Crescent, a fitted plain white T-shirt, and bare feet. Then I go to the bathroom and apply lashings of mascara and spritz my armpits with Ralph's deodorant. I feel like lying down on my bed for the rest of the day, reading *I Capture the Castle* for the thirtieth time and weeping, but I know that along with the privilege of living on a communal garden comes duty. I must join in. Everyone must join in the super fun. It is our duty.

Five minutes later, all three children are outside, practicing for the three-legged race, along with a gang of other kids, some in trees, others kicking a football over the bunting. Men with bulging calves are doing stretches against trees, wearing toweling socks pulled a fraction too high and brand-new trainers, polo shirts in amusing colors, and shapeless shorts.

Patrick is painting a white finishing line on the grass, while Marguerite is setting out a table with bowls of sweets for prizes and an array of red, white, and blue rosettes with "1st," "2nd," and "3rd" on them. I notice that the big bowl containing fun-size packs of Smarties and mini Mars Bars has undergone a change of contents and that, this year, the lucky winners are receiving Wildberry Fruit Leather strips and gelatin-free Gummy VegeBears from Fresh & Wild. I decide not to draw the children's attention to this development.

As I walk toward the Moltons' to see if I can help (I should have been out earlier but Ralph did come out for hours this morning, hammering and so on, so I felt that the Fleming family had pulled its weight), I spot that Mirabel and Posy are using a knitted belt that I spent £75 on in a moment of madness in a boutique on Kensington Park Road as a tie for the three-legged race, and the red mist descends.

I've been feeling more fractious than usual since Con and Gretchen cornered me with purposeful expressions at the weekend while I was washing up after Sunday lunch. They stood behind me and very kindly invited me and Ralph to join them on a marriage course at the Holy Trinity, Brompton.

They said that going on the course would be a wonderful journey and that, on the way, Ralph and I would discover that Christian lovemaking was the most powerful gift the Creator had given us and that married love was the most passionate and playful expression of human sexuality of all, not to mention all sorts of other important things.

I was doing fine until Gretchen used the word *playful*, which, in the context of married love was simply almost too much to bear. "Playful?" I repeated, wondering whether throwing an earthenware dish that had contained a baked ham and noodle thing called *Schinkerheckerl* at my sister-in-law's golden head would constitute an aggressive act. "It's a lovely thought, Gretchen, but Ralph's away so much at the moment . . ." I trailed off, and for the first time found an encrusted *rösti* dish a welcome distraction.

Now I run toward my daughters, screaming.

"My Missoni belt!" I yell (though I don't think it is Missoni —it just looks like it could be). "Take it off! Off! Right now!"

They stand there rolling their eyes as I grab them by their shoulders in an unnecessarily fierce grip. Then I kneel and try to untie the knot, fail, and start gnawing at it with my teeth.

"You're always in a bad mood at the moment, Mum," I hear Posy say in a low, sad voice.

"If you take One More Thing of mine without asking," I mumble, teeth yanking at the delicate silk and cashmere artefact, "I will beat you."

"For God's sake, Mum, chill pill," replies Mirabel. "It's only a belt."

"Looking forward to the races, are we, Mummy?" calls out Patrick, who has been watching this pleasant exchange with my darling children with interest. "Got your spikes on, I hope? I think there's going to be stiff competition this year. Sally Avery's been kickboxing and jogging at least twice a week—"

"Well, there's going to be no competition from me," says Marguerite, making sure each tiny rosette's tiny safety pin is secure. "When it comes to the garden sports, I am most definitely Off Games."

I decide to cheer up. Posy's right. I mustn't be in a bad mood, at least not today. This is a shimmering highlight of the garden year, the one day when absolutely everyone, even misanthropic hermits who never set foot in the garden, will make their one annual appearance.

And participation is almost impossible to avoid anyway.

From horribly early in the morning, men have been out in the garden erecting the marquee, clanking metal poles around, hammering stakes into the ground, painting white lines on the lawn, hanging out bunting and shouting to each other in the lusty voices of professional men engaged in the rare act of manual labor. The marquee is now up on the Colville side of the garden, where it will remain for the disco, and come down sometime on Sunday.

It's sticky out here, even in my T-shirt and skirt, and I envy the naked children splashing duckily in paddling pools and drenching each other with supersoakers. I also envy Ralph his nap—he's sleeping inside with his feet on the bed. He went out to help with the setting up, to borrow a hammer from Clare, he said. He was gone ages, so long that I fed the children lunch without him, feeling somewhat aggrieved.

When he came back, he was singing, "If I Had a Hammer," and announced that all the setting up had "really taken it out of him" and could I wake him up just before the races started. I didn't whinge because he did look tired. More than tired, in fact. He looked *spent*.

Clare must be inside making lemonade. I hope she brings it out in the cream enamel urn I gave her. I saw it was on sale in Laura Ashley and couldn't resist buying it for her—I even pointed out she could use it as a container if she didn't want it cluttering up the kitchen.

I felt that the enamel lemonade urn would grace any larder and was only slightly deterred by the thought that Clare doesn't have a larder, she has a post-minimalist (i.e., completely empty) kitchen with open shelving . . .

Patrick is now blaring into a loudhailer at a crowd of residents gathered at the track. The running order doesn't change from year to year: first, sprinting races for every age group up to thirteen, then thirteen to fifteen. Then there are the egg-and-spoon races, for which we use Jersey Royals and wooden spoons, then running races for the sixteen to thirty-nines and above, the sack race, the three-legged race, family relays, the dog race, the Marathon (all the way round the garden once), and the afternoon fun finishes with a shouty tug-of-war between the Lonsdale and the Colville sides of the garden.

The sports take a good two hours to get through, after which there are refreshments of Clare's homemade lemonade, and ice-cream cones courtesy of the garden committee.

Less sprightly residents, familiar with the lengthy nature of the proceedings, have brought out deck chairs and are sitting with "Isn't this lovely" beams on their cozily lined faces.

The toddlers are lining up at the starting line, stumbling, sitting down, wailing, while their parents try to steer them from the shoulders. After two false starts, Cosmo Forster (twenty-two months) is declared the victor of the race and is borne on Alexander's shoulders to the winner's table, where Marguerite offers him a choice of a leather strip or some gummy bears.

I reckon there's at least twenty minutes till the egg and spoon—so I wander off to see what Clare's up to. She's not much of a joiner-inner, and I feel that on days like this, when it's so much about children and family, it's only right to make a special effort to include her.

Clare

"I thought you might need a hand with the lemonade."

Mimi. As usual, she's marched straight in, boldly, to my house. It's lucky she didn't do this an hour or so ago—though I did take the precaution of locking the kitchen doors out to the garden to preclude any such eventuality. On the day of the summer party, the unscheduled traffic between houses is busier than ever.

Thank goodness I remembered to use her urn. I did consider giving it straight to Oxfam, but I hesitated, and the large cream object (though I loathe retro kitchenalia with a passion) with its swirly black lettering saying "*Lemonade*" is sitting on my pale bleached oak table, waiting to be filled with blended and strained ice, lemon quarters, and caster sugar. It's a lot of work, but I know everyone appreciates the effort.

"Oh, Mimi," I reply, not looking at her, as I wipe down all the surfaces in the kitchen absolutely clean of any stray spots or splatters of sticky liquid, feeling like Bree in *Desperate Housewives*. "You are sweet. No. I think I'm good."

"Are you coming out for the races?" she asks. She is tasting my lemonade straight from the ladle, wrinkling her nose as the sourness hits her tongue and giving me a thumbs-up sign. She's looking trim but not overtly athletic in a blue skirt and white tee. "You know you want to. Did Ralph come and borrow a hammer?"

"In a minute," I reply. I find her presence in the kitchen unnerving, to say the least. I wonder whether I'll ever be able to sit down for a long, pleasurable girly gossip where we take everyone who lives on the garden apart in turn, ever again. I don't answer the question about Ralph and the hammer, because I'm not sure what he said to her when he went back.

She flits back into the garden, back to where her children and neighbors are, drawn to the loudhailer like a child to the glutinous jingle of an ice-cream van.

"I'll join you in a sec," I call after her, trying to sound normal, light.

I carry the urn out and put it on a table I've covered with a heavy linen cloth. Then I stack the plastic cups in two towers of equal height by a ladle. It pains me to serve anything in plastic tumblers, but I don't see what else I can do. Then I join the crowd at the racetrack, having reserved some ice and lemonade in a pitcher in the Smeg for later, for refills when all the races including the tug-of-war are over.

Parents are standing with digital cameras at the finishing line to record their children's performances. There are plenty of smiles and laughter, but this day never passes off without tears and temper tantrums. Marguerite has to give out an awful lot of rosettes saying "1st" on them, as a rule, even to those who only came second and third.

"Come on, Posy," I cheer, to encourage her. She's standing at the far end, clad in an adorable lawn smock and Start-Rite sandals, concentrating hard, egg and spoon in hand. This alerts Mimi to something. She rushes up to Patrick.

"Short interruption to proceedings while Mrs. Fleming fetches Mr. Fleming to watch Miss Posy Fleming compete in the under-seven's egg and spoon," Patrick informs the crowd. And my heart does something inside my chest. I can't believe that I am standing here, as if everything is completely normal. But my ability to pretend makes me wonder what other dark or sinister or strange secrets all these jolly garden residents in their shorts and sundresses are concealing beneath their everyday faces.

"Perhaps this is a good moment to partake of the excellent

homemade lemonade kindly provided by Mrs. Sturgis," he bellows, and people start drifting over. I feel I have to go and stand at my lemonade stall and dole it out, which I do, until Ralph emerges looking if possible more rumpled than ever with a pleased-looking Mimi.

Patrick then hustles all the children through a succession of races, and the parents all continue to cheer their children on wildly. Dogs tied to benches bark frenziedly in sympathy. Then my heart sinks, because I know everyone will try to make me join in the Mothers' Race, which is what the women's sixteen-to-thirty-nine race is always slightly tactlessly called. Then I realize I'm off the hook. I turned forty last year, and so I am too old.

Virginie, Trish, Mimi, Lucy Forster, and Priscilla Forster are among those milling at the starting end. Their children are lining the track, peering over the bunting, and clumped at the finishing line. They are all shouting, "Come on, Mummy," "come on, Mummy," and jumping up and down, trailing sweet papers, which blow across the browning grass.

"*Treesh, what are you doing in thees race?*" Virginie is saying, tightening her bra strap underneath her sundress. "*Don't try to pretend to everayone you're under fortay!*"

"I most certainly am!" Trish colors and replies hotly. She is wearing a wraparound dress but gives the impression that, as soon as the race is underway, she will rip it off Superwoman-style to reveal an aerodynamic unitard underneath. We all went to Trish's fortieth last year (and a memorable party that was—we were all chauffeured to Little Sodbury, and there were 150 to dinner, and each table had its own *sommelier,* and if the ladies got cold, butlers rushed up with cashmere blankets), but we all decided to let her pretend she's still thirty-nine. After such hospitality, it's the least we can do.

Mimi is in bare feet, but all the others are in trainers—well, Virginie is too chic to wear trainers and is wearing white plimsolls and a pale lemon backless dress that makes her flesh look as if it's been carved out of bronze, by angels.

"*Allez, Clare,*" calls out Virginie, to me. "*If Treesh is in this race, you might as well be in eet too.*"

"That's a very tempting invitation, Virginie," I call back, trying not to feel like a sad old trout. "But I think I'll pass."

Then I see a figure sprinting along the path, darting through the groups of seated spectators. It's Sally Avery, looking lithe and tomboyish in some Lycra running shorts and vest. She's had her hair cut shorter, and it suits her sporty style. It makes me remember that this is the Averys' first garden sports and they clearly haven't grasped that the trick is to look as if you're not trying hard at all while trying very hard indeed, underneath. Though I have to say—brave of Sally and Bob to come out at all, given they are, without question, the *personae non gratae* of the year.

Sally joins the lineup next to Virginie and Mimi, who is in the middle of telling everyone very loudly that she needs to pee and hasn't been to the gym all year and she's worried that halfway between here and the finishing line she may have to squat on the grass and "do a Paula Radcliffe." The others shriek with nervous laughter as Mimi suddenly hoicks her skirt and goes down on her haunches, as if caught short.

"I would like to make an announcement," comes Patrick's disembodied voice. "To do with 'ealth and safety, ha ha. I've unilaterally made some changes to the adult races, and I hope that these will make the athletics even more fun, if that's possible." The mothers all look expectant and nervous, and shuffle about. Sally and Trish are doing hamstring stretches.

"The mums—I mean, ladies—will all have to run barefoot," Patrick blares. "And the menfolk will just have to wait to find out what the drill is for them."

All the women start obediently removing their shoes. All apart from Sally Avery, that is. She stands there.

"Come on, we all have to," says Lucy Forster to her, as if to a bolshie toddler. "Chop chop."

"But I never run in bare feet," says Sally. "I don't know what's on the grass. Why should I? What's with this garden?" I begin to feel even gladder that I haven't taken up Virginie's invitation.

"Oh, come on, Sally, don't be a spoilsport," says Mimi. "Let's just humor Patrick, shall we?"

"If you don't remove your trainers, it'll be cheating," says Trish. "We can't have cheating."

"*Well, Mimi always cheats, actually,*" points out Virginie, in Sally's defense. "*Last year, she went on steaday instead of go.*"

"Hold on, you know that's not true," says Mimi. "How dare you accuse me of cheating?"

"For Christ's sake. I thought this was supposed to be fun," snaps Sally. She takes off her trainers. Then she throws them on to the track and walks off. "There's way too much estrogen flowing here for this to be a healthy activity for us all to do," is her parting shot.

The women all look at each other, secretly thrilled that things have taken this turn. There's nothing like a public display of hostility to liven things up.

Patrick calmly walks over to the shoes. "Spirited filly," he remarks calmly, and plucks the two white trainers from the grass, tucks them under his arm and raises the loudhailer to his lips.

I leave the lemonade stall and walk quickly to the finishing line, two or even three deep in spectators. The sight of all the yummy mummies in a fight to the finish is too good to miss.

And then I see that Si Kasparian has manifested himself for the first time, I think, ever, in the communal garden. He must have taken to heart my advice, which is that it's important to make an appearance on Sports Day, Bonfire Night, and the AGM, if you possibly can.

He looks very much at home out here.

He has taken up a position to the right of the finishing line. For the first time, I can see why Mimi secretly fancies him (she denies it but is the worst liar I've ever encountered, completely transparent).

Si is tanned and wholesome-looking in jeans, moccasins and no socks and a white shirt from Façonnable. He has opened one button too many but somehow gets away with it, and my eyes linger, for a second, on his thatch of chest hair.

Then Patrick shouts, "Go!" and all eyes turn to the race-track. As ever, it is an extremely close race, and Trish and Mimi lead the pack from the start and thunder over the grass the hundred yards toward us neck and neck, Mimi's generous boobs whirling round like windmills under her T-shirt, while Trish's neck is corded with effort and her arms are working like pistons.

Both are grimacing, and I wonder if they have any idea how unattractive they look. I hear Si laughing quietly to himself.

Mimi gets to the line, just ahead, and throws up her arms in victory, jumps up and down, then picks up Posy and whirls her round in triumph. Then she heads to the table with rosettes and prizes.

Si approaches her as she's pinning her rosette on to her T-shirt with difficulty and handing her prize packet of sweeties to a proud Posy. When she catches sight of him, her flush deepens, and her mouth falls open. Something flits across her face.

"I knew you were fast, but I didn't know you were that fast," he tells her, and pats Posy, who skips away.

I don't hear her reply, because then Trish bears down on her. "You didn't come first, Mimi, I did," I hear her say loudly and aggressively.

"Oh, I thought I did," Mimi says. "Well . . . Si, this is my friend Clare, she lives two doors down from me in Colville," Mimi says, hauling me to her side.

"But I know Clare, we met at the Dodd Nobles," replies Si, to my surprise. I'm so used to reminding alpha men that they've met me and who I am. "Clare is my gardener. And I think you've done a great job," he adds, giving me a smile, which I return.

Then we stand and watch the next race, the over-forties women's race, which Mimi points out is even more hotly contested than the under-forties, as women over forty have "more time to go to the gym," and have therefore "invested more time and money in maintaining a high level of fitness."

Then we watch the men's races. Patrick announces that all the men have to run backward instead of forward, following an incident last year when the men stampeded so fast over the finishing line they plowed into the spectators and knocked several small children flying.

"At Ponsonby, the Fathers' Race has become so competitive that they make the men skip," Mimi tells Si.

"Ponsonby?" inquires Si, attentively. "Do you mean Ponsonby Preparatory School?"

"Yes—we're all Ponsonby parents round here," she replies, popping a Gummy VegeBear into her mouth.

"Are you now," says Si.

Patrick wants to run in this race, as his three boys are watching and egging him on. So he hands the loudhailer over to Ralph, who has announced that wild horses couldn't make him run.

The men line up at the far end, a great burly mass of them, all straining to win. Seeing them makes me wonder how these aggressive men could spend five minutes penned in City offices, let alone twelve hours. As they jog backward, bottoms first, calves pumping, twisting round to see the way ahead over the grass, Bob Avery manages to trip up Patrick, who falls heavily on his rump. I hear Marguerite cry out in alarm.

"Man down," says Si.

But Bob doesn't stop to see if Patrick's all right but hurdles over him backward as if he's been practicing for this all his life and powers on to win the under-forty race. All the other men try not to look too cross.

Bob punches the air, high-fives his children, and heads over to Marguerite, who is more concerned about Patrick than finding a rosette with "1st" on it for Bob. This makes me think there's still hope for them. Then I hear her ask Bob whether he would mind having a rosette saying "2nd" on it, as she is reserving the ones saying "1st" for the children, but he says he does mind and makes some remark about coming second being for losers.

Then Calypso wins the dog race, to great Fleming excitement but, it has to be said, she mainly wins because Mimi is standing at the touchline holding a Beggin' Strip which Posy has taken out from a pocket and let Calypso smell before the start of the race. Another dog owner, Sarah Pilcher, who had high hopes for her retriever, Butter, shouts "You bitch," as Calypso streaks over to Mimi like an arrow, and all the other dogs, with Butter in the middle of the fray, end up in a snarling pack on the grass.

"I'm assuming you're referring to my dog not me," responds Mimi, who seems extraordinarily happy all of a sudden.

Bob Avery then easily wins the Marathon, assisted by the fact that Patrick Molton has retired injured. Then he walks around wearing his two "1st" rosettes on his polo shirt and looks pleased with himself and not at all as if everyone on the garden hates him and resents the eyesore.

Then we all line up for the tug-of-war. It's Colville versus Lonsdale. This is always an opportunity for those who aren't bankers but media folk or architects or writers or consultants and who live in smaller houses on the "wrong side" of the garden gently to tease the Lonsdale Gardens residents on the "right side" who live in five-story mansions with tradesmen's entrances and earn millions in financial services.

"Come on, you bloated plutocrats, show us what you're made of," roars Ralph as he strains at the rope, veins on his neck standing out. My hands are hurting, and I am pulling with all my might, having taken a position a little way away from Ralph. "Show us little people how strong and powerful and important you are with your big houses and your seven-figure salaries and multimillion-pound annual bonuses!" he bellows. "Heave, Colville, HEAVE."

But, as usual, Lonsdale wins. And then, it's over for another year. I make some remark to Ralph and Patrick that it's all been a bit quiet.

"With just the one spat in the Mummies' Race, I think we can say that this year's garden sports have been tamer than usual," agrees Ralph, clapping Patrick on the back and congratulating him on his "excellent turn" as master of ceremonies.

"That's very kind of you, Ralph," says Patrick. The day has really cheered him up, I think. Especially Sally's strop. "I like to think that at least one merchant banker will end up in casualty thanks to my refereeing, so I'm a bit disappointed, to be honest, as this year I'm the only one who's ended up hurt." He makes a strange expression. "Even though I have only managed to injure my coccyx, apparently one of the many parts of the male body that are surplus to modern require-ments, it's still jolly painful." He rubs at the small of his back and wanders over to Marguerite.

The children all run into the marquee in a pack to be enter-tained by Mr. Sausageman, who has turned up wearing a spectacular, phallic shirt hung with dangling frankfurters. I look for Mimi, to have a giggle over it together, but then I remember that I am avoiding Mimi and, anyway, even though Posy and co. are still out, she's disappeared.

As I wander about, picking up discarded plastic tumblers, I pass Lucy Forster. "Weren't the races the most super, super super fun?" she asks. "I do think that our garden is simply the nicest, nicest, nicest in Notting Hill, don't you?" I can't think how to answer this, but I don't have to, as Lucy presses on regardless.

"Everyone just gets on so *well*, don't they?"

Mimi

"Oh, I think you knew right from the start that I don't ever hang about," I say, heart thumping. "If I want something, I just get out there."

"Yes, I think I may have noticed that, at some point," he says, in his slow transatlantic drawl.

He watches me try to pin my rosette to my T-shirt, but the thing is flimsily attached to a tiny safety pin and my fingers aren't working.

He does it instead for me. When I see his strong brown fingers with their clean fingernails working carefully just above my heaving chest, I feel weak. I knew that my plan to greet Si with dazzling *hauteur* when I saw him again was going to take all my strength, but nothing prepared me for the fact that when I saw him again, I would feel flakier than *mille-feuille*. My promise to myself that when I next saw him I would be remote and unattainable has vanished into the midsummer air, as if sublimated by heat and lust.

I successfully hold myself back from suggesting we nip into his house and go up to his bedroom for an unbridled session of wild jungle sex. One can't be *too* forward. But I think I might have done had not Trish zoomed up to us and tried to rip off the rosette that Si has just pinned to my bosom.

"You didn't come first, Mimi, I did," she is saying, in an unjokey voice.

"Oh. I thought I did," I say, longing for her to go away.

"Well, let's ask Si," she says. "Who won, Si? Me or Mimi? You were watching."

"Count me out," he protests, backing away. "I was just an innocent bystander. You were both pretty fast. Anyway, it's over—and I thought it was all about taking part. In your country."

"Well, you're wrong," I say. "The taking part couldn't matter less, it's the winning that counts."

"I'm not sure I get Trish," he says, after she leaves us. I like the fact that even though Trish looks twangingly fit in her short clingy dress, he doesn't get her.

"I'm not sure anyone does," I reply. "I think every communal garden has a Trish. Most of the time she's rubbing everyone up the wrong way, but then she goes and does something incredibly kind like sneak you a garden key to replace the one you've lost, and you realize it's not her fault she's so ghastly, she just can't help it." I watch Trish stomp off, and suddenly remember the famous Trish dinner-party story and decide Si is ready for it.

"I must tell you what she did once . . ." I begin, thinking that it's too late to stop now. "She once had a bunch of us to dinner and really pushed the boat out, waiters and the silver out and had it all catered, and the next day her housekeeper, Estelita, called me up. 'Madam, I sorry, Meeses Dodd Noble she asks me to call you, do you have Meeses Dodd Noble's spoon?' she asks me." I do a passable imitation of a Colombian housekeeper.

"I told the housekeeper that no, by some strange coincidence I hadn't taken Trish's spoon," I continue. "And then I hear Trish in the background, hissing, 'Go on, Estelita! Ask her again! It was one of the silver dessert spoons.' So, almost in tears, Estelita repeats the question, and I tell her I don't have it, and this all goes on for some time and then, get this! A couple of hours later she calls back yet again, and says that Mrs. Dodd Noble has asked her to ring again and could I look through my bag and pockets in case it slipped into them by mistake."

I am beginning to regret embarking on this anecdote for several reasons, among them that Si gets the impression I am for some reason a well-known klepto or—even worse—a *raconteur*.

"Well, it's not as if it's the first time the dish ran away with the spoon, is it?" he smiles at me. I let out my breath.

I am hemmed in by friends and neighbors. Patrick is making a series of seriocomic announcements about the tug-of-war, the Marathon, and Mr. Sausageman. But, still, I feel as if Si and I are alone, the two of us. A soft breeze is cooling my cheeks and lightly lifting my damp curls away from my neck, which feels delicious.

"Lemonade?" I suggest, suddenly. "Clare is famous for her lemonade. It's homemade. You know, in Clare's home. In the old-fashioned, you know, traditional way."

There is a pause. I feel Si is weighing me up, and I am hanging in the balance. And then, as the pause lengthens, I feel my heart turn to ice. It's always me who makes the running, I realize. It's the wrong way round. I've never been able to think of myself as a soft, mysterious cat, as the dating gurus recommend—I've always been an untrained puppy . . .

My cheeks burning with humiliation and rejection, I leave Si and start walking toward Clare's little table with the lemonade urn on it, next to the willow, just to show him that I don't care, either way.

"Hold on, Pussy," Si murmurs in my ear, staying me, his hand on my arm, "Don't go. I can think of something, um, equally *traditional* and *old-fashioned* and *refreshing* I'd like even more than Mrs. Sturgis's lemonade . . ."

Then he says loudly, "Mimi, I'd like to ask you a favor. Will you come and have a look at my window boxes? I'm still trying to find someone to come *feng shui* them."

"Oh, are you?" I say, also loudly. "All right, I'll have a look to see if it's the sort of thing that Donna might be interested in, if you like."

I take a quick look around the garden. Ralph is in a group over by the lemonade stall with Clare and Patrick. Marguerite is packing up her table. Jeremy Dodd Noble is playing football with small boys, among them my Cas and the three Molton boys. Very casually, we stroll to his garden gate. He pushes it open for me. It creaks, and I lead on, without looking back to see if anyone is watching. His garden is one of the nicest in the row: Clare does it very well. She's divided it up into her trademark horizontal beds, planted a mixture of grasses and vegetables and whatnot so there's lots going on, with low beds full of stuff and tall stalky things waving above. It's pretty. As I pass, I pluck some lavender and roll it between my fingers, which are still smarting with rope-burn from the tug-of-war, and sniff.

"Do you mean these window boxes," I say, turning to Si when we reach his kitchen door. There aren't any window boxes out here.

"No, I mean the ones upstairs," he says. "There aren't window boxes down here in your friend Clare's . . ." he pauses as he struggles to remember the word *"potager."* He says it "po-tah-zhay," with a heavy emphasis on the last syllable.

Making a mental note to tell Clare not to get too pretentious—I mean, Latin names are reasonable enough but French horticultural terms sound silly—I follow him into his kitchen.

It is filled with light, pouring in from large plate-glass windows at both ends. It is gleamingly, glowingly clean, in that way that makes you realize true luxury is all about having other people polish your Boffi worktops with soft cloths all day, not just someone to wash your floor every now and then.

I scoot into the middle, where I think I won't be visible either from the street or from the garden, and lean against his sleek stainless-steel worktop, waiting for him to kiss me.

"No," he orders, leaning into me with his hands planted on either side of my body, on the worktop, where they will leave a smudge. I can smell cigarettes, sun-warmed skin, roasted coffee beans, and a sweeter citrus note I haven't noticed before. I wonder briefly about this scent.

"On the table," he says. I know what he means. Something happened with complete success on the long kitchen table during the earlier episode, before we repaired upstairs to the deep luxury of his designer bedroom.

But I can't move. He's blocking me. My mouth is dry. I duck under his arm and, for some reason, I run. I want to go up to his bedroom. I'd be crackers to do anything down here. Everyone can see us here.

I make it up to the ground floor, which is all masses of space with long low sofas and huge bunches of scented lilies and cream rugs. I don't stop but bolt round the corner to the stairs up to the first floor, to where his bedroom is. I am already imagining throwing myself down on his huge bed, squirming naked underneath the fur throw and watching him unbuckle his belt.

But when I start heading up the flight of stairs to the first floor, he catches hold of my ankle. I twitch and wriggle to try to free myself, but he pulls me back down the stairs toward him, unbuckling his jeans as I come down, bump bump bump, like Winnie-the-Pooh carelessly brought downstairs by Christopher Robin shortly before boy and bear head out to Hundred Acre Wood.

"Ouch," I scream, in a way intended to incite feral rather than medical treatment.

But he, rightly, ignores me.

He puts his hands up my skirt and pulls down my pants, right down over my knees and ankles and bare, grass-stained feet. He doesn't look at them, thank goodness—sadly, they're not undercrackers but white M&S cotton—before dropping them at the foot of the stairs. Now I'm facing him, lying on the three prongs of the treads, which are digging into my back, but not too painfully, and then he snaps open his belt, without looking down but into my eyes.

Now, ordinarily, I wouldn't be up for this at all. Whenever I see movies where someone gets fucked somewhere like a kitchen table (Jessica Lange and Jack Nicholson in *The Postman Always Rings Twice*, the *locus classicus*) or on a beach (*From Here to Eternity*), I'm thinking, "That looks terribly floury/sandy/dangerous/uncomfortable," as they set about each other. I wonder how expensive the dress that a masterful male has just ripped was. I wonder who's going to clear up the flat after Cybill Shepherd and Bruce Willis have finally, chaotically got it on after sixty-nine episodes.

And I always find it implausible that our panting lovers can't delay their ardor just for a second or two so that they can make it into the bedroom and on to a nice, comfy, well-sprung bed.

Well, turns out I haven't felt real lust before. Real lust makes you care more about well-hung than well-sprung. Real lust makes you have sex in lifts and cupboards and at unergonomic angles. It makes you forget that you're lying uncomfortably, and that another man, a man who is neither your husband nor your obstetrician, can see your front fur and quite a lot of your naked back bottom in broad daylight.

Real lust takes you from *From Here to Osteopathy* and costs a fortune in private medical bills for spinal realignment later. It's like labor. If you have to ask whether you're in labor, or whether you're experiencing real lust, the answer is . . . probably not.

"It's all about freedom to, not freedom from," says Si, as he pushes a glass against a button and ice tumbles from the fridge into it. He pours Badoit over the ice, and hands it to me. I don't like Badoit, but I sip it thirstily and place Si's hand on a tender place in my back, so he can knead it.

We are back down in the kitchen. Si is talking about his yacht. I am beginning to understand why he doesn't have ties like a wife and children. It's because he has a yacht, basically.

The only photograph in the whole house is upstairs in Si's dressing room. It is a picture of Si surrounded by the crew of *Salome*. Si is in his jeans and a navy sweater. The crew are spotlessly turned out in white ducks, with epaulettes in navy braid and gilt frogging. He is incandescent with happiness, his teeth shining whitely in his tanned face, at ease while the captain and crew stand upright to attention.

"I'm free to do, free to go, is how I see it. Who wants to see the world through the window of a Gulfstream?"

Well, I wouldn't mind slumming it in a Gulfstream, but I don't say so. It's too humbling. I don't want Si to think for a second that I am attracted by his wealth. No way. I want him to think I am utterly indifferent to it.

"Last trip I took on a Gulfstream, I was with Ed, this L.A. producer, and Tom Cruise," Si continues, even though he's just told me how tired he is of private jets. "They wanted to talk finance. So we flew from L.A. to meet with these screen-writers in New York. We had dinner on the jet. It was fabulous. Scrambled eggs with truffles, Château Lafite, the works. But all I could think was, I'm stuck on this fucking plane with Tom Cruise having to listen to him talk about Scientology for five hours, when I could be on *Salome,* with only the sea and stars for company."

"How dreadful," I say. Again, I can think of marginally worse fates than being at close quarters with Tom Cruise in the leather and walnut cabin of "Ed's" Gulfstream, noshing off a tray, but I refrain from saying so.

"So, have you finished?" I ask. I want to know, in other words, whether I can expect to see more of Si. Again, it's me doing the asking.

"Well," he says, "we're not there yet."

"But how much does refitting a yacht actually cost?" I yelp. When people are rich beyond the dreams of avarice, I can't help but wonder exactly how rich they are and how much they spend, and on what . . . and why.

"Depends on the yacht you have. Depends on the toys you want. Depends on the materials, designer, craftsmen you use," answers Si, moving in for a clinch. I can sense he is stealing a glance at his Cartier tank watch behind my back as he nuzzles the damp curls around my ear and neck.

"Let me tell you something. A yacht is the ultimate statement of wealth. A jet, a mansion, they're the starter packs for those who are playing at being rich. A yacht is for real. For the big boys. It's the most expensive thing you can have, but it gives you pleasure like nothing else."

"Is that right?" I ask, playing with his hair and stroking his cheek.

"Almost nothing else," he corrects himself. I sense I should go.

I decide to leave by the front door, as it's so busy in the garden, on this day of all days. I give him a chaste kiss on his cheek. Keep it light, keep it light, I tell myself. Don't ask when you're going to see him again. You are a married woman. With children. And with a reputation as a solid citizen of Notting Hill to maintain.

"So are you around next week?" I ask and, as the words fall from my mouth, I am cursing myself.

"Yes and no," is his answer. "Are you?"

"Yes and no," I lie, my heart sinking again. He hasn't made a plan to see me again. And next week, I am the Olympic flame. I'm not going out at all.

I close the door behind me and dart down the path into Lonsdale Gardens, keeping my head down as, if anyone's on the street, I don't want to catch their eye. I manage to get around twenty yards before someone greets me. "Hello, there, Posy's mummy," comes a sweet voice I know well.

Anoushka.

"Oh, *hi*," I say, stretching out the word into a whinny. I am pleased to see her. I've been a bit distracted on the school run, what with everything that's been going on (or not going on, to be precise), and suddenly feel out of touch with the school run at Ponsonby.

"What are you doing here?" I ask, pleasantly, thinking she must be here to do some tutoring, as all the children round here are tutored, in everything, as well as attending expensive private schools.

"I'm seeing, I've, um, got an appointment," she smiles. "Anyway, I must run—I'm late . . ."

I am tempted to look back to see which house, if any, she is visiting. I suspect it is the Moltons', who are sneaking some extra lessons for Max, who is sitting the Eton test any minute, but I press on, turn the corner, and jog back home.

Clare

Gideon's punishing me, I think, for what I said this afternoon. I accused him of deception, betrayal, lying, and worst of all, not being on my side. Given what he's done, I think I've been rather soft on him. Given what I've done, I'm amazed I had the guts to manufacture any sort of confrontation at all.

Of course, he went thermonuclear straightaway. Men always do that when they're in the wrong.

First, he asked me whether I was having my period. I was just getting something out of the fridge, and I had to grip the shiny steel column of the Smeg handle for strength.

"What are you doing to the Smeg?" Gideon asked. "Giving it a Reiki massage?" Gideon is vastly amused that in what Donna calls the timeless fabric of *feng shui,* all objects in the living world are endowed, even limited-edition Smeg fridge doors, with the living energy of *chi.*

Then he said I had no right to interfere in his professional life, and he could choose whom he pleased as clients. He said he didn't interfere with my garden-design business, did he? I pointed out that Gideon knew that I had almost made myself ill over the Avery garage all year, and he muttered something about "transference."

Having done years of therapy, I know what he means. He thinks that I became upset over the garage as a way of avoiding the real issue of my own infertility. And I know the real reason he's angry is because he's feeling guilty, both about the garage perfidy and his lack of compliance over the other thing. Gideon's always flatly refused to see the doctor himself on the grounds that, as a poor student, he sold sperm for beer money and was told by some lab technician that his seed was packed with thrashing, wiggling, champion Olympic backstrokers. I think the message I was supposed to take away from this was that the problem of our "unexplained" infertility was nothing whatsoever to do with him, and I will receive a dusty answer if I ever, again, have the temerity to ask Mr. Spermatozoa to have himself checked out.

"Well, if you're so proud of your involvement in the garage, why haven't you put your sign saying 'Sturgis Group Architects' outside?" I asked him. "You put it up everywhere else."

Instead of watching the garden sports, he came home from his meeting and lunch and avoided interrogation by watching a DVD on the plasma screen in the drawing room, lounging on the new Linea Italia sofa in one of his twenty-five pairs of identical red cashmere socks.

"It's only a garage, Clare," he repeated.

"What does that mean?" I hissed back, driven by my righteous fury that, after the last four months, during which I have even contemplated setting fire to the garage, and other sundry, criminal acts, he's neglected to tell me the minor detail that he has been appointed architect-in-chief of the edifice in question.

"It's only a garage *ergo* it doesn't merit my practice sign, or it's only a garage *ergo* I shouldn't mind so much about it, even if it is ruining for perpetuity the integrity of the communal garden?"

"Both," said Gideon, and picked up the Weekend *FT*. "*Et in Arcadia ergo,*" he pronounced, as if the subject was closed.

When the disco starts, around 8:30 P.M., I drag him out. But he won't dance. The fairy lights do look magical, their colored blobs glowing brightly in the greenery. When we cross the tired summer grass to reach the marquee, there are fewer out here than I expect. The city exhales its exhaust all around us, but the garden gives us sweet, fresh air that smells of the English countryside in summer.

Mimi is there in the same skirt and T-shirt she's been wearing all day, with the rosette saying "1st" on it still pinned to her chest, twirling with gusto while Jeremy Dodd Noble gyrates in front of her with toe-curling vigor.

Thank God we don't have guests tonight. Mimi does, as usual—she loves showing off the fact that she lives on a communal garden in W11 to her friends from what she calls, to their faces, "less favored postcodes."

She is all flushed and tanned from this afternoon's athletic triumph—and doesn't seem to mind in the least that she's got black-soled feet.

Also in the tent are Trish, who's dancing with Alexander Forster to the strains of "Dancing Queen," Marguerite, who is dancing with her eldest, Max, Humphrey the terrier, and a gang of children, including Mimi's, who are clustering around the karaoke machine and singing in tuneless voices, a racket that carries from one end of the garden to the other. Patrick Molton is sitting on a bench.

"Greetings, you two," he says, shifting along a bit. We sit down and watch the writhing and jiving in front of us, feeling grateful in a middle-aged way that we are the observers and not the observed. "How's your injury?" I ask, in relation to his nasty fall in the Daddies' Race.

"Actually, I've just been to A&E, and I've managed to break a finger as well as my bottom," he says, holding up a bandaged index finger. "Thanks to Bob Avery."

"But that's perfect, Patrick," says Gideon, excited, twisting on the bench toward Patrick and talking loudly across me. "He's American! He's a banker! You're his neighbor! *He* broke *your* finger. You can take him to the cleaners, old chum. If you don't sue, he'll think you're pussy."

"I know he will," says Patrick, looking at his finger glumly. "But that's just the sort of ghastly behavior I became chairman of the garden committee to try to prevent, on the whole."

"Have you got guests?" I ask. Most residents are like Mimi

and use the presence of the disco and marquee in the garden to invite people to a social function without making too much effort on their own account.

"No," says Patrick. "Margy and I only just got back from Casualty. We're going to try to get the boys in bed before ten, if we can. And just pray that it all packs in at midnight as promised."

At this moment, just as "Dancing Queen" is fading out, and I'm thinking, he called her *"Margy,"* two more disco-goers prance into the tent. Bob Avery goes up to the deejay, who nods. Then he holds out a hand to Virginie Lacoste, who is still wearing her Jersey-butter-colored backless sundress. They take to the dance floor as the rocking opening bars of "Start Me Up" by the Rolling Stones thump up Notting Hill and down dale.

Patrick starts tapping his foot. We all watch Virginie and Bob. Bob is doing exaggerated backward leans and hip thrusts forward while Virginie has perfected a sort of Bardot-esque wriggle that only seems to incite Bob to further extremes of movement. When he sees me watching him, he waves and does a pirouette, and I give a little wave back. I am grateful. At least we've made eye contact since that awful episode by the Lazy-Man.

" 'If you start me up, I'll never stop, never stop never stop,' " sings Gideon, his eyes on the jutting buttocks and scissoring long legs and golden shoulder blades of Madame Lacoste.

" 'You'll make a grown man *cr-y-y-y*.' "

"You'll make a dead man *currrm*," sings Patrick, and their bass voices blend in agreement.

"Speaking of which," Gideon adds, "that Si Kasparian's a dirty bugger."

"Is he?" I ask my husband. "Why's that?" I sort of know, but I don't let on.

"Well, he hasn't got any children, has he?"

"Not that I know of," I say.

"Well, what on earth would that delicious teacher at

Ponsonby, you know, that tallish one with the black hair and long legs called Agnieska or something, be doing in his house on Lonsdale Gardens this afternoon then, if he didn't have any children that needed tutoring?"

As he speaks, Sally boogies on out, so I absorb what I've heard without replying.

She appears to have recovered from her hissy fit over the trainers during the races and is grinning as she limbos toward Virginie and Bob.

"I have a pretty good idea," says Patrick, shortly. "I think the question to ask is what on earth would Anoushka Brooks"—his mouth twists down bitterly—"and Si Kasparian *not* be doing in his house on Lonsdale Gardens on a lazy Saturday afternoon."

Then Patrick spots Marguerite on the grass, hand in hand with her dear-looking middle son, Charlie. He goes up to her and leads her by the hand to the tent, where they start dancing. Unfortunately, the Stones song ends and is replaced by the new track from 50 Cent, which contains very unsuitable lyrics about hos and bitches and rape and is quite impossible to dance to without seeming old, and sad, so the Moltons give up and wander on home—arm in arm!

Gideon and I pretend not to notice and not to feel too pleased and hopeful of a reunion. Our tactful efforts are slightly undermined by all the children, who have been drinking the dregs from glasses left on fairy-lit tables and catcalling hooting remarks about parents "sexing" each other, and there is a lot of nudging about "Max 'n' Charlie 'n' Sam's mummy 'n' daddy going home together" even among the children, who seem to know almost as much about what's going down on in Lonsdale Gardens as I do.

I reach over and take Gideon by the hand.

It is time to break the news—part one, anyway.

Mimi

So.

Back in the saddle at Colville Crescent. Sitting at my desk, in our bedroom, looking out over the blowsy garden, where the trees are already shedding their leaves.

I was dreading, in a way, coming back. It's been a long six-week break first in Cornwall with the children, staying in a big Victorian house on the cliffs at Minack with Con and Gretchen and their Gang of Four . . . and next on the Dorset coast on our own in a "grottage" (i.e., rented cottage) while Ralph worked as a consultant on the Oolite site for South West Petroleum.

I complained like buggery, just to keep up appearances really, but we had the most lovely time despite everything—windy walks on beaches and cozy pubs and bracing swims . . .

And then, lastly, to Slinky and Perry in the Borders, where I ate my own bodyweight in Penrith toffee between meals (more addictive than crack cocaine). I had to, we seemed to be subsisting, as usual, on luridly pink sausages that the children complained looked like newborn gerbils, floury baps, and whatever Selina said was abundant in the kitchen garden. So it was runner beans for one week and spinach the next, till we all literally went green at the sight of my mother-in-law's trug.

We were all ravenous, all the time. In one way, this was encouraging, as it suggested I am not physically, emotionally, and bodily in thrall to a man who seems perfectly happy not to see me for weeks at a time, but in another, it was lowering, as I am now way north of nine stone again.

Anyway, we're back. Clare went on yoga safari with Donna

to some eco-hotel in Lamu, while Gideon gave some seminars on the West Coast and presumably "mentored" a succession of lissom, willing Californian girls.

Patrick and Marguerite have been in Scotland all summer, surrounded by ghillies and rods and "Brazilians" of midges, according to an e-mail Max sent Cas. This good news was confirmed by an e-mail I got from Marguerite.

"I had to allow him back," she e-mailed from Eilean Aigas. "Even if the house was so much tidier with him gone—during his three-month absence, I even imposed a Japanese-style edict forbidding any outdoor shoes to be worn in the house, which he's agreed to as one of his many conditions of return. I think you can imagine some of the others! Oh, well. Hope I'm doing the right thing and not being a complete doormat. After all, it is his house. He works all hours to keep me in the style. I want for nothing, as you know. And the boys miss him."

Virginie and Mathieu are in the Île de Rey.

The Averys are on the family compound in Nantucket.

We are all alone, it seems, on Lonsdale Gardens. The house is looking almost habitable as Fatima has been coming in twice a week and she sweetly left us an eggy golden tortilla rich with red pepper and leaking with oily orangey chorizo for our first supper back, so I didn't resent in the slightest paying her full whack over the summer.

And, as usual, we've managed to hit town just in the nick of time for the lowlight of the calendar, which goes by its local, technical name of "the dreaded carnival."

The two-day street party which defines Notting Hill to millions globally is loathed without reservation by almost everyone who lives here, all apart from Cas and Mirabel, who thinks it's "mint."

I am deliberately sitting on the garden side of the house, because if I sit street-side, I am forced to watch a parade of revelers saunter past my door, gobbling goat stew from tin punnets purveyed by Mr. Yum Yum.

Then they'll casually toss the container into my front garden or unzip their flies and pee into my rubbish bin. All to the accompaniment of pumping reggae and soca and hip hop crashing out from three sound systems on Ladbroke Grove at the same time.

No wonder, then, the property-owning class either sensibly stays away in Provence or Umbria or leaves their Notting Hill residences for the long weekend and only returns after it's safely over, and the streets are lined again with new cars, drivers waiting in Lexuses, and gently exfoliating trees rather than sole traders hawking soulfood to the great unwashed.

The dreaded carnival may be lovely for everyone else, but it's hellish for us. I'd rather still be away, too, comfortable and quiet somewhere else, with people I've chosen to be with (plus chef and driver preferably), rather than with half a million uninvited guests who lack access to proper toilet facilities.

Plus, it's hard not to resent the fact that the whole character of the neighborhood changes, if only for two days.

The shops board up their fronts, and restaurants the rich treat like office canteens, like Mediterraneo and E&O, unapologetically close, secure in the knowledge that they're not pissing off their regular clientele, because none of them are there anyway; and, if that's not bad enough, all this shutting-up-shop is followed by the arrival of half a million uninvited, marauding, drug taking, goat-stew-eating, skanking reggae lovers who proceed to commit the cardinal sin of actually enjoying themselves without having recourse to a seven-figure income to do so.

Which is unforgivable.

"If you won't come with us, we're going without you."

I don't look round. My desk faces the window. When Donna came round in March, after she'd been *feng-shui*-ing Clare, the same time she told me to lose the TV, she also pointed out that my desk wasn't in the power position and that I had to place a mirror and hang a crystal 1. so I could command the room and see the door, and 2. so I could circulate the stagnant *chi*. That was her last visit.

I think it was then that I realized that my flirtation with Eastern therapies was going nowhere. My desk still faces the window, but then I don't exactly need to turn around to see that a mutinous-faced Mirabel will be standing in the doorway, in a wisp of a skirt and unsuitable footwear, such as *my* party shoes.

I have to say, I agree totally with Ralph about their clothes. He sometimes looks at Cas and Mirabel, in their homey gear of hoodies and combat trousers or slutwear and mildly remarks that he sees the point of Children in Need but would be even more keen on Children in Tweed.

I close my laptop and sigh. I know resistance will be futile. The beat of carnival is stirring my children's blood, and I can no more stop that than I can prevent collies from whining excitedly when they scent sheep on a hillside.

"Okay, but no more than half an hour, then—I'm getting deaf enough as it is."

The music's too loud to talk, so I lead them to Ladbroke Grove, one of the main arteries clogged by floats and processions, and we stand on the corner of Elgin Cres. I feel my mobile vibrating in my pocket. It's a text.

"Ring bell of 61 Elgin and come up to Flat 4," it says.

"Okay," I text back, not knowing who it is, and not caring. It's been a long, and not particularly hot, summer.

Patrick is standing at the open door of the top flat. He hands me a cold Red Stripe.

"Coke, kids?" he says.

Patrick's fuck-flat is very nice. I say so. Not in so many words, though. "Only got it till tomorrow, so I thought I might as well make the most of it," he says. "Three-month lease expires Monday."

"Fab," I say. We all move to the window. "When's Marguerite back?"

"Wednesday," says Patrick. "She thought she'd stay up in Inverness with the boys while I came down and sorted out my domestic arrangements, which is fair enough given it's the dreaded carnival. I've taught them all how to fly-fish on the Beauly," he continues happily. "Max caught a two-pound trout, just under Lovat Bridge."

I know how much this sort of thing means to men, so I give him a moist look and clasp his arm. It's too noisy to respond, but he knows (because I'm married to Ralph) that I will at least understand if not share the joy he feels, and I really do. Then we all move to the window.

As I look down on the scene, I try hard to describe it to myself, as a sort of test. But it's impossible. The scene is too rich, too big, too dense, too seething.

Beneath us, fifty plump black women in batty riders (i.e., ultra-short shorts) are shaking their booties and their puppies (and their mittens and their kittens for all I know) to the deafening sounds of "Reggae Bump Bump" featuring Elephant Man.

I love how these women only have to twitch their bums from side to side and splay their feet, splat, splat, as they waddle in time to the beat, and they're dancing. I can sense they feel the beat not just with their hips and elbows but with their eyeballs and earlobes, as they meld with the thumping, rib-rocking, jowl-shaking pumping of the music as naturally as breathing.

I'm slightly distracted by a young white man trailing in the wake of the float. He's in ironed jeans, a striped shirt, and he's clearly in finance. I can almost see the bubble above his head that reads, "I'm dancing. People are watching me. Please let this be over soon. And please, Lord, if I get home tonight alive, I'll have Linda renew my Give As You Earn pledge as soon as I get back to my desk."

As I look down, I feel almost benevolent. I have a drink in my hand. I'm back in London. And in some ways, today's fine.

Sunday, it's Children's Day, which starts after some touching multi-faith opening ceremony officiated by the Mayor of Kensington.

Float after float is majestically processing down Ladbroke Grove, sound systems blaring megadecibels that shake your heart in the solar plexus and gently scramble the brain within the skull.

I suppose this is, once a year, just about bearable—for no more than half an hour, anyway.

What I like about today is that everywhere I look, shouldering costumes bigger and more feathery and more daring than Big Bird, are beautiful, dark children.

From my eyrie, I look straight down at a cavalcade of little girls in flamenco-tiered dresses of many colors swirling their skirts out and back, looking like anemones expanding and retracting under seawater.

Behind them, a glittering procession of chocolate-colored children in sunflower headdresses and gold-tinfoil costumes, looking just like twirling half-eaten Crunchies still in their wrappers, and just as edible.

Still, as it's Children's Day, the God squad are out in force on the corner of Elgin Crescent and Ladbroke Grove, just to put a Christian dampener on pagan high spirits, and to confirm one in the general feeling that English people are uncomfortable with any musical expression of abandon unless it involves the massed singing of "Land of Hope and Glory," bobbing up and down in white tie, and tambourines.

The Christians are wearing tabards. The tabards are shouting messages, so we proclaim them to each other in fervent voices.

"'I Recommend My Savior to You,'" says Cas.

"'I am not Ashamed of the Gospel of Christ,'" says Mirabel.

We notice that no one takes the outstretched leaflets.

"I feel like ringing Con and Gretchen and telling them to

get their asses up from Petts Bottom, this is a big missionary opportunity they're missing here," I say, disloyally, and then add, "Only kidding, guys!"

Cas and Mirabel adore their Christian uncle and aunt and cousins, and give me sharp, direct looks.

"Petts Bottom?" queries Patrick, his lip twitching.

"'Fraid so," I confirm. "It's in the Kentish weald."

Cas and Mirabel and Patrick are giggling as they try to come up with alternative slogans, designed to appeal to the crowd below.

"'What The Fuck Would Jesus Do?'" suggests Patrick. "Oops—am I allowed to say that in front of the children, Mimi?"

"Don't worry, Mum says 'fuck' all the time," Cas says diplomatically, and I mark him down for a long and distinguished career in the Foreign Office. "How about 'God Made You—He Can Also Destroy You'?" Cas offers.

"'Jesus Died for Your Sorry Ass,'" adds Mirabel, as we watch an HM Prison Service float trundle by. It is draped with a big banner on the front which proclaims "Valuing Diversity," underneath a Whitehall portcullis.

Yes, it's all right up here, with a Red Stripe in my hand, right now, but I wouldn't dream of coming again tomorrow.

Bank Holiday Monday. Tomorrow, loads more people come. And the people who come have knives and guns, so helicopters buzz overhead all day and all but the most dedicated skankers must be quite glad when it's all over, until the last weekend in August this time next year.

"Hey, I've got some news about the Avery garage," Patrick says, as we leave. The children have begun to toy listlessly with their empty Coke cans, and we are standing in the little hall. The whole place has the unloved transience of a single man's bachelor pad, with junk mail littering the mat and a faint mustiness perfuming the air.

"Oh, God, that—I haven't thought about it all summer."

"Well, I hope it's good news," says Patrick.

"The only good news I can imagine is that the council is going to pull it down after all and admit they committed a blunder of historic proportions," I reply, checking my bag is firmly zipped before braving the throng. "I mean, I just can't get over how negligent they've been, giving planning permission for a garage and not spotting it's a house and the Averys haven't even once, even for the sake of appearances, put their car in it."

"We got a trellis," he interrupts me. He can't contain himself.

"Trellis?"

"We, the garden committee, as in 'We, the People,' have put up a trellis," Patrick says proudly. "With the Averys' knowledge of course. Sally and Bob even came to the meetings—they were most cooperative in fact. Anyway, it's to screen off the garage so you can't see it from the garden and, more importantly, to screen off the new windows so they don't shed light pollution on to the precious green space that is Lonsdale Gardens."

"Oh," I say, encouragingly, not sure whether I follow the thread of all this, and not sure I even knew about the new windows, or if I did know, whether I'd forgotten. "That sounds really good."

"Then Stephen's going to train clematis and wisteria and other climbing plants up it—Clare's advising him—to hide the trellis itself. It all went through the garden committee, so it's completely kosher. According to Clare according to Gideon, if you get me, there's apparently some issue about any temporary structures over six foot in a Conservation Area needing planning permission, but as the Averys haven't objected, I don't see why the planning department at RBK&C should either. I mean, if a brand-new huge house with brand-new huge windows overlooking the communal garden can be okay, what can possibly be wrong with a flimsy wooden screen?" he asks, his voice rising triumphantly at the end.

"How brilliant!" I say. "So we have a Trellis Towers on Lonsdale Gardens. Gosh. Did you think of leylandii? Maybe not . . . anyway! Good work, Patrick."

As I'm wittering and leaving the flat, children trailing in my wake, I realize that I am pleased about the trellis, and not only because it promises finally to draw a line under the tedious unpleasantness over the new garage once and for all. And I also realize that the fact that I am pleased means I am back, not just in person after a long holiday, but in the Celia Johnson sense of the word.

I love the bit in *Brief Encounter* when Fred says to Laura, as they sit reading after supper in the sitting room one evening, the rain gusting outside, "You've been a long way away." And she says, "Yes." And then her husband says, "Thank you for coming back to me." This tender reticence is so much more unspeakably poignant and so much more English than if Fred and Laura had unpacked their marital problems and looked at them with a couples counselor, I always think.

So, yes, I've been away, but I'm back. It feels good. Better than I thought it would, anyway. I'm doing well.

And Patrick is back too, which is nice, after his excursion, with Marguerite. Less nice, I suppose, for the girl he shagged here. Unless, that is, she has managed to do the thing we are under such pressure to do all the time, which is to close the door and *move on*.

Autumn

Clare

I quite like it when term starts again in September. I like the way terms' beginnings and ends provide a contrapuntal rhythm to the natural beat of the changing seasons.

All my clients come home after their six weeks away, settle their children back into school, and my telephone starts ringing. I should be exhausted—I'm working four-hour days—but I find I am charged with energy and purpose.

Mimi called, to complain she'd been back since before the carnival as usual and while everyone else was still away, and to say what a relief it was that all the children had at last gone back.

"I'm just so lucky all three of mine are at Ponsonby and I don't have to go around sighing about being in three different places at once," she said. She seemed at a loose end, for her, and when I put the telephone down, I realized that there wasn't any point to her call; she didn't suggest meeting for lunch or coffee, she didn't ask when the next yoga class was, and it was only after she'd hung up that I realized that, for once, Mimi had rung without wanting something and, in fact, I got something out of her.

I almost rang her back and asked her over for coffee . . . but something held me back.

Anyway. Just hearing her voice, talking about the back-to-school routine, and the school, started me thinking.

Clearly, one can't hang around when it comes to education, and schools round here aren't just difficult to get into, according to Mimi—they're impregnable. It is something I must definitely bear in mind, when the time comes.

Take Ponsonby Prep, which I managed to make the subject of our relatively brief conversation just now.

When I asked, Mimi said it was a lovely school and boasted, of course, the supreme advantage of being near. She described it as coed, old-fashioned yet caring, with a catholic intake.

I think I know what that's code for. That doesn't mean it's broad church. Catholic intake means that it may be academically comprehensive but, socially, it is rigorously selective.

Mimi then claimed to be unmoved by the fact that there were so many celebrity parents at Ponsonby. In fact, she said she wished celebrity parents tried a little harder to fade into the background, and the reason they didn't was because they too clearly understood the PR benefits that followed from visibly performing an everyday duty shared by most parents in the land accessorized by a cute towheaded child or two.

Then we moved on to the headmaster, Dr. Alan Hamilton. All the parents call him Doc H. and have him over to dinner, as a matter of course.

Mimi said that he announced with some pride at the beginning of term assembly the good news that the school was so oversubscribed that it was harder to get a place at Ponsonby than a table at the Ivy—even for siblings.

I wasn't sure how to take that. Of course, the parents who had already got their children in (i.e., Mimi, the Moltons) are secretly thrilled, but as a lesser being who has not—quite yet—managed to produce a baby let alone manage to wangle a firm place at Ponsonby for it, I can see how others could react differently to that piece of "good" news. I wondered whether I could persuade Mimi to have me and Gideon over with Doc H. and his wife for a casual kitchen supper and decided that it was a stretch under current circumstances.

Lastly, Mimi told me that Doc H. was somewhat celebrity-struck, but in a very nice way.

"I'll never forget Doc H., after some movie star had dropped off her child before heading to LAX in her private jet, saying to me earnestly, 'I know everyone thinks Marla is just a Hollywood starlet, but when she's at Ponsonby, she just wants to be a *Mum* like *everyone else.*'" Mimi continued, and I could just picture the curl of her lip.

So we're back to the daily Notting Hill drill involving jostling egos and temper tantrums and private jets and alpha behavior (and that's just the nannies). As a sharp-eyed observer of some years' standing, this is how it goes.

7 A.M.   *The driver arrives to take the man of the house to the City in a three-liter Lexus towncar. (When I asked Gideon why men round here didn't go by Tube, which is so much quicker, Giddy explained that top bankers are so impatient that their private doctors have forbidden them from ever using public transport. "Taking the Tube's like illicit sex or squash. It can induce sudden fatal heart attacks," he said.)*

Driver waits in the car, its huge engine belching, in a black suit and white shirt, reading the Express, *till Daddy emerges from his £4m house with his briefcase containing BlackBerry, Prozac, Viagra and copies of* The Wall Street Journal *and* FT. *This can take up to an hour, but the driver never switches his engine off, as if there's some law against it.*

7:45 A.M.   *The nanny takes the kids off to school in her brand-new nanny car, picking up one or more children en route, always observing the code of the Notting Hill school run (according to my oracle, Mimi: no tardiness; no honking; and no nuts, no traces of nuts, nor any other potentially fatal allergens nor mood-altering foodstuffs containing sugar ever to be allowed onboard).*

8 A.M.   *Mummy drives off to Pilates or her private trainer in her Porsche Cayenne with sat. nav. and in-car DVD. On her return, she will double-park outside Starbucks on Holland Park Avenue, where she will get a £50 ticket, which*

she will stuff into the glove compartment as she sips her daily cup of soy half-caff latte.

8:05 A.M.   *The dog walker from Pets in the City rings bell to take the family pet for his nature ramble or puppy playdate in the park.*

8:05 A.M.–3 P.M.   *The housekeeper cleans and irons, often with the assistance of a Polish girl and ironing lady. During these hours, the house has to be occupied throughout the day by paid help, as someone has to be in to open the door in order to admit frequent deliveries and service purveyors including Mr. Michanichou the grocer, Mr. Lidgate the butcher, Ocado and Food Ferry and Nappy Express for essentials, Mr. Armit for wine, D-Stress Direct for Mummy's shiatsu massage, and various other experts, including a special man who weekly comes to polish all of Daddy's shoes and valet his clothes.*

3 P.M.   *Mummy or nanny drives to school to pick up children and drops them home continuously observing the NH school run rules for the way back (no sugary snacks in case children go into glycemic orbit, and no driving off until children safely back home with adult).*

4 P.M.–8 P.M.   *The children follow up seven-hour intensive school day with music lessons, music practice, private tutoring, homework sessions, Ritalin, Kumon, art classes, and so on, only breaking for some fresh air in the communal garden and a supper of organic chicken nuggets (no ketchup—ketchup is banned) and broccoli.*

9:30 P.M.   *Daddy arrives back to a sparkling home, equally fragrant Mummy and Montignac supper of green beans and fillet steak laid in dining room with heavy white-linen tablecloth, linen napkins, candles, and flowers, all to make Daddy feel his twelve-hour day in the City money factory is worth it.*

10 A.M.   *Daddy falls asleep in front of the news while*

Mummy alphabetizes the spice rack while watching
Desperate Housewives on DVD in the kitchen.

At least I know what I'm in for, I suppose.

And Gideon is being amazing about it all.

I've decided that his attitude to my plan has been so generous, so tender, and so accepting that I've decided he can have
a free rein when it comes to the major changes I've planned
for the New Year.

I'm going to get Donna on board, of course, for making
major decisions in terms of the bagua map and to make the
most of the year's energy cycle for the new house but, otherwise, I'm decided. Even though I bought it, it's his as much
as, if not more than, mine.

Mimi

Beep beep beep. Beep beep beep. Beep beep—oh *nooo* . . . morning has broken, again. Just can't get used to it after the endless summer.

Instead of getting up and getting the day off to a nice early start, I lie there, thinking and putting off the evil moment.

There was a time when ancient-looking adults (who were, I now realize with a slight shock, *years* younger then than I am now) seemed to relish breaking to the younger me the news that life speeded up as "one" got older.

One had simply to learn to try to live in the moment and make the most of now, they would tend to continue importantly, especially when one has children, because they *grow up so fast*, you *wait*, they'll be gone *before you know it.*

Well, yes. Now I'm officially biologically extinct (as is every female over thirty-five, according to the *Daily Mail*), I know exactly what they're driving at.

Yup, I seem to be buying three pairs of new trainers every other day. Yup, birthdays, Christmas, PTA summer fêtes, sports days, do indeed whiz round with nosebleed-inducing velocity. But I also find that while these gala occasions accelerate just as quickly as threatened, problem is, while they're happening, one doesn't want to live "in the moment," let alone "live the moment," let alone the new imperative, which is to "make the most of now" at all.

So much pressure!

I can think of a lot of things one wants to hurry past, not linger over. Sunday afternoons. The hours between 4 P.M. and 8 P.M. every winter weekday. All magical or mythical children's films over two hours long, with specific reference to the Lord of the Rings and Narnia cycles. Special assemblies where each child, of every age, and whatever their ability, plays an instrument, and if they do not play an instrument, peeps out "Go, Tell Aunt Rhody" on the recorder.

Nor have I ever, even once, heard time's wingèd chariot rushing near during any of the long hours I have recently spent in the school uniform department of John Lewis. By the time I've finished getting Casimir's new kit, sports equipment, and numerous other important sundries before the start of every term, an exercise that now involves a ticketed queuing system and individual time slots for all the Back to School Mums as well as the taking out of a second mortgage, he's usually grown out of it.

Children's parties. Cas's tenth birthday party, a festivity that clearly fell far short of the prevailing standard for our area (we made the mistake of having it *chez nous* rather than, say, helicoptering the entire class for a bog-standard affair at the tree-house at Hogwarts, i.e., Alnwick Castle), seemed to go on for days . . . to be honest, just thinking about children's parties makes me feel weak; other mothers round here do set the bar *so high*.

As for summer holidays, once they've finally started, after a whole month of school fêtes, end-of-term assemblies, leavers' events, concerts and sports days, they then seem to go on for longer than the Jurassic Period and, before the first day of the new year, I almost camped out on the pavement the night before in order to be the first mother to hurl rose petals at the school gates.

Plus, the beginning of the school year is always a bit chaotic. The first two weeks of September are a blur. Today, we're leaving for school the back way, through the communal garden. We're even more laden than usual, and term's only been going two weeks.

Posy is in the middle of telling me, in Proustian detail, the plot of the latest six-hundred page Harry Potter book. I am nodding eagerly at timed intervals.

I am so thrilled that any of my children read anything at all—cereal packets, Enid Blyton, Jacqueline Wilson, you name it—I am prepared to pretend to listen intently to plot summaries for as long as it takes.

We're letting Calypso powder her nose by the back door. I am about to accompany all three plus dog across the garden, then through the gate and up to school that way.

As Calypso lowers her hindquarters and Posy plows on about Snape and Dumbledore, Cas asks me why it is that when I buy orange juice without pulp, it says the equivalent of lovely smooth juice, no nasty, horrid bits on the side of the carton, but when I buy orange juice with pulp, it, like, says, contains lovely, juicy bits.

"That's a very good question, Cas," I say (my default answer, as I wonder whether I can fit this into an article). "But I'm just listening to Posy explain something . . . look at the beautiful colors of the leaves as they turn."

Cas and Mirabel roll their eyes. Posy is still childlike and delightful in that she 1. allows me to dress her in Viyella and corduroy, 2. thinks that Prêt à Manger is something to do with Baby Jesus, and 3. when asked what she wanted to be when she was a grown-up, answered, after much thought, "a dressing gown."

But I find it rather sad that almost nothing impresses her older siblings anymore, apart from things like iPods, Top Shop, football, and dirge-like songs from the band they call Coalplay. Indeed, I am just mourning the fact that they are growing up as overstimulated, materialistic London children with no imaginations and no character-forming experience of being bored even for two minutes let alone for a whole rainy two-month summer, when suddenly Posy interrupts her narrative with a loud squeal.

"Christ, Posy, careful you don't drop *Hengist*," I squeal back. "What?"

Hengist is a model of a Viking longship, anatomically correct in all particulars—curved keel; dragon's head; cloth sail; benches for oarsmen, etc. Every time Posy moves a muscle I snap, "Be careful of the mast," or "Make sure you hold it both ends, Posy," as if she's carrying a newborn baby.

Not that we made her. She's better than that. I sourced *Hengist* off a mother with an architect husband and a son, Nat, at Westminster Under School, whom I had been stalking with this aim in mind for some time.

When Nat was leaving, I casually inquired whether he would be wanting his seaworthy Viking longship (which I knew his RIBA-trained father took several days off work to make) when he went to "the Great School" or was he perhaps—I added in a meaning way—too old for it now? I'm ashamed to say I even offered to pay.

So every time the children have to make a Viking ship for homework, which is often, all I need to do is lift *Hengist* off the top shelf of the playroom, blow the dust off a bit, and *ta-daaa*!

I find this allows us to relax for a few precious seconds during weekends, whereas all the other London parents we know are cutting out bits of cloth and going to craft shops for balsa wood and waterproof paint in authentic Nordic colors.

And now Posy is bearing our trophy with pride undiminished by the knowledge that she is the third Fleming child to do so.

Mirabel continues downloading a Gwen Stefani ringtone on my mobile. Cas ostentatiously opens the Sports section of the *Telegraph*, which he is taking to school for the football reports. I remove *Hengist* from Posy's arms and she runs over to the gravelly path that encircles the outside edge of the garden. Her feet kick up the pea shingle as she runs, and her blond curls bounce over the nape of her neck and sailor-suit collar.

"Look, there's a tiny little baby bird that's fallen out of her nest, and the Mummy bird is trying to help her! Do you think she's just been borned?"

"Oooh, yes," I say, following her. "Look, children, over there on the path by Clare and Wussy's house."

A nestling, about the size of a grapefruit, with stubby chicken wings and downy feathers, is bobbling about on the gravel. As we approach, a large black bird that has been attending to the chick retreats, but stays close.

"The Mummy bird must be trying to help it off the path before Wussy comes out and mauls it to death," I say. "How sweet is that!"

"Mum," chides Mirabel. "Please. Sad."

Then the crow walks up to the nestling. We all think the crow is going to pick up the chick with her beak and pop her in a nest somewhere. We all stand expectantly waiting for the bird to prove just how far she is prepared to go to protect her own chick in a cockle-warming display of mother-love.

Then I realize the bird is a carrion crow. And she's not saving, she's stabbing the poor baby chick, gashing a hole in the chick's neck with her sharp beak.

Oh, God, this is ghastly, is all I can think. This is . . . breakfast time in the garden of good and evil!

The nestling flaps and flops about hopelessly as the crow pecks and stabs. Posy runs forward, waving her arms. The big bird hops away again and eyes us with a steely resolve I haven't seen since Trish Dodd Noble was trying to get Melissa into St Paul's Girls' School.

We walk up to the baby chick—if that's what it is. It is past saving. Not even soft-hearted Posy is moved to rescue it and nurse it back to health with milk from an ink-dropper. It is large-boned, with sallow skin goosebumping underneath stubby feathers. It is, in other words, not nearly cute and fluffy enough to deserve life, not round here, anyway.

"Mummy," Posy whispers in horror.

"G.O.," murmurs Mirabel. She is still talking only in acronyms, presumably in order to complicate dialogue with the older generations, so she says "G.O." instead of "gross out," "T.M.I." for "too much information," "P.S." for "plastic surgery," etc.

"Why did the baby bird's mummy try to kill her?" Posy carries on, shocked.

I explain that it's against nature for mothers to kill their own children, and that the horrid crow's probably not the chick's mummy but only following her predatory instincts. I think I may have used the phrase *red in tooth and claw* more than once.

"Can't we just shut up about the birds now, Mum, please," says Cas, as I open the gate at the far end with my garden key, which never leaves my possession (I am keenly aware that once it's lost, you have virtually to buy another house on the garden to get another). "I mean, big deal," Cas says. "Like, who cares? Let's just bring on the boring day at boring school, okay?"

After that, we walk to school in thoughtful silence.

But it's not over yet.

As we're crossing the road, Calypso, who is off the lead, almost runs under the wheels of a black Range Rover with tinted windows. The rear bumper superfluously announces that the six-litre vehicle is *SUPERCHARGED*. For some reason, this irritates—especially as we are all walking not driving and therefore our ozone footprint is so much smaller than theirs.

"Mum, now Calypso almost got smushed by that massive car," Posy screams.

"Watch where you're going, will you?" I yell.

Unfortunately, we are within earshot of the wiggling crocodile of parents and nannies and children making their way to Ponsonby Preparatory School.

Mirabel hisses at me through her teeth. *"Mum!"* she hisses. "How often do I have to tell you it's *inappropriate* to shout! Like, T.E.! My whole class can hear you, not to mention *Miss Forster.*"

We walk on, me mulling over the fact that everything I do is wrong in my children's eyes and pondering the moral role reversal between parents and children this sadly flags up and also the fact that everything I do remains a cause of T.E. (i.e., total embarrassment) to my firstborn daughter.

Ahead of us, manning the pavement by the white zigzags, is the usual phalanx of yummy mummies and groovy daddies in unattractive neon tabards opening car doors and escorting able-bodied and in some cases fairly large children the danger-ous few steps to the security-coded school gates during the hazardous morning school run.

"Hello, Lucy," I say. "Hello, Miss Forster," chorus the Flem-ing children.

Lucy Forster sticks out like a sore thumb. The mothers are all in their Juicy and Asquith designer jogging and yogawear and look like overgrown babies, while the uniformed children are all mini-mes of the Royal Family en route to church at Balmoral, looking serious, even stately, in their tweed tailoring and wool princess coats. In the middle of the group, Lucy is there in her sensible skirt of deep forest green, her matching green polo-neck, her lucky cardigan with Palo-mino ponies appliquéd to the front and loafers with brass snaffles on them. And Alice band, of course. Lucy is the Lone Sloane. One feels she should have a preservation order slapped on her.

"Hullo, Posypie, hullo, Cazzy, hullo, Mirabel, hullo, Mummy, hullo, Calypso," replies Lucy. "Haven't seen you for yonks," she says, and strokes Calypso. "Yonks, absolutely yonks! Did you have a good summer? Are you going jogging round Hyde Park?" she asks me, and does a little run on the spot.

"Erm, yes, I am," I answer vaguely, realizing that this is the only explanation possible for being kitted out in such a slovenly way at this time of the morning.

"But, Mum, you hate jogging," Mirabel corrects me audibly. "You're wearing the clothes you always wear, it's not as if it's special sportswear."

Unfortunately, Mirabel is accurate. These are indeed clothes that I wear every day, not for sport: a tatty pair of gray Lonsdale sweatpants, bagging around the seat, an old tracksuit top of Cas's and sneakers.

Just then, the overbearingly large Range Rover stops noiselessly on a double-yellow on the corner nearby. The driver gets out, wearing wraparound dark glasses, and opens the passenger door.

It is one of those moments when you know something very Notting Hill is going to happen, any second.

The buttery morning autumn light is bathing the fresh cream-painted semidetached stucco villas that line Pembridge Square, home to Ponsonby Prep, with a bright glow of privilege, the trees inside the garden square are soughing in the light September breeze, and a breathless expression of pure delight is wreathing Lucy Forster's face and brow.

The supermodel Belle MacDonald unfolds herself and a child's scooter from the backseat. She tactically smiles at Miss Pierson, the gym mistress, and Miss Forster, the remedial English teacher. This causes such joyous consternation that Miss Forster drops some papers, which Belle herself stoops to collect, actually kneeling on the pavement, while Lucy cries, "No no, don't you pick them up, thank you. Gosh, thank you." Belle's sports gear is in quite another league from mine, I can see that.

She is in tight black leggings and a top that is both cropped and hooded, by Adidas by Stella McCartney. On her size seven feet, she has bulky glo-white trainers which make her whippet-thin legs, rangily lean all the way up, thighs no wider than her calves, look even thinner. I check to see whether her head is too big for her body, but it all seems in enviably perfect proportion to me.

The Range Rover glides off, and Belle stands holding a scooter. I feel desperate to please her in some way, for her to notice me—Belle has that effect on us all. It's no one's fault. She ignores my apologetic smile. This is standard operating procedure when international celebrities have to come into contact with random civilians.

When Cas came home from Ponsonby without his history book last term, he told us that Tom, the son of a legendary rock god, had taken it. So I called Tom's vast residence up the road in such a stratospherically expensive part of WII they probably need oxygen masks just to breathe and tried to reach Tom's mummy, who is very thin, very blond and very Californian.

I got the full-time housekeeper, Carmen, which was a blow, as Carmen's Engleesh she not very good. Still, I asked Carmen whether Tom. Had. Casimir's. Book. In reply to this simple question, there was a ten-minute delay. I hung on grimly, imagining Carmen wandering around the huge, rock'n'roll mansion, in and out of rooms with white baby grands in them, Jacuzzis, recording studios, and so on.

Finally, the domestic slave came back on the line, her leg chains clanking audibly, and said that Tom didn't have the book. Actually, what she said was, "Tom he no have book."

At 8:30 P.M. the Californian blond called. She admitted straight out without apology that Tom did have Cas's history textbook, without which Cas hadn't been able to do his homework. "Sorry," I said, as she had cleverly managed to make me feel this was my fault and certainly not hers.

Then she went on to say that "the snafu" was all very inconvenient as they had "film people over."

After a long discussion, she grudgingly agreed to let me come and pick it up, but only if she could "have her housekeeper stand in the street with it." So we did the hand-over in the dark, in the middle of the road, as if we were standing in communist East Berlin and not in one of the premiere residential streets in London.

Yup, that's how reluctant the superrich are to interact with even vaguely normal people like me. Ever since, I've kicked myself for not simply purring, "No problem! Just have your driver drop it over," when she called.

So Belle ignores me, as I am unlikely to be of any social or educational use to her, unlike, say, Miss Pierson, who might pick her son for the football team and therefore holds the emotional well-being of the small boy in her palm.

"Come on, darling, hop on board," she says, to her son. "Let's go!" She speaks in a caressing voice that is designed to persuade all within earshot that she may be a multimillionairess with her own lingerie empire lacily straddling the globe, but there is nothing—*nothing*—more important to her than her own child.

She steps aft and grabs the handles, and they streak down the pavement in the direction of Ponsonby Prep, her mane streaming sexily out behind her and trailing a starburst of glamour and money and fame in her slipstream. The crocodile wriggles on to the gates where the cocktail chat is at full throttle.

". . . we're very pleased, actually . . . yes, Tallulah got into St. Paul's . . . a music scholarship . . . flute and violoncello . . ." (Faint cries of "Well done, Tallulah" from other mothers, who are trying not to gnash perfect whitened teeth too loudly.)

". . . Samson's got a singing role in the Children's Opera this Christmas . . . cricket nets . . . Lords . . ."

". . . no, we're going to Barbados, in December . . . the Lockharts are coming, bringing the nanny, thank goodness . . . and a macrobiotic chef . . ."

And, amid but not above this chatter, stands Belle, head and shoulders taller than the other yummy mummies, in deep conversation with Cookie, another supermodel, about the washability of cashmere babygros and how many pairs of lacy frillies a woman should have.

"I believe every woman should have seven sets of beautiful lingerie," says Belle to Cookie, with the same earnestness that men talk about the Kyoto protocol on climate change. "That's the absolute minimum . . . I personally have about fifty . . ."

They move on to how long they each take to get ready to go out.

"With me, it's twenty minutes, tops," claims Cookie. "I just rub some Vaseline into my eyelashes and pull on some jeans."

"With me, it's not even ten," brags Belle. "I don't do my hair, and just put on lip gloss and blusher. Focusing on the way I look makes me uncomfortable. I try to focus on the way I feel, and reading my child a bedtime story makes me feel great, and having my hair done doesn't."

I stand there in a clump with the children, trying to look happy, relaxed, and generally yummy as I tune in to the beauty secrets of the supermodel set.

The mother behind me is American and also eavesdropping. I can't remember her name but know she is the wardrobe mistress for WII Children's Opera, i.e., the woman gives up hours of her time and whole weekends for months, all in the sacred cause of introducing kids to the dubious joys of modern opera, and, like many American moms around here, she is a tireless, cheerleading, school-governing brownie-baker who hides an iron fist inside a velvet glove.

The mom is holding a white-and-green paper cup containing her morning coffee from Starbucks, only she's removed the sippy lid and is imbibing the hot liquid up through a straw.

"Why are you drinking coffee out of a straw?" I ask, and shoo the children forward, out of earshot.

The children surge up the stairs without looking back.

"I bleach," answers the American mom, matter of factly. "So I can't allow my teeth to come into contact with any beverages that stain."

I'm not sure what the appropriate answer to this is, but the truth is I'm waiting for Belle to hop back into the huge Range Rover and thus confirm my suspicion that she only scooters the last few yards to school . . . just to Show Off.

But the Range Rover glides away instead of chauffeuring the supermodel into Hyde Park. Belle folds up the scooter, tucks it under her arm, and mounts the steps hand in hand with her child.

She's laughing in a relaxed, friendly way with Lucy Forster, and I hear the words "nit check" and "my lucky day" float down to me.

So it's Belle's turn to do nit check for year three. That's why she hasn't legged it into the Range Rover. One would have thought she would have delegated this duty to a slavishly grateful member of staff, but no. Celebrities know exactly when to follow the principle of subsidiarity and when not to.

Rats, I think, stomping to the park.

Just when you think it's safe to slate some local sleb, they go and do something really selfless and socially responsible.

Just to throw you.

Clare

"No, no, I'll go," I say to Mimi.

I've been avoiding Mimi, for obvious reasons. "I'm meeting, um, er . . ." I stutter, and then pick up, "Marguerite. For lunch. So I'll pick up most of it in the market en route. I've got cloves, and I'm going to the Portobello Road anyway to Kingsland, for the beef fillet."

"Mm," Mimi says. "No, don't worry. I said I would. It's fine."

It's Guy Fawkes night on Lonsdale Gardens tonight. Mimi had called to see if I had any cloves. And lemons. And oranges. And a large saucepan, the size of a stockpot. The only ingredient she did have at home, she admitted, was cheap red wine.

All this is, I presume, her oh-so-subtle way of letting me know she's having to make the mulled wine for the Bonfire Night revelers tonight. Trish rang and asked her, and it's so difficult to refuse Trish. Whenever Mimi complains about having so much to do, her voice carries an undertone I know only too well, the suggestion that I cannot possibly know her burden as she has children, whereas I don't.

"Mimi, love, you must learn how to say no, even to Trish," I go on, in my most caring voice. "You've got so much on your plate. Why don't you let *me* make the mulled wine? It's no trouble. Donna's coming over for an hour, then I'm only going to run up some anchovy and Parmesan tartlets, and I'm not even making the puff pastry. I've got plenty of time."

I mean it. I don't want Mimi to have to do one more extra thing. She always has so much to do.

Though the truth is, Mimi doesn't have the first idea quite

276

how high her plate is heaped, now we have a result—I think, though, as Ralph says, there's "many a slip." It's been difficult, of course it has, but Ralph has bent over backward to make the whole transaction—well, series of transactions—as painless as humanly possible.

I grab my pink *agneau toscane* gilet from Joseph and head out. My toes feel snug in my fur-lined boots from Coco Ribbon.

I notice the builders working on houses all the way down Elgin Crescent, their radios tuned to pop songs that make me want to cry, and they look at me as I walk past, and I like it. I can smell autumn in the air strongly, the tang of bonfire and the mulchy smell of the golden leaves on the pavement, and my heart is lighter than it's been for ages.

Back in June, he was all for telling Mimi about our arrangement straightaway. He said it was only fair to her, and she would be furious at what we'd done but more furious at his attempts to conceal it.

I told Ralph we should wait until Donna had checked the Zi Wei Dou Shu almanac; and then Donna said it would be better to wait till we'd reached the autumn equinox—and Ralph, to his credit, didn't bat an eyelid at either delay.

He seemed much more understanding after I gave him *Feng Shui 101*, on the art of placement in relation to energy and cosmic breath and some other basics. I went over some of the commonsense building blocks and avoided the way-out leftfield stuff best left to the hardcore disciples, and it really seemed to work.

I explained I had enough to deal with working through all the fallout of Gideon's reaction. Gideon's in a better place now and, needless to say, Donna has been endlessly giving, to us both. I'm not talking about the beautiful fertility hanging crystal she gave me, which now nestles between my strangely bigger breasts but of her generosity with time, and in imparting her deep knowledge of Eastern therapies.

She's really put herself out to explain to Gideon, in private, exactly why we've had to take this route.

I'm in line in Kingsland, the so-called Edwardian Butcher on the Portobello Road, waiting while the woman in front of me buys a pound of green smoked streaky bacon, and I begin to feel nauseated.

Luckily, another butcher comes out from the back, where he's been hacking marrow-bones, and asks me what I want. I point and pay quickly for the beef, peeling off twenties while he's trimming, twining, and wrapping, then dash from the shop.

There's a stall selling fireworks next to the stall selling magic mushrooms underneath a sign on the awning that says *Antiquities, Curiosities, Clocks*. I am tempted to report this obvious felony to the pair of community police officers in yellow jackets I saw outside Mr. Christian's, but I don't have the strength. I must remember to conserve my energies, to aid flow to the *hara chakra*, of course.

I cut left down Lonsdale Road, en route to Fresh & Wild first, for the citrus and cloves and, next, lunch at 202.

I pass the shop window of Myla, painted a sugar-almond lilac, with its two mannequins wearing plum-colored satin push-up bras trimmed with silk the color of greengages and standing beneath shiny disco balls hanging from the ceiling. I enter on a whim, the plastic carrier from Kingsland clunking fleshily against my leg, which is, I work out, the weight of a premature baby.

I browse among the hanging rails and finger wistfully the little wisps of lace and satin and cotton, the French cami-knickers and teddies, the cantilevered basques, the thongs in packs of two, mainly in a soothing palette of neutrals: nude, flesh, pink and black. Myla's got color right. It just shows how the careful application of design and a literate eye can render the trashy and vulgar into something desirable.

"Can I help you?"

The black shop assistant keeps a respectful distance. I am examining the pleat on the hem of a nut-brown balconette brassiere, trimmed with pink. I have also just noticed that, on a sort of plinth, against the opposite wall, sits a range of sculptural, elegant vibrators in black and ivory.

"Actually, I do need a bra, but something for everyday," I answer, just in case she thinks I'm here for a sex toy but am too shy to ask. "I've gone up two cup sizes, and I need something that's pretty and supportive, but more supportive than pretty."

"Like a really good girlfriend, right?" the young woman says, breaking into a smile.

"Exactly," I beam back, marveling at how easy it is for women to bond over fripperies but how hard it is to communicate honestly over more important things, like houses, and husbands, and children.

She browses briefly in the rail along the side of the shop floor, then hands me a cotton underwired bra on a padded hanger and pushes open the door of the changing room. Mirror down one wall, bench, wooden floor. It's warm inside and I'm so hot all the time, so I push the door ajar. Then I slowly remove my gilet, then my cashmere sweater, then my agnès b vest—actually, no wonder I'm hot—and then, finally, my bra.

I'm admiring my bigger breasts with satisfaction when I hear a voice I know well rattling out a request.

"Excuse me, but are zeez all you 'ave?"

Well, not such a surprise. She's born to shop, she's French, and this is an upscale lingerie boutique round the corner from her house . . .

"And what is thees? What doz eet do?"

"Oh, that's Pebble," I hear the shop assistant reply, then a small sound as she removes it from the plinth, and a soft whirring noise. "It's for external use, as a massage toy. For both sexes."

"And zees one?"

"That's called Bone, it's designed by Tom Dixon, and it's also for both sexes. And it's fully rechargeable, no batteries. Look." A stronger whir.

There is a silence, during which I pitch myself forward and lower my breasts into the cups in the approved Rigby and Peller manner, waggle from side to side, and then reach behind, clasp and straighten. I stand up straight. My breasts are bulging out of the top, and the sides—and this is a DD cup.

"Eez eet internal, or external, zees bone?" The shopgirl gives a confiding, unshockable giggle. "Whatever, I should imagine," she says huskily. "If you don't mind me asking, what sort of use do you have in mind?"

My mind begins to race. I don't imagine for a second that Virginie's in here uxoriously trying to spice up her sex life with the colorless Mathieu, who's never around anyway. Nor can she claim to be doing some sly market research for her clothes catalogue. Still. I never pegged Bob as the sort of man who goes for sex toys. He's plain vanilla, with those very straight clothes he wears, the ironed jeans, the sporty weekend casuals. . . . It just goes to show, I think, as I take off the cotton bra and replace it on the hanger without making a sound, that you can never tell when it comes to between the sheets.

There is a pause. Virginie doesn't answer. Then she says, *"I'm looking for a present. For my girlfriend's bursday. I'm not sure she would like any of zose."*

My girlfriend or a girlfriend? My mind is racing.

"Well, can I tempt you with some lingerie?" the shop assistant asks. I hear steps as they move around the shop.

I place a hand against the wall for support. I am finding it hard to breathe. Virginie is going to come in to the changing room next door to mine and try on some lacy lingerie—for her *girlfriend*.

"A lovely choice, if I may say so," says the shop assistant, as I hear the rustle of tissue paper. Then the puff of the scent-

spray into the shiny carrier bag, which is how Myla likes to round off the purchase of anything saucy. "Very feminine."
While the elaborate transaction continues, Virginie fills the silence.

"*I came here, speciallay. I love eet 'ere, Myla's so much more sophisticated zan ze magasin Anne Summers, which is not only veray vulgair, ze couleurs are terribul . . .*"

"Well, I think your girlfriend will be delighted with this pantie set," the assistant purrs. "I've had my eye on this polka dot lacy peephole bra for some time, and the knickers are dead cute, too."

"*Mais zay're not for her,*" Virginie shoots back, gaily. "*My friend would nevair wear anytheeng like thees . . . she is veray, ow you say, sportive—she keeckboxes, so she only wear white pants, like schoolgirl, tu sais, plutôt comme Anna Kournikova! Ze lingerie is for me,*"—Virginie confides with a husky giggle—"*she loves me to wear eet, so in zat sense eet's a present for her, comprenez?*"

At some moment during the revelation which followed her spot-on analysis of the Myla appeal, I go into shock. The shop assistant is trying to flog boycut briefs to Virginie now, but it's astonishing—as if my body now registers things before the brain, and not the other way round. I have to leave.

But how am I going to leave without manifesting in front of Virginie?

I layer on my tops quickly and zip up my gilet. I push the door of the changing room softly and walk past Virginie as if I haven't seen her at all. She is playing with the speed controls of a blue rubber steel-tipped dildo with a look of deep concentration on her face. A bunch of lilies and a baguette extrude picturesquely from the basket she has placed on the floor at her feet. As I open the door, out into Lonsdale Road, I cannot resist looking back.

She is still holding Steel, the blue dildo. As our eyes meet, she pushes a button, and the tip vibrates. A high-pitched whine starts. She carries on looking at me, and I feel myself blushing —as if I've been caught doing something shameful, not her. I feel an appalled, almost aroused fascination. Trust Virginie to have passed on the dubious muscled attractions of the gingery Bob Avery and plumped for the boyish, slight, cropped allure of Sally instead.

Say what you like about Virginie—and I certainly have—but she has always had impeccable taste. In clothes, food, interiors, houses—and now I cannot fault her choice in either females or dildos either.

Virginie raises an elegant, arched eyebrow at me, as a sort of humming starts in my head, and replaces Steel on his plinth.

I go into Fresh & Wild on autopilot and start grabbing from the dewy display of organic produce in the front, piling knobbly Sicilian lemons and navel oranges into my arms until one of the security guards hands me a basket, which is the only time any member of staff has ever been helpful without prompting, so I give him a grateful smile.

As I smile at the man, I wonder wildly whether I am a lesbian too, then put it down to hormone overload. I discard the thought and mentally checklist the basket, realize cinnamon sticks are missing, retrieve cinnamon sticks from the basement, queue to pay, pack away the shopping in a Hessian carrier bag I use for these occasions, and go to 202 next door for an early lunch.

"Well, have I got news for you," I say, as my date scans a menu. I feel more together now. I don't need a menu. I've been here so often, I know it off by heart and always have the fried green tomatoes with mozzarella followed by the grilled chicken with pecorino shavings and roasted pumpkin.

But Ralph is looking drily amused to find himself, on a weekday, amid a chattering roomful of ladies who lunch, surrounded by cabinets containing lapsang-souchong–scented candles, salad bowls, and green chunky glassware and hemmed in on all sides by menswear and low mahogany tables. It may not be very Ralph, 202, I allow (I think he goes to Simpson's, the Beefsteak, and White's, in that order), but the food is good, and the gossip is even better.

"You've decided not to go through with it," he says, closing his menu, and looking at me directly, so my heart does a little backflip.

"On the contrary, we are going through with it." I deliberately use the first person plural.

"Right," he says, studying the menu again. "I suppose I'd better break the happy news to Mimi. And, in that case, I'll need a drink. Maybe a nice glass of . . . I know . . . hock."

I cast around for a waiter and notice for the first time the two young women sitting virtually on top of us, on a table for two on my right. One is plump and bottle blond, the other is skinny and bottle blond, and both are wearing low-slung combats, trainers, tight vests and hooded tops from Miss Sixty. They have Australian accents, and the topic is the forthcoming weekend of drinking in the Slut and Legless, which is what Antipodean nannies call the Slug and Lettuce on Ladbroke Grove.

As I'm hailing the waiter to order Ralph's wine, the plump blond one opens her mouth and speaks, and I realize what amazing serendipity it is that I am not having lunch with Marguerite, but with Ralph. For the second time in twenty minutes, I find myself frozen with horrified curiosity.

"And then his weird yucky wife found out he had a girlfriend in a flet, he hadn't deleted his texts, so Anoushka had to stop it," the blonde is saying. "Petrick was terrified his wife would find out, I mean, she was at the school and all, and so he pretinded it was someone else he'd known from work . . . some timp!"

Ralph is gazing across the shop-cum-restaurant with an expression of Olympian detachment, which can only mean one thing. He's listening as hard as I am.

"You know, I think the bitch wife would have gone nuts if she'd found out it was her own son's teacher," she continues. "At Ponsonby Prip! Ken you believe it? She'd have shut the whole school down! So Anoushka had to move out of thet flet on the corner of Ladbroke Grove, and Petrick crawled back to his huge pile after his three-month exile from his anal"—she pauses to try to think of the worst insult she could pay the innocent Marguerite, giving me and Ralph a moment to ponder the congruity of the words pile and anal—"starter wife."

Fascinating though this is, and highly informative too, I cannot afford to let time slip by. I know Ralph is going to tell Mimi about one part of what's being going on between us, at least—Lord forbid he ever breathes a word about the other part—but I still need to give him that little extra push.

"But I thought Petrick was, like, totally hot for her?" meanwhile continues the skinny blonde. "She said the six was, like, great?"

"So she said," replies the fat one. "But Anoushka always says thet."

"I could have found out, you know," confides the skinny one, "but I turned Petrick down, I never said, in case it got back to Noush. The man's got a six drive, at least. You can't say that for many English blokes."

"Hee hee," sniggers the fat blonde.

"Her her," sniggers the skinny one.

I clear my throat.

"Ralph," I say.

"Yes, Clare," he says.

"There's something I need to tell you."

"Oh, no," he groans. "The most ominous words in the English language. Do you have to?"

"Actually, there're two things I need to tell you. Good news and bad news kind of thing."

"If you must." Luckily, the waiter brings his drink and my still Welsh spring water (I find fizzy water tastes too strong) at this moment, and he cheers up a little as he takes a large sip.

"Well, first, not to put too fine a point on it, it turns out, that . . ." I trail off, searching for the right words.

"Clare, talk faster," Ralph says. "I've got to write a report on the spike in the gas price after the attack on that pipeline, and I've only got till close of play."

"Well, that Virginie Lacoste isn't, after all, having an affair with Bob Avery."

"I could have told you that in March." He rolls his eyes and checks his watch.

"Maybe." I sip my water, and look at him, grinning. I am enjoying this, in an as-flies-to-wanton-boys sort of way.

"I know for a fact that she's not having an affair with Bob Avery," I go on.

"Yeeees . . ." says Ralph. "Pray continue."

"Bob Avery was on a plane with Patrick the night I saw Virginie flitting around in her nightie," I say, deftly hiding the fact that I am one of the last to know that these two shared a cabin on that fateful night.

"I do fervently hope you're not going to tell me those three are in the middle of some sort of threesome," interrupts Ralph, "because I don't think I could eat this mushroom and goat's cheese thing if you did."

"I think we can be confident they're not, just as I can be reasonably confident that the reason Virginie isn't having an affair with Bob is because . . ." I pause triumphantly to deliver the knockout blow, "Virginie's having an affair with Sally."

"Christ on a bike!" ejaculates Ralph. "Lord, Heavens above! How do you know?" He then typically undermines my satisfaction by adding, "And, er—who's Sally?"

Ralph doesn't know his way round the garden and its residents like I do, but I'm pretty sure he's teasing—he must know who Sally is, especially as the dramas over the so-called garage really put them on the map.

I tell Ralph how I know, an account which ends with Ralph

pointing out that flings ain't what they used to be and begging me to tell him who else on the communal garden is "concealing Sapphic inclinations."

Then he narrows his search and asks me how I know it was Sally that Virginie was buying "the items" for, and I tell him about Virginie mentioning a girlfriend who kickboxes, about the boycut panties and so on. Then I remind him that Virginie was spotted leaving the Averys' that night in March.

Ralph is clearly enjoying this hugely, so I feel bad about delivering the bad, personal news that affects *him* next. But I give it to him fairly straight and, to his eternal credit, he doesn't seem too bent out of shape about it. I tell *what* I know and, more importantly, I tell him *why* I'm telling him, because the information, in my view, which is very much shared by Donna, helps to make sense of what we have done.

Ralph signals to the waiter, who brings the bill. "This is on me," I try, protesting, but I know it's no good. Ralph would never let a lady pay for lunch.

"Thanks for telling me, Clare," he says, taking out a Coutts card. "Though I have to say I still think there's an awful lot to be said sometimes for leaving things unspoken." He gives me a manly stare, his chin up. "Hey ho," he says. "At least now I know what sort of things you girls talk about over lunch, and what you eat, and with whom," he says, keying in a pin number when the waiter returns and adding on too much for service.

He shrugs on his tweed overcoat. "In fact, all I need now is a big strong banker husband to take care of me, and life would be complete."

We skirt past the Aussie nannies, who are jabbing two spoons into a dish of sticky toffee pudding, while I wait for the waiter to bring my gilet. Ralph wanders toward the door, where he waits, looking rather out of place among the racks of suede coats for men with tippet collars. The urgency of writing his report seemed to leave him at the arrival of his second glass of hock. The nannies are still at it.

286

"George and Sam are out tonight, some cherity benefit, so I'm on from three till midnight," says the skinny blonde. "Can't complain, though. Five hundred quid a week, cesh, it's not bed, I s'pose."

Ralph is waiting for me by the door, so he doesn't hear what they say next.

"Well, I think it's greet, as you get your own flet. Oh yiss—did I tell you the latest about Anoushka?" says Fatty. "She's moved on, after Petrick."

"Oh, yiss?" says Skinny.

"Yiss. She's found herself an unmarried man for the first time ever and, what's more, he's a billionaire. And he has a yacht," continues Fatty. "And a house on a communal garden. She called me from the Jacuzzi in his house in Lonsdale Gardens last night. To think she was a nenny like us until she got that cushy job at the Prip. The lucky cow," she concludes, as her spoon scrapes the last skidmarks of toffee from the bottom of the thick, white china bowl.

As Ralph walks me home, I use the last ten minutes in his company to relay this touching postscript, one that seems neatly to tie up the loose ends of both the Molton and Kasparian affairs to him in full.

Mimi

"Isn't this exciting? Isn't this your absolute favorite, favorite, favorite night on the garden?" asks Lucy Forster, who is bent double finding wood to put on the bonfire.

I am breathing deeply the scent of rotting leaves and wet grass and letting Calypso out before I shut her in Ralph's study before the fireworks start. She's gun-shy and hates loud bangs.

Stephen has cut a large square patch of turf within which sits a high teepee of wood awaiting immolation. I helpfully chuck on a stick; must be seen to do one's bit on these occasions. It lodges in the side of the teepee, and Calypso, who is even more of a stick-chaser than Patrick's a skirt-chaser, gives it a longing look and quivers. "So who's making the guy then, this year?" trills Lucy.

"We are," I say.

In the kitchen, as I speak, about ten children in school uniform are stuffing balls of newspaper into some pressed khaki chinos of Jeremy Dodd Noble's, and a blue, old, New and Lingwood shirt with frayed cuffs of Ralph's.

A pair of only slightly down-at-heel Lobb's brogues has been procured from Patrick Molton. Clare has added a Boston Red Sox replica baseball cap she's had Fed-Exed for the event specially. She wants everyone at the bonfire to get that we are all still so cross with the Averys in particular and the Americans in general (the garage and the war in Iraq have blended into one seamless global offense) that we have deliberately modeled the guy in the image of Bob. Just in case there remains any doubt whatsoever about the identity of the guy, she has also donated a pair of red cashmere socks of Gideon's.

At 6.30 P.M. we will all go out into the garden to light the bonfire and roast Bob, have nibbles and mulled wine and then crowd around a roped-off enclosure to watch the fireworks. I'm looking forward to it.

Lucy's right. With the bobble-hatted children holding sparklers in their mittened hands . . . the bankers main-lining mulled wine . . . the lawyers rubbing their hands and hoping for a firework to go off at a tangent into the crowd, causing injury . . . the crackle of the pyre . . . the sparks shooting orange flecks into the night . . . the fireworks exploding in the night sky, the fizzing, crackling, the *son et lumière* splendor of the annual, tradition-encrusted event . . . it is definitely a highlight of the garden year, with a lovely, fizzy atmosphere.

Ralph's coming back from Westminster early. He tried to tell me that he was having an "important drink" with Fucker and Hooray, but I told him it was a three-line whip, he had to be there, and what on earth could be more important than interacting with his own children and neighbors on Bonfire Night, especially as it was our turn to do the mulled wine?

"I'll tell you later," he'd said. I am duly bracing myself to hear that he has booked a boys' fishing trip to Iceland, no doubt the exact week of half-term.

Lucy Forster goes to help Jeremy Dodd Noble string the colored lights in the trees, and I wander in, bamboo stake in hand, given to me by Patrick Molton with firm instructions to "ream that arsehole Bob Avery from end to end."

I duly thrust the bamboo, voodoo style, up one chino-leg, past the belt and up through the torso so it sticks out of the dummy's neck. The children look impressed. The effigy looks spookily like Bob. Even I am feeling cross with Bob now.

I thought that, with the trellis, we could draw a line under the whole business. But no. Apparently, the Averys have written to the planning committee squealing about the trellis and reporting the garden committee for putting it up without planning permission, which was, everyone agrees, sneaky and unsporting of them. Last summer, the garden decided not to seek planning permission on the grounds that, if the council didn't object to the Averys erecting a massive new million-pound dwelling with underfloor heating and broadband and passing it off as a garage, then they were unlikely to object to the unanimous wish of the garden residents to put up a flimsy wooden fence to screen it off.

Turns out, the garden committee was wrong on that point.

So now Patrick and everyone else is livid, all over again, about the fact that we have to seek retrospective planning consent, for a piece of wood, requiring architects and paper-work and hours of fiddling about and huge fees.

Just now, Patrick muttered to me that if the trellis does come down, we are going not only to grow forty-foot leylandii in its place, we are going to install a nice, clean, fragrant and commodious "Canine Toilet" in the flowerbed just underneath the "garage" window.

"Mimi!" wails Ralph, as if in pain, as he walks through the back door. He is home early after all.

"Why on earth did you give that shirt of mine to the children? It's perfectly good. I was planning to wear it at least until I retired—and as for these shoes! I can't believe you're letting them put them on the guy." Ralph reaches for them, then groans, "Oh, my sweet Lord. These shoes happen to be a five-hundred-pound pair of hand-stitched bench-made brogues from John Lobb."

As he speaks, he is removing his own scuffed suede shoes (he says the rule never brown in town only applies to women wearing fake tan) and putting them on.

All the children, including ours, look on in horror. It's not done to possess anything that's been pre-owned. There are no hand-me-downs in Notting Hill, no secondhand cars, and even housekeepers reject their bosses' offerings of designer clothes unless they still have their price tags on them, presumably so they can flog them on eBay.

"You can't take them," chirrups Max Molton. "We need them for the guy."

"Yeah, we do," chorus Lilac, Saffron, Willow, Casimir, Posy, Mirabel, Zebedee, Panda, Daffodil, Aida, and Jack, all of whom are crowding the kitchen, too.

"But I need them more than he does," says Ralph, slipping them on. "I'm sorry, children, but I've always wanted a pair of Lobbs, and they fit me like the proverbial glove. I'll find you something else, if you give me a minute or two. I'm sure I've got a pair of niffy trainers upstairs."

But he doesn't go upstairs. He comes over to me and puts his arms around me, from behind. I'm standing, stirring and gazing at the oranges and cinnamon sticks and cloves swirling in the wine-dark depths of the stockpot. Neither of us speaks.

There is in his manner a stillness, a seriousness, that tells me.

This is it.

"Darling," he says. Then he lets out a heavy, pent-up sigh. "I've got something to tell you. But do you want me to tell you now, while all this is going on"—we hear whoops from outside, the crackle of the bonfire, excited cries—"or when it's all over, the fireworks and everything?"

My heart starts thumping. I do not move, I merely carry on stirring, allowing the winy steam from the saucepan to heat my face with alcoholic dew. It's going right up into my hair, frizzing it, but I'm past caring. I'm standing in my warm Aga kitchen with my nice, handsome, clever, and kind husband, a man who has given me three healthy children and a cozy home and whose only two faults I've so far detected, in twelve years of marriage, are dropping damp towels and reading out loud in a slightly overemphatic voice to the children. And I have set all that at risk by falling for a billionaire who promised to take good care of me, who told me I made him feel like a moose in the mating season, but didn't try my mobile once all summer.

At this moment, I will do anything. I will give up my so-called career, my friends, even my shopping habit. I will give up lattes at Tom's. I'll start drinking Nescafé. I'll snip my credit cards. I'll burn my books—so long as I can hold on to Ralph.

"It depends on what it is you want to talk about," I answer lightly, as if I have never, ever done so much as lusted after another man, not even in my heart. "If it's something major, such as you having Christmas with your mother and father in Scotland, I think we should wait till a calmer moment." Ralph doesn't react. "But if you want to go on a boys' fishing trip with Fucker and Hooray, then let's get it over with."

Not in my wildest dreams do I think that it's about fishing. As for Christmas, if that's what it is, which I doubt, I'd go to Perry and Slinky like a shot. For the whole Christmas holidays. And play bridge.

I'd even dance eightsome reels with ancient Lord Clydesmuir in full Highland evening dress, even though he touches my breasts as he turns me and makes my goat alert go off like a car alarm on a new BMW in Elgin Crescent, all without a murmur of complaint. So long as it's not about me and Si, I can cope.

I've never seen this sorrowful expression in Ralph's eyes before—well, actually I have, when I had Calypso spayed and Ralph cried, twice, and asked me how could I, a mother, do that to "another woman."

My husband looks around his kitchen, with that strange expression on his face, as if he's trying to imprint the scene on his memory.

The children have put the head on Bob and are sticking orangey-brown wool to it, for hair, and sliding some old trainers of Ralph's that Mirabel has located onto his feet.

Ralph takes a ladle and pours himself a tumbler of mulled wine, which looks purple-dark and blood-thickening.

"No. Let's talk later, I think," he murmurs, and heads out.

"Ralph!" I scream after him. He turns around, stiffening. And he gives me his steady look, the look that conveys that if you were going to choose any one man to enter the trenches with, it would be Ralph.

"Don't wear the Lobb brogues outside!" I call in a softer voice.

I can cope with almost anything from my husband, and Lord knows what he plans for me later. But still. If you live on the garden, tramping back into the house with muddy shoes on or wearing smart shoes out into the garden are both against the rules, whatever's going on.

Ralph obediently puts on some Hunter Wellingtons by the back door. Then I shout, "Quickly, children, it's six thirty, time to head out." I find the Cath Kidston oven gloves, and tie on my Cath Kidston floral apron.

"But the clock on the microwave says seven thirty," points out Zebedee accurately. "I know," I say, without further explanation. I haven't changed it from British Summer Time because it helps me get Posy into bed.

I remain in the kitchen for about ten minutes, putting things to rights.

Then I take the mulled wine pan in two gloved hands and follow Ralph out into the garden.

Ralph is standing by what Posy calls the "bombfire" with a glass in hand. I go up and deposit the lidded saucepan of wine on a fold-up table, then extract towers of plastic tumblers from the front of my apron and leave them alongside, with the silver soup ladle.

The fire is blazing merrily, having made short work of the

effigy of Bob Avery in his Red Sox cap, his dress-down Friday on Wall Street wear, and Gideon's red cashmere socks. The children are waving sparklers. There are Lidgates sausages and buns, accurately spiced red cabbage, Boston baked beans with bacon and molasses, and packets of crisps on the table. All is as it should be. So far.

"So, what's the news?" I say, my heart beating uncomfortably fast. This isn't helped by the fact that several lights have just blazed on at the back of Si's house. Which means he's there. Si. It is, after all, one of the communal garden gala nights, when everyone makes an appearance—but still. Just thinking I am going to see him makes me think I'm going to be sick.

"Did Crusty and Hooray, I mean Hooray and Johnny, I mean Fucker and Hooray, take it on the chin?" I'm so nervous, I muddle up all his friends' nicknames, which always annoys him.

"Take what on the chin?" Ralph says. My heart begins to sink toward my boots again. "Well, that you're not having this important drink with them," I remind him, in a light voice. I ladle myself some mulled wine and start walking toward the bonfire. Ralph follows.

All the younger children are now running in a squealing pack from one side of the garden to the other with sparklers. The older children, the preteens and teens, are looking at the fire with faces ruddy and aglow with imminent sexual awakening, as if the fire is kindling something inside them from within. I make a note to make sure that there is no sneaking off into the shrubberies during the prolonged fireworks display.

We stand gazing into the leaping flames in what I hope is companionable silence for a minute or so. Then Ralph heaves a sigh, drains his tumbler and drops it on the grass. He then takes out a gatefold, glossy folder from the extra-large pocket in his Barbour, the one designed for storing dead pheasants in. My heart soars with relief. The fire is so bright I can see that he is holding illustrated property particulars.

"Ooooh," I say, moving up to him. "What's this then?"

"Our new house," says Ralph.

"What!" I scream.

I snatch the brochure. First I feast my gaze on the front photograph, which shows a honey-stoned, sweet-faced, wisteria-clad farmhouse and a selection of unspoiled outbuildings all with mullioned windows nestling in a plump green valley. Sheep graze in a field beyond a rustic iron fence. Cotton-wool clouds dot a cornflower-blue sky and, in the distance, a heart-stopping glimpse of a deeper blue that can only be the sea.

"Live the rural dream in Hugh Fearnley-Whittingstall country," commands the blurb from Humberts, the estate agent. The fire is so bright I could be reading this in daylight.

I open the folder and start reading out loud. "Home Farm. First time on the market for forty years, a rare opportunity to purchase Grade II listed small country estate on the Jurassic Coast."

I make an enthusiastic smacking sound with my lips.

I run through its glories rapidly: "Slate floors, oak paneling, Aga kitchen, scullery, larder"—I break off, eyes shining, to beam at Ralph—we always love to joke about houses with a "wealth" of period features, before resuming—"Four bedrooms, mature gardens, walled garden, *kitchen* garden, paddock, land comprising three acres in all. Bothy and stables. Guide price . . ." I glance at the guide price, and scream.

I fling my arms around Ralph, inhaling the sour smell of old oilcloth, guns, cigars, Land Rovers, and Labradors that hangs around his Barbour. "Wowwww! How did you swing that, darling? Have the American oil people given you a big bonus? I can't believe that we've finally got our own second home! It's the dream!"

I start doing a little dance around the bonfire and singing, "We've got a house in Dorset, we've got a house in Dorset!" quite loudly, even though Jeremy and Doors to Manual are both within earshot, as is Clare. I rush up to her and hug her, and she returns my embrace stiffly.

Then Ralph marches up to me. He grabs my arm and drags me, like a naughty child, away from Clare to under the willow tree. Then he puts me up against the trunk, so we are both shielded from the garden by a canopy of branches. I hear a whistle blow and the sound of people calling to each other, "Fireworks, everyone" and "Other end of the garden, quick, quick," in the firelit dark and the generalized movement of booted feet on grass and gravel. His eyes are glittering. I begin to feel afraid. There is a loud bang, and I can see cascades of gold tracery in the night sky above Lonsdale Gardens through the winter-bare willow branches. He puts his face closer to mine.

"Just listen to me, for once, please," he hisses. "I think I can handle, just, that you have cuckolded me with a man whose command of the English language is only slightly better than my own dog's."

So he knows about Si, is the thought that flits across my panicked brain.

"And who apparently spent three million pounds on essential accessories for a floating penis extension. I can't help your poor taste, your lack of judgment," Ralph spits out. So he knows about Si's yacht, too, I think. It is all I can do, to think, because I'm not breathing. I don't dare.

"Anyway. I'm too angry to talk about that now. Much too angry." My heart sinks further. I am going to take a terrible beating in the headmaster's study after prayers for my all-too-brief moments of madness . . . which is my just deserts, I suppose, given my doomed attempt to snare a billionaire and somehow, somehow shore up my tenure in Notting Hill . . . not to mention indulge in wild bouts of hot monkey sex with a man I found (well, still find) irresistibly attractive. . . .

But Ralph hasn't finished with me yet. Not by a long chalk.

"But what I cannot stomach, now, or ever, is your adamantine refusal to live in the real world, Imogen. For goodness' sake. Do you honestly think I, we've, got that sort of money just lying around?"

Oh, God. He's calling me by my real name rather than the name that I've been called since I was in OshKosh B'Gosh. This means things are really bad. The only time he's ever called me Imogen before was when I wrote off his vintage Jag (lovingly called "The Shag") when we were courting by driving her into a parked car after I'd had one Pimms in a pub in Cookham.

"Do you honestly think, in a million years, that we could afford Home Farm if I hadn't sold Colville Crescent? Jesus Christ, woman. Where's your common sense?"

I exhale. I know this is my only chance for a fightback. I am reeling from a succession of knockout blows—but I can still feebly try to land a punch of my own.

After all, I tell myself. This *is* Notting Hill.

A spot of extramarital nookie with a close neighbor is one thing. We're all grown-ups here. But selling a rare-to-the-market mid-Victorian house—not merely a house but our children's ancestral *family home*—on a communal garden, the sort of house that a banker would trample over his own grandmother to spend his City bonus on—is another thing entirely! It's . . . *wrong*.

Ralph owns it outright but, still. We are married. It's as much mine, morally, as his. Not that I will use the word *morally* in what I'm about to say.

"Well, fuck you, Ralph," I say. "Who do you think you are, accusing me of adultery and then using that as a convenient reason to sell the children's home since they were born, the only place they know? I mean, really! Are you serious? Have you really sold the house?" My voice is rising to a shriek, but I don't care. I have to yell, in order to be heard. The fireworks are reaching a climax.

The air is smoking with the smell of burning leaves and cordite, and the sky is lit up with yellow, green, white, and pink and filled with crack, bang, and crump as thousands of pounds' worth of fireworks go up in smoke. As each one detonates, the crowd shrieks and oohs and aahs as one. Soon, the neighboring gardens on Lansdowne Road and Elgin Crescent will light the blue touchpaper, and displays of willy-waving fireworks even longer and more costly than those on humble Lonsdale Gardens will begin. Not for nothing are tonight's festivities known as the "vanity of the bonfires."

"Actually, yes," says Ralph. "I have."

"How much for?" I can't help asking. At their peak, terraced houses in Colville Crescent were exchanging hands at an eye-watering £2 million, yes, TWO MILLION POUNDS, but then, ours definitely won first prize for shabbiest in row . . .

"I'm surprised you're even interested, given how clueless you are about our finances," replies Ralph. "Though since you ask, I sold the house and banked enough to pay all the school fees and university fees for all three children and buy Home Farm."

"But what about work?" I know how much having the money for school fees means to Ralph, who has been selling off what our American friends call "heirlooms" to pay them, in arrears. "What about your job?" I say, remembering all too well the time he told me, after one dinner at E&O, that we had "largely eaten the Georgian silver candlesticks."

Ralph's face brightens in the firelight.

"The Isle of Purbeck site has finally been greenlighted," he says. I struggle to remember what site he's talking about.

"The exploration well's now licensed to test prospects at both the Jurassic Great Oolite and the Triassic Sherwood Sandstone levels with an estimate in place of upwards of two hundred million barrels, perhaps with an upside of four hundred million," continues Ralph. He so loves anything to do with oil and gas and his work that he's almost speaking to me in a normal voice, I feel pathetically relieved, even if I can't follow the thread of what he's saying that well.

"I love it when you talk science," I say. "But what does that mean . . . for us . . . if there still is an . . . us, I mean," I continue, more meekly.

"It means I'm going into industry, to work for South West Petroleum. They've been after me for ages, but there's no way I could commute from London to the Isle of Purbeck. I can, though, do the job from Home Farm and go to London once or twice a month, and still do the newsletter, from home. Home . . . at Home Farm."

"But what about the children?" I ask. "They're at Ponsonby, and we haven't given a term's notice."

"I am aware that our children are at Ponsonby, Mimi," Ralph says.

"I know you are, but if we hoick them out, we'll have to pay three times double sets of school fees. We're stuffed." At this stage, I don't dare ask the main question, which is, of course, "What about me?"

"I think that when I tell Doc Hamilton about the activities of a certain member of his staff, he'll be prepared to waive the school fees for next term," says Ralph. He glances over to Si's mansion, which is blazing like the *Titanic*. "Which brings me to the next piece of bad news, Imogen."

Which I think I might have guessed already.

Through the willow branches, I, too, look over at the lights at 104 Lonsdale Gardens, the Kasparian residence. Golden light pours out from the architect-redesigned windows. There are two figures standing silhouetted on the balcony, and one of them is smoking a cigarette.

The other is a willowy young woman with sleek dark hair in a demure princess coat. They are watching the display, which is reaching its crescendo with the Catherine wheel, followed by a firework that whizzes along a string and back. This, for reasons lost in the mist of time, is known as the "Flying

Pigeon." As each firework detonates its ordance, the faces of the happy couple are illuminated—and everything is illuminated.

I feel as if the bottom has dropped out of Lonsdale Gardens. I lean against the willow tree for support and close my eyes, as I grapple with this new horror.

Si has his arm protectively around Anoushka's narrow shoulders. He is blowing his smoke away from her face, even though the air is filled with the smoky tang from the bonfire and the sausages and the fireworks anyway.

Tears prickle at the back of my eyes. I don't want Ralph to hear the sob in my voice. "Fire away," I say to my husband. "It can't get any worse, frankly."

"Yes, it can," says Ralph. "Your smoothychops prick of a lover has been two-timing you with Posy's teacher."

I don't answer.

"Who has landed on her feet after being ejected from her cozy Ladbroke Grove fuck-flat, where she was graciously accommodated by Patrick Molton. The easier to service her in."

I continue to maintain what I hope is a dignified silence.

"And they're getting married on his yacht on Christmas Day," Ralph says. "Your lover and Posy's teacher, who happens to be Patrick's ex-mistress. Isn't that cozy?"

"Won't it be a bit cold on deck?" I hear myself asking.

I can't think what else to say. And I do think that the mooring on St. Catherine's Dock in the City, which is where *Salome* was when Si last mentioned her, will be a little bleak at Christmas.

"Not in the British Virgin Islands, I shouldn't imagine," says Ralph. "They've got to do it by Christmas, because the silly bitch is in pup, according to Clare. She's sprogging in March."

I struggle to recall Anoushka looking anything but regally slim at school, and fail. Some women reach term without being visibly pregnant at all. Clearly, Anoushka is one of them.

"You women are all the same. All you want to do is find a man and . . ." he pauses, struggling to find the right word . . . "and then, as soon as you've got him in bed, you *sperm-nap* him." I wonder where Ralph found this awful expression from. And why he sounds so worked up about Anoushka's pregnancy.

"You seem to know an awful lot about the happy couple," I say, in a cold voice. "May I ask how?"

"The new purchaser of 67 Colville Crescent told me all about it," answers Ralph.

"And who is he?" I demand to know.

"She, actually," says Ralph.

"All right then, Ralph, who is *she*?" I repeat, shouting, and lower my voice quickly.

The display is over. The crowd is walking swiftly away from the roped enclosure, murmuring, away from the little tent where my stockpot of simmering mulled wine lies empty amid the wreckage of the wintervalian feast of Lidgates' finest chipolatas and red cabbage.

"I've sold it to Clare," he says, almost sulkily. "For more than two million." I look around for Clare, but she's gone inside and, no doubt, tonight she has locked her back door carefully behind her.

Only a few teens are left, chucking sticks onto the embers. This garden's fireworks are over—and the Fleming family fireworks are no doubt about to begin.

And that will be it, in Lonsdale Gardens, until next spring.

Winter is a dead time. Nothing happens, as all the children and adulterers stay inside, and it's almost possible to forget that there's a big green space out here at all, except for after Christmas dinner, when engorged families might stagger from the groaning board to take one ceremonious turn around the path before collapsing in front of the *Little Britain Xmas Message*.

For the next few months the five acres of grass and trees and flower beds, and new compost heap and shrubby borders, will wait, under their blanket of snow or brittle coating of frost, receiving only weekly ministrations from Stephen and occasional reconnaissance by Clare, and dog packets, until spring—when the first shoots of new life, the thrusting crocuses and primroses, the damp green grass and soft air, bring the children and lovers and meddlers out to play again, and a new garden year begins. Only next year, it will all be different.

And minus me.

Spring

Clare

I send a text to Gideon in New York to call me as soon as he wakes up. Then I send a text to Donna. "Great news. Am coming over to celebrate!! Put kettle on, Clare S."

Donna's got a new flat in Shepherd's Bush—I know because I had no cash to give her at my last session, and so Donna texted me the address to which to send a check. I've never been there. Which isn't surprising. Since she's been sensibly concentrating less on *feng shui* and more on acupuncture and herbal medicine and holistic design, she's almost exclusively doing home visits with her clients, which is lovely, as her presence is so calming. She doesn't text me back, but I've got to tell her my news, in person.

I'm pregnant! At last! Of course, I know it's early days, but I just know that this one is a stayer. I was so upset that I miscarried on Bonfire Night, but this time, I've done everything right, and I was pregnant again by early in the New Year, by the same method, I suspect (it's impossible to know for sure, unless I do a DNA test which, for obvious reasons, I will do my utmost to avoid).

I switched to the whole wheat grain diet and drank eight glasses of water a day: it made me bloated and my chest inflated so much that Gideon started openly referring to my "rack." I ate so much oily fish I thought I'd develop gills.

It's such a relief that I grasped the nettle over the house situation. I'm sure I've done the right thing. I'll never forget, in the spring of last year, when Donna gave it to me straight.

"You're yanging yourself to death in this house," she pointed out. We were sipping green tea in my sunny, peaceful kitchen one morning in April, as we gazed out at my *potager*, with its promise of wild garlic, columbine, and salvia interspersed with herbs and lettuce and spinach.

"It's all sharp edges, corners, stainless steel, and stone floors. There are no pictures on the walls to soften the atmosphere. All the finishes are speeding up the *chi* too much. The crystal is a start, but you need to do more. You need somewhere with soft furnishings, wooden floors, carpets, rugs, preferably with children and a pet, musical instruments, with cream rather than white walls. In the kitchen, your range is too near the sink, your stove should be positioned to the east to capture the tree *chi* energy of that location," she went on.

"What you've described sounds ominously like Mimi's house," I said.

"Well, what you need is exactly like Mimi's house," Donna replied. "It's time we tried extreme *feng shui*, my dear. Couldn't you consider, I don't know, some sort of *life-swap* for a while, where you and Gideon move into her house and she moves into yours while you carry on trying? I know it sounds mad, but it could be your only hope. Obviously, you'd need to give the place a thorough going-over and clear-out, of course, before it could be habitable for you and Gideon."

"Are you kidding?" I replied. "She'd trash the place. She's not nearly anal enough. I only allow her in for coffee and grown-up supper, and even then I have to supervise her fairly closely. And they've got a dog."

"Well, you should think about it," said Donna. "I mean, the master bedroom in Mimi's house doesn't have an ensuite, and it has that dreary green Flemish tapestry . . . but it's all very *yin*, you know. As I don't need to remind you: Mimi and Ralph had three babies in six years. Your bedroom is all shiny surfaces. You have a bathroom, or should I say wet room, ensuite, and you don't even have a door to separate your sleeping and washing areas. Don't you see how that literally introduces a dampener on things? And you've been trying to conceive for what, five years . . ." She trailed off, and gave me a meaningful look.

Of course, Donna was spot-on. I couldn't stop thinking about what she'd said, and I realized that she was right. I couldn't stop thinking about how Trish and Jeremy were going through a bad patch. Donna came on a home visit, and she went through their whole house with a dowsing rod and discovered the problem: their new bathroom was, quite literally, an open sewer. The builders had left a cap off the soil pipe so all the *chi* was fetid and stagnant.

Obviously, they called in the builders, first, but second, Trish went with Donna to buy an amethyst to hang there to dispel the *sha chi*—and it worked. Jeremy got a pay raise literally the next day, and Trish's Shropshire house was featured in *House and Garden* a couple of months later, which given the lead times of magazine production schedules, dates the uplift in their fortunes exactly to Donna's visit.

In my bones, I knew what Donna had suggested wouldn't just unblock my energy channels. It would also sort out Ralph's financial problems.

All I had to do was make him an offer he simply couldn't refuse, so I did. End of October last year. I offered him the full whack, top dollar. Two million plus.

I emptied my portfolio of shares. I liquidated everything. It was worth it just to see his brow clear the day we finally exchanged contracts.

"You know you're paying me way over the odds?" he said, running his hand through his brown hair, leaving it ruffled like a naughty schoolboy's. Ralph is too honest not to point out he thinks I am paying him more than his father's old house is worth.

It was the day his solicitor had called to tell him the balance had arrived, and we were having a quick coffee in Inn the Park, in St James's Park, near his office, to iron out the final wrinkles.

"Of course I do," I had answered.

"But why?" he said.

"Because you're worth it," I had answered. "And because of the extras. And the top-ups," I'd added, using his phrase.

After the miscarriage on Bonfire Night, I asked if Ralph wouldn't mind repeating our earlier transaction until I got a positive result again.

He was no trouble about it. He said it was a lot more pleasant and considerably cheaper than topping up Mirabel's mobile phone, and he would carry on "supplying the needful" for as long as I wanted.

"Well, I'm jolly grateful, I can't deny," he said, as we watched some greylag geese waddling onshore and shared a slice of celebration shortbread. "I didn't realize the Fleming, er, fixtures and fittings, bits and bobs . . . not to mention the odd, er, *top-up* were worth so much. My *feng shui*p has finally come in."

And then he said that as he was two and a half million in the black, we might as well push the boat out and have another cappuccino and slice of shortbread on him to celebrate.

Still no text back from Donna. I just can't wait to give her a hug. And her present. I've found a perfectly hideous pair of earthenware clay birds kissing, and I know that's the sort of thing she likes. I know just what she'll say when I present them to her—something about how romantic figurines boost the playful romantic energy of the west.

Well, here I am: 23 Stowe Road. I'm looking at the lists of names on the buzzer. I'm looking for her name, Donna Linnet. There's only a D. Thrush, though, in the basement. I try that, while getting out my mobile to call her again.

The sound of bolts being unfastened, of double locks unlocked. Then a door below me opens. "Who is it?" comes Donna's dear, clear voice. It lifts my spirits just to hear her—I'm always a bit nervous in Shepherd's Bush. Coming from the very smartest part of Notting Hill, it's all a bit gritty for me around here.

"It's me—Clare!" I say, and descend. The steps are slimy with moss and, in the well of the house, it smells damp.

Donna is standing just inside the door. Her face has that lit-from-within quality that makes her so attractive, like a Halloween pumpkin almost, and her blond hair gleams. Her eyes are clear and blue, empty of toxins and full of compassion. She is smiling, pleased to see me as ever—but she's not holding the door open as I expect and welcoming me in.

"*Namaste*, Clare," she says. "I wasn't expecting you, is everything all right?"

"*Namaste*," I reply (this is the standard salutation of the yoga practicer). "I did text to say I was coming."

"I've lost my mobile," says Donna. "I left it at Marguerite's yesterday."

"Things are more than all right . . . can I come in for a second?"

There is a hesitation.

"Of course," says Donna, opening the door wider. I step inside, into a small hall. It is very dark, and full of coats, and boots, a shopping trolley, and a fold-up bike. There are umbrellas leaning against the walls, and a loo that smells faintly of damp off to the left. A litter tray emits a high odor, so I breathe through my mouth.

"Not much flow of *chi* here," I joke. But Donna doesn't reply and leads me into the main room, which has an unmade sofa bed, piles of books on the floor and a TV. I immediately notice that the TV is not only positioned so it faces the bed head and sends radiation straight at the sleeping Donna, but it's on, and what's more, it's tuned to *Trisha*. Most of the floor space is taken up with a rowing machine.

Which is all most odd, as, according to Donna, a bedroom should be a restful cocoon, free from the following: spiky plants, exercise equipment, electrical items, and sharp objects.

I suppose some of my shock must have showed in my face, as Donna opens her mouth to talk.

"I've got you a present," I say, forestalling her. All I want to do, to be honest, is give her the clay figurines and get out of there. I'm pregnant. I've bought a house. At least one of those developments, perhaps both, is because of her.

But, right now, I cannot believe what I am seeing. I cannot believe this sighting of Donna Linnet in her own habitat. Donna Linnet, who makes an extremely good living telling people to knock down walls, move bathrooms and position ourselves at all times to capture the positive *chi* energy that flows from Heaven to Earth. Look at her living conditions! Clutter, cats, litter trays . . . there can be no doubt she is a fraud and a charlatan. I mean, there's even a copy of *The Marks & Spencer Little Book of Feng Shui* by her bed—and this is a woman who claims to have studied oriental therapies for *seven years*.

I find it hard to look at her.

I open my bag and hand over the clay pigeons, wrapped in tissue paper. Donna takes them with a low cry of pleasure and half closes her eyes. She keeps them in her hand. I have decided not to tell her about my pregnancy after all. Doing so now will be, I fear, bad karma.

"I know what you're thinking, Clare," she says. "God, you're such a bad actress. You think this is my flat, don't you?"

"Well, isn't it?" I ask, trying not to look around, trying to keep my expression neutral. "Aren't you D. Thrush?"

"It's my sister Danielle's," says Donna, pointing to a large photo of a young woman exactly like Donna, only a size up, joyfully embracing a delicate black female with a shaved head. "I always hated my surname, so I changed it to Linnet. Still a songbird name, but completely different energy, I felt."

Something inside me softens. "The linnet's warble, sinking toward a close / Hints to the thrush 'tis time for their repose," I recite. "Wordsworth. I think if I was called Thrush I'd change it to Linnet, too."

310

"Wow, that's beautiful," breathes Donna. "You are clever to know that."

"Helps to have read English at Cambridge," I say, smiling now, feeling better.

"Danielle's in the Himalayas, on a hiking trip with her girl-friend, Somalia. It's a sort of prenuptial honeymoon—they're getting married, well, they're having their civil-partnership ceremony at Christmas—it's so great, isn't it? I can't wait. And I'm cat-sitting while my new flat in the Portobello Road's being refurbished." I ask what she's having done.

"I'm installing an outdoor shower using rainwater on the roof, replacing the loo with a wet room, and doing some other little improvements, like creating a meditation space where I can get into the zone for some proper chanting and contem-plation. I'm greening it, basically, taking down the satellite dish and replacing it with a wind turbine. I can't wait to get back in there. Green tea?"

"Actually, a *chai* would be lovely," I say. "If you've got the wherewithal to make it."

Then I tell her my news, and she explodes like a firework. Tears run down both our cheeks and we grip each other in a long, silent hug. We both mop our eyes, and I clear my throat and ask for *her* news in an enough-about-me voice.

She tells me that she's been round to the Moltons, and Patrick's agreed to have the entire house *feng-shui'd*, even though Marguerite has only just finished redecorating—she does it on a loop, like most Notting Hill housewives. As soon as the builders finish one look—steel, limestone, marble, rubber—it's time to rip it all up and start over again, with a new interior designer.

"You see, I could immediately sense that the downstairs toilet, the one Patrick calls the Rod Room and where he hangs all his framed Eton team photographs up and down the walls and keeps his fishing stuff, will have to go," continues Donna.

"Go where?" I ask. "What do you mean?"

"They'll just have to move it, reposition it somewhere else. It's no big deal. If the Taiwanese government's just shifted the entire capital lock, stock, and barrel on the advice of a *feng shui* guru, I don't see why the Moltons can't move the gents."

"I still don't see why, though . . ."

"The first thing I did was to compare the floor plan of their house to the bagua octagon, which is how I start with every house, and it leapt out at me. Patrick's not going to get the seven-figure bonus he's looking for from Goldman Sachs unless they reposition the loo, because the toilet's sitting over the money corner."

"Oh," I say, sipping the creamy sweet *chai*.

"And what this means is, every time one of the Moltons flushes the toilet, his wealth is going straight down the pan."

"If you put it like that," I say, "I'm sure that Patrick will give the go-ahead. 1. He's desperate for Marguerite to be nice to him again, and 2. like all extremely rich people, he's always in the market for new ways of saving his money."

I leave Donna and get back into my new Prius to drive back to Notting Hill, to the house, to rest. It's spring. If all goes well, my autumn crocus, Junior (who I am planning to call Gertie, if it's a girl, after Gertrude Jekyll, and Joe, after Joseph Paxton, if it's not), will be in her pram, out in the garden, under the willow, by this time next year.

I haven't decided what, exactly, we should do with the Fleming house. It is just sitting there, empty, since we refurbished it. We didn't do much—I just had a team from Gideon's firm rip out the Aga, the tacky country kitchen, the fitted cupboards, the dirty carpets, the dusty curtains, the paneling in Ralph's study, and do a very simple job on it, the minimum.

And we had to replace the bathrooms, of course. Donna

came in (she found a ghost in the downstairs loo, and we had to buy a very expensive amethyst crystal to move him on), and I felt it was right to pay her at least 5 percent of the budget.

Gideon is keen to sell it at a huge profit now it looks like a posh house rather than a seventies time capsule, but I'm holding him off. Of course, we could make a big turn on it. But I don't want to, and not merely out of respect for Ralph.

As I've explained to Gideon, we need it. After all, when Gertie is born, I'll need somewhere for a maternity nurse and a nanny to sleep, and there's also the question of Fatima.

I don't like the idea of her having to commute to and from the Golborne Road, getting tired, waiting for buses. I want her to be completely alert and rested when she's on duty, and I want her to work full time—so my plan is to keep the old Fleming house as a combined office space for me and a flat for Fatima and the nanny.

"What, you mean we keep the whole house as a separate residence, pay the community charge, in W11, just for your vanity garden design job and the staff?" Gideon demanded.

I soothed him, told him it was a great idea, and how convenient it would be, and that everyone around here is too psychologically fragile to share houses with the paid help if they can afford not to. He bought it.

Still, I can't believe I persuaded him. I can just hear Mimi's reaction.

"You may have taken slightly longer than the Jurassic period to get pregnant, Clare, but I've never known someone turn from a quite normal, unscary person into a Notting Hill Mummy quite as fast as you."

Spring, the Following Year

Mimi

"So, come on, give me all the gossip," I say to Marguerite, invitingly. "I've been away for fifteen months, so I'm expecting a full update. How's the new crop of babies?"

I have got out a large tray, and as I talk I'm loading it with Cornishware mugs, impressively matching sideplates, butter and clotted cream from the marble in the larder, homemade jam (homemade in this home, no less), a sugar bowl, and a cake Mirabel and Posy made yesterday with their new Hugh Fearnley-Whittingstall family cookbook, which we use all the time now, of course. When in Rome . . .

The golden scones—both crumbly and buttery, though I say so myself, since I discovered a lighter touch at baking—are cooling on a rack on the deep windowsill, beyond which I can see Ralph snoozing on his back on a tartan rug.

The Emma Bridgewater cream pottery gallon teapot is sitting on the kitchen table, lapsang souchong already spooned in, waiting to receive two kettles' worth of boiling water. Next to it is a mixed bunch of flowers and ferns from the garden, which Posy has stuck into an old enamel milk jug. It's taken over a year to get the place right, but now each room is a tableau straight out of *Country Living*, and a strange contentment, a contentment I never knew it was possible to feel, steals over me.

The window is open, and a fresh sweet breeze blows through the room, with its ancient flagstoned floor and laundry rack, upon which a lurid assortment of darling Mirabel's unsuitable fashion items, including her first proper bra, are drying droopily among five pairs of jeans and innumerable odd socks. The smell of clean country air mingles with the toasty smell of scones and warm laundry and, if I sniff deeply, I catch a whiff of woodsmoke from the drawing room, where we like to slump with Calypso after an exhausting day doing very little and seeing no one.

I lift the shiny silver lid of the Aga and slide the kettle on to the hotplate. "Tea in five minutes," I shout through the open window.

Posy is on Trumpet, her shaggy Exmoor pony, in the orchard. She isn't wearing a hard hat but, if she falls, it will only be on the soft ground of West Dorset. Casimir, who loves bowling and plays cricket for the village team, is bowling to Mirabel, who has discovered she loves batting. And swimming in the sea. And lying on her back in the orchard reading *Black Beauty* . . .

"I said it was tip and run, silly," he shouts, as she thwacks the tennis ball over the fence and stands there like a dummy.

"Can I help?" calls Ralph without even twitching.

"No," I shout through the open window, still on the phone to Marguerite.

"You first," she says. "So . . . how's it going in Dorset?" What Marguerite means, of course, is, How is it going since Ralph sold your home from under your feet to your best friend, behind your back, and bought a farm in the West Country? And how is your marriage going since Ralph was told, again by your best friend, that you'd been screwing the billionaire next door? In other words, nothing too close to the knuckle!

"The house is absolutely peachy," I say. "You must come. It's this old stone farmhouse with the proverbial wealth of period features. Ralph's idea of bliss, and now mine, too. It's amazing. Back in Notting Hill, I literally couldn't conceive of anyone wanting to live anywhere else than Notting Hill. You know how difficult it was getting me outside the confines of W11—I mean, even W2 was alien territory . . ."

"Still is," says Marguerite. "I try never to cross the line over Chepstow Place into Westminster, even now."

"I was incredibly small-minded, had no horizons at all, no spirit of adventure. But now . . . it's lovely. We all have space to breathe. The children all have their own rooms. I walk up the hill behind the stables, and I can see the sea, but I can't see another house. Posy has a pony, and Mirabel is, thank God, almost back to normal now—it's wonderful, she's so much nicer in the country. We don't have to interact with anyone—apart from the Bodens . . . did I tell you they are the nearest neighbors? All the children have started hunting together . . . and we both love Sophie and Johnnie, of course . . . isn't that a *hoot*?"

Marguerite makes sounds to convey that it is.

"You know, I really thought I'd miss the communal garden, the turf wars, the infighting, the socializing, not to mention the lesbian intrigues, but I don't. Ralph was right. It was time to . . . move on. I'd never have done it myself, and I'm glad it happened. If not the way it happened, which was a bit scary."

"I know it was," says Marguerite. "I was really worried about you. And Ralph."

"God, so was I," I say. "I thought I was going to get my marching orders. That Bonfire Night. Ralph tells me he knows about Si. And he tells me he's sold the house to Clare. And then I go round to Clare's in a fury and find an ambulance outside, waiting to take her to hospital, so I don't even get a chance to thrash it out with her. That was a great evening, on the whole."

"And how are you and Ralph?"

"Better," I say, staunchly. Marguerite is in the picture about me and Si, but no one else on the garden (I pray) knows. "I have to say, being married to a member of the upper classes who regards disloyalty as far worse than infidelity has been a great blessing. His father's had mistresses since Ralph can remember and of course Slinky's been the mistress of some belted earl for years." I say "of course," but I actually only found out when we had our problems over Si and the move and so on.

"That's not to say we haven't had our sticky moments, though," I continue. "Ralph kept saying it wasn't the fact that I'd slept with someone else that upset him; it was the fact I'd allowed myself to be seduced by big money that really upset him. There was some truth in that, I accept now, but the truth is, money *is* terribly sexy. Ralph doesn't understand that."

"I know," Marguerite sighs. "I think it's just too threatening for men, that."

"Nor did I let on that I made all the running after Si anyway, and not vice versa."

"Did I tell you that I saw Anoushka, too, that night?" suddenly asks Marguerite.

I'm not sure what to say. I thought that the identity of Patrick's "floozy" was still under wraps. I didn't think Marguerite knew. My pause is a giveaway.

"What, you didn't think I didn't know who Patrick was seeing, did you?" she shoots into the silence. "I knew in five minutes flat, Mimi! I hired a private investigator. I'm not dumb. I had to. Once I'd found out that he was screwing Charlie's teacher, I had him over a barrel. I mean, my family lawyer told me that it amounts to *virtual child abuse*. I could have taken him for everything. And more. He's been putty in my hands ever since. Ask Donna."

"I haven't seen Donna for years," I say. "I'm *beyond* Donna now. You told me when we had lunch in Fresh & Wild that you didn't know and you didn't care who she was."

"I lied, Mimi," says Marguerite.

"I don't blame you. Anyway. So what did you say to Anoushka?"

"I didn't say anything to *her*, she came up to *me*, holding a sparkler. She was with Posy, in fact. Then she said, the silly cow, 'Do you still hold me responsible for the breakdown in your marriage?' and I just looked at her and said, 'You flatter yourself.' Then I very pointedly went up to Patrick and gave him a big kiss. She looked mildly put out, I must say, and she made a big point of snuggling up to Si during the display, later."

"Well done," I say, removing the kettle with one hand and pouring water in the teapot.

"What's the baby like?"

"Darius," says Marguerite. "She keeps coming out into the garden with him, showing off, very Queen of the May. You wouldn't know for a second that she'd been sacked from Ponsonby for screwing the father of a child in her charge. She's very much at home, obviously, in the Kasparian residence in Lonsdale Gardens. She keeps saying that as soon as she's less tired—even though she has two nannies and a personal trainer—she's going to start doing some serious charity work."

"Of course she is," I say, finding the cake knife. "Of course she is. And how are the Dodd Nobles?"

"Well, thank god, I've persuaded Patrick to hand over the chairmanship of the garden committee to Trish," she reports. "That business over the trellis was the last straw. I was fed up with him being chairman. I made him write letters, to the Dodd Nobles and Forsters—not the old Forsters, but to Priscilla and Alexander, who've moved next door to your old house, now Clare's new house, since he became shadow home secretary and very busy and important—and to everyone else round the garden. In the letter he said he'd done it for four years and he was going to resign.

"Anyway, no one wrote back, which was par for the course, as it's such a poisoned chalice, so he sent out another letter saying that if one of *them* didn't become chairman, then *an American* would. The prospect of Bob Avery or whoever being in charge galvanized everyone. Jeremy and Trish moved pretty fast after that. It's such a relief not to be caught up in garden wars any more. Especially since the Averys took the garden committee to court over the trellis and, naturally, the only resident who refused to sign the petition to keep the trellis was . . ."

"The foxy Frenchy," we say in unison, and then giggle. As I hear her laugh, I realize what a rare sound it is.

"La Belle Virginie," I say, transferring the scones to a willow-patterned plate. "Is she still going at it like the clappers with Sally Avery?"

"Nobody knows," says Marguerite. "And since Clare's in baby bliss with baby Joe—who is an absolute sweetie by the way—there's no one around to do our spying anymore. But Clare does have a theory that Virginie is pansexual or bisexual or something. She seems to think Virginie's not just having a thing with Sally but she's had threesomes with both of them, Bob and Sally."

"Oh, God, I must ring Clare," I say. "It's too good, all this gossip. I'm so out of the loop. I've got to catch up. I'll give her a call. I might even get her here for a weekend, to do the garden, give me some ideas." As I speak, I imagine a pleached lime walk . . . an espaliered orchard . . . the neat bushy rows of a Peter Rabbit vegetable patch bursting with crunchy green goodness.

"I think you should, you know, Mimi. You were such good friends."

"I know. We were. And what's the small matter of her stealing my house and my housekeeper between friends, eh?"

I say good bye to Marguerite, who has allowed my retrospective promotion of Fatima, who came to clean three times a week, to the position of housekeeper to pass without comment. I haven't asked about the Alexander Forsters or whether the Averys ever actually parked the kids or the Chrysler in the "garage," or about Patrick, much, or about Clare's baby, or about Si and Anoushka, or what Clare's done to what was my house.

I also make a mental note to call Marguerite back, at some

point, to ask whether it's true that Gideon and Donna have . . . become close. I wouldn't be surprised.

Frankly, if Gideon and Donna have found love over recycling gray water and solar photovoltaic panels, well, good luck to them. I can't find it in me to feel too sorry for Clare, especially as Clare has got my house, my housekeeper and now the crowning glory—the baby she always wanted.

I stand in the dark hallway looking out into the garden beyond, a bright green idyll beckoning me, full of sunlight, spring flowers and waving blossom. Before I step over the stone threshold, I allow myself to think back.

Back to Bonfire Night, when we lay in bed, like marble effigies, side by side, not knowing when to begin, both seeking refuge in silence—which I was the first to break. I attacked him—best form of defense—over the sale of the house to Clare.

Ralph mildly pointed out that, like it or not, it was his house; and that he was beginning to worry that he'd need industrial heavy lifting machinery ever to get me out of it, and that he'd decided a *fait accompli* was the only option I'd left him.

He also said something wise—about Donna, amazingly, who, it turns out, sort of brokered the deal between Clare and Ralph.

He said he'd been completely skeptical until he realized that she was just a New Age management consultant cleverly persuading us to pay her to tell us things we already knew. He said that when Clare made the proposal to buy our house (apparently, there was endless chart consulting and dowsing and so forth that had to go on in secret), what she was saying, in so many words, was that *Clare* wanted what *I* had.

That made me think. It made me think a lot, in fact.

Then he went on to say that the reason everyone carries on using her is because much of what she says is common sense and not Eastern mumbo-jumbo at all, and we're all so unconfident about our own instincts that we only follow them when we've paid someone £100 an hour to tell us to.

And then when Clare, finally, after years of trying, got pregnant, I was quite surprised by Ralph's response to that, too.

It was almost as if he was moved by her happy news when, normally, Ralph wants nothing to do with pregnancy and even less with what Donna calls the beautiful and empowering birthing experience, even of his own children.

He goes pale if he overhears even a tiny snatch of the most Victorian and reticent account of someone's labor. As for anything to do with periods or front bottoms—once, I had a full waxing of my nether regions to celebrate our tenth wedding anniversary. It was going to be a lovely surprise for Ralph.

After our romantic dinner, we repaired up to bed in Colville Crescent. I removed my frilly Myla event knickers and gave him a twirl. "Ta daaaa!" I trilled, showing off my all. Ralph took one look at my gleaming private (Posy's word), staggered across the bedroom, clutched at the curtains for support and fainted clean away, bringing down not only the curtains but a six-foot mahogany pole onto my head. Which was one way, I pointed out later, of putting the *ka-boom* back into bedtime.

And when Clare's baby was born Ralph actually 1. asked whether it was a boy or a girl and 2. asked whether it had a name yet. And 3. unbelievably, what the baby looked like.

I almost fell over in shock. Whenever any of my friends has had babies before, he has shown not the slightest interest in the confinement or eventual product as, according to Ralph, all newborn babies are the same, whether male or female.

As for the other stuff—my flingette with Si—the curious thing is, we never spoke of it again.

Ralph said that he had never before asked any woman about the wrong-side-of-the-blanket sorts of things, that was private business between consenting adults, and he wasn't going to start with "his current wife." And then, he added, which was strange, and shocking, as he used my name again: "And I hope you will extend the same courtesy to me, Imogen."

So what I've learnt, finally, is this. Ralph's not an Eton mess at all. He's more together than anyone I've ever known.

I carry the tray through, out of the kitchen, into the wide hall, and across the porch to my waiting family on the lawn, to where Ralph is now reading my latest "It's Your Funeral" column, which is another thing that has miraculously survived our move to the country, along with our marriage and Posy's unparalleled collection of moist cleansing wipes.

Look at him, now. He's skimming my piece, a smile playing about his lips, completely cool about the fact that my subject this week is . . . Si Kasparian.

I did think, after his betrayal of me with Anoushka, the least Si could do was give me a few more column inches this way. Even Faint Praiser thought it was a great idea, too, especially as I was too busy getting my kit off with him to have written up my exclusive interview with the mysterious billionaire this time two years ago.

Si told me he wanted to be buried at sea, after a service on the deck of his yacht, *Salome*. And he wanted a fireworks display, and no hymns. He wanted his crew to line up on deck in their naval ducks and throw lilies onto the waves as Anoushka played her flute and little Darius Kasparian, the son and heir, precociously read from *The Prophet*.

"What a prat that man is," Ralph says, cutting himself a second slice of cake and inserting it expertly into his jaws. "I never liked him very much. He never had very good taste. As for choosing Kahlil Gibran." He groans, as I ponder the fact that Ralph regards Si as having very poor taste, "Christ. What a cliché."

In answer, I take a scone and almost dispose of it in one bite. "Fabulous scones," I say, through my ambrosial mouthful. "Though I say so myself."

Then I scoot down on the rug, my head gratefully on his lap, thinking, I may have been betrayed by my husband, my best friend, and my lover, and in more ways than I will ever know, but what a bonus and a blessing those betrayals have turned out to be. . . .

Together, we stare up at the façade of our honey-stoned house with its wisteria-clad porch, over to green hills and blue sky.

If this was a Richard Curtis movie, the camera would pan away from this touching vignette and rise rapidly airborne to show the happy nuclear family living in a jewel of a house buried deep in the unspoiled glories of the ancient Dorset countryside.

Posy is riding Trumpet into the kitchen, Casimir is climbing too high in the apple tree, and Mirabel is wandering round in her pants, but I don't care. Since we moved to the country, she's been a changed girl, and soooo much nicer since she gave up saying "like" for Lent.

It's a far cry from Kensington and Chelsea, now we're hundreds of miles away from the mayhem and madness of Notting Hill communal gardens and in an English country garden of our own.

We've found a piece of heaven, and all I can say is, thank God, estate agents, ecocoaches, and all the lifestyle gurus in the land, for that.

Acknowledgments

I would like to thank my editors and publishers, Trish Todd, Juliet Annan, and Carly Cook; my agent, Peter Straus; my copyeditors, Sarah Day and Sarah Hulbert; my friends Giles Wood, Mary Killen, Sebastian Faulks, Henry Porter, Henrietta Courtauld, Helena Fosh; and Jenni Russell for textual and moral support and inspiration; and last but not least, my family and dog, Coco.

Notting Hill for Beginners

Agent Provocateur—shop on Westbourne Grove selling peephole bras and other saucy, frilly items mainly to men.

agnes b.—clothing retailer selling edgy urban chic clothes for *homme*, *femme*, and *bébé*. Its vests—long enough to tuck in—are justly renowned. Large store on Westbourne Grove opposite Tom's (q.v.) and Fresh & Wild (q.v.).

John Armit—West London wine merchant whose devotion to the wines of Pomerol earned him, for a time, exclusive rights to distribute Château Petrus, so very much the vintner to have in your BlackBerry around Notting Hill parts.

B&Q—a DIY chain frequented by the sort of person who doesn't pick up the phone any time something needs doing/fixing but actually trudges along in person (i.e., no one in Notting Hill).

Babington House—country house hotel owned by Nick Scott, owner of the Electric Cinema and Brasserie and Club (q.v.) near Frome in Somerset where rock 'n' roll lifestyle meets rustic comfort in rooms equipped with all essentials for townie-friendly country house weekends such as plasma screens, hot tubs, spa treatments, and so on.

bagua map—pronounced "ba-gwa," a chart used in *feng shui*, pronounced "fung schway," to ascertain which part of your home relates to your life via the "guas," or areas representing prosperity, fame, relationships, family, creativity, and children, etc. It is not wise to use the term *bagua map* in conversation with dates you are seeking to impress as grounded. Actually, don't talk about baguas with any men you're not paying by the hour for something.

Peter Bazalgette—a local resident and some say inventor of the Big Brother format.

Beautcamp Pilates—a fitness studio that claims to be a "staple of core living" for many local slebs.

The Beefsteak—like Pratts, is a private gentlemen's club founded in the eighteenth century where all the waiters are called George and where nothing ever changes—thank God.

Belgravia—the statement address for London's numerous resident sheikhs and oligarchs.

Belstaff—a brand retailer of cool rocker and biker gear like, er, leather jackets.

Berol—a maker of black marker pens and other stationery.

Bodens—the family of Johnnie Boden of the catalogue fame, who live, when business permits, in a rambling spread near Bridport (q.v.) in Dorset.

Boffi—brand of minimalist, high-maintenance bathrooms and kitchens based on, and I quote, "specific design philosophies," one of the philosophies being, one darkly suspects, that it is absolutely essential to spend a six-figure sum every twenty-four months on refreshing your kitchen.

Bonpoint—Parisian children's outfitters supplying all your pale pink cashmere and organdy requirements, outlet in Westbourne Grove, now owned by Edmond de Rothschild.

Bonsoir—purveyor of pajamas and other nightwear in quality cotton poplin.

bothy—a tumbledown farm laborer's dwelling place generally ripe for conversion into a swanky holiday rental/second home.

Emma Bridgewater—a potter who sells the country way of life to town-bound middle-class mummies via adorable spotted/painted/spongeware china.

Bridport—scenic West Dorset market town where hippies, foodies, and country lovers can indulge almost orgiastically in their love of all things seasonal, wholesome, and organic, much championed by Hugh Fearnley-Whittingstall (q.v.) an enthusiastic but compassionate meat eater, rural chef, and deliberately uncoiffed TV personality and food writer.

British bulldog—a game played by two sides of children who run toward each other at speed while the bulldog, positioned midfield, tries to catch them. Serious injuries are inevitable and expected.

Fiona Bruce—gamine BBC newscaster of cut-glass vowels and plunging necklines and appreciative male audience.

Bucks—short for Buckinghamshire, a Home County near London.

Builder's Arms—traditional name for a traditional English pub where, traditionally, much drink is taken.

Cheeky Monkeys—toy shop in Kensington Park Road selling charming wooden toys that appeal to parents but are immediately discarded as "sad" by all children.

Chelsea—bijou district with residential squares and terraced streets and charming shops that so entranced the Clintons they named their only child in its honor.

chillout room—a multimedia den with surround sound, plasma screens, recording facilities, full drum kit, etc., for jam sessions.

Chilterns—rolling chalk hills a few miles northwest of London with magnificent beechwoods, nestling villages, and brick and flint villages.

Chiswick—the leafy, chlorophyll-drenched West London suburb boasting numerous good restaurants, French patisseries, and schools, dwelt in by high-income families including the Bodens (q.v.).

Chobham—Surrey village much favored by upwardly mobile noovs, i.e., nouveau riches, lying conveniently between the M3 and M25 motorways.

Clarke's—restaurant and deli owned by Sally Clarke, in Kensington Church Street, where fabulous home cooking eaten in reverentially hushed tones meets stratospheric prices.

Coco Ribbon—über-girlie boutique on Ken Park Road selling chiffon shirts and spaghetti-strap dresses and scented candles and silky thongs.

council block—public housing, project housing.

Crocus—website and online catalogue supplying plants, bulbs, and garden accessories (your search for that £100 wood and steel painted child's wheelbarrow and cute kiddy trowels and hoes is so over!)

Also supplies cut flowers "arranged by celebrity florists" and online advice offering bespoke advice to ungreen-thumbed customers by the site's resident "plant doctors."

Crusty, Fucker, etc.—all upper-crust Englishmen like Ralph have nicknames and went to either Summerfields and Sunningdale and then Eton, where they made their six closest friends (male, it goes without saying). These friends do not change. Ergo, nor do their nicknames.

Daily Express—downmarket Tory tabloid.

Daily Telegraph—house newspaper of the Tory party, still in broadsheet form, with rapidly aging and testy readership of retired, huff-puffing, high-cholesterol Colonels in the Home Counties.

dekko—slang for "look."

"do a Paula Radcliffe"—refers to the long-distance runner's being caught very short during the Athens marathon, live on worldwide TV.

Iain Duncan Smith—forgettable former leader of the Tory party who stepped down in 2003.

E&O—Asian/Pacific fusion restaurant on Kensington Park Road (q.v.). Eastern and Oriental, always puhlease known as E&O, is a destination venue for all neighborhood showoffs and sleb watchers, with its plate-glass windows and cleverly angled mirrored interiors. Together E&O and the Electric (q.v.) private club, cinema, and brasseries, provide an axis of excitement along Blenheim Crescent.

Easy Living—new Condé Nast magazine aimed at the thirty-five-plus lady reader.

Electric Cinema—a cinema on the Portobello Road where locals can view latest releases in sumptuous surrounds in leather armchairs while sipping wine and nibbling tapas. A historic venue dating from 1910, with its plaster paneling and gilded vaulted ceiling, this is one of the oldest working cinemas in the U.K.

Gavin Esler—television presenter of highbrow BBC *Newsnight* program and News 24 anchor with dark hair, active eyebrows, emphatic delivery, and distractingly mobile mouth.

Eton Fourth of June—the principal annual celebration of the legendarily upper-crust school, held on the birthday of King George III, a day replete with archaic sporting ritual and pageant and very contemporary displays of conspicuous consumption and wealth, with parents arriving on Agar's Plough by helicopter (if they could) while their sons and heirs wander around in garlanded boaters pursued by miniskirted girls from St. Mary's, Ascot.

Farrow and Ball—manufacturer of traditional paints and wallpapers much used by the many English people who live (or would like to live) in historic houses, with paint names like Tallow, Ointment Pink, Book Room Red, Dorset Cream, Clunch, and Wainscot.

Felicitous—neighborhood deli and coffee shop owned by Lady (Felicity) Osborne, mother of Tory shadow Chancellor George.

Hugh Fearnley-Whittingstall (q.v.) Country—the area around Bridport (q.v.) made chic by the arrival of foodie subsistence farmer and TV personality Hugh F-W.

The Food Doctor—clinic on Holland Park Avenue which charges grateful clients £60 simply to tell them not to eat "anything white."

Fresh & Wild—whole-food organic store and café on Westbourne Grove, selling food free of hydrogenated fats, artificial sweeteners, colorings, and flavorings. If you ever doubted food is the religion of our age, a brief visit to this temple of all things raw and crunchy will convert you once and for all.

Emma Freud—the dark and skinny TV presenter and writer married to Richard Curtis, the screenwriter and director, and great granddaughter of Sigmund. They are, without question, Emperor and Empress of Notting Hill, with four adorable and gifted children. The couple combines horrible amounts of talent and industry and success with a burning and quite obviously genuine desire to improve the lot of those less fortunate than themselves (into which category everyone else in the world, apart from perhaps Bill and Melinda, fall).

Gaggia—Italian maker of espresso machines.

Gharani Strok—fashion label of Croatian/Italian design duo Nargess

Gharani and Vanya Strok, worn by Madonna, Nicole, Kate, Keira, Kylie, Gwyneth, and lots of other women known only by their first names.

Gloucestershire—county to the west of the capital famous for its honey-stoned market towns, antique shops, rolling hills, and cloth-cap-wearing celebrities. More expensive per square foot than Knightsbridge and bitterly called "Poshtershire" by those who cannot conceal their resentment of the townie takeover of the Shires.

Grade II listed—English Heritage, a government quango, lists all houses/barns/buildings of architectural/historic/industrial interest.

The Grocer on Elgin—shop and deli and café on Elgin Crescent where food is appetizingly presented for sale like blood and plasma product, in shrink-wrapped cellophane.

The Guardian—influential, serious, leftish daily paper first printed in the north in Manchester, now in easy-to-digest tabloid format, about the closest thing to *Le Monde* in the Anglosphere.

Lulu Guinness—pint-size, wasp-waisted designer of vampish, girly 1950s handbags, couture, and shoes.

Hampstead—North London village suburb synonymous with Jewish intelligentsia (Marx and Freud both lived here) now colonized by polenta-eating Liberals, writers, and media tarts.

Hanger Lane Gyratory—a big roundabout where the North Circular Road and Western Avenue meet—and that's making it sound a lot more exciting than it actually is.

Heat!—influential celebrity weekly.

Allegra Hicks—the stylish Italian designer, married to Ashley Hicks, whose wafty, trippy clothes and rugs and homeware have earned her the accolade "Queen of Kaftans."

Highgrove—the name of HRH the Prince of Wales' private seat in Gloucestershire (q.v.), near Tetbury.

Hilditch and Key—Jermyn Street (q.v.) shirtmaker, est. 1899.

Anya Hindmarch—one of the many celebrity Notting Hill handbag designers. See also Lulu Guinness.

Holland Park Lawn Tennis Club—WII members-only tennis club with less than Wimbledon-style grass courts and equally persnickety rules.

IT—acronym for "information technology," a boring computer class held in all primary schools.

Ilse Jacobsen—a Danish footwear brand that has pulled off the impossible—making Wellington-style boots sexy. Her trademark Hornbaeck lace-up gumboots come in twenty colors and are guaranteed the wearer any number of Mellors moments in the woods.

Celia Johnson—English actress who played Laura in *Brief Encounter*, a film during which Mimi always cries noisily.

Kensington—full of Royal Parks, Princess Diana walks and exhibitions, Royal Palaces, Peter Pan statues, and lots of little old ladies with tiny dogs and power-walking yummy mummies in Juicy Couture and Masai Barefoot Technology trainers.

Cath Kidston—delightful English Rose and designer of spriggy retro chintzy homeware.

Ladybird—the brand of children's clothes and underwear available in Woolworth on the Portobello Road.

Lakeland Plastics, Scotts of Stow, and Picketts—all shops with mail-order catalogues that arrive in the weekend papers like tempting spam.

Lisboa—working class Portuguese café on Golborne Road famous for its custard and coconut tartlets and milky coffee served in tall glasses.

Little Sodbury—town in Gloucestershire (q.v.).

LK Bennett—brand retailer of shoes and officewear.

Lobb's of Jermyn Street (q.v.)—a shop selling bench-made and bespoke brogues. "A Gentleman," Churchill once observed, "buys his hats at Lock's, his shoes at Lobb's, his shirts at Harvie and Hudson, his suits at Huntsman, and his cheese at Paxton and Whitfield." Ralph would heartily concur.

M&S—acronym for Marks and Spencer, the food and clothing retailer to Middle England, claims to have popularized the avocado and frozen seafood tagliatelle.

Maison Blanc—patisserie on Holland Park Avenue where the baguettes are not as good as the snooty francophone staff thinks they are.

Andrew Marr—BBC presenter of important Sunday morning politics show; he has jug ears and a devoted female following.

Meditteraneo—Italian restaurant on Ken Park Road, aka the Hi Street.

David Mellor—aka the Cutlery King, the eponymous owner of the shop selling pared-down, clean-limbed kitchenware to those who find traditional flatware just too . . . frilly.

Miss Sixty—brand retailer of trashy teenwear.

Jóse Mourinho—darkly brooding Portuguese manager of Chelsea Football Team, and total sex god.

Myla—lingerie and sex toy boutique on Lonsdale Road.

The Napoleon of Notting Hill—novel by G. K. Chesterton, first published in 1904, about a hidebound London suburb at war with its modernizing neighbors.

nets at Lords—boys' cricket training sessions held at Lords Cricket Ground in St. John's Wood, home of the Marylebone Cricket Club (MCC). Also mistily called the "Home of Cricket" by English ex–public schoolboys.

New and Lingwood—a Jermyn Street (q.v.) tailor also on Eton (q.v.) High Street.

Nicole Farhi/202—a shop cum restaurant on Westbourne Grove selling Nicole Farhi branded goods where lunch can cost up to £4,000 (if you fall for the French oak table as well as the lobster rolls with shoestring fries, which, let's face it, you probably will).

nitcheck rota—London schoolchildren are all so infested with vermin that schools now require parents—even celebrity ones—to take turns to come in and comb for headlice.

Nuline on Westbourne Park Road—a parade of builder's merchants supplying builders with all they need for area's perpetual round of expensive property refurbishment.

Ocado—online grocery delivery service associated with Waitrose supermarket.

Ottolenghi—deli/café selling sublime, ambrosial prepared dishes to go, and baked goods of such succulence that even supermodels abandon a lifetime of fasting to scoff. Also has large table downstairs for even more serious troughing.

Anita Pallenberg—a swinging rock chick of the sixties and Rolling Stones girlfriend, who starred, along with Mick Jagger, in Nic Roeg's Notting Hill movie, *Performance* (1970).

Michael Parkinson—veteran Yorkshire broadcaster with Saturday talkshow who an unimpressed Meg Ryan called "nutty." Often referred to cozily as Parky.

Guy Parsons—hairdresser in Westbourne Grove.

John Pawson—architect and high priest of minimalism, designer of both Cistercian monasteries in Bohemia and the flagship Calvin Klein store in Manhattan, which figures.

Perivale—unsought-after lower-middle-class west London suburb.

Peter Jones—mumsy Sloane Square emporium on five floors supplying all your haberdashery and soft furnishing needs as well as everything else.

Petts Bottom—village in the Kentish weald, hard by Lynsore (I kid you not) Bottom.

Ponsonby Prep—imaginary but representative-of-area private school, the only place to send your precious sprog age five to thirteen. Parents stop at nothing to secure entrance for their offspring. Nothing. Actually, you don't want to know.

posecode—wordplay on *postcode*.

Primark—bargain basement chain of young fashion shops selling schmutter at below-sweatshop prices. Think how cheap sales are at Gap—and then divide by half again.

Private Eye—fortnightly scandal sheet with brilliantly funny covers, cartoons, and satire much read by chattering classes.

Question Air—boutique selling "directional," i.e., "unwearable" designer "pieces" and designer jeans.

Rassells—nursery and garden shop in Earl's Court.

Rachman—as in Peter Rachman, Notting Hill landlord whose name has long been synonymous with squalid and exploitative tenant housing.

Ribena—black-currant purple cordial for children famous for its tooth-rotting and clothes-staining properties.

Rigby and Peller—corsetiere to Her Majesty the Queen, where the middle-aged saleswomen pride themselves in determining your brassiere requirements with one raking glance.

Lord Sainsbury of Turville—the grocer peer with supermarket chain of the same name.

Savoir Beds—the bespoke beds company supplying riffraff such as the late King Hussein of Morocco, who ordered forty-six for his palaces, Liza Minelli, and the Savoy Hotel. Prices start at £4,300—but can you put a price on sleeping on a cloud?

Selfridges—famous London department store on Oxford Street with excellent food hall and wacky window displays.

Seven For All Mankind jeans—trademark skinny jeans made from frayed denim.

Shepherd's Bush—raffish suburb of Notting Hill and Chiswick for those who cannot afford either the W11 or W12 postcodes.

Shropshire—western county adjoining Wales with foodie capital, slow food city Ludlow.

Simpson's-on-the-Strand—a bastion of English trenchermen since the early nineteenth century, its famous roast viands carved from a trolley, with potted shrimp, steak and kidney pud, and treacle sponge all popular choices from the "nursery food" menu.

Slug and Lettuce—a pub favored by Antipodean drinkers.

Smeg—high-tech retailer of vast stainless-steel appliances, with a name that public-school-educated males cannot say out loud without schoolboy snigger.

Lolly Stirk—a pre- and postnatal yoga guru who teaches Notting Hill mummies just what a positive and empowering experience a natural birth is . . . . NOT (author's capitals).

St. James's and Jermyn Streets—the two key shopping streets for gentlemen in the heart of London's Clubland, selling luxuries such as cigars, hard cheeses, guns, handmade shoes, and tweedy clothes with complicated pockets for shooting things in.

Start Rite—children's shoe company, started in 1792 by the cordwainer James Smith.

Stickle Bricks—plastic first construction toy set for babies and toddlers that very efficiently picks up fluff, pet hair, and chewing gum.

Suchard—Swiss chocolatier.

TE—acronym for "total embarrassment."

Tea and Coffee Plant—Fair trade boutique on Portobello Road selling huge range of compassionately produced tea, coffee, herb teas, and cocoa.

Tesco—name of ubiquitous supermarket chain where average Briton spends one in every eight pounds.

The Test—legendary chalkstream that makes fly-fishermen all over the world go moist-eyed; so clean its waters are used to wash the paper used for British bank notes.

TMI—acronym standing for "too much information."

Toast—a catalogue and online shopping site for those affronted by the bright colors and splashy patterns of the Boden (q.v.) catalogue. Toast features sludgy-colored loose-fitting clothes in linen and cotton, which are photographed in locations as convenient as Patagonia, the Peruvian altiplano, and the Argentinian pampas. The catalogue showcases gaucho and hippie chic, Spanish riding boots, cashmere throws, and soulful-looking models placed decoratively in inhospitable wildernesses staring moodily into the distant horizon, while clutching mugs in fingerless mittens. You know the look.

Tom's—deli owned by Tom Conran of the hospitality dynasty, much frequented for power breakfasts (the blueberry porridge . . . the honey-drizzled muesli!) by A-listers.

TopShop—brand retailer for teens and preteens and fashion-sensitive grown women.

Totty—slang for gorgeous female flesh.

202—the restaurant in Nicole Farhi (q.v.) on Westbourne Grove.

Viyella—fabric of 80 percent cotton and 20 percent wool that has made sporting gentlemen snuggly since 1784.

Westminster Great School and St. Paul's Girls' School—the *numero uno assoluto* private day schools for boys and girls respectively, and virtually impregnable to all but the scarily bright offspring of London's pushiest.

Whistles—brand retailer on Westbourne Grove, selling women's fashion.

White's—a private gentlemen's club at the top of St. James's Street (q.v.) whose members include the arch-dandy Beau Brummel and currently David Cameron, the young leader of the Conservative Party.

wotcher—slang for "hi" or "hello."

Yates Buchanan—shop on Kensington Park Road where Kate Moss first clapped eyes on a pair of rabbit-fur-trimmed, pom-pom mukluk moon boots, and a universally silly trend was born.

Young England—Elizabeth Street SW1 store selling old-fashioned children's clothes in bygone fabrics and styles like corduroy, smocking, and velvet.

Zucca—restaurant, well, more like canteen for the young, trendy Cameron Conservatives, designed by the eco-architect to the stars, Alex Michaelis. Social death to be seen eating pumpkin risotto and spicy sausage farfalle anywhere but upstairs.

Notting Hell

"If you live on the garden, you can't help but see things. We all see straight into each others' back gardens, rear windows—and should live our lives accordingly."

Something smells dodgy in Lonsdale Gardens and it's not the primroses sprouting from the flower boxes. It's what lies beneath this private upscale community in the Notting Hill district of London that is creating quite a stink. Here residents are blessed with the key to the beautiful communal garden . . . and cursed with having to share it with their neighbors:

- The Sturgises: Clare is too busy trying to be a garden-design consultant, neighborhood snoop, and mummy to be to notice that her eco-architect husband Gideon has a naughty little secret.

- The Flemings: Mimi, a freelance journalist, is passionate about living in the elite neighborhood even though her husband Ralph knows they are living well beyond their means.

- The Moltons: Marguerite, a typical NHM (Notting Hill mummy) with food issues, is married to Patrick, a banker with an appetite for other women.

- The Lacostes: Virginie and Mathieu are a French couple who out-chic everyone else, but Virginie is spotted sneaking around the garden at night half naked when her husband is out of town.

- The Averys: The token Americans, Bob and Sally are putting off some neighbors with their renovation plans and getting quite chummy with others.

- Si Kasparian: The new billionaire on the block is looking for the perfect woman to accessorize his yacht . . . even if she is another man's wife.

Parties, high-end shopping, *feng shui* debriefings, private yoga classes, and celebrity sightings all flourish in Lonsdale Gardens. But fertilized with betrayal and backstabbings, life in this picture-perfect garden neighborhood is about to grow out of control.

Discussion Questions

1. There are two narrators in this novel, Clare and Mimi. How do they differ in their storytelling styles? Do you think it is important to have two narrators? Why or why not?

2. "Clutter is anything that gets in the way of the ability to move through the day with grace, serenity, and self-respect" (page 13). Residents of Lonsdale Gardens are obsessed with *feng shui*. Why is this ironic? At the end of the novel, are all things harmonious in the characters' lives?

3. "We're all charming and considerate when we're on our own turf, or in each other's houses, but anything to do with the communal garden manages to bring out the two-year-old in all of us" (page 34). What does the communal garden symbolize in this novel?

4. Mimi broke the First Law of Adultery. What is it? Why does she risk her family's happiness by having an affair?

5. "The taking part couldn't matter less, it's the winning that counts" (page 234). What does each woman—Clare, Mimi, Marguerite, Virginie, and Sally—hope to achieve in her own life?

6. "I tell *what* I know and, more importantly, I tell him *why* I'm telling him" (page 286). What transpires between Clare and Ralph? Do you approve or disapprove of their actions? How much do you think Mimi knows about their conspiracy?

7. "I may have been betrayed by my husband, my best friend, and my lover, and in more ways than I will ever know, but

what a bonus and a blessing those betrayals have turned out to be" (page 326). Why does Mimi think these betrayals are blessings? Do all the betrayals in this book turn out to be blessings?

8. After reading this book, would you like a key to Lonsdale Gardens? Why or why not?

9. *The Sunday Times* says: "There are plenty of wicked one-liners in this read." Which one is your favorite?

10. Mimi regards Clare as her "closest chum on the garden." What do you think of their friendship? Do you think any of the women in *Notting Hell* are true friends to each other?

11. This novel is full of men who are either deceitful or dim . . . or both. Are there any decent male characters in Rachel Johnson's Lonsdale Gardens? If so, name them.

12. Are you a believer in *feng shui*? If so, does the room you are sitting in now have flow? How would you rearrange the room in order to be *feng shui* friendly?

Reader's Tips

Give a great garden party: If you don't live on a communal garden like the ladies of *Notting Hell*, host your book club meeting in a public garden. (To find a public garden in your area, do an advanced search at www.publicgardens.org/Custom/GardenSearch.aspx.)

Test your Notting Hill knowledge: Use the glossary in the back of the book to quiz your book club members on their Notting Hill vocabulary.

Fantasize about your funeral: Mimi's always looking for interesting people to describe their final send-offs for her column, "It's Your Funeral." Have your book club members share their ideas for their last rites.

Q&A with Rachel Johnson

Are these characters based on your neighbors, friends, enemies, and/or celebrities?

According to the English newspapers—who all tried to nail each character to a well-known West London name—yes. According to this author, no. All the main characters are invented; that was the most fun part. Yes, I come into daily contact with celebrities and world-famous architects and bankers and so on, and yes, my kids go to school with the children of rock stars and Turner Prize–winning artists, so early on in the creative process I decided to do the following. If I was going to put a real person in, I would name him in order to make it clear that my characters were—repeat, *were*—invented.

So you will find the names of supermodels (Kate Moss, for example) and of bestselling authors (Sebastian Faulks, Salman Rushdie) and architects (the minimalist John Pawson, who happens to live bang next door to me).

I hoped this would forestall the whole who's-in-Rachel's-naughty-roman-à-clef-type arch guessing games, both in the neighborhood and in the media, but it didn't. There was a lot of speculation, especially about the character of Si Kasparian. Sadly, as I told interviewers, he was completely made up. I sigh wistfully.

Then I would add that, if a brooding single billionaire did move onto the garden, could I please be the first to know? (Everyone wrote Kasparian was Peter Soros, the nephew of George Soros, who is a dear friend of mine but, it has to be admitted, not the sort of fatally irresistible man for whom Mimi would risk all.)

Basically, though, everyone thought they were in it and they weren't, but they couldn't decide whether to be in it or not in it was more insufferable. (The author says the latter, but she would, wouldn't she?)

I can't count the number of red-faced men who come up to me in the street or at parties, huffing and puffing at the way I've put them in my book. It's always news to me that these boring, striped-shirt, investment bankers on massive annual salaries are so fascinating!

But I know how to deal with them now. I smile sweetly and say, "Oh, you noticed! Well, it's true I always have been obsessed with you, for ages . . . " and trail off.

That usually shuts them up.

Why did you want to dig into the stereotypes of the NHMs?

I remember walking around the streets of Notting Hill and seeing these rail-thin women, driving their huge 4X4 Mercedeses and Porsches—with their perfect blow-dried hair and expensive makeup, with tiny children in Duke of Windsorish tweed uniforms and herringbone overcoats, laden with cellos and sports kit in the back—and thinking how unhappy they looked despite their three fully staffed houses in superprime locations, their high-rolling husbands, their daily treadmill of Pilates and yoga and treatments. I thought, This is my subject—I must write about them before someone else gets there first. I felt drawn to the paradox the NHMs represented. These women, who have everything you could dream of, always looked so wretched, so down.

I put it down to the transferred stress from their husbands' careers (that's a bit like referred pain, such as when you have a heart attack but it hurts in your shoulder) and a terrible, nagging suspicion that living a life of excess without the sharpener of paid work is not as fulfilling as it might look to envious outsiders like me.

You live in Notting Hill. Do you share Clare's sentiment: "There is nowhere, absolutely nowhere, quite so worth living as in a Notting Hill communal garden"? How did your neighbors react to the book's publication?

I absolutely love the 'hood, and my communal garden is like a little Garden of Eden in the middle of London—it's perfectly quiet and bosky, and I can smell the blossom. It is the very garden, in fact, that Hugh Grant jumped into with Julia Roberts in that famous scene from That Film, as the movie *Notting Hill* is known in my neck of the woods.

I feel very, very lucky to be here. I couldn't possibly afford to live here now (we bought our house when it was affordable and this was a funkapolitan, raffish postcode to live in, not a ghetto for the superrich).

But I don't think my neighbors—who have in fact been wonderfully elastic and generous on the whole—feel quite so fortunate to have me as a neighbor. Basically, I was not flavor of the month for a while, but we all hung in there and we can all look each other in the eye again and say "good morning" to each other, which is all I can really hope for.

Of all the *Notting Hell* characters, why did you choose Clare and Mimi as the narrators of your story? And why was it important to have two narrators instead of one?

I tried writing the book in the third person. That didn't work. It sounded too formal and remote. So then I tried first person and found the mother ship, but I thought it would be too tiring for the reader if the whole book was in Mimi's scatty, self-centered, ditzy voice. So I wanted to contrast Mimi with a woman who is utterly unlike her: childless, perfectionist (trying not to say anal), married to an immoral aesthete (rather than to an upright, reserved English gent like Ralph). Clare is a complete visual snob who used to work for *House & Garden* and sees everything as a possible photo shoot—because she just can't help it. Mimi is what we now call a "slummy mummy." And lo, the dual narrative of the book was born. Clare, needless to say, was much harder to write than Mimi, because so much of me is in Mimi (which is why I call the heroine Mimi, in case you were wondering).

Adultery runs rampant in *Notting Hell*. How should readers feel about this?

Really chilled. It's fiction! Like, relax.

all of that was what was going on while I was writing *Notting Hell*.

Will we see the characters from *Notting Hell* again in a future book? What are you working on now?

I am writing a book that centers again on the Fleming family, but relocates them to deepest Dorset in the southwest of England, which is very, very green and remote. You will not be surprised to hear that Mimi manages to find the only serpent in this paradise quite quickly. Some of the plot of *Notting Hell* reaches a denouement in the next book. I've really enjoyed writing this one, which is called *In a Good Place*, but be prepared for something darker and with fewer brand names and—even bigger shock—almost no puns!

If Mimi were to interview you for "It's Your Funeral," what would you tell her?

I would like my closest friends and family to gather for a highly traditional funeral in the West Country village church where I was christened, near where my family still has a farm. I would like my children to choose the service, but I will have left instructions that the following must be in the order: Psalm 23 ("The Lord is my shepherd"), the hymn "Abide with Me," "Jerusalem," Psalm 121 ("I will lift up mine eyes unto the hills") because the church is set on a green hill far away. Afterwards, I would want everyone to repair to the pub and drink to me with pint tankards of tawny Exmoor ale from the local brewery, and cry openly.

References to *feng shui* are throughout the novel. Why? Do you think *feng shui* is a valuable practice or merely "nineties nonsense for women with too much time and money on their hands"?

Well, what do you think I think? Yes. Of course it is utter mumbo jumbo.

Are there plans to adapt this book into a film? If so, which actors will be starring in it? Or which actors would you like to see represent your characters?

I am hoping that when I publish the sequel, there will be enough material to tempt Harvey Weinstein into making an offer I simply cannot refuse.

***Notting Hell* received good reviews in the UK. How do you think American audiences will react to this book?**

I am worried that American audiences will fixate on the anti-U.S. sentiments currently prevailing in Western Europe and think I am out to get them. And that I'm anti-American. Please believe me, I'm not. What I do in the novel is to reflect a weariness with the cult of the U.S. banker family in Notting Hill (they are very domineering, to be honest) and a sense of outrage over the ongoing Iraq war, because